ALSO BY LISA GRUNWALD

Summer

The
Theory
of
Everything

The
Theory
of
Everything

~

LISA
GRUNWALD

ALFRED A. KNOPF · NEW YORK 1991

THIS IS A BORZOI BOOK
PUBLISHED BY ALFRED A. KNOPF, INC.

An excerpt of this work was originally published in Esquire.

Library of Congress Cataloging-in-Publication Data
Adlor, Lisa Grunwald.
The theory of everything : a novel / by Lisa Grunwald Adler.—
1st ed.
p. cm.
ISBN 0-394-58149-0
I. Title.
PS3557.R837T4   1991
813'.54—dc20   90-52910   CIP

MANUFACTURED IN THE UNITED STATES OF AMERICA

FIRST EDITION

FOR STEPHEN,
AND THE THEORY OF EVERYTHING ELSE

Always keep Ithaca fixed in your mind.
To arrive there is your ultimate goal.
But do not hurry the voyage at all.
It is better to let it last for long years;
and even to anchor at the isle when you are old,
rich with all that you have gained on the way,
not expecting that Ithaca will offer you riches.

Ithaca has given you the beautiful voyage.
Without her, you would never have taken the road.

—CAVAFY

Angel, teach me right.

—JOHN FREDERICK HELVETIUS

The
Theory
of
Everything

Part One

I

THE DREAM

"WHERE ARE WE?" Alexander asked his mother.

"We're here," Alice said, and stopped the car.

She wiped the foggy windshield with her hand, her gold wedding ring tapping against the glass.

"Has it come yet?" Alexander asked.

"No. Just watch."

"But I can't see anything. Did I miss it? Was I sleeping?"

"No. You will."

"Mom."

"What, cookie?"

"Tell me again."

Alice turned to her husband. "What time is it?" she asked him.

In the darkness of the car, Sam peered closely at his watch, then looked up slowly, staring straight ahead. "Eleven forty-five," he said quietly.

"Fifteen minutes!" Alexander told Alice. "We've still got fifteen minutes."

"Well—"

"It was a long time ago," Alexander said, prompting her.

"It was a long time ago," she said, smiling.

Sam drew a magazine from the straw bag at his feet. It was too dark in the car to read it, but he wanted to do something to prove he wasn't listening.

"A very long time ago," Alice said, turning to face her son. "There was a storm, a huge storm, and it washed out the bridge that goes over the river."

"The one we just passed?"

"Yes. The one we just passed."

"The stationmaster," Alexander said.

Alice nodded and wet her thumb to rub a smudge of chocolate from Alexander's cheek. "The stationmaster knew that the train was coming," she said. "So he took his lantern, and he walked out on the tracks. It was raining very hard. The stationmaster waved the lantern in big circles so the engineer would see the lights and stop."

"But he didn't stop," Alexander said.

"No," Alice said. "He didn't stop. The train ran him over. Then it went off the bridge and into the river."

"And everybody—" Alexander whispered.

"Everybody died," Alice said.

"Oh, for God's sake," Sam said, turning to Alice.

"So now," Alice continued, "now, once a year, on the same night, at the same time, people around here see the Railroad Ghost. A light turning in big circles, and then going out."

"Maybe it's just a firefly," Alexander said, running the tips of his fingers along the stitches on the vinyl seat.

"No."

"Maybe it's some kind of reflection," Alexander said.

"Why don't you see for yourself?" Alice asked.

Then she left them both sitting in the car.

Alexander's eyes shone. His right foot pinned his left foot to the floor of the car. His hands grasped the headrest of his mother's empty seat. "Dad," he pleaded. "Come with me."

"No, Ex, I can't."

"Please."

"I can't."

"But don't you want to see it?"

"There's nothing to see."

"But how do you *know* that?"

Sam turned in his seat and forced a smile of reassurance. "You go if you want to, Ex," he said. "Really. And I'll want a full report."

Alexander waited as long as he could. Then he slid out the door like a shadow, running after the dark shape of his mother. Fog covered the field in a fine light gray blanket. Alexander's head came up to Alice's waist. He reached out a chubby hand for her, but she either ignored it or didn't know. Her steps were firm and rapid. Out of breath, Alexander struggled to keep up, walking double time beside her, four steps inside her every two. Panting, he finally reached out and touched his mother's leg. She stopped and looked down at him. She seemed surprised. Then she smiled.

"Mom," Alexander said, near tears.

"What, cupcake?"

"Too fast."

"You think?" she said, and laughed. Her laugh was high and cruel.

"Mom."

"We're here anyhow. Want me to pick you up?"

He did but shook his head no. In the black sky, two clouds parted, and the moon and the stars appeared, as if they had just stepped through an open door. Alexander shivered and looked at the ground, but the ground, like the stars, seemed to sparkle. It was covered, for as far as he could see, with a layer of flattened beer cans.

"This is where the college boys come for their initiations," Alice explained. "Do you know what an initiation is?"

"I thought it was magic," Alexander said, still looking at the shining surface. "I thought it was silver."

"Magic isn't silver," Alice said. "It's gold."

Then they waited.

2

THE IDEA

THE LIGHT TRACED a large shining arc in the air. His mother's necklace. His mother's grin. Its path described a man's arm. But there was more to it than that. There was the man himself, remembered, a middle-aged man in black foul-weather gear with a mustache and a policeman's hat, standing on the doomed tracks in the rain, wanting his dinner.

"Don't!" Alexander screamed in his sleep.

He felt Linda touch his shoulder.

"Don't!" he screamed again.

"Hey," Linda said softly. "Hey."

Alexander lay beside her, quiet.

"You awake?" she asked him, fitting her hand around the back of his neck.

"Sorry," he said.

"Wake up or else you'll have it again."

She moved to put both her arms around him. He settled against her and kissed her shoulder.

"Awake," he murmured. "I'm awake. Sorry," he said, and fell back to sleep.

HE HAD HAD another nightmare. That much he could tell by the way that Linda was standing there beside the bed, looking at him with a wry, bright smile. She held a cup of coffee. She wore a terry robe. Sunlight came in the windows behind her, lighting her face and hair. "Let me guess," she said. "You don't want to talk about it."

"Is there coffee in there?" he asked her.

"Yes."

"Is there a catch?"

Linda handed him the cup and shook her head and put a hand on her hip.

Alexander took a sip and saw his eyes dance in the coffee's surface as it broke. He looked up at Linda. "Delicious," he said.

"Come on, you *screamed*, Alexander," she told him. She was almost laughing. "You screamed, 'Don't!' Don't what? What were they *doing* to you?"

"What time is it?"

"Who were you screaming at?"

"What time is it?"

Linda sighed. "It's just past seven."

"*Damn.*"

Linda flinched.

Alexander put his mug down, threw off his covers, and rushed toward the bathroom, not looking at her.

"I love these early-morning chats we have," Linda said.

In the bathroom, he turned the shower on.

"Don't you?" Linda shouted after him.

He went to the doorway. "Work," he said. "I'm late," he said, and shut the door behind him.

BY SEVEN FORTY-FIVE, he was waiting on line at the token booth in the Seventy-second Street subway station. He tapped his right foot and checked his watch. He smoothed his hair. He smiled to himself. Linda was not going to worry him now, and neither was his nightmare.

He bought a package of tokens and stepped toward the grimy turnstiles. A homeless man was standing nearby, holding a sign that asked for money. The crowd was moving past the man like water flowing around a rock. Alexander thought about the different wave patterns that water could make.

Alexander was a physicist. He was thirty years old. For most of his life, he had wanted to find one thing true that no one else had found true. For three weeks now, it had finally started to look as if he'd done what he'd always wanted to do.

There was probably not a single person in the crowd of sleepy, well-dressed New Yorkers around him who could understand his discovery. Breakthroughs in theoretical physics weren't like finding stars, or medical cures. But in a sense, he'd often told himself, every one of their lives might be changed if he was right.

"How?" Linda had asked him once.

"Science," he had said.

Now he was almost happy. In his pocket were notes he had made outlining the article he would need to write. The article would have to put his countless pages of numbers into a few thousand assertive words and a couple of clean equations. Alexander had been checking his final calculations for nearly a month

now, and he was almost done. He had kept the extent of his
progress to himself, but all along he had been nurturing the
fantasy of how it would feel to be finished.

He thought it would feel fantastic.

And in waiting for that moment to come and alter everything,
Alexander felt safer, and more certain, than he'd felt for years.

Below ground on the subway platform, he stared into the
darkened tunnel, watching for the glimmer of light on the
tracks.

WILSON NATIONAL LABORATORIES sat in the center of Long
Island, fifty minutes from Penn Station, where the trains left
twice an hour. Alexander enjoyed the ride. The cars were quiet,
traveling against the rush of incoming commuters, and the time
was utterly his. He never had to listen. He never had to talk.

It was only five miles from the Wilson station to the lab
itself, and Alexander kept a bicycle at the depot. Most people
rode bikes around Wilson, a huge complex of more than a
hundred buildings and more than a thousand full-time employees. The main attraction was a four-mile-long atomic accelerator that was laid out in a circle like a giant train set. The
experimental buildings stood on the circle's western rim, two
huge warehouses with ninety-foot ceilings and vast overhead
cranes and mammoth detectors. Nearby was the building that
housed the physics department: room after room of dingy walls
and ancient computer terminals and badly painted bookshelves,
physicists on grants and professors on collaborations, graduate
students and technicians and administrators and hangers-on.

Alexander spent most of his time on the second floor of the
physics building in a small office that had a desk, a computer,
two chairs, a bookshelf, and one tiny, unopenable window. On
either side of his office were the identical offices of his two grad
students, Fred Talbot and George Heinz. Talbot and Heinz

were working on their theses. They helped Alexander crunch the equations and sometimes helped him to think.

Alexander had had similar offices at Wilson for six years now, ever since he had finished graduate school and gotten his thesis published, and *Nature*, the prestigious science weekly, had declared it one of the ten most promising pieces of work on the physics horizon. After that, he had won a "genius" grant of $30,000 a year for five years from the MacArthur Foundation. He had also had all sorts of offers from universities, including several full professorships. The offer from the people at Wilson had been the most generous: they were desperate for some in-house academics to give them credibility. Essentially, Alexander had been hired to be smart. He had chosen Wilson because it was offering a good salary and he wanted to save the genius money. He had chosen it because it was a perfect refuge from the vortex of teaching. And finally he had chosen it because working there meant he could live in New York, which was where he'd grown up and where his father still lived.

The corridors of the physics building were deserted when Alexander arrived that morning. He walked into his office, quickly shut the door behind him, put his coffee on the desk, hung his jacket on the coatrack, and then stood by the small window, looking out at the lush lawn. Something would have to happen, he knew: either outside the window, or inside his head.

Alexander could stand by the window looking out at the lawn for hours. Sometimes, when he stood there, he didn't think about physics at all. Sometimes he thought about Linda, and sometimes he thought about his father, Sam. But always the work drew him back, as if along a private current.

This morning, he thought about the pages of notes that were tucked into his right-hand pocket, and he touched them, as if for luck, and thought: It's really going to happen, this is really going to happen.

He wished that his article was already written. It struck him that when it was published, he would probably be famous.

ALL ALEXANDER had to do every day was show up and seem brilliant. There was nothing he needed to tell anyone at the end of a week or a month. Every few months, he and Heinz and Talbot would take stock, Heinz inevitably pushing for them to publish, Alexander inevitably saying that it was too soon, and Talbot inevitably saying nothing, just looking like the quantum geek he was. Every six months or so, Alexander would let Heinz write up a progress report to Bruce Biner, the head of the lab. But beyond that, Alexander was free to do whatever he wanted. For the last three years, that had meant working on his version of a theory that physicists spoke of as the Theory of Everything.

The Theory of Everything, if anyone ever found it, would be exactly what its name suggested: a theory of physics that would explain, with equal precision, the pattern of the tides and the invisible violence of the atom. It would explain the existence of light and account for the presence of gravity.

Physicists sometimes said that the Theory of Everything would be an equation that could fit neatly onto one side of a T-shirt: an $E = Mc^2$ that would explain why $E = Mc^2$ was true—and explain a thousand other equations as well, and make still other equations extinct. The Theory of Everything would unify the two great but contradictory foundations of modern physics: quantum theory, which explained the atom, and relativity, which explained the stars. Finding the Theory of Everything might even mean the end of physics as physicists knew it. It could open up the universe, and close down the blackboards, and for a long time now, in one form or another, it had obsessed Alexander, like a childhood love.

. . .

OF COURSE by average human standards, Alexander was brilliant. But how brilliant was brilliant enough? In several weeks he would be thirty-one, and for a physicist, thirty-one was fairly old to have so much ambition. Newton had been twenty-three when he'd come up with the theory of gravity. Einstein had been twenty-six when he'd hit on relativity. Heisenberg had been twenty-six when he'd found the uncertainty principle. These breakthroughs had had overwhelming importance to the progress of science and history, but the genius of their authors had gone hand in hand with a kind of naiveté that age and experience seemed to dull. The conventional wisdom said that if you knew too much, you'd think you'd know what wouldn't work, and you'd be that much less tempted to try new things. The assumption was that you had to be unschooled, unpolluted by the old ways of asking: you had to discover the questions yourself in order to find the answers. Often Alexander had thought he couldn't be the real thing.

But physics, for Alexander, was a lot like love. It began with curiosity and changed into compulsion. It needed energy and attention and grace. It offered answers, then destroyed them. And it usually ended in mystery that changed back to compulsion.

Alexander hadn't known about the last part when he had started. In junior high school, it had been the certainty, not the mystery, that he'd found so compelling. He had loved the predictability of steel balls rolling down wooden ramps. He had loved the measurement, the laws, the equations. If you knew the acceleration and the time, you could know the velocity. If you knew the velocity and the acceleration, you could know the time. If you knew the time and the velocity, you could know the acceleration. This was how the world worked: three variables running back and forth across the border of an equals sign. *A* equals *B* times *C*. *B* equals *A* over *C*. *C* equals *A* over *B*. Put the letters in a box and *sink* them, and the sentences would still be true.

He had grown up to be a physicist because a childhood of waiting for magic had made him fall in love with facts. And though facts had almost nothing to do with his work—with the pages of calculus and brackets and Greek letters that cluttered his desk and his memory—the possibility of finding the truth still got him up in the morning, still kept him up, surprised, at night.

AT NINE FORTY-FIVE that morning, Alexander's phone rang. It was an extraordinary occurrence in an office that required no information and provided none, and Alexander watched it ring, then watched it after the ringing had stopped. He didn't want interruptions. He only wanted to work. He thought: It's really going to happen, this is really going to happen.

Alexander sat at his desk and called up a file on his computer. The strength of his approach depended on linking eight complex mathematical proofs together: breaking one wildly esoteric equation down into eight more manageable steps. The file he was concerned with now was the fifth of these very crucial proofs. He had already checked through the first four, searching for errors and contradictions, trying to guess what a critic would say.

His phone continued to ring, and he continued to ignore it.

Sometime past ten, Bruce Biner's long-suffering secretary appeared at Alexander's door, a small notebook in her hand and a wild look on her face.

"He wants to see me?" Alexander asked.

"I've been calling you all morning!" she said.

"I've been working all morning."

"We're all working, Mr. Simon."

"I bet it can wait," Alexander said. "I bet it can wait until he gets back."

"You want Dr. Biner to *wait?*" she said.

BINER HAD BEEN invited to lecture in Switzerland at CERN, one of the top three physics labs in the world. Downstairs, on the main floor, he was standing behind the desk in his office, which was just as drab as Alexander's but three times as large. Frenetically, he was stuffing files and notebooks into a shiny leather briefcase. Biner was fifty-eight years old. He conveyed an extraordinary mixture of accomplishment and anxiety. He was a man who spoke constantly about himself without prompting or humor, who stole ideas from younger colleagues without subtlety or remorse, but who could be, with people whose work he needed, sickeningly obsequious. To Alexander, he had seemed a caricature of himself from the moment they had met.

"You're late," Biner said when Alexander walked in.

"I came straight down."

"*I'm* late," Biner said. "You'd think I could get to an airport on time. Why can't I get to an airport on time? These people are *Swiss*. These people make *watches*. These people don't tolerate *lateness*."

Alexander smiled impatiently and wondered what he could say that would help him seem more sympathetic.

"What's wrong with you?" Biner asked, smoothing first his jacket pockets, then his lapels.

"Nothing's wrong with me."

"You look worried."

"Just curious."

"Ah," Biner said.

"You wanted to see me."

"Ah."

His favorite syllable, Alexander thought. It was usually a stall tactic. Biner smiled almost shyly now, planted his knuckles on the desk, and leaned across it, trying to look imposing. "I just wanted to know, Mr. Simon," he said, "if there was anything you had to tell me that I might, should the occasion arise, be able to tell the Swiss."

"Anything—"

"Of course I don't want you to feel any pressure," Biner said, backing down immediately. "I mean I want you to feel no pressure at all. But I gather that you've made quite a bit of progress on your recent calculations."

"How do you gather that?"

Biner gazed back uncomfortably.

"Heinz?" Alexander asked.

"Well, yes."

Alexander's cheeks flushed, and he felt a sudden hollowness in his stomach. He tried to sound nonchalant. "What did he tell you exactly?"

"Well, nothing exactly enough," Biner said. "And of course I didn't really believe him. But that's why I wanted to talk to you."

"We're not ready to publish yet."

"Of course not, of course not," Biner said quickly.

"Heinz is a dweeb," Alexander said.

"Fine, fine," Biner said. "No problem, then. That's fine." He seemed truly stricken.

"It's still too soon to talk," Alexander said, more gently. "I don't want to promise something I can't deliver."

"Of course not," Biner said again.

Alexander hoped that he had sounded convincing. The truth was that a part of him would have loved to tell Biner all about his theory, and to see Biner's face light up with wonder, and to have Biner tell the Swiss. But Alexander knew that there was much too much at stake. He watched as Biner threw his

Burberry raincoat over his arm, picked up his bags, and stopped at the door. "Sorry for asking," Biner said. His bushy eyebrows had straightened into one anxious line.

"You'll miss your plane," Alexander said.

Biner groaned and looked at his watch.

Again, Alexander fought the impulse to tell him how far along he really was. He managed to say nothing. He watched as Biner walked down the empty hallway and turned the corner at the end. Again, but more intensely, Alexander felt what he'd been feeling all morning: the wild, specific fear of having nothing in his way.

His legs were actually shaking. Back in his office, he put his arms on his desk and his head in his arms, and he thought about his Theory of Everything, and he thought: It's really going to happen, this is really going to happen.

ALEXANDER LOCKED his door and unplugged his phone and worked straight through the morning. But the reminder that Biner was waiting had made it hard to concentrate. Intermittently, Alexander tried to track down Heinz, but if Heinz had been dumb enough to spill the beans, he had also been smart enough to clear out of Alexander's way.

Despite himself, Alexander liked Heinz. Heinz was lanky and pale and spectacled, the template for a thousand aspiring physicists who would have been engineers if they'd been less good at math. But Heinz had balance the way that Alexander had dreams. Heinz knew how to enjoy himself. He had a gift for happiness in all things that struck Alexander alternately with wonder and contempt.

Looking out his window, Alexander rehearsed the lecture he would give to Heinz, if he ever got hold of him. Think of cold fusion, he would say: Remember Pons and Fleischman, because soon nobody else would. Think of Blas Cabrera, he'd say: the

Stanford physicist who'd discovered a rare particle, let others hype his findings too soon, and then become a laughingstock for not having had the proof. The world of physics was filled with premature headlines and Nobel-seeking jerks. Alexander didn't want to be one of them. He wanted to be the real thing.

He returned to his desk and worked through lunch. By midafternoon, he had forgotten about Biner, forgotten about Heinz, and was safely inside the numbers. To be inside the numbers meant to be so steeped in their language and shape that the world regained its old and awesome purity. This was a world of symbols and proportions, a world with a kind of beauty both magnificent and hard, and it was the one world that Alexander had never been forced to share.

STILL STRUGGLING with the fifth proof, he missed his usual train back into the city. It was seven-thirty by the time he came home, and he climbed the stairs of the brownstone, past his own apartment to Linda's. Her front door was wide open, and her living room was empty. "Linda?" he shouted, mildly alarmed.

"In here," she called to him. "Rowing."

He dropped his keys on her kitchen counter and walked into her bedroom. It was identical only in size to his, cluttered by the evidence of a hundred remembered choices: this sofa over the blue one she'd seen; this china; these glasses; these things from home. Alexander's apartment was thoroughly different from Linda's, an uneasy mix of stark, useful things he had bought for himself out of need, not want, and a number of others he didn't need and hadn't chosen but felt he should keep. Linda's place was infinitely nicer, but she spent most nights downstairs at his.

He paused at her bedroom door, watching her from behind as she moved back and forth on the rowing machine. She was wearing a faded gray T-shirt and a pair of short black shorts, and she was rowing as if she was being chased. Her head was tucked, her arms taut, and a thin line of perspiration showed on her back. She didn't look up when he walked into the room, and her concentration delighted him. Alexander loved to watch Linda when she didn't know he was watching her. Often in the evenings he would come upstairs and find her sitting at her coffee table, correcting her students' spelling tests. Small shiny piles of colored stars would be spread out before her, and she would be tapping her foot to unheard music, and she would be so intent and so absent from him that he'd find it oddly stirring.

Most kinds of scientific discovery depended on observation at a distance, and what Alexander discovered when he watched Linda at a distance always seemed more solid to him than what he could see close up.

"You shouldn't leave the door open," he told her.

"I know," she said, and kept rowing.

"Anyone could walk in."

"I know."

He settled on the bed. Linda was always leaving doors unlocked and wanting to walk through Central Park at night, and Alexander was always giving her speeches about her safety. Physical danger was one of the things he thought he could control. Others were money, neatness, health, sobriety, and memories. Alexander liked control. He didn't want to lecture now to Linda, though. He watched her row. "Where are we this evening?" he asked her.

"The Thames," she said without slowing down.

Her hair, blond and red, straight and short, hid her eyes.

"The Thames!" he said. "That's where you were yesterday."

"It's a big river," she said.

He sighed. "I'll never know how you can do that without getting angry that you're not getting somewhere."

"Never know?" she said. "You'll figure it out someday." She

looked up at him and smiled. It was the same smile he'd seen that morning. It was a smile that suggested she knew something vital about him, and that he would have to keep her if he wanted to find out what it was. He had been with Linda for two years now, and he still wasn't sure if her smile was a bluff or a promise.

He leaned over the edge of the bed to tuck a flap of her bedspread in. Even if Linda knew him, he thought, that wouldn't change what there was to know. He stared out the windows at the flowers she had planted. This was the other big difference between their apartments. Linda's had a door to a private roof. The roof was the size of a whole other room, and Linda had made it a garden. Impatiens hung from the railing, and geraniums came up pink and red in the sooty air, not knowing that their colors should be any less vivid in the filthy city.

Looking at the flowers, Alexander thought about the first weekend they had spent up here, how he'd seen Linda tanned from the sun, sweating, her oldest clothes smeared with soil and dried paint. She had been humming to herself, and then she had stopped when she'd seen him watching. "What?" she had asked him.

"Just listening," he'd said.

Linda had turned back to her plants and had gone on humming, and in that sweet, ample moment of her self-assurance, Alexander had looked back through the windows to contemplate her bed.

Now he thought about all the fine dinners Linda had made for him and that they had shared on her roof in the late summer light. He thought about how her presence had helped to shield him from his obsession with work. There was something fierce and glorious about her, which he understood as an absence of fear. Half the time, he wanted to share it. The other half, he told himself that it wasn't an absence of fear, but of thought.

"Tell me what you're going through. *Explain* it," she was saying now.

Alexander sighed.

"I know you're not going to tell me about your nightmare," Linda said.

"I didn't have a nightmare."

"Right. As I say. I know that's not, like, up for major discussion. But what about work?" she said. "You're nervous, right? Or excited."

"Right."

"Which?"

"I don't know, Linda." He had never liked telling his worries to her, and least of all his worries with work. All he had said to her lately was that he thought he'd be writing his article soon. He didn't understand why he couldn't tell her more. His reticence often angered her. He tried to oblige her in other ways.

Now Linda glided to a stop, and the shining arms of the rowing machine let out a long, exhausted hiss. "You know," she said, "you don't talk about this stuff, and tiny, nasty beasties start tromping around in your brain and doing the polka and hurting you."

"Look, Linda, I really don't understand it myself."

"I know," she said.

"So stop," he said.

Linda leaned over to undo one of her Velcro foot straps. The muscle in her thigh flexed, clear as a bone.

"How was school?" Alexander asked her.

She laughed. "Oh, the CPA flipped out at recess," she said. Linda had names for some of her students; the CPA was a six-year-old who kept track of his classmates' daily grades. "One of the girls wouldn't tell him what she got on the quiz," Linda said, "and so he tried to bribe her with a cookie, but she was hanging tough."

She undid the other strap and effortlessly stretched her body until her chin rested on her knees.

"Doesn't that hurt?" Alexander asked as Linda tugged on the soles of her feet.

"That's not what hurts," she said, sitting up.

He put a hand on the top of her head. "It's not that I think you won't get it," he told her. "It's just that I don't want to talk about it."

Linda rose from the machine, picked it up, and propped it against the wall. Then she curled up next to him on the bed. "Well, for once I know something you don't know," she said.

"You know lots of things I don't know."

"I mean really. I've got news," she said. She ran her fingers through her bangs.

"What?"

"Guess."

"I love your hair," he said. He had never said that he loved just her. He had never liked making statements that were based more on hunch than on absolute proof.

"Guess," Linda said again.

"You got home early and you cooked us a great dinner."

"Guess."

"I got home late and I'm *going* to cook us a great dinner."

"God, I've got to take a shower," Linda said.

"*What*, already?" Alexander asked.

"The guys are starting Thursday."

After a winter of doubt and debate, Linda and Alexander had decided to break through her floor to his ceiling, tear out his kitchen, rip down some walls, and turn the two apartments into one large duplex. Linda was handling the details.

"Of what month?" Alexander asked her.

"Alexander."

He laughed, and she frowned.

"They said the same thing last week."

"No. Really. George—you know, the one who speaks English? He called today and said this time they're really going to be here. Ten o'clock sharp. I got a substitute and everything. To take homeroom tomorrow. I'm going to spend the whole day packing. Isn't it great?"

"It's great," he told her.

She took his hand, and they sat on the edge of the bed together, silent, like children waiting for punishment.

She nuzzled against his shoulder. "Let's not get cranky," she said.

"We won't."

"Good. I'll take care of this. You take care of work."

Alexander stood up and took off his jacket, walking toward the bedroom door. "I've got to get out of these clothes," he said.

"Are you hungry?" she asked.

He shrugged.

The cat, whose name was Rogue, leapt up onto Linda's lap, and she lay back, lifting him in the air, then holding him tight against her.

LINDA HAD HAD only the sketchiest idea of what a physicist did when Alexander first told her that he was one. But Linda, Alexander learned later, had not been very pleased. Her automatic image had been of Robert Laster, the eleventh- and twelfth-grade physics teacher whom the girls said they hated because of the large mole on his chin and because of the way he rubbed his stomach whenever he got excited. Linda had gone to the science department office once and found Mr. Laster lying on the floor, chuckling merrily over two pages of an equation that he'd told her was thirty-one pages long. She'd asked him for an aspirin, he'd pointed to a shelf, and he'd chuckled again, more wistfully, as he'd turned to the next page.

A physicist. Great, she'd thought.

"But don't worry," Alexander had added. "I only think about work when I'm there."

She had been wary, but it had taken no time at all to convince her. He'd been funny and helpful and normal. He was handsome, in a nerdy way: dark eyes, dark curly hair, a lanky body, strong arms. He had asked her a lot about herself, and sometimes he'd even read short stories or novels after dinner. Of course there had been the sex, too, and all the daily embraces. He could be both gentle and sweet with her. He told her that he felt lucky he'd met her, and she said that made her feel lucky as well.

Occasionally, emptying out his pockets for the wash, Linda would find a scrap of paper on which he'd scribbled some strange notations, but he'd never made notes like that when he was home.

Instead, she had wound up begging him to talk about his work, and when she really pressed him, he would tell her about the geeks who worked at Wilson, and he'd make fun of Heinz and Talbot—"nerd savants," he called them—and then he would ask her how her day had been. Every once in a great while, he would offer analogies to explain something in physics, simple stories that charmed her but that she knew were far too simple.

She loved the stories despite herself. She hated the condescension. Sometimes—more and more, recently—she would tell him that their romance was doomed because he would need someone or meet someone whom he deemed smart enough to understand his work. Then Alexander would tell her that it had nothing to do with smartness. He would say that he didn't want to *be* like all those wacko scientists who spoke and thought about nothing else, that what he wanted instead was to come *home* at night. They both loved the idea of home.

At the beginning, Linda had seemed to believe him, but

more often now, she would give him the knowing smile. She
told him that by keeping his work to himself, he kept a crucial
part of himself secure, unchanged by the relationship, and that
much more invulnerable. She told him that that gave him
control, but he didn't know if she understood how much more
than his work he kept hidden. Mostly what he was hiding was
the depth of his own fear.

THE FEAR HAD to do with what was unknown. To Alexander,
some mysteries seemed less inevitable than others. Since childhood, he had felt helpless before the mystery of things that were
large. Ever since the Railroad Ghost, the night sky had always
terrified and reduced him. Even now, at thirty, he was grateful
when the city smog obscured the stars. Caught on clear nights
out on Linda's roof, he would try to remind himself that everything in his body and his line of sight was made up from the
dust of stars. He would try to imagine the stars and himself as
geometric points. He would try to imagine lines that reached
up from him to the heavens, as if he were a part of them.

It had never worked. Planets and stars spun like wheels in
the night sky, rolling away from him, flattening ideas and
intentions, insisting on forever. The number of stars was infinite. Infinity scared him more than death.

The mystery of the atom had been a totally different thing:
for some reason, it had never seemed as inevitable, as huge. In
sixth grade, Mr. Caldwell had drawn the atom on the blackboard, and it had even looked like the solar system, with elec-
trons orbiting the nucleus the way the planets orbited the sun.
But atoms had seemed more manageable, less mystical, less
ancient. Atoms had never beamed down on lovers; they had
never guided sailors; they had never been wished on. People
had found them. People had wanted to know what the world
was built with, how it all could work.

As an idea, the atom had existed since before the birth of Christ, since the Greeks first sat in the Aegean sun and studied a handful of sand. Every human impulse had always dictated the same thing: if you kept looking, you would find something basic, something with which the world was made. Bodies were made of cells. Photographs were made of dots. Beaches were made of sand.

But then they took the sand apart, and the world kept getting smaller. They found that inside the sand were atoms, billions in a single grain. They found that inside the atom there existed a tiny nucleus. The nucleus was so tiny compared to the atom itself that to picture how small it was, one had to imagine a grape in the middle of a football field. And then they found things even smaller that were inside the grape, things called quarks and gluons, and the things that they found did not make sense. They didn't behave like grains of sand. They weren't alike. They wouldn't stack up. They wouldn't exist in normal time. They weren't logical, and they weren't pretty. The world shouldn't have worked.

It was as though someone had taken apart a beautiful ticking clock and found that the insides were only cotton. The cover had gently been put back on. The clock went on ticking, but the sound was hollow, and no one could trust the time.

This was the mystery that Alexander had not accepted. At first, like the mystery of the sky at night, it had made him depressed and frightened. But then, unlike that mystery, it had made him feel defiant. He was going to be a physicist, he'd said when people asked him. He was going to find the thing inside the clock that made it work.

"WHAT DO PEOPLE *do* out there at the lab?" Linda would ask.

"They're trying to prove that the world is real," Alexander would tell her.

"I wish you'd take me seriously."

"I do take you seriously."

"You don't think I'm smart enough."

"Of course I think you're smart enough."

"Then tell me," she would say.

"I *am* telling you," he would insist—and he was. Because what the people at the lab were doing was using the accelerator to break the world down into its smallest parts. That was why they referred to the huge machines as atom smashers. The machines took particles of atoms and sent them around in circles at enormous speeds, and then made them collide so that smaller particles would be formed. Physicists were still trying to find out what the world was made of, but the more they looked for it, the more elusive it seemed to be.

"Let's say you hear about a certain house," Alexander had said to Linda once, trying to explain. "A friend of yours has seen it, and he knows you're in the market. He calls you to say that he's seen this house. It's right over there in Brooklyn. It's got three bedrooms and a nice kitchen. It's in a nice residential area with lots of other houses.

" 'What's it made of?' you ask him.

" 'Brick,' he says.

" 'Great,' you say. 'Brick. I love brick.'

"So you go to the house, and the house is great, but you've got to make sure it's solid.

" 'Let's take a look at these bricks,' you say.

"You sneak into the basement and you find a whole pile of them lying there. You pick one up, but the second you do, it turns into dust.

"What the hell is this? you think. How can this thing be standing?

"You go outside, and you look at the house again. It's solid. It's standing, so the bricks must be real. Maybe it's only the fact that you touched them that made them fall apart.

"But something's either there or it's not there, you think. And if it's there, you should be able to pick it up and examine it. Tough luck. You can't. And that's nuclear physics."

LINDA WASN'T beside him when Alexander woke up the next morning, and he found her upstairs in her apartment, already dressed and working. She was taking her books from the bookshelf—grabbing clumps of them with both hands and humming as she did. Alexander stood by the couch, looking at the stacks of books all around her.

"Don't you want to keep them in order?" he asked.

"Morning!" she said. "What order?"

"Don't you want to keep them alphabetized?"

"They've never *been* alphabetized," she said.

"Oh, God."

"Relax, Alexander," she said. "Relax."

"Well, how do you ever find a book?"

Linda turned from the bookshelf and smiled with exaggerated calm. "Tell you what," she said as if she was talking to one of her students. "When it's all done, and the new bookshelves are built, I'll let you put all the books together and organize them any way you like."

"But what are you planning to *do* with all this?"

"Well," Linda said, "after you go to work, I'm going to go to the grocery store and get a lot of boxes. You're going to pick up more boxes on your way home. And then I'll put all the books in all the boxes."

Alexander stared at the empty shelf above her head.

"Alexander," Linda said.

"I was thinking none of this is going to look the same after today."

"Yes," Linda said. "That's the general idea. Boy, you gotta

get up pretty early in the morning to put one over on you."
"I don't know," he said.
"Go to work. You'll feel better. Write some squiggles. Smash
an atom."
He knew she would want a kiss, and so he kissed her, watch-
ing her eyes close.
"I'll try to leave early," he said, hating the Boy Scout tone
in his voice. "Get back and help you."
"Lighten up," she said.

WAITING FOR the subway car to come, he leaned against a
steel post, trying not to inhale because the smell of urine was
so overpowering. A black man in cutoff blue jeans and a
stained yellow shirt approached him ferociously. "Jesus!" the
man shouted.
    Alexander took a step back.
    "Jesus!" the man shouted again, then reached into his pocket.
Alexander looked around the platform wildly. But the man
merely pulled out a tiny Bible. "He's coming," the man said
quietly.
    Alexander smiled politely and looked into the dark tunnel.
    At first there was utter blackness, and then the sense of
possible light. Silver beams from the approaching train crept
forward on the tracks like mercury. Then there was the rush of
the stale air, and he was safely inside the crowded car.
    Pressed between two made-up women on the train to Penn
Station, he heard their voices but not their words. The subway
shook from side to side and then ground to a halt, the lights
out. In the darkness, Alexander thought of the man on the
platform and wondered what it would be like to believe in God.
Then he thought about his angel, whom he never allowed himself to call an angel. It wasn't too fitting for a physicist to have

an angel, but Alexander had one. He had had one for years. "Touch me," Alexander always said to her. She came to him in strange dreams, and she left him with strange memories.

"WILL IT HURT US?" Alexander asked.

He looked up at Alice when she didn't answer, but her face was too high above his, and she wouldn't look down. He could see her chin, which was pointed at the darkness like a hound's snout, and he could see the cushiony folds of her purple sweater and the gold locket that fell over its turtleneck collar and swung back and forth like a pendulum. "Mom," he said as bravely as he could. "I'm scared."

Her hand rested briefly on his head. "Me too," she said gaily, "but that's the fun of it, isn't it?"

"No," he whispered.

With his right hand, Alexander made a tight fist around the folds in his mother's sweater, and he didn't let go.

AT THIRTY, Alexander still had one memory of his mother that was more vivid than the rest, and it was of standing with her in a misty field and waiting for a ghost to come. Sometimes he remembered that it had come, but most times he hated that memory and would make himself think of something else.

Alice had believed in ghosts, of course. She had also believed in horoscopes. In palmistry. Numerology. She had spoken about past lives the way some people recall great dinners. She had told her husband about his Aries and her son about his Saturn. She had gloated about her Taurus.

She had wanted everything Sam couldn't give her—principally money and magic.

When Alexander was eleven, Alice had gone to a numerologist, and she'd won the New York lottery after following his advice.

Well, Alexander had said as a child when friends or teachers asked him. Well, he'd said, she decided to travel. Well, he'd said, we don't really know. Well, he'd said, she just wanted to live a different kind of life for a while.

What had really happened to Alice was that in one stroke, she had won more money than she'd ever made Sam feel guilty about not earning. Then she'd gone a little bit crazy. She had tried to spend it all so she could want something again.

Sam went on teaching high school science in a New York private girls school, and Alice filled their apartment with furniture and paintings and workmen making "improvements." Then one day, with no warning, Alice took off, alone, for Europe. The first year, she sent Alexander postcards with colorful stamps, and she sent Sam a lot more furniture and artwork with explicit instructions on what to put where. Then there was a silence. And then, on Alexander's twelfth birthday, he received a nineteenth-century armoire and a long, too-chatty letter.

He had eighteen such letters now, filed chronologically in an accordion folder that he kept in the bottom drawer of his desk. Alice had never come back. She had never explained why. She had sent Alexander two armoires, four tables, six ugly paintings, two beautiful lithographs, one umbrella stand, one mirror, and one miniature chest of drawers inlaid with ivory. He kept the chest, the umbrella stand, and the smaller paintings in one of the armoires. He kept his clothes in the other. He had put two of the tables beneath his stereo speakers, one in front of his couch, and one in the back of his closet, along with the bigger paintings. The lithographs, which were spectral images of women drawn by Matisse, he hung above his bed.

It had been nearly twenty years since Alexander had seen his mother. Sam hadn't seen her either. She had left their lives like pain, leaving nothing to grab onto when they tried to say how it had been.

THE SUBWAY swung into motion again. The lights came back on, and around Alexander, the passengers blinked and adjusted their clothes.

Alexander watched as a passing train flew by on a parallel track, and then the field and the ghost and his mother departed, and the work filled up his mind again, the way a substance under pressure will rush into an open vessel.

THE BASIS OF any Theory of Everything was a search for or-der—not just inside the atom, but throughout the universe. To do the work on his theory, Alexander had to see beyond all the particles and subparticles. He had to ponder forces.

The dictionary defines a force as a strength exerted or brought to bear, as a cause of change or motion, as an active power. Love can be a force, therefore, and so can fear. So can the moon and the wind and the sea, and a million other things that move.

Forces, though, in physics, are a great deal more specific, and a lot harder to find. In fact, only four are known to exist: two that are known from the visible world, and two whose effects remain beyond sight. Gravity and electromagnetism are the forces that act on the world we know. The strong force and the weak force keep our atoms from blowing apart. But every known action in every known place in the known universe can be explained by one of these forces.

You'd think that realizing this would be a comfort. You'd think that it would be like finding out that anyone you ever met, anywhere in the world, would speak in one of four languages.

But physicists like Alexander ask this question: Why four? They ask: Why not twelve? Why not seven?

Above all, they ask: Why not one?

Physicists who search for the Theory of Everything say maybe the four forces are part of a whole—not really different languages, just different dialects. Since they would like to find out that relativity and quantum theory are two sides of the same coin, they say gravity, the force essential to relativity, the force that swings the moon around the earth, must be reconciled with the other forces, the ones essential to quantum theory, the ones that work on atoms. They say maybe there was just one force in that flash when the universe was new, but then the force broke into pieces. And they spend their lives trying to put the pieces back together again. The theory they are searching for is meant to unite the four forces, and thus the moon and the atoms.

In the complicated mathematics that they use to conduct their search, they keep finding illogical numbers—numbers they call infinities, and sometimes call ghosts. Like nonsense words, the ghosts can be very useful, but they don't really have any meaning. Physicists go to great lengths to get rid of the ghosts.

Given Alexander's memories and his dreams, the irony of fighting ghosts had never been lost on him. But as with most things he didn't understand and didn't think he was going to, he tended to push it from his mind.

AT THE LAB that day, Alexander stayed by the window for most of the morning, and he played through equations in his head like songs.

He knew what he was doing. It was one of the good days. He had the sense of his own power, the slightly guilty sense of having something that was rare. It was the same feeling he had

had as a boy, climbing trees with Sam in Central Park—nimble enough and brave enough to go a branch beyond him.

"What's it like up there?" Sam had always asked. Sam had never said, "Come down," which was just what Alice would have said. Sam had never seemed to mind.

"It's great up here!" Alexander had shouted, a little sorry he'd climbed ahead but not enough to stop climbing.

That was how he felt now, struggling for the next step, giddy, knowing that at times his mind could work as well as a machine.

ON THE WAY BACK from the subway that evening, Alexander bought flowers for Linda, and he braced himself for chaos and climbed the stairs to her apartment. He soothed himself with an old game he had—counting off the stairs with the names of the chemical elements. It was a pointless game, he knew, but it usually calmed him down. Hydrogen, helium, lithium. Seventy-two was hafnium. He caught his breath and stood at Linda's door, reading the note she had left for him.

"I'm downstairs taking a bath," it said. "Come on and join me. The door's unlocked."

Alexander shook his head and crumpled the note in his hand. This was New York City, he thought, and she leaves an open invitation on her door. He walked back down the flight of stairs. Everything in nature had an essential characteristic, he thought; in Linda, it was probably trust.

"In here!" she shouted when he called her name. He walked into his bedroom. "Come on in!" she shouted, and he opened the bathroom door.

"How could you leave this note just sitting there for anyone to—" Alexander stopped.

She was lying back in the bathtub wearing a large pair of

fuzzy white and pink rabbit ears. The pink of the ears matched the pink tops of her knees.

He leaned against the door. Despite himself, he grinned.

Linda giggled. "I found them when I was packing things up."

"Do you know how cute you look?"

"How was your day?" she asked him.

"Fine," he said.

He put the flowers in the sink, unbuttoned his shirt collar, and loosened his tie.

"Dinner!" Linda said, pointing to the flowers. "Great!"

She watched as Alexander removed his shirt. "Anything much happen today?" she asked.

He smiled at her again. "Don't forget to wash behind your ears," he said.

She laughed. She looked at him. "Come on in," she said. "The water's fine."

He tossed his jeans into the wicker hamper and took off his underwear. Then he stepped into the bathtub. He grabbed the handle of the soap holder and lowered himself into the cool water, arranging his legs around Linda's. Then he put his hands on her shoulders, and pulled her toward him. He straightened her ears, which had skewed to one side.

"You know," she said, "if we had another pair of these, we could fuck like rabbits."

LINDA WENT UPSTAIRS to call out for sandwiches, and when Alexander joined her, she was kneeling on the floor against her couch, reaching behind the cushions. Alexander watched her as she pulled out a book of matches and a dollar bill, shifted them into her left hand, then dug up some loose coins. She turned around as soon as she heard the door close.

"Look what I found," she said. She opened her fist and counted the change. "A buck forty-eight. That makes—what's a buck forty-eight and six dollars and thirteen cents?"

"Seven sixty-one," Alexander said, distracted. He was looking around the room. Her bookshelves, he saw, were completely bare, but they would need to be dismantled. Her paintings and drawings and antique signs had been removed from the walls, with the exception of the old phone company sign she had put up with an elaborate system of bolts and braces.

"That makes seven sixty-one," Linda said. She walked to the empty bookshelf, where other coins were strewn like winning chips.

"Like it?" she said, gesturing to the stacks of carton boxes and roped-up paintings.

"Give me a minute," Alexander said. It had suddenly occurred to him that she would always be there.

Linda smiled and led him, as if he were an invalid, to the center of the couch. She rested her head against his shoulder, and he stroked her back.

"How'd it really go today?" she asked him.

"It really went fine," he said.

She had rolled back her old hooked rug, and along with the couch, the chairs, and the coffee table, it would need to be stacked in a corner somewhere and covered with sheets or tarpaulins. He realized that he'd forgotten to bring home the boxes he'd promised that morning, and he felt a brief pang of guilt, seeing all the ones she had brought up on her own.

"Do we need more boxes?" he asked.

"No. Not yet."

"Sorry."

"For what?"

"That I didn't bring you boxes."

"That's okay," she said. "I managed."

"Where'd you put the phone book?" he asked her.

"The phone book," she said.

"Yes."

"I packed it," she said. "Why? You need to make a call?"

"Which box?" he asked, hating the way their voices seemed to echo in the foreign room.

"Which box? I don't know," she said.

"Didn't you mark it?"

"No."

"Linda!"

"I have a system."

He glared at her.

"Oh come *on*," she said. "Give me a break."

"I can't *believe* you're just throwing all this stuff in without marking it."

"Yes you can," she said evenly. "We've known each other for two years."

"I can't believe it."

"Oh, honestly," Linda said. "It's just for a few weeks, and anyway, it's my stuff, and it would have taken me *twice* as long to mark it all up. You want to do a filing system for your stuff, that's fine."

"I don't want to do a *filing* system," Alexander said. "I just want to know where things are. If we're going to live together, I just want to know where things are."

Linda stared at him sideways, then stood up and stared at him head-on. "You're scared to death, aren't you?" she asked.

He looked at his feet and thought about the question, and then looked up at her and smiled.

"Well that's just peachy," she said. "But don't take it out on me."

IN HIS DREAM that night, Alexander said, "The secret. I can keep the secret. Tell me what it is."

The angel said: "I know things that will make you understand the whole universe."

Alexander said: "Touch me."

The angel didn't touch him, but she held out a finger, like God in the Sistine Chapel, and then she disappeared. In his bed, next to Linda, Alexander woke up utterly certain that someone had just left the room.

THE FIRST HEAT of the summer settled on the city the next evening, early and startling, dense as lead. With all the windows open, Linda and Alexander could still find no breeze. The dust seemed to engulf them. Alexander worked in his apartment through the evening, packing his things away into boxes. He paused only once: to reread his mother's letters. But he slammed the accordion file shut when he heard Linda coming downstairs. She kept him company, marking his boxes for him with her large, neat blackboard lettering. By ten o'clock, they were nearly done. Alexander had taken off his shirt, but his back and chest were slick with sweat. Linda and he resorted to the bathtub, facing each other, knees up, taking turns with the soap.

"*Christ*. It's only *May*," Alexander said.

"We need to get that air conditioner."

"No shit," he said.

"Well, why don't we do it this weekend?"

"I'm going to have to work," he said.

"Work," Linda repeated. "All weekend?" she asked.

"Why don't you pick one out and get one of the guys to bring it over?"

"I'll see," Linda said. She reached behind Alexander to turn on the water. A deep groan rose from the pipes.

"God," she said. "We've got to get that fixed."

"Not much we can do," he said. "It's just the cavitation in

the pipes. They make oscillations, and the oscillations get amplified."

Linda turned off the faucet and glared. The groaning stopped, and there was silence.

"Sorry," Alexander said.

"Cavitation?" she asked.

"Bubbles."

"You could have said so." She leaned back again and picked up the soap. "All weekend?" she asked again.

Alexander nodded, and then he watched as she soaped her arms. He thought how incredible it was that he had become accustomed to her body. That the mere factor of time—two years was longer than he'd spent with anyone—had so radically changed compulsion to regimen. She was absolutely no less pretty than the first time they had met. She was small but feisty, her hair red and gold, gold and red, depending on the season. Her eyelashes were still impossibly long, her body still impossibly fit, her smile still impossibly present, and yet she was different. She was overwhelmingly *there*. She was inescapably possible.

Linda had grown up in Chicago, but she'd spent summers on her grandparents' farm in South Dakota, and when she walked down Columbus Avenue she looked as if she were striding home to supper through fields of wheat. Her cheeks were always a little pink. Alexander was floored by the fact that she had milked a cow.

They had met on a mild autumn night, the night the brownstone next to theirs had caught fire. It had been three in the morning, and Linda had spotted Alexander at the bottom of the stoop. He had been wearing blue jeans, penny loafers, and a baggy blue wool sweater; he had been jiggling his keys in one hand and holding a wallet and comb in the other. The rest of the dozen or so tenants had been dressed in bathrobes or pajamas. Linda herself had been wearing a ratty black wool coat over a man's dress shirt. Alexander had looked at her and wondered where the man was. Linda had looked at him and wondered why he had brought a comb.

"A comb?" she had asked him, smiling, hoarse with sleep.

"Force of habit," he had said. He'd seemed only dimly embarrassed, maybe not embarrassed at all. Linda told him later that she hadn't been able to decide which she thought was more intriguing, or which she had hoped would be true.

"I've got a cat," she had said. "He's up there. I should get him. Don't you think?"

Alexander had smiled and walked over quickly to one of the firemen. "There's a cat up there," Alexander had said. "Should I go get him or is everything okay?"

"That's all right," the fireman had said. "We've got it all under control."

"It's all right," Alexander had said to Linda. "They've got it all under control."

"Thanks."

"What's the cat's name?"

"Rogue," Linda had told him.

"That's a good name for a cat."

"What's yours?"

Months later, Linda would tell Alexander that she had fallen for him because he hadn't been embarrassed that he'd had a comb in his hand and because his voice had sounded so deep and sure when he'd asked the fireman about Rogue. "You were just so grown-up," she had said to him. He thought that she probably didn't believe that now. But still, she would stroke the front of his neck and say, "You know, I love the sound of your voice." She had never let herself say that she loved all of him either. Alexander was sure that she would have said it if he had said it himself. The thought of her self-restraint touched him and also made him nervous.

Now she picked up her blue teddy bear sponge and soaped the place between her legs, looking up at him shyly. The teddy bear had been a gift from a former boyfriend, and it was one of the many odd remnants of Linda's past that cluttered her apartment like pieces of ancient armor. He didn't like to think about Linda's past, or about her future.

Alexander reached out for her hand and kissed her knuckles, which tasted of soap.

"That tickles!" she said.

"Let's make love."

"Here? The water will slosh all over the place."

"Not if we're careful with the volume of displacement."

"I know a way that's neater," she said, bending down.

In her bed hours later, with his eyes adjusting to the darkness, and his heartbeat to the rhythm of her breathing, he touched her hair guiltily and studied her face. She even smiled when she slept.

ON THURSDAY, Heinz finally resurfaced. He stood in the doorway to Alexander's office, twisting a rubber band in his hands and smiling through the diatribe.

"You don't," Alexander said, "tell the head of the whole goddamn lab that we are ready when we're not."

Heinz nodded tragically.

"You don't," Alexander said, "go shooting your mouth off about stuff that isn't yours to boast about in the first place."

Heinz hung his head.

"Think," Alexander said, "of what happened to Blas Cabrera. Do you want the same thing to happen to us?"

Still looking down, Heinz shook his head no.

"Do you want," Alexander finally asked, "for this whole thing to blow up in my face?"

Heinz looked up at Alexander, a trace of a grin on his face.

"You're right," he said. "It's all my fault."

Then he shut the door to the office, stretched the rubber band over his index finger, and shot it at his head. He fell to the floor with a deathly groan.

"Oh, get the hell up," Alexander said.

"I killed myself," Heinz whispered back from the floor.

"Biner's going to be back in ten days. It would be awfully nice if we had something *real* to tell him."

IN 1906, a well-known Viennese scientist named Ludwig Boltzmann blew his brains out with a shotgun. Gossipy scientists blamed Ernst Mach. Mach had ridiculed Boltzmann for believing in the atom. No one believed in the atom then, and Mach said it was absurd to believe in anything that could not be seen. In effect, Mach said that Ludwig Boltzmann might as well have believed in ghosts.

The prejudice in those days was that truth could only be proven by the evidence of the senses. By Alexander's time, of course, the prejudice had changed.

Ever since the 1920s, when Heisenberg had come up with the uncertainty principle, physicists had fallen in love with an esoteric, unprovable world. The uncertainty principle basically said that you could never know exactly what was happening inside an atom, because whenever you looked, you changed what was there. The particles of light that you needed to see by would always knock things around.

Explaining to Linda the way physics was now, Alexander would say that it was kind of like trying to find out if a light bulb stayed on inside a refrigerator when the door was closed. Once you opened the door to look, you altered the experiment. Physicists like Alexander who still craved a more rational view of the world were usually seen as old-fashioned and quaint.

Einstein, strangely enough, had been one of those physicists.

He had never accepted the mystical implications of quantum theory. "God does not play dice with the universe!" had been his famous response to the randomness that lay at its heart. It hadn't made sense to Einstein that the laws that seemed to apply so perfectly to large things wouldn't work for things that were small. Einstein spent the last thirty years of his life looking for a theory that would link the moon to the atom.

"Why does there have to be just one theory?" Linda had asked Alexander once.

"Because there just does," he had told her.

"Why?"

"Linda."

"Why?"

"I don't know. It just makes *sense*, that's all."

"Why should things make sense?" she had asked.

3

THE ANGEL

AS PROMISED, the men did show up at the apartment that Thursday. It was the first of June. Linda broke an unspoken rule and called Alexander at the lab to tell him.

"They're here!" she cried. "Four of them! One's wearing a hard hat, I swear! There's paper, there's plaster everywhere—"

Her voice had the breathy enthusiasm that he'd once told her he loved and that he'd never been able to trust since then.

"Are you all right?" Alexander asked, cutting her off.

"Sure. I'm fine. I just wanted to tell you."

"Well, it's great," Alexander said.

"Are you busy?"

"Yes."

"How's it going?"

"Fine."

She sighed. "Well, hurry home, pal," Linda said to him.

But it would be hours before he would have to face the mess at home—hours in which he could finish rechecking the sixth of his proofs, and then hours in which he could tell Sam all about what he had done. On Thursdays, Alexander always went to see his father. The ritual was drinks, chess, dinner, and at least one reference by Sam to someone else's grandchild or daughter-in-law.

Alexander had chosen Thursday nights—as he chose most things, when he had to make a choice—only after much thought. He felt that Sam needed the visit to help him through the weekend. Friday nights would have helped Sam more. But Friday nights would have been too clear an admission that neither one of them expected Sam's life to change.

AT SEVEN that evening, Alexander stood in the hallway outside his father's apartment, a full bag of deli food in his arms. This was the apartment where he had grown up, where he and Sam had gone on living alone after Alice had left them.

Beneath Alexander's feet were the ugly green and black floor tiles with which Sam had taught him to multiply. Alexander knew without counting that there were exactly 126 of them: six tiles across, twenty-one tiles down. He remembered when his feet had fit together inside one square. He thought about when he had first told Sam his hopes for the Theory of Everything. Alexander grinned, remembering how skeptical Sam had been. He shifted the bag to one arm, rang the doorbell, and smoothed his hair.

"Is it my son?" Sam asked as he opened the door. He was wearing a pair of crumpled khakis and a bright red turtleneck shirt, and he stood with his arms open, a tall, thin, balding, beak-nosed man.

"Red?" Alexander asked as they hugged the bag between them, the heavy door falling against their elbows.

"What's wrong with red?"

"Nothing. I've just never seen you wear it."

Sam closed the door and locked it behind them. He shrugged. "It was on sale." This was a reference to Alice. Alice had lived for sales. "Drink?" Sam asked.

"Sure." Alexander wanted to wait before telling Sam his progress. He wanted to savor the moment.

"Scotch?" Sam asked him.

"Sure."

A bottle was already sitting on the counter in the kitchen. Alexander brought out the ice. Sam poured. They clinked glasses.

"I'm going to cream you tonight," Alexander said, but knew that he wouldn't allow himself to.

"This way, Ex," Sam told him, smiling. He turned off the kitchen light. "The study's a mess. I set up the game in the living room."

Warily, Alexander followed him in. The living room had been Alice's pride, the room that she'd filled with fragile things and had never allowed him to play in—the room that had smelled of floor wax and that she'd taught Alexander to tiptoe through. It had a wall of six windows that had never seen the sun. The windows faced the northeast, and the light only hit for about seven seconds a day, but years ago, years even before Alexander was born, Alice had gladly sacrificed light for location. The point was to live on Park Avenue, no matter how unfashionably north (Ninety-eighth Street), no matter how close (third floor) to the ground.

The room was still an odd, pale blue—paler perhaps with age—and it was still very large by city standards. The wooden floors now needed waxing; the shelves badly needed dusting.

The room was nearly as burdened with furniture as it was with the past.

Sam settled onto the sofa behind the coffee table, and Alexander took the ornate, once-grand French armchair, laughing as he nearly slid off its worn silk upholstery.

"Don't you think it's time you maybe did a little work on this place?" he asked.

"Ready?" Sam said, not looking up from the board. He moved the white pawn that he always moved. Alexander answered with the black pawn that he always moved. Their opening gambits, never changing, were the greetings of a lifelong conversation. They had played thousands of games of chess together; when Alice had left, they had done little else.

There was a silence for three or four minutes as they each developed positions.

"You through grading finals yet?" Alexander asked.

"Almost."

"When does summer session start?"

"Two weeks."

"Your move, Dad."

"Stop talking then," Sam said. He sipped his Scotch and studied the board. "How's Linda?" he asked.

"Fine. It's your move."

Sam hesitated briefly, then moved a knight.

"Sure you want to do that?" Alexander asked.

"Who taught you this game? Who taught you that question?"

Alexander looked up. "I can pin your queen," he said.

"Go ahead," Sam said cheerfully. "Do your worst."

It had been many years since Alexander would have fallen for his father's bluff. Now he tried to decide if he should act as though he had.

"I did it," he said to Sam instead.

"Did what?" Sam asked.

"*It*," Alexander said.

Sam's eyes darted to his son's. "Ex," he said, softly. "Really?"

"Yes."

"Everything?"

"Yes. Everything."

Sam started to take another sip of Scotch, then put his glass down and stood up to pace.

"Now don't get too excited," Alexander said, but his own heart, he realized, was suddenly racing.

"You're done? It all works?" Sam asked him nervously.

"Yes."

"You're sure?"

"*Yes*, Dad. Of course I'm sure. Well, almost sure. I've still got two more proofs to recheck before I start writing the article."

"And does it—what about the ghosts? Does it get rid of the ghosts?"

Alexander smiled. "No ghosts," he said.

"I want to read it when it's done," Sam said gruffly.

"Yes, Dad," Alexander said. For most of his life, he had known more about science than Sam, and he had always tried, gently, to pretend that he didn't.

"Are they going to make you leave the lab?"

"What?"

"Once you finish. Will the deal there end? Will they make you leave the lab?"

"Dad. You don't understand. When I finish this thing, I won't need the damned lab. I'll lecture, I'll teach. I'll be very hot."

"Only if you're right."

"Dad."

"You have to be right."

"Dad. I'm telling you. I'm right."

Alexander looked at his father, who was standing by one of

the dusty windows. "Why aren't you more excited?" he said to Sam's back.

"I'm just trying to think about your future. You should, too."

"God, Dad. I thought you'd say, 'This is it. My son is going to be someone I *teach* about.' I thought you'd be thrilled."

Sam turned back from the window.

"I am thrilled, Ex," he said. "I just think—you've waited so long for this to happen. I just want you to be sure that you're right. How long till you're finished?"

"I don't know. A few weeks. I'm working like crazy."

"Don't tell anyone till you're really finished," Sam said. "You don't want to look like you're shooting your mouth off."

Alexander looked down at the chessboard and took another long sip of Scotch. He moved a pawn, not pinning the queen. "Biner already knows," he said softly.

"You *told* him? How could you tell him! Remember what happened to Blas—"

"Blas Cabrera. Yes, Dad. I know. I *didn't* tell him."

"How did he find out?"

"Heinz. Heinz told him."

"How could you let him do that?"

"I didn't *let* him do it. He just did it."

"So Biner must be going nuts."

"I just told him that Heinz was wrong. He looked like he was going to cry. He felt so bad for pushing me."

"Well, he should," Sam said reflexively. He finished off his own Scotch, and stared at the chessboard as well.

Alexander stood and took Sam's glass, letting his hand rest on his father's shoulder. "Don't worry," he told Sam. "Everything's going to work out fine."

Sam snapped back to attention. "Of course it will," he said. "I've got no doubts," he said. "No doubts at all. If anyone can do it, Ex, you can. I know you can." For the first time, Sam smiled a true smile. "How about some champagne? Don't you think this calls for champagne?" he asked.

"Let's wait till I finish the article."

"How does it feel?" Sam asked his son.

What's it like up there? Alexander could hear his father saying. "It feels fine," Alexander said. "But you're stalling. When I come back, we *play*."

Then he went into the kitchen to refill his father's glass. Standing by the window there, he looked out at the lights across the way and remembered something he hadn't thought about for years. It had taken place on the night in the misty field, on the trip to North Carolina. Alexander saw himself as a boy running through the darkness toward the white lights of the rented car, running like a demon through the vacant field that stretched between his mother and his father.

He remembered how he had seen his father's foot and leg emerge below the opened car door.

"Ex?" Sam had called out to him urgently. "Ex? Are you all right?"

"Daddy! Dad!" Alexander had shouted.

His father had lifted him up.

In the kitchen, Alexander poured out the Scotch and tried to shake off the memory.

After dinner, they started another game, because they both said that they had lost track of the first.

Sam moved his pawn, and Alexander moved his, and then they traded other moves, and Alexander looked at the pale blue walls and wondered what color his father would have chosen instead, or if he had always needed someone to do the choosing for him. Alexander wondered, as he had many times, what his father might have been and done if not for the fact of Alice. He wondered if, by leaving, she had ruined Sam's chances for greatness, or if she had left him because he'd never wanted to be great. Alexander wondered if his father had ever had dreams.

"You should paint this place one of these days," Alexander said.

"I know. Your move. Don't stall. I've got you scared."

"HE'S NEVER going to do it," Alexander said to Linda that night as he set the alarm clock, sitting on the edge of her bed. "He'll never get the place painted, and he'll never get rid of all that junk. It's like he still thinks that she's going to come back."

"And you don't?" Linda asked him.

IN ALEXANDER'S DREAM that night, he saw a gold light move in a broad arc, tracing the length of a man's arm. The light had a fuzzy glow, as if covered in gauze or a deep fog. Then it went out. The angel appeared. She wore a yellow dress with high puffed sleeves that looked like wings. Her hair was yellow, too, twisted into elaborate braids that made a halo on her head. Her eyes were brown, and deeper than his convictions.

"I'm watching you," she said, floating several feet above his bed.

"Touch me."

"Not yet."

"But I want to know."

"You will."

"What do I do?"

"You'll know."

"Give it to me."

"Not yet."

.   .   .

"GIVE IT! Give it!"

"Hey, fellah," Linda said, tugging the sheet around his shoulders, letting her hand travel up the warm bony ridge of his shoulder blade.

"Was I asking for something?" Alexander asked, his face still pressed against the pillow.

"Yes. You said, 'Give it.' Give what?"

"Oh."

"Want to tell me?"

"No."

"Want to repress it really well and get, like, a disease?"

Alexander rolled over and pulled Linda's body on top of his own. She shrieked. In his mind, the gold light again flickered out.

"Give it," he whispered to the sweaty part of Linda's neck.

As she tightened her legs around him, she said, "This wasn't what you wanted, was it?"

IT HAD ONLY BEEN half an hour or so from the railroad tracks to the fancy hotel where Alice had persuaded Sam to let them stay the night. She had raved about the room, and eaten the mint from her pillow, and fallen into a deep, obstinate sleep. So Sam had tucked Alexander in, letting him keep a night-light on.

They were on the road heading back to New York by nine. With stops for lunch and dinner, the trip took twelve hours. Sam and Alice traded turns at the wheel, and Alexander was quiet. A few hours outside the city, they stopped for gas, and coming back from the men's room with Sam, Alexander paused before the doors on the passenger side, staring at the bent reflection of himself in the thin chrome door handles.

"Dad," Alexander whispered.

Sam bent down to meet his son's eyes—something he would do all his life, even when Alexander was a grown-up himself, and only a few inches shorter than Sam.

"What is it?" Sam asked.

"Can I sit with you?"

"Come on."

In the front seat, Alexander leaned more closely toward his father so as not to bother Alice, who seemed somehow bothered enough as it was.

They didn't say anything. The car smelled of French fries and vinyl. Driving, they slipped down the humid highway, with glimpses of the yellow lights of houses off the road. For several miles, Alexander leaned his head against his father's arm, leaning into the safety of childhood, so uniquely physical. For once, though, his father's arm, and the slight sense of his breath, did not seem to be enough. Alexander felt something that couldn't be touched. What he felt was a grown-up sadness, and it was defined by the way that it seemed to cut him off from his father, from the lights in the houses. For the first time in his life, he felt alone in his body. He closed his eyes and saw the field of the night before. He opened his eyes, and above him the taut steel cables of a city bridge seemed to spin like the spokes of a turning wheel—forward into the starry sky.

"Why are we here?" he whispered to his father, tears in his eyes and in his voice.

There was no doubt in Sam's mind about what his son had meant by the question. He had always known that the question would come, and if he was startled that Alexander was only eight, he was quietly thrilled as well.

"Why do you think we're here?" Sam asked.

"I don't know," Alexander said.

Sam stroked his son's hair. "Listen to me very carefully," he said. "I don't know why we're here either."

Alexander looked down to where his feet disappeared in the darkness of the car. "Grown-ups know everything," he whispered to the darkness.

"No," Sam said. "They don't."

"Mom says," Alexander said.

Sam looked at his wife. Oblivious to their conversation, she was staring intently at the road, driving with one hand while with the other she ran her gold locket back and forth over its chain.

"She doesn't mean *everything*," Sam said softly. "She means like when to clean up your room, and how many aspirins to take when you're sick."

"Oh."

"Some people believe in God."

"Do you?"

"No."

"Why not?"

"Same reason I don't believe in ghosts."

"I don't believe in God either," Alexander announced, and Sam was grateful for the darkness, which hid his smile.

There was a long silence then, but a little later, just as Alice turned off from the FDR Drive, Alexander touched his father's arm. "Tell me," he said to Sam. "I promise I won't tell anyone else."

"I don't know, Ex," Sam said.

"Is it because I'm not old enough to know?"

"Ex. It's because I don't know."

Alexander shivered and wanted to cry, and every golden light off the highway glowed like the light he had seen in the field. That night, in a dream, Alexander invented a private fantasy. The fantasy was that Sam did know the answer but was not allowed to tell him. The fantasy was that an angel would touch Alexander when he deserved to be touched, and that she would tell him what he needed to know when he'd earned the right to know it. The fantasy was that all grown-ups were touched by angels and sworn to silence, and that was how they became grown-ups.

"I will touch you someday," the angel said to him that night in that first dream.

He had never told a word of this to anyone he'd known, but for years he had nurtured the fantasy as if it was a secret vice.

"I TELL YOU my dreams," Linda said as she lay in bed with Rogue on her stomach, stroking the short fur between his ears. It was Saturday morning, and Alexander had slept till ten. The construction had started in his apartment, and they had spent the night upstairs.

"I know you do, Linda."

"And you don't tell me yours."

"Sure I do. Remember the one where I won the marathon? Remember the one where the Good Humor truck was chasing me down the street?"

"I mean it."

"We're just different that way," he said.

He slipped out of bed and immediately bent to smooth out his side of the tangled blankets.

Linda laughed. "I can't believe it," she said. "This place looks like Times Square, and you're straightening out the sheets."

"You've got to start somewhere," Alexander said. He lifted his side of the mattress gently, tucking in the sheet and blanket and standing back to appraise the perfect geometry of his hospital corner.

"Don't you trust me?" Linda asked, her lips against Rogue's neck.

"Of course I trust you," Alexander said.

"Don't you think I'll understand?"

"Linda," he said. "Let's not start this." He smiled and stretched out across the bed. He lifted the cat from her face and dropped him gently on the floor, and then he looked at Linda, an inch away. Her eyes were as large as lights. He dreamed about ghosts and angels, and he knew he could never tell her that. "Just because you need to tell me your dreams doesn't mean I should need to tell you mine," he said. "Don't you see? It doesn't mean I trust you less. There are lots of ways an equation can balance. A can sometimes equal B. It doesn't have to equal A."

He tugged at a strand of her hair, and she ran a finger along the outside of his ear.

"But if B equals A," she said slowly, "doesn't that mean that B should *be* A?"

"You know what I'm saying," Alexander answered. "All that counts is the equals sign."

"Oh, gee," Linda finally whispered back. "I love it when you talk math to me."

Then it turned into a wordless hour that drowned out the moment of talk.

ALEXANDER ARRIVED at the lab just before lunchtime. For a Saturday morning, the place was uncharacteristically busy. Something was clearly going on. Clusters of physicists stood in the corridors, sipping coffee and looking worried, their hands fluttering through the air. Happy physicists, Alexander thought.

It turned out that there had been what was known as an event at the accelerator. It seemed that a new subnuclear particle had been found.

Hearing the news again and again as he walked through the crowded hallways, Alexander tried to act excited, but the truth was that such breakthroughs no longer did much for him.

Despite the way they were always touted in the press, they seemed, to Alexander, too predictable somehow. For several decades now, physicists had known by the particles already discovered that several similar particles would have to exist. To find them, they had had to construct ever-larger accelerators with ever-greater energies, and the debates raged in Congress about the prudence of spending billions of dollars to discover what everyone knew was there.

To Alexander, finding these particles seemed rather like filling in the final holes in the table of chemical elements, or putting the last few pieces of a jigsaw puzzle in place. It was nice to think about the thing being completed, but the work that required the real imagination had already been done. To finish the jigsaw puzzle would do nothing to explain why the picture in the puzzle was a landscape, say, not a still life, or why it was made of two hundred pieces and not of two thousand or twenty.

Alexander's work involved not finishing the puzzle but exploring why and how it had come to be in the first place.

THE SUCCESS OF Alexander's Theory of Everything depended on two unprovable and essentially unimaginable premises.

The first unimaginable premise was that the fundamental stuff inside the grape inside the football field was not made up of tiny dimensionless dots but of tiny one-dimensional lines. These lines were called strings. Like the strings inside a piano or on a guitar, the strings inside the nucleus of an atom would vibrate with different frequencies. But instead of producing F sharps and B flats and chords, they would produce different kinds of particles, as well as the forces that acted on them. The main reason why this was unimaginable was that the strings were supposed to be 10^{-23} millimeters small.

The second unimaginable premise in the Theory of Everything was that these strings existed not in the three dimensions (width, height, and length) that we see, or even in the fourth dimension (time) that Einstein explored, but in a total of ten dimensions, the last six of which had no shape and no name. The reason for all the dimensions was to get rid of the ghosts. In higher dimensions, those illogical numbers cancelled themselves out. Earlier theories had put the number at twenty-six dimensions, then at ten, but had always assumed that the extra dimensions were somehow curled up inside the others. Alexander's big breakthrough was to ignore the physical implications of the extra "curled-up" dimensions, and to reduce them mathematically to two dimensions instead. In two dimensions, all the ghosts cancelled out, and the strings became actual physical things, not merely ideas. Of course the universe wasn't any easier to imagine, but there was a beauty to the math that suggested he was right. Mathematically, Alexander's theory worked. Mathematically, it united the four forces and everything they acted on. But only in two dimensions. And only if the universe was made up of strings.

In its own way, it was simple, but only in its own way.

ALEXANDER WORKED on the last of his proofs long into the late, sunlit afternoon. Linda called him once to ask when he was coming home. In the background on the phone, he could hear car horns blaring up from the street, and the tinkle of the copper bells that hung on the neighbors' roof. He could picture Linda up there, sitting back in one of the rusted white lawn chairs, looking out over the many buildings where life, she was probably telling herself, was really going on.

Alexander told Linda that he wouldn't be home for dinner.

When he finally walked into her bedroom late that night, he found her hidden by the sheets and blankets, sleeping very soundly, like some lost part of him.

. . .

MOST PEOPLE—and even many physicists—felt daunted by the notion of extra dimensions. What did it mean to say a fifth dimension, or a sixth, or a seventh? But Alexander had always loved to think about such things. As a teenager, he had read a wonderful book called *Flatland*, an early-nineteenth-century satire by a Shakespearean scholar named Edwin Abbott. *Flatland* explained the fourth dimension by analogy to the third. It was a brilliant and wonderfully simple book.

The hero of *Flatland* was a being named A. Square. He lived in a world that had length and width and no depth, a world like a giant table top. One day, he was miraculously lifted out of Flatland by a fabulous creature called A. Cube. From his new perspective in the third dimension, A. Square could look down on his own land and see things as they really were. The neighbors and relatives he had previously known only by the different shadows that the sun cast on their angles were suddenly whole shapes to him—squares, triangles, pentagons. He saw his world the way we see a printed page. He could look inside houses, see inside rooms. He could understand that a sphere passing through Flatland would have scared the daylights out of him, seeming to come from nowhere (since "up" didn't exist) and passing through his single plane of vision as a rapid succession of widening, then shrinking circles.

Deposited back home in Flatland, A. Square promptly told the world about his newfound knowledge and was imprisoned as an anarchist and a lunatic.

Flatland showed how vibrant a world could seem, no matter how limited. It showed how groundless a fear could be, no matter how natural.

Sometimes, when Alexander remembered his ghost, or woke up from a dream of it, he would make himself think of the *Flatland* sphere. He would tell himself the two things were the same—that the ghost would make sense in the fourth dimension, just as the sphere had made sense in the third. And then he would play the old math game of trying to picture a four-dimensional cube. He would fall back to sleep, or lean back in the subway, folding up all sorts of shapes in his head.

LINDA'S SCHOOL'S graduation was on Thursday of the coming week, and Alexander had promised to take the morning off and go with her. He had done the same thing the year before. He had loved the way she'd acted with her colleagues and her students.

He was sleeping every night in her apartment now, her bedroom the one refuge from the sawdust and the mess, and when he woke up Thursday morning, she was standing, looking nervous, at the foot of the bed.

"What is it?" he asked. "Did we oversleep?"

Linda sighed. "It's Alice," she said. She held up a business envelope.

"What is it?" he asked.

"Hey. Try to wake up. It's a letter. It's from your mom."

Slowly, Alexander sat up in bed. "Where's the rest of it?" he asked.

"This is it."

"Just that? Where are the wooden crates? Where are the old delivery men with asthma?"

He punched up the pillows behind him and leaned back. Linda gave him the envelope.

"It's almost a week early," she said with awe. "Has she ever been early before?"

"Not this early."

"What do you think it is this time?"

Alexander rubbed his eyes. "I think," he said, "it's an envelope."

"Aren't you going to open it?"

"It's not my birthday yet."

"*Open* it," Linda said.

He grinned at her and opened the envelope. Inside, there was a letter, handwritten in tiny script. He read it first to himself, twice through, then read it out loud to Linda.

June 7

My darling son,

Next week is your thirty-first birthday. I was thirty-one when you were born, and so this birthday has a special importance. I have waited for it, many years, knowing what I would give you. This is the last present I will give you. It is nothing. Well, not nothing, of course, but nothing that is tangible. (Don't you hate clutter? I'm sick of it.)

I think it is time for us to meet. That is my present. I'd explain what the planets are doing right now, and why this is a good idea, but though I gather you're a scientist, I don't think you'd really get it. But it's a good time. Trust me. I'm your mother, and I wouldn't lie to you.

Please call Cleo Cole. She is a woman I have known for many years and she has helped me in the past. She has also sent you your birthday presents. Her phone number is 984-2835. It's a good number, by the way. She had it checked numerologically. But that's hard to explain, too. Did I mention that Cleo is a palm reader? She is. Call her.

Love,
your mother

They were late leaving the apartment. Alexander took longer than usual in the shower, and then Linda couldn't remember where she had packed her white straw handbag.

"Don't say you told me so," she called over her shoulder as she knelt beside her bed, dragging out one carton box after another.

"What's wrong with the black one?" Alexander asked.

"It's *summer*."

"You had the black one yesterday."

"Yesterday I wasn't going to see all the parents."

Alexander put a towel on top of the drop cloth that covered Linda's couch, and he sat very still as Linda whirled around her apartment, digging through all the boxes. He watched her spin out the door on her way down to his place. She was wearing a beige linen dress. She looked very pretty. He heard her voice but couldn't tell if she was talking to herself or to him. He didn't wonder enough to ask. He sat at an eerie distance, his hand on the letter, which he'd stuffed into his pocket. He already knew the letter by heart. His throat was tight, his hands too cold. Why now? was what he kept thinking.

"Darn!" Linda screamed from down below. "Darn, darn, darn! That's it! I'm giving up! Let's go!"

Slowly, he walked down the stairs to join her. She was standing on the landing outside his front door. She was buoyant, exasperated, slightly sweaty.

"Take these?" she asked him, handing him her lipstick and keys.

Alexander touched the letter again as he put Linda's things in his pocket.

In the cab, she laughed about her lack of organization, apologizing to him, blaming herself, dusting the ivory plaster from her beige leather shoes. Finally, though, she caught his mood and waited a moment, silent.

"I know what you're thinking," Linda said. "You're thinking you're going to hate this whole palm reader mumbo jumbo, right? But it really isn't that big a deal."

"I know."

"Really," she said.

"That isn't it."

"It isn't?"

"No."

"What is it, then?"

"Not now," Alexander said. "We're here."

"We've still got five blocks to go."

"Later."

"I'm worried about you."

"I'm fine. I am." He put his hand on the back of her neck and leaned over quickly to kiss her cheek.

"More," Linda said, her eyes full of play.

"Not now. Look. There are munchkins."

He pointed out the cab window, where children were moving over the steps of the school like particles at great heat.

"You liked this last year," Linda said. "The graduation, I mean. Didn't you?"

"I liked seeing you as Miss Williams," Alexander said. He paid the fare and got out beside her.

"It won't last too long," she said. "I promise. It won't."

Inside, the folding chairs set up on the main floor of the auditorium were already filled with parents and students. Linda took Alexander's hand and led him up to the balcony, where they settled in among the teachers.

A tall, thin man with a thick dark mustache came by and put his hand on Linda's shoulder and said hello.

"Jerry," Linda said. She removed his hand. "This is Jerry," she told Alexander. "He teaches fifth- and sixth-grade English."

"Don't hold it against me," Jerry said, pumping Alexander's hand. "I'm a masochist. But Linda knows that better than anyone. Don't you?" he asked.

"Idealistic teacher talk," Linda said. She was actually blushing. "You're not a masochist." Linda said. "You're a twerp."

"See? I love it, I love it," Jerry said, and squeezed Linda's shoulder again, and disappeared.

She began to read the commencement program, and Alexander studied her.

"What?" she finally said.

"He was flirting with you."

"He flirts with everyone."

"Is he married?"

"No. Don't look at me like that."

Alexander smiled. He felt oddly proud of her.

"Shh," Linda said. "It's starting."

A bitter-looking man with curly gray hair was seated at the piano, looking down the aisle of the auditorium, his hands poised like counterweights above the keys. There was a silence, and then he started—the Pachelbel Canon, arranged for piano, a desperate emphasis at every measure to give the girls their pace. Finally they entered, by twos and by height. Twenty-four white dresses, twenty-four pairs of short white gloves, and twenty-four pairs of flat white shoes. Friends separated by height were given away by details—two girls had daisies in their hair. Four had gone wild with makeup. Identical bouquets of delicate flowers quivered in their arms.

When the girls reached the stage, they turned to the audience.

"They look terrified," Alexander whispered.

Linda smiled and touched his sleeve.

The headmistress stood up, a boxy lady in a navy blue suit, and talked of beginnings and endings and pride. Alexander looked down from the balcony on the heads of two hundred schoolgirls. He saw them pass notes and whisper things and exchange bracelets and giggles. He saw a pure exuberance that made him ache. Then he looked at Linda. She was leaning forward on her chair. Her cheeks were flushed, and her eyes were bright. She looked like one of the children, and he suddenly wanted to love her more than he'd ever wanted to love her before.

"She's winding down," Linda whispered to him.

They stood up to sing the school song, then a hymn, then sat while the diplomas were handed out one by one. The head-mistress had asked everyone to save their applause until the end, but somewhere early in the alphabet, one set of parents hadn't been able to resist, and after that the other parents clapped for their children, too.

Sam had had his own school's commencement the day that Alexander had graduated, and so Alexander had gone home alone and worked on a prime-number problem that he'd known he wouldn't be able to solve.

There was a flutter of bodies in the front rows down below as the youngest girls were shepherded onto the stage. Then one of them balked like a horse entering a stall, and a teacher took her aside, bending down to her, talking softly, an arm around her waist. The girl's face grew redder, and she burst into tears. There were clucks of sympathy from the audience as the teacher led the girl gently outside. Her classmates were looking on, rapt, ignoring the pianist's snapping fingers. Finally, they re-membered and shyly faced the man for their cue. The hymn they sang came out high and clean. It made Alexander listen. They sang:

> Holy, holy, holy,
> Lord God almighty
> Early in the morning
> Our song shall rise to thee.

After the hymn was over, the little girl was led back inside by the teacher. The parents started clapping for her, and the girl burst into tears again. As the girl grabbed at the teacher's skirt, Alexander felt Linda clutch his hand. He tried to squeeze her hand back, but her grasp was so tight that he knew she couldn't feel his own. Her eyes were fixed on the young child, and her hold was so tight around his hand that his fingers could barely move.

LINDA STOOD in the sun on the school steps, chatting with parents and students and teachers. Her hair shone in the bright light, and she squinted as she smiled. Alexander stayed by her side, pretending to be a part of her. He wondered how it was that she had gotten so full of life. He felt, by comparison, half evil and half sad. He knew he was what he was, though. He knew that he thought too much, and said too little, and he also knew that he wasn't very likely to change.

He said good-bye to Linda quickly and walked to the corner, hearing the children's voices fade.

There were certain theories of time that came less from science than science fiction. They said that time could be seen as a vast terrain, with stretches of empty desert and then clusters of life and activity. Maybe, Alexander thought as he rode a cab to Penn Station, that view could explain why everything seemed to be happening to him all at once. Or maybe, he thought, there was no explanation, and no way to understand it at all.

The work at the lab seemed easy by comparison.

OF ALL THE inexplicable discoveries that had changed the way scientists saw the world, the one that intrigued Alexander most was known as the double-slit experiment.

The double-slit experiment was an incredibly simple one to perform. By way of apparatus, all it required were some sheets of photographic film, a screen with two small slits in it, a patch to cover one of the slits, and a kind of gun that could fire one particle of light—one photon—at a time.

If you covered up the first slit and sent photons, one by one, through the second, the photons would hit the film and leave a certain, predictable pattern. Fine. But if you *opened* the first slit, and again sent photons, one by one, through the second, the photons would hit the film and leave a totally *different* pattern.

This was more bizarre than it seemed. In both cases—with the slit covered and open—a single photon started from the same place, then went through the same slit at the same angle and speed. Newton had said that if you knew the position and speed and direction of something, you could compute where it would go. But the photons went different places. How could a single photon being fired through one of the slits "know" where it was supposed to go? How could it "know" to behave differently depending on how many slits were open?

Questions like these were among the means by which the old universe had come crashing down. Years after the first time the experiment had been performed, the questions still could not be answered and still could not be ignored.

Alexander stood by the window in his office, opening and closing the dusty venetian blinds and thinking about this experiment and wanting, more than anything, for the world to make sense to him.

BY THE TIME that Alexander came home late that night, he was almost too exhausted to think anymore, and long past the point where he knew what to feel. The work had gone well. He had finally finished checking the last proof. That was all he seemed to know, and almost all that mattered. The work had gone well. It was basically done.

It was too late to do anything else. The day was finally over. It was too late to call Sam and tell him that he'd finished, though Alexander had missed their weekly game of chess. It was too late to call the palm reader, even if he'd wanted to.

Alexander knew that he should go upstairs to Linda, but he didn't want to do that either. He wanted to be alone. He stopped at the fourth-floor landing and, for the first time in nearly a week, he opened the door to his own apartment instead.

Apart from his couch, which was still in its place by the windows, there was nothing around him that seemed even vaguely familiar. All of his mother's furniture had been pushed unceremoniously into the corners of the room and covered with clear plastic. A large wooden sawhorse stood solidly in the center. Alexander almost smiled. He sensed that he had come to a foreign, neutral place. He found that he liked its foreignness.

The bedroom was totally empty, except for a set of half-finished bookshelves. Dimly, he tried to remember what Linda had said she had done with his bed. In the kitchen, the refrigerator was empty and dark. The power had been turned off. The cabinets were empty, too, except for a package of Ritz crackers. He took them into the living room and folded back a drop cloth to sit on the couch. He ate a few soggy crackers, staring, exhausted, at the triangle of light that came under the front door. He tried to guess what its angles were. He put the box of crackers down, and he lay back on the couch with the drop cloth as a blanket. He was sure that he would be too tired to dream.

Beyond the living room windows, Alexander caught a glimpse of the moon as it rose between the two brick buildings that loomed like distant parents over the roof. Quickly he turned away again. He would rather have stared at the sun than the moon. Often in his childhood he had imagined the moon getting larger and closer, like lights along a railroad track.

. . .

THE ANGEL'S HAIR was blond, of course, shiny and halolike. Her dress was white in his dream that night, like a graduation dress, and as she flew about the living room, moving from one pile of things to another, Alexander could see her wings.

"What am I going to do?" he asked her.

"What do you want to do?"

"I want to know everything. I want you to touch me."

The angel smiled, hovering above Alice's armoires.

"Touch me," Alexander said. "I want to hold you in my arms. Aren't you tired of flying?"

"I can't touch you yet," she said.

When Alexander woke up, there were tears on the sides of his neck.

SAM CALLED on Sunday, gruff and distracted.

"Sorry I missed chess the other night," Alexander said. "But Biner is due back tomorrow, and—"

"Yes, Ex, I know." Sam's voice was terse; it was almost harsh.

"Sorry. I said I was sorry, Dad."

There was silence.

"Dad. What's wrong?"

"I think you should just get over here."

"Tell me what's wrong, Dad."

"Just come over."

"Are you sick?"

"No. I'm fine."

"Then what the hell is going on?"

Sam cleared his throat. "Your mother," he said. "I think she's finally lost her mind."

.   .   .

"OH MY GOD," Alexander said.

He was standing in Sam's doorway, numb and appalled. The front hall before him was gridlocked by dozens of large wooden crates. They were stacked to the ceiling, obscuring the walls, packed into each other like the pieces of a Chinese puzzle. Most of the boxes were still nailed shut. Those that had been tugged open held ice-white marble statues, ornate furniture, antique lamps.

"The *Citizen Kane* look," Sam said, and laughed.

Alexander did not laugh back. What he wanted to do was leave.

"There's more," Sam told him.

"More?"

"In there." Sam pointed to the living room, then slipped through a narrow alley between two stacks of crates and pushed against the double doors. Grimly, Alexander followed him in. The living room was a warehouse. Clumps of green excelsior rolled like hills across the parquet floor. Unlikely sculptures stood side by side. Tables were stacked like acrobats.

When Alexander was little, Alice had loved going to auction houses. Often, she had taken him along, holding his hand and pulling him down row after row of dusty, forbidding objects. When Alexander could break free, he had searched the aisles and corners for the inevitable out-of-tune piano, and then he had taught himself scales and arpeggios, letting the quest for precision comfort and carry him away.

"God," Alexander said now. "This is all from Alice?"

Intentionally, for once, he tried to remember his mother—how she must have felt and what she must have hoped for as she made these pointless purchases. Where she had been living. Where there had been room for this. And finally, where she was now. He half expected to see her emerge from behind one of the wooden crates.

Sam followed Alexander to a pair of heavy, hideous pedestals that were carved in the shape of women carrying baskets on their heads. "I think she's hitting an ascetic streak," Sam said.

"You find this funny?"

"What choice have I got?"

Together they snaked their way back to the front hall.

Alexander sat down heavily on an unopened crate. "Where is she?" he asked.

"I don't know," Sam said.

"You saw her."

"No. I only talked to her. She won't let me see her. But she says she's decided that, as she put it, materialism is for the birds. She wants me to have all her stuff."

"What are you going to do with it?"

"Sell it, I guess. Give it away. I don't know. She may actually be crazy." Sam was trying to meet Alexander's eyes. He settled beside him on the crate. "Also she wants to see you," he said.

Alexander was silent.

"She told me she wrote you a letter."

"Yeah, Dad, I know."

"She said that you haven't called that woman."

"No, Dad. I haven't."

Alexander started to walk toward the kitchen. Sam leapt up to follow him. "Why, Ex?" he asked. "Why not?"

"Drink?" Alexander asked, reaching for the Scotch.

Sam nodded and waited, silent, as Alexander poured their drinks.

"I finished the last proof, Dad," Alexander said. "I'm finally ready to start writing the article."

"Why haven't you called her, Ex?"

Alexander handed Sam the drink. "I just don't want to deal with it."

"Why didn't you call *me*?"

"I didn't think you'd want to deal with it either."

They sipped their drinks at the same moment, then laughed

at their timing. Alexander knew that Sam was trying to understand.

"What's so hard?" Sam asked. "She says she's ready to do this for you."

"It's for her," Alexander said.

Sam thought. "Maybe," he said.

"It's the law," Alexander said.

"What law?"

"Conservation of Guilt."

Sam laughed.

"Guilt," Alexander said, "can neither be created nor destroyed. There's a finite amount, you see, and it just keeps getting passed around."

"You want to meet her, don't you?" Sam said.

"No."

"I don't believe you."

"Not now," Alexander said. "Do you have any idea what is going *on* in my life?"

"Do you?" Sam asked.

ALEXANDER WOKE at dawn on Monday and couldn't get back to sleep. He showered quickly and dressed, and then he went downstairs to his old apartment, found the box marked "desk," and shoved the new letter from his mother into the file that held the others. He didn't stop to reread the letter. He didn't copy the phone number down. He knew that he wouldn't call.

He left Linda sleeping and took an early train to Wilson. He would let the work take over. There had been something grotesque, he thought, about what he had seen in Sam's apartment. He felt he had seen something grown out of control, like a cancer, he thought, or a ninety-page number.

The early sun beyond the train window lit the city and the fields too brightly. Alexander closed his eyes against the power of the light. Hydrogen, helium, lithium, he thought. Beryllium, boron, carbon, nitrogen . . .

He felt defiant and scared and sick.

THE GENERAL SENSE of ease that had pervaded Wilson in Biner's absence had thoroughly evaporated with his return. The large mainframes in the computer room were working at full tilt when Alexander arrived at the lab. The laser printers were humming. Up and down the corridors, Alexander could hear the frantic tapping of computer keyboards.

Alexander braced himself, but he found no message from Biner in his office. He stood by the window, waiting for the phone to ring. Biner would want to see progress, he knew. Biner would want the article. Biner would be crestfallen if there wasn't something to see. Alexander felt sorry and sad. But by ten o'clock, when no word had come, Alexander sat down at his desk and tried to begin the article. The sick feeling he had had on the train came back: an emptiness in his stomach and a sense of dread.

He turned on his computer, opened a new file, and promptly spilled his coffee all over the keyboard. It took the rest of the morning to track down the dweeb in requisitions and ask for a replacement. Alexander got nothing done.

At lunchtime, he bypassed his usual sandwich-at-the-desk routine and actually sat down in the cafeteria with a tray. Instantly, Talbot and Heinz appeared, as if they were some kind of hologram.

Talbot immediately opened a book, and Heinz unwrapped his sandwich.

"Hi," Alexander said to them.

Talbot silently turned a page, and Heinz painstakingly folded his wax paper into perfect halves.

"Hi," Alexander said again.

Heinz looked up at him. "You never call, you never write," he said.

"I've been finishing the proofs," Alexander said. "Christ, I've *finished* the proofs. I thought you were going to do the same."

"We're almost done," Heinz told him. "You'll have them by midweek."

"Good."

"They look just fine, you know. We haven't found a thing."

"Keep looking."

Alexander scanned the room for some sign of Biner. He realized he had a headache, and he felt mildly feverish. Maybe he was sick, he thought.

"Did you know," Heinz was asking, "that no matter how large a piece of paper you have, you can only fold it seven times?"

"Yes, actually," Alexander said. "And how useful for you to bring that up now."

Heinz shrugged and flicked his folded-up sandwich paper at Talbot's nose. Talbot did not look up. "Bingo," Heinz said.

"Have you got a mother?" Alexander asked him.

"Have I what?"

"Have you got a mother?"

"What kind of question is that?" Heinz said. "Of course I've got a mother. What do you think, I got here by spontaneous creation?"

"Well, do you see her a lot?" Alexander asked. "I mean, do you talk to her a lot?"

Heinz smiled. He leaned back in his chair. "No, no, I've got her down now to about twice a month. I've been training her. I've been weaning her, ever since college."

Alexander nodded. Absentmindedly, he put his hands inside his jacket pockets, as if feeling for the letter he had carried there all weekend.

"Your mother giving you a hard time?" Heinz asked.

"Sort of."

"Well, they're like children, you know. You've got to be firm with them."

Alexander smiled.

There was a bit of a buzz in the cafeteria as Biner entered and scanned the room.

"Look," Heinz said to Alexander.

"I know."

"He's going nuts about this new particle."

"Well, that figures," Alexander said, though for some reason it hadn't occurred to him. He felt a strange pang of jealousy. He knew he should be happy to have Biner riding someone else's wave, but nothing seemed to be making him happy. He looked out across the cafeteria at the parallel lines of the tables, and he wondered what everyone else there wanted. He wondered if they were going to get it, and what the hell they would do if they did.

BINER DIDN'T CALL for Alexander until late the next afternoon.

"Welcome back," Alexander said as he walked into the office. "I hear that your lecture went wonderfully."

"Oh, it went fine," Biner said. His face was deeply tanned except for two half-circles under his eyes that made him look owlish and quizzical. He was standing behind his desk and studying three huge sheets of ledger paper. "Have a seat," he said to Alexander, motioning to a chair.

"I've made a lot of progress," Alexander said.

Biner looked up. "That's good," he said. "That's awfully good. Now. I'm counting the house here. Just a few questions. You have two research assistants, correct?"

"That's right," Alexander said. "It's Fred Talbot and George Heinz."

"And they are both doing graduate work, is that right?"
Alexander nodded.

"And they'll be with you for how long?" Biner asked.

"I guess until we're done," Alexander said. "Or until fall
term starts. Whichever comes first."

"And which do you think will come first?" Biner asked.

Alexander wondered if it was possible that Biner had forgotten
their last conversation. He wondered why he suddenly cared.

Biner's face remained expressionless. "I'm only curious," he
added, "because we're going to be short on office space now,
and I'm trying to find some room."

"We should be done before the month's out," Alexander said
carefully.

Biner made a note on one of the ledger pages, but didn't
seem to react any further. "Fine," he said. "That's all I need
to know right now. I'll see you later. Thanks for your help."
He buzzed his secretary and asked who was next.

JUNE FOURTEENTH, the morning of his thirty-first birthday,
Alexander woke a few minutes before seven. For once, his dreams
had been square and unhaunted. He had dreamed about the
article and had seen it completed, printed in a magazine, underneath his name.

Linda was still asleep. Her face was blotchy, and there was
a wry smile on her lips. Beyond the bedroom window, the sky
was a sickly blue, and the clouds and paler buildings were made
pink by the early sun. Pigeons scrambled after some crumbs on
the roof, but aside from them the only motion was a huge
broken tarpaulin flapping in the unfinished window of a new
building far in the distance.

. He realized that, if he wanted to, he could see his mother
today. The thought made him feel sick. Or maybe he really
was sick, he thought again. Maybe he could spend the whole

day in bed, and Linda would take care of him, and he wouldn't have to think.

When she stirred beside him, he closed his eyes. He knew that she would have planned this morning, and that waking him up would be part of the plan.

He felt her sit up slowly, so that the mattress springs wouldn't make any noise, and he listened to her tiptoe out the door and into the kitchen.

Later, after she had brought him his breakfast in bed, she covered him first with her kisses and then with a large blue blanket she had crocheted for him.

"It's beautiful," he said.

"It needs one more row of squares," she said. "I ran out of time."

"It's beautiful."

"What's wrong?"

"Nothing's wrong. It's beautiful." He kissed her. He wondered if she had ever given him anything that hadn't made him feel guilty.

"Now listen, pal. Don't get all weird over the time it took," she said. "I really enjoyed making it."

"Okay," he said.

"Now, look. Are you going to call about your mom today?" she asked.

"She's not my mom," Alexander said. "She's barely my mother."

"Are you going to call?"

"I don't know."

"I think you should call her."

"I don't know, all right?"

SAM PHONED the office just after lunchtime.

"How's the article coming?" he asked.

"Fine," Alexander said, though he hadn't yet managed to write a single sentence.

"Have you gotten in touch with your mother yet?"

"No."

"Why don't you just let her wish you happy birthday?"

"Why don't you just get off of my back?"

WHEN HE CAME HOME that evening, there were three children jumping rope outside the front door. On the stoop of the neighboring brownstone, two women sat watching. They were wearing shorts and smoking cigarettes and keeping an eye on their children as the summer evening cooled.

Alice had given Alexander only one birthday party that he could remember, but it had been one of her finest hours. Instead of the usual party standards like Pin the Tail on the Donkey, Alice had made up her own games, and Alexander had thought they were great. One game just involved Alice bringing a tray full of objects into the room—batteries, glasses, pencils, notepads, matches, anything—and letting the children look at it and then taking it away. Then Alice had handed out pencils and paper and told everyone to write down what they'd seen. Alexander had won this game, but that hadn't seemed fair to Alice, and so she'd given the winner's prize to the boy who had come in second.

What did she want from him now?

Linda's apartment door was open again, and Alexander stepped in, calling her name. The men had finally gotten to her living room, he could see. The floor was covered now by their stiff pink-brown paper—pieces taped together in an odd mosaic, the white lines of the tape like the lines in a playground game. The room smelled of sawdust and men's sweat. They had knocked through the old kitchen wall and had put up three beams for the new one.

Linda snuck up behind him and circled his neck with her arms.

"Happy birthday!" she said.

"This place is a firetrap," he said to her. He took a step forward, but she didn't let go. She took the step with him, their bodies touching, as if they were vaudeville partners.

"Happy birthday!" she said again.

Alexander tried to look over his shoulder at her, but she held on tight.

"You left the door open again," he said. "Anyone could walk right in."

"God, you're such a grump," she said. She let go of him quickly, then ruffled his hair. "It's your *birthday*, for God's sake. Look at this," she said. "This is going to be the kitchen to end all kitchens." She stood up on tiptoes and kissed his forehead. "Ooh, what I will cook for us in this kitchen."

Alexander put a hand around one of the beams and looked up to where it met the ceiling. "You think this is stable?" he asked.

"It's not done."

"It wobbles."

She laughed. "I love the things you don't know."

Alexander walked over to the windows, which were opaque now with dust. Enviously, he looked back at the room, with its evidence of practical men: a shovel, a level, several measuring tapes, a large box of tools, and a red tin case for a special kind of saw.

"Let's go out for dinner," he said to Linda.

"Oh," Linda said. "No—I bought groceries and everything. Your birthday dinner."

"It's going to taste like plaster."

"My special chicken."

"You convinced me."

"Did you call her?"

"No."

"Oh, Alexander."

He followed her into the kitchen and sat on the papered floor, leaning against the broom closet and watching while she cooked.

His life, he thought, was almost past waiting for, past being a condition to be fulfilled. Like if he graduated with honors. Or if he got a great job. Or if he met a great woman. Or if they moved in together.

Listening now while Linda hummed and worked in the kitchen, he thought of all the sentences he'd started with an "if" and that he'd never quite bothered to complete with a "then." If . . . then. A standard of logic. But what had ever been his thens? *Then* he'd be happy? *Then* he'd be real? *Then* he would stop being troubled by dreams? The ifs had always been simpler. Now the ifs had all come true. Except for one, he thought. If he could just write this article, he thought. Then he'd be happy. Then he'd be real. Then he would stop being troubled by dreams. Then, he thought, he might marry Linda.

For dinner, they sat up on Linda's roof ("*Our* roof," she said when he called it hers). While he'd washed up below, she had set the table with straw place mats and her grandmother's blue and white china and the two pale porcelain candlesticks she had bought as a wedding present for a friend whose fiancé had wound up backing out.

Linda had made enough chicken, but not too much, and he told her how good it tasted. The sky seemed to go from deep red to dark blue with no kind of warning in between.

The candles kept going out in the breeze, and Linda kept relighting them, never seeming to lose her patience or humor, never seeming to be diminished. Again Alexander wondered, as he had so often before, if Linda's happiness was something learned or something she had been born with. There were some equations in physics that were simple because they were meant to be simple, and others that were simple because their complexities had been worked out.

If people were like equations, Alexander thought, then he still hadn't figured out what kind of simplicity Linda's was.

"Look at them," she said suddenly. She had raised her wine glass to a window across the way. "Don't they look happy?"

Alexander followed her glance and saw two dark figures leaning across a table to kiss.

"We're happy," he said.

"There *is* more to life than work," Linda told him.

"I know that," he said. "I wouldn't be here if I didn't know that. I wouldn't have gotten you if I didn't know that."

Looking thrilled, Linda sipped her wine and put her feet up on the large geranium planter.

Alexander folded his napkin into perfect fourths.

"You got a call today," Linda said. "I was downstairs with one of the guys. So I picked it up."

"Who was it?" Alexander asked.

"It was the palm reader."

"Oh."

"She wanted to know why you hadn't called. She knew it was your birthday."

"Great."

"Do me one favor," Linda said.

"Anything."

"A birthday present for me."

"Name it."

"Promise me you'll call that woman. It's no big deal."

Alexander forced a grin. He turned toward the darkening city and watched as a light was turned on in a distant building and two small square windows appeared. He shivered and turned back to Linda.

"Alexander?" she asked.

"Are you done eating?" he said.

"Sure," she said.

"Then let's go in."

"Not yet. It's so nice."

"But it's dark."

"No it's not," she said, laughing. "Come on. It's so warm. Let's stay a while."

"You stay," he said. "I've got dishes to do."

"Don't you feel well?"

"I'm fine."

But he rose much too quickly, loading the tray with the dishes and hurrying toward the doorway.

He watched her tilt her head back and drain her glass, and see in the darkening distance the small rising moon he had seen himself and had been frightened by.

FOR WEEKS AFTERWARDS, Alexander would tell Linda and Sam that the reason he'd finally called Cleo was that they had both kept asking him to. And for months afterwards, he continued to believe that.

ALEXANDER CALLED Cleo Cole for the first time late that evening, when the moon had finally gone behind a cloud, and Linda was taking a shower.

Alexander stood in the rubble of his old apartment and thought to himself: Oh, what the hell.

4

THE ANSWER

ALEXANDER HAD HAD to leave a message on Cleo Cole's answering machine, and by the time she finally called back late the next Sunday afternoon, he had almost convinced himself that Alice had changed her mind.

He was out on the roof with Linda, and she dashed for the phone when she heard it ring. Eagerly, she handed it out to him through the bedroom window.

"Is that Alexander?" Cleo asked him when he picked up the phone.

"Hello?" he said thickly.

"That *is* Alexander!" Cleo exclaimed. "I'm Cleo. Cleo Cole. You know. You called. I'm calling back. And look, what took you so damned long?"

Cleo's voice surprised him: it was younger than he had ex-

pected, and it was cheerful, and it was Southern. He realized
that he had imagined someone brittle and dark.

"What took *me* so long?" he said.

"Well, yes, I know I didn't call you back," Cleo said, "but
I've been working like a maniac. A total maniac. *You* waited
almost a week, though. Personally, I thought you'd call right
away, but Alice said it was probably going to take you even
longer."

"She did?"

"She said you probably hate her."

"Hate her?" Alexander repeated. He felt strangely dull. "Oh.
No. Hate her? I don't hate her."

Linda, who had returned to the roof and was lying back in
the sun, sat up sharply when she heard the word *hate*.

"Bully for you, then, doll!" Cleo said. She sounded as cheerful
as a stewardess. "Bully for you! So. When do I get to meet
Alice's boy?"

"I don't think," he said, almost laughing, "that you should
call me Alice's boy."

"Well, fine, but she really wants to see you, you know. She
came all this way, you know."

"No, I don't know," Alexander said. "All what way? Where
was she before?"

"Oh, that's right," Cleo said. "I almost forgot. You're not
supposed to know that."

Alexander looked through the windows at the paint that was
blistering on the bedroom ceiling. He felt Linda's eyes behind
him, and Cleo waiting for him to speak.

"Honey," Cleo said. "Is there a problem?"

"There's no problem," Alexander said.

"She's a little flaky, you know," Cleo said.

Alexander laughed. And you're not, he thought.

"Don't you want to meet her?" Cleo asked.

"Sure I do."

"Well, then, let me call her and find out what's a good day and time."

"I work during the day."

"Yes, but Alice will want to do this according to the planets."

"Oh God," Alexander said.

Cleo laughed, and he thought she was probably laughing at him. That was all right, he figured, since he had just laughed at her. In the background on the telephone, he could hear an old Bob Dylan song:

> *Time is a jet plane, it moves too fast.*
> *Oh, but what a shame that all we've shared can't last.*
> *I can change, I swear. See what you can do . . .*

"How long has it been?" Cleo asked.

"Since I've seen her?" he said. "Nineteen years. No, twenty now. She left when I was eleven."

> *Love is so simple, to quote a phrase.*
> *You've known it all the time,*
> *I'm learning it these days . . .*

"Oh, Alice," Cleo said. Then there was a sigh in her voice, and it sounded like a parent's sigh.

"Alice," Alexander said, and for a moment he saw his mother's gold chain and the glimmer of her gold locket—and then he could see the gold light approaching, as if it were an idea.

"I'll get back to you, soon as I can," Cleo said.

LATE THAT NIGHT, long after Linda had turned away from him in sleep, Alexander lay in bed and wondered if he did hate Alice. He decided that he didn't think it was possible to hate what he'd never loved, and he honestly didn't think that he had ever loved her. But riding the train to work that week, and plowing through the introduction for his article, he found that his mind kept drifting to the crates in Sam's apartment and the chaos they had made. What did it mean, he wondered, to want to buy up the world as Alice had, piece by antique piece? Alexander tried to own the world, too, but own it in another way. Acquisitive, inquisitive: There wasn't that much difference, he thought.

He and his mother had stood on different shores, casting wide nets over different seas. But they both had hauled in as much as their arms could bear, and they both had kept their backs to the world behind them.

FOR A SOLID WEEK, Alexander worked late at the lab. Heinz and Talbot had handed in their write-ups and had found no contradictions in his calculations. They were hanging on for another few weeks, ostensibly to help him if he wound up needing them, but really just in case there was any early glory to share. Biner had still shown no interest, though, and Alexander went happily back to not giving a damn what he thought.

By Friday, Alexander had finished the introduction to his article, the difficult summation of what the whole thing would prove, and late Friday night, waiting for the last train home, he sat in the Wilson station, rereading the pages he'd written and feeling quietly thrilled. Cleo had once again not called him back, but it had been easy, immersing himself in work, to forget all about the meeting, or at least to be glad it was out of his hands.

ON SATURDAY, Linda tended the flowers on the roof, and Alexander lay in a deck chair, feeling the sweat gather in the small of his back. The air was thick and humid, and the heat was overwhelming, but inside, the apartment was even worse.

After more than three weeks of construction, there was still not a single room in the entire place that could really be considered finished. Only Linda's bedroom had remained untouched, and yet on Wednesday night Alexander had come home to find all their clothes hanging above the bed there on a makeshift closet pole.

The one air conditioner that Linda had talked the men into installing hummed and groaned in the bedroom at night like a troubled sleeper.

Linda told Alexander that the One Who Spoke English kept muttering things about walls not being plumb, and about edging pieces not being delivered, and when she'd complained, he'd looked at her as if she didn't understand some fundamental truth of the universe. Alexander didn't know how she had kept herself sane. Her annual three-week trip to her grandparents' farm kept being postponed. She didn't want to leave, she said, until the men were gone.

His eyes half-shut, Alexander listened to the desperate whine of an oboe across the street. He wanted to go somewhere. The lab would be quiet and cool, he thought, but he knew that he had been there all week, and that he owed Linda some time.

He had always hated the city in summer. The wackos all came out of hiding, and the streets filled with sound. The garbage reeked, and the traffic crawled. Sidewalks were narrowed by outdoor cafés, and at night, on Columbus Avenue, women would lean against cars with their drinks, flirting with strangers in khaki suits.

Alexander looked at Linda, squinting against the sunlight. She was humming softly, trimming back the leaves from a crowded flower, and he decided it was a good thing that he wasn't on his own. "Hi there," he said to her. "Come here often?"

Linda smiled.

"How are you?" he said.

"Did you see the Rattners' rosebush?" she asked him.

"What?"

"Over there." Linda gestured to their neighbors' terrace. "The Rattners bought a rosebush. They must have gotten it upstate somewhere."

"Nice."

"Nice!" she said. "It's beautiful!"

"How would you like me to try to find you one of your own?" he asked.

Linda gave him the look—half sarcastic, half blindly loving—that was the whole reason to be with someone like Linda, and might be the reason to leave her as well.

SUNDAY, Alexander put on his jeans and his Einstein T-shirt, helped Linda carry a bunch of posters to the framing store, kissed her good-bye, and then walked across Central Park to Sam's. On the vast green lawn, single women with tans and string bikinis sprayed themselves with water, as if they were flowering plants. Objectively, Alexander thought, not one of them was as attractive as Linda, but each of them was a mystery, and each of them would have had to be won. He wasn't sure when or how it had happened, but Linda, he knew, had already been won.

The plan for the day was to open the crates, take inventory of the crates, organize the crates, and mark the crates. Sam had called an auction house, and there were people coming Wednesday to do a full appraisal. Linda had offered to help with the sorting, but Alexander had told her that he and Sam would be able to manage alone.

"Hope you're rested," Sam said when he met Alexander at the door.

"I'm all set," Alexander said.

They went straight to the living room.

"Mind if I put on some show tunes?" Sam asked.

Alexander smiled and shrugged. "It's your place, Dad," he said.

Sam put the sound track from *South Pacific* on the living room stereo, and for more than an hour, he and Alexander worked without speaking. They pried the crates open with screwdrivers, pulled back the excelsior, made notes of what they found. Joyfully, Sam sang along with the record, tune after sentimental tune that Alexander recognized without knowing.

When the record stopped, there was silence, and then Sam said: "I really did love her once."

"Oh, Dad," Alexander said.

"I know that's probably hard for you to believe," he said, "but when I met her, God, she was just amazing. She used to laugh. *With* me, I mean. And God, she was beautiful. I'd fall apart just thinking about her. She was smart, and she was classy. God, she was classy. She knew how to get around, you know. How much to tip a maître d'. She knew what you shouldn't wear. She showed me things—"

"She wanted to change you," Alexander said.

"Not at first."

"All along."

"Well. I didn't know that then," Sam said. "We had good times. It was exciting. In bed—"

"*Dad.*"

"I'd never wanted anyone so much. She made me feel like I could just—"

"*Dad.*"

"All right. But you've got to know. I think it's important that you know. She was so *convincing*, you see. How much she loved me. Wanted me. Said I was great. Said I was good. Loved that I was a teacher. Called me Professor. Did you know that she called me Professor? I still think sometimes that she fooled herself too."

"Hand me the hammer," Alexander said brusquely.

Startled, Sam turned from the crate he'd been unpacking.

"Ex," Sam said. He put his screwdriver down and moved, concerned, to Alexander's side. He looked down at him. He waited. He tried to meet his eyes.

"I hate what she did," Alexander finally said. "I'll always hate it. I hate the fact that she couldn't just love you for what you were." He looked up then, and saw Sam's smile.

"And is that how you love Linda?" Sam asked. "Is that how you love yourself?"

THE STREETS HAD barely cooled at all by six o'clock. The air was still damp and heavy, but Alexander decided that he was in no hurry to get home. Walking back across the park, he saw couples strolling the fields and paths, attached by their shoulders and hands. Children scampered for dandelions and chased after squirrels and birds.

Alexander knew that it was not enough for him to be happy. He thought that was probably why he so rarely was. In the years since finishing graduate school, he had made a lot of progress in accepting other people—Linda, Sam, Heinz—who wanted to be happy. He had even learned to respect their contentment as a different kind of talent. He hadn't yet learned to envy it, though, to want it for himself. *Just living* was still a foreign country, and living there seemed to mean that he'd have to lose the best part of himself.

"You need a *lobotomy!*"

That had been Ruth, his college girlfriend, one late night during one long autumn. Alexander had been awake for two days, filling pages with his theories, and he had been in bed with Ruth for hours, wired, trying to explain his work, rattling on until she hadn't been able to stand it anymore.

"Can't you *ever* just turn it off?" she had asked.

The truth was that he could turn it off, but that to do so made him frightened. He *could* lose himself sometimes—to talking, to sex, to watching a movie. But always, afterwards, he would come back to himself, scared that he had been wasting time.

"Can't you just *enjoy* yourself?"

That had been Linda, their first winter together, when a blizzard had hit, and the trains had stopped, and he hadn't been able to get to work.

Sure, he had thought then. If someone could just tell me that I'll never be great.

Then, he figured, he would either have to change or die. But no one had ever said never to him. Instead what they said was when.

And when would he know if he didn't have it? And what would he do then? Would he find another line of work? Would he have children and dump all his dreams on them? What would he think about when he took a shower or rode a train? What would there be to want?

"WELL, *hi*," Cleo said on the phone when she called him back, finally, late that Sunday night. Her hi was more like *hhah*. "Hi there, Alexander. Mr. Alexander. No, that's no good. That's just miserable. What if I call you Al?"

"Please don't. I mean, I wish you wouldn't."

Al.

Even after a week of trying, he still couldn't picture her. Maybe, he thought, it was just her accent that made her sound so young.

"This is Cleo Cole," she said.

"I know."

"The flaky palm reader."

"I know."

"The one who knows your mother."

"I *know*." Jesus, he thought.

"My," she said. "I'll bet you've got this really thick thumb. I'll bet you've got short fingers and a huge Mount of Mars. Those things tell us about drive, you know. And impatience. I'll bet you learned to walk before you were two."

"You'd have to ask Alice," Alexander said coldly. He didn't know what the Mount of Mars was, but she was right about his fingers.

"Well, you can ask her yourself," Cleo said.

"Did you talk to her?"

"Well, sure. We talk all the time."

"And?"

"And you're supposed to come here Friday. June the thirtieth. Be here at four o'clock. It's Five Fifty-five East Eighty-fifth Street. I've always liked the number five."

"She'll *be* there?"

"Well, she told me the time and the place."

"Great. But will she be there or not?"

"You've got to watch that Mount of Mars, now."

Alexander said nothing.

"She's going to meditate on it and throw the I Ching," Cleo said. "I told her good. I can't do better than that."

"I'm sorry. It's not you I'm mad at," he said.

"Well, gee, doll, I know that."

OVER LUNCH at the lab on Thursday, Alexander told Heinz that he had a doctor's appointment the following day, and that he'd be out of the office, just in case Biner was looking for him.

"Anything wrong?" Heinz asked.

"Just a checkup," Alexander said.

"You should get more exercise," Heinz said.

"Fuck off."

Heinz looked suspicious. "Something you're not telling me?"

Alexander laughed. "No," he said.

And he wondered what Heinz would think if he knew the real reason for his absence. He wondered what Talbot would say. Or Biner. A Wilson National Laboratories physicist. MacArthur winner. MIT graduate. Theory of Everything.

Hey, where the hell were you yesterday, Simon?

Went to a palm reader, gentlemen.

CRATES STILL obscured the periphery of Sam's living room, but he'd set up the chessboard there anyway.

"It bothered you, didn't it, my talking about Alice last week?" he asked once they had settled down with their drinks that night.

"No, Dad. It was okay."

"It bothers you, this whole palm reader business."

"No. I've gotten used to it."

"Don't expect too much when you meet her tomorrow. Your mother, I mean."

"I won't."

"Like hell."

Sam had the white pieces, but he opened with the queen's pawn instead of his usual king's.

"What are you doing?" Alexander said.

"Just trying to keep you on your toes."

They moved their pieces in silence.

"How's the apartment coming along?" Sam asked.

"Looks about like this," Alexander said, gesturing to the

boxes around them. "I can't stand it anymore. They keep telling Linda they'll be finished in ten days. Doesn't this mess drive you crazy?"

"They're taking the rest of the stuff tomorrow."

"Good."

"It'll be a big relief," Sam said.

Alexander moved a bishop. "What are you going to do with the money?" he asked.

Sam grinned. "I don't know," he said. "I'd like to give some of it away. I'd like to keep some, I guess. What I'd really like to do is set up a trust fund."

"For what?"

"For a grandchild."

"You don't have a grandchild."

"Work on it," Sam said.

He peered down at Alexander's last move. "You sure you wanted to do that?" he asked.

Alexander nodded casually. Sam moved a bishop. "Check," he said.

Stung, Alexander looked down at the board. "God," he said. "I didn't even see that."

"Keep the broad view at all times," Sam said. "Never forget where you are," he said.

Alexander looked back from the game to Sam's face, and then, earnestly, back to the board again.

IT WAS NEARLY ten o'clock when he got home from Sam's. From the corner of the street, he could see Linda at their front door, holding a paper bag in one hand and rifling through her purse for keys.

"We needed milk and coffee," she said.

"You shouldn't stand outside the door like that," he said.

"You shouldn't look through your purse like that. Any creep could just come up behind you and make you let him in."

"Isn't that what you're doing?" she asked, and kissed him.

"I'm serious, Linda," Alexander said.

"Of course you're serious, sweetheart. You're always serious."

"Linda."

"Stop it. I just feel safe, okay?"

"It's not okay. You shouldn't feel safe." He pushed past her to open the door with his own key and saw as he held the door open for her that he had made her angry.

"I'm sorry," he said as they climbed the stairs. "It's just that I worry about you."

"You don't worry about me," she said. "You just want to stir things up. You just want to get a rise out of me."

"*Christ*," he said to her harshly, but he was startled to realize how right she was.

"How'd it go?" she asked him. "How was Sam?"

"Sam was fine."

"What'd you eat?"

"Scotch and deli."

"Again?"

"Again."

They paused to catch their breath on the third-floor landing. Alexander noticed that the tenants had installed a new electronic alarm system.

"How many games did you play?" Linda asked.

"Two."

"And he won both."

"Yes."

"Because you let him."

"No."

Alexander began climbing the stairs again.

"No?" Linda asked after him.

"No. Not this time. He really won."

Linda shook her head and followed Alexander up the stairs. "Well, that's great," she said. "Isn't it?"

"Sure."

"Was something wrong with you?"

He had reached his front door and said nothing as he turned the key in the lock.

"Alexander?" she asked. "Were you okay?"

"Just a killer headache."

She blocked his entrance playfully. Her mood had already brightened again. "Wait till you see this!" she said to him.

They stepped inside, and she turned on the light, waving to the room as if it were a miracle or a game show prize. All that seemed to have changed was that another pile of his furniture had been moved into the center of the room.

"Come on!" Linda said, rushing toward the corner where the furniture had been.

Slowly, Alexander followed her in. They were looking up at the ceiling, where a hole had been cut for the staircase to go. A circle of light shone down from above.

"Fantastic," he said. "Great."

She hugged him. He kissed her. She pulled on his sleeve. "You want some wine or something?" she asked.

"No. I've got to get some sleep."

"Fresh sheets tonight," she said.

"I think I'll sleep down here."

"Here? Don't be silly. It's a mess," she said.

"I've got this killer headache."

"I'll rub your head."

"No. You know how I am. With a headache, I mean. I'll just keep you up."

Linda looked down. "Are you angry at something?" she asked him.

"Don't be silly."

"Are you worried about tomorrow?"

"No."

"About seeing your mother?"

"No."

Linda bit her lip and frowned, and at the same time, her eyes lost their focus. It was a look Alexander knew by now: fear and courage, anger and self-restraint. He had seen it every time that he had pushed her to the edge, every time that he had pretended, consciously or not, that he was being perfectly normal and that she was the one who was acting strange.

"Don't," Linda said, her gaze still frozen.

"Don't what?"

"Don't lie to me."

Alexander began to unbutton his shirt. He felt wild and exhausted and unable to cope. He tried to think of something to say, but in his mind he was measuring the length of the couch and picturing his body fitting into it. He was thinking that if the couch was a rectangle three feet by six feet, then it would have a diagonal line of six and seven-tenths feet, because to get the diagonal of a parallelogram, you had to take the square root of the length squared plus the width squared. And he was thinking that he would be able to fit with eight inches to spare.

"Alexander," Linda was saying to the stack of boxes in front of her. "Just don't treat me like I'm some bimbo."

He touched her arm. "You are nothing like a bimbo," he said.

"Just don't act like I don't know you."

Alexander took her hand and kissed her fingertips.

"Twenty years," she said. "It's been twenty years since you've seen your mother. Do you really think I buy it that you're not worried? Tell me you don't want to talk about it, but don't tell me there's nothing to talk about."

He squeezed her hands tight. "Linda, I'm sorry," he said. "I'm not lying. Nobody knows me better than you."

"You know," she said, "it's like you always think that love is supposed to be some sort of equation or something. Like it has something to do with *worth*. Like all these parts of people get added up, and if they come to a certain value, then they'll be worth loving. Well, love has *nothing* to do with worth, pal. You either love someone or you don't. Love is an accident. That's all."

"All right." Alexander said. He pulled Linda toward him and kissed her, and then he looked up to watch her face as it changed and her eyes as they regained their focus.

He finally did fall asleep downstairs. Silently, Linda made up the couch with the blanket she'd given him for his birthday. She kissed him good night and went upstairs. She was still angry with him, but not enough.

If only, he thought, she was harder to get, then he might understand how to want her again.

When they had first met, Linda had been finishing her master's while teaching grade school part-time to pay her rent and keep her summers free. Her energy had amazed him then; her confidence had been extraordinary. She had seemed both bright and elusive, infinite mischief in her eyes. He wondered again how she'd turned into this woman who made up couches for him. He wondered if he had changed her.

It seemed sometimes that he had taken her independence from her as if it were a coat, and he now stood at the ready whenever she was cold, politely offering her first one sleeve and then the other, smoothing the shoulders, even kissing her neck, and casually obscuring the fact that it was he who had taken the coat in the first place. He understood the stalemate, and could not find a solution for it: If he loved her more, she would need him less; if she needed him less, he would love her more.

Alexander lay on his diagonal, and above him, the hole in

the ceiling loomed, a white circle of light. Then he heard Linda's footsteps as she moved across her living room floor, and he heard the sound of something scraping as she pulled it, and then he saw a piece of plywood slowly cover the high, bright circle like a cloud covering the moon.

Rogue woke him in the morning, a claw scratching against his neck, and then the sweep of fur.

"Linda?" Alexander asked.

There was no answer.

He prowled the rooms. There wasn't a note. He went upstairs. He looked in her kitchen. No coffee. No toast. No note there, either.

Good girl, he thought then. It's your goddamn coat.

CLEO COLE'S apartment was on the thirteenth floor of a prewar building so old, so overlooked, and so far east that the elevators were still run by actual elevator men. Later, Alexander would learn that Cleo had had an affair with one of those elevator men. He would also learn that Cleo believed in the power of the number thirteen, that her living on the thirteenth floor was no accident, and that Cleo, in general, did not believe in accidents. But when they first met, she didn't even say hello. She opened the door and immediately gripped his hand, staring at him with ridiculous intensity. Alexander was too surprised to squeeze her hand back, but he managed to mirror her gaze exactly. Contests had never bothered him. People who tried to stare him down had. Then Cleo surprised him again. She looked away, laughing, and her laugh was the absolute inverse of her stare. Her laugh was giddy and throaty and frivolous. She ushered him in, still holding his hand.

When they reached the living room, she let go. "What kind of handshake was *that?*" she said.

Alexander stood beside her, absentmindedly flexing his fingers. The first thing he noticed was the sunniness of the room: the yellow fabric on the couches and chairs, the high windows, the white walls, the plain glass tables. The second thing he noticed was a low wooden stool where a clear Lucite slipper sat centered on a green velvet pillow. Then he noticed Cleo herself. She was blond. She was tall. She was, in fact, stunning. She was wearing a pair of khaki shorts and a man's white shirt that was buttoned all the way up to the collar. Around her waist was a woven multicolored belt with little tassels that played off each other like atoms when she moved.

She pointed to the couch, and Alexander sat down. She settled next to him, crossing her legs easily into what looked like a yoga position. Her legs were tan. She was wearing gold lamé loafers. On her wrist there was a tan line, where a watch should have been. Her posture was so correct that he found it disconcerting. She looked at him again, still smiling.

"Well," he said.

She reached for a pack of Salems, lit one, and blew a line of smoke at the ceiling.

"This isn't all bullshit, Alexander," she said. "What I do, I mean."

"Where did you grow up?" he asked her.

She smiled, shaking her head. "The South."

"Well yeah. I sort of figured. But—"

"Virginia."

"Is she coming?"

"She's not here yet."

"I can see that."

"So. You're nervous. And let's just say you think this is a lot of crap."

"Let's just say I'm kind of new to the game."

"All right. Let's just say that."

There was a pause. "Can you call her?" Alexander asked.

"No. She only calls me," Cleo said.

"So when you told me that you'd get right back to me, you just had a hunch that she was going to call you that week?"

"Oh, no. She calls me every week."

Alexander was stunned. He looked away. He noticed that Cleo's ceiling and the top of her bookshelves were not exactly parallel. "When she's in New York, you mean," he said quietly.

"Oh, no. Every week."

"For how long?" he said.

"Well." Cleo looked at him apologetically. "For fifteen years," she said.

"How old are you?" he asked her.

"Thirty-eight," she said.

Alexander couldn't think of anything to say that wasn't another question. He didn't want to ask questions here. He tried to figure out which was crooked, the ceiling or the bookshelves.

"Why don't I tell you about how we met," Cleo said. "I was new to all this too, once, you know."

Alexander was speechless.

"All right?" Cleo said.

He nodded.

"I met a guy," she said. "He was a numerologist. I was a model then. But I fell in love. Wiped out. And so I bought his act for a while, you know? We lived by the numbers. I even let him change my name. But frankly I still think all that stuff is a lot of horseshit."

Alexander had to laugh.

"No, really." Cleo raised her hands. "Palms are different. You'll see. But anyway, your mother was one of his clients. He was the one who gave her the big numbers, right? To help her win that lottery? Well, she took off, right? Beat it. Split. Didn't give him a penny. And she was not our favorite person on this planet for a while. Zoll—that was the name he gave himself; his real name was Richard—Zoll even lit a special candle and put a spell on her once." Abruptly, Cleo stopped talking. She looked closely at the heel of her left hand, and then lit another Salem.

"So how did you wind up being friends?"

"Whoa, doll. I'm not sure I'd call her exactly my friend."

"Well, what, then?"

"A few months after Alice took off, Zoll turned to me one night and said he had something to tell me. He said that he had finally done the one thing he had never agreed to do for his clients. He'd charted out his own death, and guess what, it was only six weeks away. Okay, I know that sounds ridiculous, but you have to understand, Zoll had shown me over and over again how all sorts of famous people's deaths were right there in their numbers. He had shown me how to do it. He gave me Jayne Mansfield's birth date and—I didn't know who she was then—he told me to predict when and how she would die. So I figured it all out by the numbers, and the numbers said she was going to be guillotined on June 29, 1967. Guillotined. Crazy, right? Then he told me Jayne Mansfield had died on that very day in a car crash and that the glass from the windshield had cut off her head."

Alexander looked down at his watch. It was just past four-thirty.

"So Zoll split," Cleo continued. "Left me a note that said there were a couple of things he was destined to do before he died. *Right*. And so I was a wreck. I go around like a maniac, go to all our old places. Cafés. Clubs. Bookstores. Looking for him. At one place, I meet Faith. Faith was a famous palm reader. Really famous. If she had been a scientist, she would have been Einstein. Anyway, she does my hands, and she says I've got the goods, and she becomes my teacher. A few weeks later I get a cable from Zoll's parents saying that *Richard* was in the hospital. Two broken legs. Seems he had gotten right through the big day and nothing had happened, so just before midnight he got into a car and basically smashed it into a tree."

"Clever," Alexander said.

"Lord. What a jerk." Effortlessly, Cleo switched her right leg under her left and her left leg over her right. "A month later," she went on, "your mother calls, looking for him. She was still in the country then. Did you know that? The first place she went was Nevada. Nevada, right? Anyway, I told her all about Zoll, and she was feeling just as disillusioned as I was, and we started talking, and I told her about Faith, and when she got back to New York she came over and I read her palm. I've read her palm about once every six months since. And that's it. That's the whole story."

"Every six months?" Alexander said. "I thought she was living in Europe."

Cleo reached into a basket underneath the coffee table and brought out a sheet of ivory-colored paper, holding it from the back. "This is what the police use when they take fingerprints," she said. "It's much more accurate than just looking at your hand anyway. So she sends me prints."

"How high tech," Alexander said.

"Come on. Why don't I show you?" Gingerly, she laid the sheet of paper on the table. "All you do is just press your hand down."

Alexander looked at his hands, which were resting on his knees.

"What are you scared of?" Cleo said, grinning at him as if he was a camper. "You're a scientist, doll. You're a big-deal scientist. You know all this stuff is bullshit anyway."

Alexander smiled back at her but didn't move his hands. "You're very nice," he said icily. "But I really don't want to do this. Now, where is Alice?"

"I don't want to read them *now*, doll," Cleo said, completely unruffled. "I *won't* read them now. I promise. I'd just like to have your prints. Good Lord. The son of Alice Simon. I've been wondering about your hands for years now. I won't even *look* at the prints while you're here. I promise. Really. You can hide them somewhere and call me later. But please, doll. I'd just like a little bedtime reading."

His hand left a grayish print on the paper, and the paper left his hand black.

"You can go wash up now," she said, and pointed toward a door.

In the bathroom, there were pictures of Cleo all over the walls. Cleo with longer hair, perched on a mountaintop cross-legged, next to some guru type. On the other hand, Cleo in a modeling pose, a black strapless evening gown with a slit up the side and her hair pulled back with a velvet ribbon that looked very soft and elegant. He wondered if she was single.

He washed his hands. The ink was stubborn. He looked for a scrub brush and found one in the shape of a small pink pig: She had to be single, he thought.

Back in the living room, he found her peering over the prints. She looked up at him intently, then stashed the pages under the table.

"Just one thing," she said. "It just leapt out at me. You've got a really skeptical nature."

He had to smile then. "That's just *amazing*," he said. "Just amazing. You could tell that just by looking at those prints, huh?"

"I was right about the Mount of Mars."

"Good for you," he said, smiling.

"Would you like some tea?" she asked him.

"Not if you're going to read the leaves."

Cleo laughed. "It's Lipton."

They drank tea. He told her nothing, didn't ask about Alice, only heard about Cleo's other clients. She said she had Senators and stockbrokers and authors and actors. She said she had never had to advertise. They all came by referral. She had a cat named Boris who prowled the table and allowed Alexander to talk about cats and to tell her, as he had once told Linda, how he had believed as a boy that cats really did have nine lives and how he had borrowed a friend's cat because he had wanted to test the hypothesis experimentally.

"What happened?" Cleo asked him.

"I lost my nerve," Alexander said.

"Good." She laughed. She agreed with him that Alice wasn't coming. And he agreed with her to try once more if Alice called again.

LINDA WAS UP on the roof, pruning, when Alexander came home from Cleo's. Dead leaves striped the wooden planks of the deck like shadows.

He snuck up behind her and kissed her neck. "Hi," he said.

"Hi."

"Looks like your marigolds are starting to bloom."

"Actually, they're dying," Linda said.

"Sorry."

She crumpled some brittle leaves in her hand and tossed them over the railing. "You were a real jerk last night," she said.

"I know I was. I'm sorry," he said. He knew that she was torn between anger and curiosity, and he was happy to find that he wasn't sure which emotion would win out. He stretched out in one of the deck chairs and felt unaccountably good.

A bee buzzed around Linda's head, and she batted it away.

"Birds do it," Alexander sang. "Bees do it."

"A real jerk," she said.

"Even educated fleas do it."

"Pretending you weren't worried," she said.

"Let's do it," he sang. "Let's fall in love."

"Please tell me," she finally said, "how it went."

"She didn't show."

"Oh, Alexander."

"I kept waiting. Cleo—the palm reader—Cleo kept saying she'd come."

"Are you very disappointed?"

"I think I'm relieved."

Linda looked at him doubtfully. "Well, what was Cleo like?" she asked.

Alexander shrugged. "She was a palm reader," he said.

"Well, did she read your palm? Did she tell you your fortune? Was she all spinstery and weird?"

"Come here," Alexander said. She sat between his legs on the chair, and he held her in a tight embrace. Heat rose from her neck like perfume. "You're my girl, aren't you?" he said.

"Was she pretty?" Linda asked.

FOUR DAYS LATER, the night of July fourth, Alexander sat on the living room couch, once again rereading the introduction to his article. There were screams and shouts rising from the street like balloons.

"We're out of milk," Linda announced. "Why don't you come down with me? It's such a nice night."

On the street, she took Alexander's hand and swung it back and forth as if he were a child.

The neighboring street had been sealed off from traffic for some kind of block party, and there were a few policemen standing by the entrance on the avenue. They looked somehow strange for New York cops, and then Alexander realized that they were smiling—huge, uncynical, happy grins. Children were tumbling past them into the safety of the vacant street, dressed in patriotic costumes, waving flags, tripping on shoelaces, shrieking.

Linda stopped in front of the barricades and peered after them with unmistakable longing. Alexander put a hand on the back of her head and imagined her crocheting something small. She was thirty years old, and she had every right to want a child. Every right to be married. And she was so damned smart about him that she'd never once raised the subject with him.

"Look at the sky!" she said.

He followed her gaze. Between the buildings, they could see the pale blue summer light fading into darkness, and Alexander put both his arms around her.

"Do you know why the sky is blue?" he asked her.

"No," Linda told him. "And I don't want to know."

5

THE TOUCH

NEARLY THREE WEEKS had passed since Alice had failed to show up at Cleo's. It was still only July. Alexander could not remember any month of his life that had moved with such sickening slowness. A heat wave had hit the city. No rain had fallen since the end of June, and for the last five days, the temperature had hung insistently between ninety-four and a hundred degrees. The usual stench of the city was deepened by the heat, and the usual anger and possible violence rose from the pavements, all day, like steam.

The summers of Alexander's childhood had never been long enough for him. Every June, Sam had borrowed some equipment from the school where he taught, and together he and Alexander would turn the dining room into a makeshift lab. Then it would be the end of August, and everything would have to go back, and Alexander would watch mutely as Sam dismantled what they had built. Alexander could remember the shock and sadness of the first cool autumn day.

Now he longed for even the faintest hint of fall. At night, he and Linda slept without covers. In the morning, they woke up sticky and distant, neither of them wanting to touch. It didn't help that the construction was still in full swing. The living room bookshelves had been built, the new kitchen appliances had arrived, and the small room that would be Alexander's study finally had walls. But old appliances sat dusty and unconnected in the upstairs living room, and everything seemed to need paint. When Alexander came home one night to find the new closets finished and the clothes put away, he let out a yell, picked Linda up, and carried her to the bedroom. Lying beside her on the bed, he stared, smiling, at the ceiling where the curtain of their clothes had hung. For a moment, he felt free.

At work, the progress had been less tangible. Alexander had finished the first draft of his article, but each time he read it, he found new things to change. His mind felt sluggish, addled by the heat. Biner hadn't spoken to him in ages. Talbot and Heinz had left by now, and the other people he knew at the lab had been swept up in the excitement about the new particle and the inevitable jockeying for credit. Alexander walked through the halls of the lab each day, as unnoticed as a ghost.

"WHAT ARE WE going to do about the couch?" Linda asked him. It was Thursday night, July twentieth, and Alexander had come home from chess at Sam's to make fairly vigorous love to her. They were stretched out on the couch, with three electric fans lined up on the coffee table like scouts. Alexander's chest was slick with sweat.

"What's wrong with the couch?" he asked.

"It needs to be re-covered."

Alexander looked at her blankly.

"Don't you want this place to look nice?" she said.

He covered his face with a throw cushion.

"You just don't want to deal with it," Linda said.

"Exactly."

"You know, for someone who's supposedly so brilliant, you've got a lousy imagination."

"About couches, you mean?" Alexander asked.

"No," Linda said. "About me."

THAT SATURDAY, Cleo called. "Hey," she said. "Did you know you were going to get married when you're thirty-two and outlive your wife?"

"Oh no!" Alexander said, laughing. "I don't want to outlive my wife."

"Get a cat," Cleo said, and Alexander laughed again.

"Alice called today," she added casually, and Alexander stopped laughing.

"Yes," he said.

"She says she's sorry."

"It was three weeks ago," Alexander said.

"Yes."

"Well," he said. "I'm sorry too."

"She said she'd like to try again."

Alexander was silent. He heard Linda in the next room sweeping the daily half-inch of plaster dust from the paper that covered the floor.

"How's Monday?" Cleo asked him.

"This Monday?"

"Yes."

"Monday's fine," he said after a moment. "What time?"

"Five o'clock."

"Fine."

"Good. Watch out for those small fingers of yours now."

"Oh Christ," he said.

"And Alexander," Cleo said in a way that actually chilled him, "you know, you shouldn't be scared of the moon."

"The moon?" he repeated stupidly.

"Hell yes, doll, the moon."

HE HAD TOLD Linda that the call had been from the lab. This time, he didn't want either Linda or Sam to know what he was doing. Having them know and watch him had been too exhausting.

In Cleo's building, the elevator man eyed him with definite amusement. Another one, he seemed to be thinking. Alexander fought the need to explain that he wasn't a client, that he was a scientist, for Christ's sake, and not some gullible fool. The elevator man whistled, and Alexander kept quiet. At Cleo's floor, a man in a gray pin-striped suit who looked vaguely familiar stepped into the elevator as Alexander stepped out.

"Magic," Cleo said when she opened the door.

"What?"

"Do you have any magic in your life, Al?"

"Please don't call me that," Alexander said.

"Sorry."

"Why did you say that thing about the moon?" he asked her.

"Because," Cleo said, "you're not as complicated as you think."

"Is Alice here yet?"

"No," Cleo said. She led the way into the living room. "Hey, you call her Alice too," she said.

"I didn't have much practice calling her anything else."

They sat on the yellow couches, Cleo crossing her legs and Alexander studying the pattern in the rug.

"Do you know what she calls you?" Cleo asked.

"I think the joke here is that she *doesn't* call me."

Cleo picked some white lint from the right leg of her blue jeans.

"What does she call me?" Alexander asked.

"She calls you her cookie."

"Her cookie," he repeated. He felt the strange ache in his throat that he often felt when he dreamed, or when he caught too long a glimpse of the sky.

"Her cookie," Cleo said.

"Do you like her?" Alexander asked after a few moments. "I mean, honestly. I know she's a good client and everything. But do you like her?"

"We talk a lot," Cleo said.

"Talk."

"Yes."

"What about?"

"The stars. Her hands. We talk about numbers. We talk about magic." The cat leapt up onto Cleo's lap.

"Magic," Alexander said.

"Yes."

He looked back down at the rug and decided that there was, after all, no repetition in its pattern. "The thing my father always said," he told Cleo, surprising himself with his candor, "was that what Alice wanted most was magic."

"He was right," Cleo said. She dropped the cat to the floor and stood up, wedging her hands into the pockets of her jeans. "And guess what?" she said. "It's what you want too."

. . .

AFTER HE LEFT Cleo's, Alexander walked through the dusky humid streets and settled against an oak tree in Central Park. He saw three different men his age wearing business suits and carrying flowers wrapped in gaudy paper. Of course Alice hadn't come, and Alexander was exhausted from the double effort of anticipating her arrival and trying to pretend it didn't matter to him. He had stayed at Cleo's for nearly two hours, and now he was astonished that the hope of seeing his mother had kept him there so long. Perhaps, he thought, it was simply the need he felt to understand her.

He had found out some things, but still wanted to know others. He had found out that Alice had been in love with another man long before she had married Sam, and that the other man had been rich and not Jewish, and that his parents had kept him from marrying her, and that it was his picture that she had kept inside the locket she wore around her neck, the locket he remembered from the night of the ghost. He had found out that Alice explained every decision she'd ever made as being part of her destiny. And he had found out that, for fifteen years now, Cleo had been the kind of child to her that Alice had wanted to have.

HE HAD STAYED in the park until the time that he usually came home from work. When he walked into the apartment, he was astonished to find the wood floor uncovered and the bulk of the workmen's equipment gone.

Linda was flushed and clearly excited, kissing him intensely, then stopping every few minutes to hug him again. Alexander felt a genuine rush of fear—the fear that his life had just arrived in a neat package.

For once, Linda said she was too tired to cook, so they ordered in, and she spread an old blanket, picnic style, across the wood floor. The cracks between the planks of wood were beige with plaster dust. Linda and Alexander passed boxes of Chinese food back and forth, like toys.

Her fortune cookie said, "You must rely on your friends."

His said, "Learn to learn from your mistakes."

They finished eating and leaned back against the front of the couch. Linda looked around the room beatifically.

"Isn't it great?" she kept asking.

"It's great," he said again and again.

"I mean, I thought they'd never finish," she said.

"I know. It took forever."

"But it was worth it, wasn't it? I mean, isn't it great?"

"It's great."

Linda sighed and stretched contentedly. Then she reached for her purse and drew out several swatches of fabric. She put one on the couch, where her head had been resting. "So what do you think about this one?" she asked.

Alexander felt something inside him stop.

"I like the stripes," Linda went on, "but I just wonder if the white part won't get too dirty."

Stop it, Alexander was thinking.

"I mean I love the gray," she said.

Stop, he thought.

"But I'm just worried about the white," she said. "What do you think, sweetheart? Do you think that it's too impractical?"

"I think the place looks fine," he said quietly.

"I'm not talking about the place," Linda said, oblivious to his mood. "I'm talking about the couch."

"The couch."

"Yes. The couch. The piece of furniture that we sit on. The thing we're leaning against right now."

"Enough," he said.

"What?"

"Enough!"

Rogue leapt from his spot beside Alexander. Linda sat up straight, startled.

"Haven't you had *enough*?" Alexander said. "You've been fixing this goddamn place up for *decades*!"

Linda looked at him, shocked. "I just want it to be nice," she said.

"*Nice*," Alexander said. "It *is* nice. I don't think you just want it to be nice. I think you want it to keep going. I think you *like* spending all your time on tile samples and swatches and where should we hang the painting."

Linda crumpled the other swatches as if they were pieces of Kleenex.

"Don't yell at me," she said to the floor.

"Fuck it," he said. "I *am* yelling. I don't think you'd know what to *do* with yourself if this place was ever finished."

"I'd enjoy it," Linda said.

"You'd just be waiting for the paint to fade so you could start all over again." He stood up and sat down. He knew that he was being unfair, and that only made him want to be more so. "Christ!" he shouted. "They're *things*! They're only things! It's just like Alice."

"It's nothing like Alice."

"You could spend your whole *life* looking for new things to fix up!"

"And what about you!" she said, finally shouting back. "You could spend your whole life looking for things to take apart!"

She left the room, head down, her newly cut bangs not quite hiding her tears.

Spent, Alexander leaned back on the couch. He heard the squeak of the bathroom door and listened for the water he knew she would run to cover the sound of her crying. When it started, he felt like crying too. He hadn't cried in years. He didn't want to cry. He didn't cry. He looked around for Rogue but saw himself instead, reflected in the glass of one of the posters Linda had picked up from the framers.

FIFTEEN MINUTES later, he was on the subway heading to Penn Station, and forty-five minutes after that, he was safely inside his office, rereading the article that was already done and deciding he needed to rework its conclusion.

Alexander stood at the window, looking through his own reflection to the empty, dark grass and the lamps along the distant pathways spread out like stars. He had wanted one thing since the night in the car with Alice and Sam when his mind had woken up. He had wanted to be a great and brilliant scientist. Good and smart would not have been enough. Great might actually change the game. If he were great, he had always thought, he might leave something behind him in the muddle of people whom he passed every day in the streets and stood next to on the trains.

Now he was giving his own fears to Linda—telling her she was the one who didn't want what she had worked for. In the night sky, a cloud parted, baring the moon, and Alexander wished that he could be a boy again, just starting out on the journey and believing in the goal.

THE ANGEL WAS Cleo that night in Alexander's dream, and he woke to a dim room and a new fear. In the pale gray light, he moved across the bed to Linda and pressed his legs against the backs of her legs and locked his arms around her as if she were his life.

In the morning, while she was still asleep, Alexander retrieved one of the squares of fabric from the living room floor and left it on the dining room table with a short, sweet note. In the evening, Linda greeted him as if he were returning from a long voyage at sea.

BY THE END of the week, Alexander noticed that the fuss about the new particle had finally started to fade. A slight air of sadness hung over the lab. The normal competition for time on the accelerator seemed to have lost some of its edge. A note from Bruce Biner appeared in a box on the front page of the lab's newsletter, *The Wilson Wire*. It was addressed to all Wilson employees, thanking them for their professionalism in the midst of all the publicity, and reminding them that the business of the lab needed to continue without thoughts of press attention. "We've had a lot of national and international attention in recent weeks," the note read, "but there's no reason to feel discouraged about resuming our daily efforts now that the spotlight has shifted away from us."

Around the cafeteria, lab technicians stacked Styrofoam cups into molecular configurations and speculated that Biner was entering a deep depression.

IT WAS TUESDAY morning, the first day of August, and Alexander was sitting in his office. He had taken the contents of a package of Pepperidge Farm Goldfish and was arranging them on his desk in ever-widening circles. Physicists and mathematicians played a similar game in their heads, called sphere packing: How many spheres could fit inside one sphere? How many circles could fit inside one circle? This was the kind of question that brought physicists endless joy and debate.

Alexander heard a cough and looked up. Biner was standing before him, framed by the doorway. He was wearing an expensive-looking double-breasted suit, and there was a fine sprinkling of dandruff on each of his shoulders. He looked at the arrangement of orange fish on Alexander's desk, and then at Alexander. His right eyebrow arched acrobatically. "Simon?" he said expectantly.

"Goldfish packing," Alexander said, trying to stare him down.

Biner looked at the ground a moment. Alexander took a deep breath.

"Well," Biner said, "but you've got it all wrong." He pulled up a chair and sat on the other side of the desk.

Alexander laughed nervously. "I didn't know," he said, "that there was a right way to do this."

"May I?" Biner asked, his left hand poised above the many bright orange rings.

"Be my guest," Alexander said.

Neatly, Biner swept the goldfish to one side of the desk. "The question," he said, "is not how many goldfish can fit inside one circle. Properly, the question should be how many goldfish can fit inside one *goldfish*." Then he arranged the pieces carefully into the outline of a large, plump fish.

Alexander laughed, astonished.

Biner smiled perceptibly. "You see," he said, "there are some good things that come from not having all those reporters around here."

"Yes."

"Join me. Please," Biner said.

For the next five minutes, they were silent as they rearranged the goldfish in neat fish-shaped rings.

"There," Biner said, as they finished. He looked pleased. "At least that's one solution." He pushed back his chair and reached into his pocket for his pipe and tobacco. He thrust the pipe into the navy blue pouch, then tamped the tobacco down with his thumb. He returned the pouch to his pocket, pulled out a match, lit the pipe, and took a long, contented puff. "So," he finally said, "where the hell is your goddamn article?"

Alexander looked down at the desk. Sentences of excuse and explanation formed and re-formed in his mind. But he knew, as he had known the night he yelled at Linda, that something more courageous was going to be required of him. He reached into his top drawer and drew out the stack of pages.

"Here," Alexander said. "It's here."

He handed the article to Biner.

BY SEVEN O'CLOCK, there was still no word from Biner. Alexander couldn't remember ever having seen him leave later than that. But Alexander felt numb and exhausted from the wait and the worry, and he couldn't seem to make himself get up and go home.

At his computer, he called up a game called Castle, which Heinz had programmed in for him. The object of the game was to move a cursor through the rooms of a vast castle, picking up treasure and avoiding pitfalls. Points were awarded for the ogres and demons that one could destroy along the way, and also for the treasures that one could find and keep.

On his first few games, Alexander was killed almost immediately by an ogre in a garden that ran at his cursor furiously. By the fifth game, though, he had gotten the hang of it.

He had the sword, the helmet, the goblet, and the necklace. That was all he was allowed to carry—four things at a time. He moved the cursor back through the rooms of the castle, passing the ogres and the snake he had already killed. At the front gate, he deposited the two treasures with the other six he had found. For protection, he kept the sword and the helmet. You never knew.

Back in the corridor on the second floor of the castle, he found a sapphire ring and picked it up. Then he found a doorway.

OPEN DOOR, he typed into the computer.

NEED KEY, the screen said.

GET KEY, he typed.

GET IT YOURSELF, the screen said.

He would have to find the key.

Down a winding corridor, a trap closed around him.

GAME OVER, the screen said. PRESS 'Y' TO PLAY AGAIN.

BY THE TWENTIETH game, Alexander had found an amulet that said PROTECTION FROM TRAPS. To get down the corridor, he would need to carry this, and the sword, and the helmet. He would only be able to carry one thing more. He passed through the trap unscathed. What he found was a book.

READ BOOK, he typed.

IMPOSSIBLE, the screen said. LETTERS ARE BLURRY.

He went back for the glasses he had found in the queen's bedroom. To read the book, he would need to drop his sword or his helmet. He dropped his helmet.

READ BOOK, he typed.

BOOK SAYS, "GET WAND."

He would have to drop his sword, too.

In the corner of the third turret, a large spider killed him.

ON THE TRAIN home, he discovered that he was shaking. His hands were trembling, and his face was hot. Past midnight, he told himself, you're just very tired.

But the windows made black mirrors, and he saw that he was scared.

It was nearly one in the morning when Alexander reached Penn Station and climbed the stairs from the tracks. At that hour, the station was part shelter and part combat zone, homeless people sleeping on benches and leaning against closed stores, foreign shouts echoing through the huge hall. It seemed that a hundred eyes—pleading, dazed, haughty, menacing—tried to meet his. Alexander stared down at the sticky floor and walked as if he were late for a very important meeting.

THE NEXT DAY at the lab, he never left his desk.

He was back at the gate of the castle. He had killed two snakes, two spiders, two ogres, and one demon. He had gathered up a goblet, a cross, a gold bar, a harp, a necklace, a magic wand, a book, and a ring.

OPEN GATE, he typed.

IMPOSSIBLE. GATE LOCKED.

GET KEY, he typed.

GET IT YOURSELF.

He moved the cursor to the key and picked it up.

OPEN GATE, he typed again.

The gate opened.

Alexander stared at the blinking cursor.

Now what? he thought.

One by one he moved his treasures outside the gate until they were clustered at the bottom of the screen.

CONGRATULATIONS, the screen said, and then it went blank.

For nearly fifteen minutes, Alexander continued to stare at the blank screen, as if he were looking at a night sky and waiting for the sun to rise.

THE STRANGE THING for Alexander was to feel so nervous about Biner's response when deep down he knew that his theory was sound and that his article described it accurately. But as the hours went by on Thursday and Biner still hadn't called, Alexander began to feel unhinged. He knew he had set something in motion that he could no longer control, and it didn't help to remember that that thing was precisely what he'd always longed for. At around three o'clock, he put his head on his desk, and by the time that Biner's secretary finally buzzed him, Alexander had fallen into a strange half-sleep, the kind of sleep in which his thoughts seemed to take on physical shape. It took him a moment to clear his head.

In Biner's office, Alexander was alarmed to find a stranger. Two strangers, if he counted Biner, whose face was contorted by a hideous, forced grin.

"Ah," Biner exclaimed as he waved Alexander in. "Here he is now."

"You *look* like you've been working around the clock," the man said.

"Night and day," Biner crowed. "Alexander, meet Stanley Seligman."

Alexander shook the man's hand, trying to place his name.

"I'm from the *Times*," the reporter explained.

"Of course," Alexander managed to say. He wondered if Seligman had felt how cold his hands had just become, or if he could sense how furious he was. Alexander glared at Biner, but Biner simply beamed back as if a lifelong partnership was finally paying off.

"I figured," Biner said with seeming magnanimity, "that you would want to answer some of Mr. Seligman's questions yourself."

Alexander felt his face flush. He realized his hands were now clenched.

"Of course," he managed to say, attempting a smile that he realized must have seemed as alarming as Biner's. "I'd just like to see you for a moment in the hall."

Biner frowned.

"Please," Stanley Seligman said. "Let me. I'll be outside when you're done."

Alexander had begun to pace even before the door shut. He was trying to put his thoughts into words and trying to find a way out.

"What's the trouble?" Biner said. The new grin had been replaced by the usual anxiety.

"The trouble!" Alexander said. "Where the hell do you get off calling the goddamn newspaper? I didn't even know if you had *read* the article yet. I haven't even submitted it for *publication* anywhere. I'm not ready to tell the *New York Times* what I'm up to!"

"I think you are," Biner said simply.

"You had no right to do this."

Biner looked at Alexander with what seemed like sincere confusion. Almost politely, he asked, "Have you lost your mind?"

Alexander felt sick to his stomach, powerless to explain himself, and utterly trapped.

"You've done a great thing," Biner said. He sounded as if he was speaking to a frightened child. "You've written a brilliant article about the mystery of the whole universe. Did you want that just to be our little secret?"

SOMEHOW, Alexander answered most of the questions the reporter asked him. Seligman hadn't, of course, read the article yet, though Alexander noticed a neatly Xeroxed copy of it sitting like a party favor on the corner of Biner's desk. After five minutes of general background information, Alexander found himself fumbling for even the simplest statements of fact. Finally he looked to Biner, half warning, half imploring, and it was Biner who suggested that the interview would be more fruitful after Seligman had read the article.

"Now that you know where he is, you can call him any time," Biner said.

Alexander left the room as quickly as he could.

. . .

IN THE JOHN, which was deserted, he chose the farthest stall and slumped down on the floor, pressing the side of his face against the cold tiled wall. Then he vomited, and after he vomited, tears finally began to warm his face. His body was shaking. He pressed his arms around his knees and his face into his arms, and he thought, I did it, I got it, I did it, I got it.

"YOU LOOK like hell," Sam said when he opened the door for Alexander that night. "What's wrong with you? Are you sick? You look sick. Do you have a fever?" He reached out a hand, trying to feel Alexander's forehead.

Alexander stepped into Sam's foyer, ducking to avoid the hand. There had always been something about Sam as nurse that had seemed both brave and poignant, and it had always made Alexander feel uncomfortable. "I'm *fine*, Dad," he said. "I'll be with you in a minute."

In Sam's bathroom, Alexander stood at the sink, looking at himself in the mirror of the medicine chest. It was true that he looked gray and shaky, and he looked somehow hollow. He sighed, then turned the tap on, brushed his teeth, and gargled as quietly as he could. Then he rinsed his face with cold water and dried it vigorously, hoping to bring some color back to his cheeks.

In the kitchen, Sam was pouring the Scotch. "You were in there a long time," he said. "Are you all right?"

"Dad," Alexander said. "You know you were always lousy as a Jewish mother."

"I'm what you've got," Sam said reflexively, the echo of a hundred childhood arguments.

"Dad," Alexander said, feeling sorry.

"Can't you tell me what's wrong?"

Alexander grinned. "Why don't you ask me what's right instead?"

Sam took a sip of his drink. "What's right?" he asked doubtfully.

Alexander reached into his jacket pocket and handed the article to his father.

They moved to their usual places in the living room, sitting by the chessboard. Sam read slowly, nervously, then poured a second drink and read the article again. When he finally started speaking, the points he raised were minor ones—questions of spelling and grammar. Once, with unconcealed delight, he corrected a math error, but it turned out to be a typo. He raised no points of logic, and Alexander couldn't tell if Sam had understood what he'd read or not. For once, he felt too tired to care. He was happy to see Sam feel needed, but the exhaustion of the day began to overtake him, and in some ways he had never felt so far away from his father. Sam's excitement seemed tangible. Alexander remained immune, feeling only the pressure it created, as if Sam's apartment had somehow become a giant, sealed vessel.

SAM HAD ASKED Alexander how Linda had reacted, and he seemed completely confounded to learn that Linda didn't know that he had given the article to Biner, let alone to the *New York Times*. Alexander knew that she would want to be told, but when he got in late that night, he found her sleepy and uncommunicative. Lying next to her in bed, he whispered, "I've got good news," but she sighed and rolled over, perhaps already asleep, and Alexander had to smile at himself for feeling hurt by that.

The telephone woke them in the morning, and Linda answered it. Stanley Seligman was calling to set up an interview, and when Alexander finally hung up, Linda was sitting cross-legged on the bed, hurt and furious.

"What the hell is going on?" she said.

"I tried to tell you last night, but you were sleeping," Alexander said.

"Tell me now."

"I'll tell you tonight."

"No, damn it. Tell me now."

"I'm late, and it's going to take a while."

"Is it good?"

"I don't know yet."

"You must."

"I don't."

IT WAS REAL now, and Alexander knew he had no choice but to follow it through. He met Stanley Seligman at noon in the Wilson cafeteria. Seligman ate a pastrami sandwich and immediately began to sweat. He actually used up a thick stack of napkins blotting his forehead again and again. He explained that he had an allergy, but he seemed nearly as excited as Sam had been the night before.

"So you going to Stockholm or what?" was his first question.

"I've already found some minor errors in the article," Alexander said. "I have to correct them first, you know?"

Seligman paused for a moment. "Modest. Cautious," he said. "Fine. I'll say that. Now why don't you talk to me? I found one mistake in the computation on page ten. Was there something else? That just looked like a typo."

Alexander laughed.

"Don't forget," Seligman said, "I already talked to Biner."

"Biner may have called you too soon."

"Why don't you let me be the judge?" Seligman said.

"Because there's no rush. I think it's too soon."

"Look, I wrote a goddamn magazine cover story on string theory," Seligman said. "I don't know what the hell your problem is, but this is exciting to me."

IN THE AFTERNOON, Alexander sat at his word processor, corrected the typo in the article, and printed out the new version. He wrote the briefest of cover letters, then addressed a label to *Nature*, the British science journal that had once praised his thesis so highly.

Biner walked into the office just as Alexander was sealing the envelope.

"Ah, good," Biner said. "Who did you address the letter to?"

"To the editor," Alexander said stiffly.

"By name?"

"No."

Biner laughed, then snapped his fingers above the envelope. "Open it," he said.

Alexander shrugged and handed the envelope to Biner, who withdrew the letter and scanned it quickly. "Ever heard of a magazine slush pile?" he said. "You do it this way, and this article is going to sit in some poor secretary's in-box for weeks."

He reached into his breast pocket for his silver fountain pen and scribbled the name of an editor on the top of the page. "Address it to him," Biner said. "And mention my name."

"But—"

"We're old friends," Biner said unconvincingly. "I'll give him a jingle this afternoon."

"I can handle this myself," Alexander said.

"No you can't," Biner told him, and left the room.

.   .   .

THAT EVENING when Alexander came home, he found three
workmen on their knees in the living room, poking through
the creases of a large beige drop cloth as if they were surveyors
mining for gold. Clumps of plaster dotted the drop cloth, and
Alexander could see that the men had finally finished their one
remaining task, which was to plaster the wall beside the new
overhead cabinets. A fourth workman—Alexander thought of
him as the One Who Wears a Hard Hat—was straddling a six-
foot ladder, assessing the scene and giving directions.

"Luis lost a screw," Linda explained to Alexander in a
whisper.

"We've got a lot of screws," Alexander said.

"Not this kind. It's a special screw. It fits the doorknob.
After that, they're totally done."

"Can't we just get a new doorknob this weekend and do it
ourselves?" Alexander asked.

"It's complicated."

"We'll buy a doorknob book."

"Also it's expensive."

"Please. I want them out of here."

"Come on. Let's help them look."

For the next twenty minutes then, Alexander and Linda joined
the workmen on their knees.

"It's got to be here," Luis kept saying.

"That's just what I say all day," Alexander said over his
shoulder.

"What do you do, man?"

"Don't ask," Linda said. "He'll never tell you."

SHE COOKED DINNER after the workmen finally left, but
Alexander ate little.

"You look like you're going to cry," Linda told him as she
brought in a pot of coffee.

"I never cry," he said.

"I know."

Alexander pushed his chair back from the table and placed a hand, palm down, within one of the square white tiles in the tabletop.

"Okay," Linda told him. "I want to know what's going on."

Alexander lifted his hand and watched as the print that it had made evaporated slowly.

Two hours later, he and Linda had moved to the living room, and he was still trying to explain to her the nature of the breakthrough he'd made, and the nature of the stir it would cause and all the attention it would bring.

Linda had decided not to re-cover the couch. She had had it cleaned, though, and it was still damp, so she and Alexander sat apart from each other in the two armchairs, their feet propped up on opposite ends of the coffee table, their eyes rarely meeting. Linda mostly listened, her head down, her brow tight, her concentration heroic. From time to time, she would interrupt with a question, and Alexander kept trying to find the balance between insulting her by explaining too much and confusing her by explaining too little. At one point, he caught her looking so serious that he had to smile at her.

"What?" she said. "Did I ask something stupid?"

"I was just thinking that I wished Stanley Seligman had asked questions this good today."

"Keep going," Linda said without acknowledging the compliment. "You were telling me about quantum gravity."

Alexander walked over to Linda's chair and bent down to kiss her.

IT WAS MIDNIGHT before he had finally finished with a description of Biner's visit to the office that day. "And that's it," he said. "That's everything."

Linda looked up. "Nice story," she said lightly.

"Long story," he said.

"So you got sick in the men's room."

"It probably sounds kind of funny now. But God I felt awful," Alexander said.

"I don't think it sounds funny," Linda said. "I don't think it *is* funny. You were just terrified, that's all."

"I was. You're right," he said.

"I know."

He had never considered the possibility that telling Linda what he was feeling might actually make him feel better.

"You are such a trooper," he said.

She shrugged, and almost smirked, as if she'd been keeping a secret for many years.

He wondered, suddenly, if he knew her. The thought stirred him. He didn't feel tired. He felt curious and strangely hopeful, the way he did when he was faced with a math or physics problem to solve. Maybe, he thought as he helped Linda tidy the living room, maybe, he thought as he followed her upstairs to their bedroom, he should have told her all this long before.

He wondered, now, about the nature of her love. He had pushed her back so many times, and she had pulled herself back so many times more, and what he didn't know was whether that pattern had diminished her in some way that was hard and irreversible. Was disappointment an imperfection that could be distilled away?

Emerging from the bathroom in a large white T-shirt, Linda slid into bed beside him, regal and silent but clearly triumphant. Alexander could tell that she wanted to savor the moment: her pride, her vindication, and his obvious interest.

He reached for her.

"Something on your mind?" she said, grinning.

Alexander kissed her neck.

"Something you'd like to do?" she asked.

"Yes," he murmured to her. "Yes. I want to make love to you."

"No you don't."

"Yes," he said. "I do."

"No," she said. "You only think you do. The minute I say you can, you'll lose interest."

"I never lose interest in sex," he said.

"Not in sex," Linda said. "In me."

"Linda." He grabbed her, holding her tightly, putting one leg between her two, feeling the coolness of her thighs against him, hugging her harder.

"Oh," she said.

He kissed her again, trying to imagine that they had never had sex, thinking of the way her bed had looked when he'd seen it through her windows from the roof so long before, remembering the shock and perfection of her body, her mixture of shyness and stamina.

She opened her legs.

"Tell me," he said to her. "Tell me what you want."

She rose to meet every movement he made. He tried to move with the rhythm of her body, but when he stopped moving, she stopped, too. She followed him. She waited.

"What do *you* want?" he whispered to her.

"I want you to want me even after you've had me. Even then," she said. "Even then."

Her eyes were closed. He looked at her. And so she was Linda after all. Her sense of what she was missing was inseparable from him.

When she said she was coming, he didn't believe her.

When he came, he came quickly, and felt nothing he hadn't felt before.

They lay beside each other. Linda lightly stroked the side of Alexander's chest. He closed his eyes and felt exhausted and couldn't remember ever having felt as lonely.

"I love you," Linda whispered. The words made him feel exactly what he'd always thought they would make him feel, and so he pretended to be asleep. Linda sighed in the darkness, but he knew that she was still watching him.

SHE WAS LOOKING at him when he woke up in the morning, as if she'd been waiting all night for his reply.

"Hi," he said, and dashed for the shower.

SHE WAS IN the kitchen when he came downstairs. She had regrouped again, somehow finding her way back into the perfect stasis they both knew so well and did so many things to sustain. She said good morning and smiled as if the sex had never happened, or as if it had been wondrous, or as if she hadn't used the word *love*, or as if he had used it, also.

"I always knew you could do it," she said.

Alexander looked at her grimly. "Do what?" he asked her.

"It," she said. "The theory. The article. You know."

"How did you know?" he asked her.

"What?"

"How did you know?" His tone was icy and condescending. "What made you so *sure* I could do it?"

Linda turned off the kitchen faucet, dried her hands on the back of her blue jeans, and turned around to face him. "What's with you?" she asked.

Alexander balled up the dish towel and threw it toward the kitchen counter. Linda winced, as if he'd aimed it at her.

"I PROBABLY SHOULDN'T be telling you this," Cleo said when she called him later that day.

Alexander was in his new study, organizing his books and files. He put his hand on his forehead. "What?" he asked her. "Is it something bad?"

"You're a twenty-two."

"I'm a what?"

"You're a twenty-two. The spiritualism is just immense. Do you know what I'm saying?"

"I'm a twenty-two. This is an important moment for me. Funny, though. I always felt more like—a seventeen."

"Did I tell you that you have a skeptical nature?"

"Yes, and that's just *amazing* you guessed that."

"In numerology, we add up the month, date, and year of your birth, and all those numbers are reduced down to a number under nine."

"I don't know how to break this to you," Alexander said, "but twenty-two doesn't qualify as a number under nine."

"Smart-ass. There are two numbers that are spiritually powerful and are not reduced. They are eleven and twenty-two."

"I see."

"I knew from your Mount of Jupiter that you had a spiritual nature, but this is really remarkable. Your mother never told you this?"

"No."

"Amazing."

"What are you?" Alexander asked, laughing.

"Oh, I'm a twenty-two, too."

"And what does it really mean?"

"It means—it means we have what you'd call a guardian angel."

"A what?"

"A guardian angel. I mean an earthquake could come and this building would split in half, right here, and you and I would not fall in. We have divine protection."

"Alice," Alexander said. "When am I going to meet Alice?"

"When you do."

SHE WAS BACK again, floating in a corner of the dusty bedroom, looking down at him. And it was really her again this time— no trickery, no Cleo.

"Is it now?" he asked the angel.

"Now?" she said.

"The Touch," he said.

She drifted toward the bed and hung above him in the cold air. Her body was above his, but she hovered at the ceiling like a figure in a painting.

"Now?" she asked him gently. "Why?"

"Because," he said. "I did it."

"Yes," she said.

"I worked. I learned. I waited."

"Yes," she said.

"So touch me."

"Now? Are you sure you really want me to now?"

Slowly, her body moved down above his, holding a perfect parallel.

He reached up with both hands for her, but she was still several feet beyond him.

"It may not be what you think," she said.

"Why? What should I be scared of?"

ALEXANDER WOKE from the dream with a start. The sun was rising, and the sky was so furiously red that it colored every window in the skyscape. Alexander's first thought was that the city was on fire. He closed his eyes, and when he opened them only a moment later, the sky had changed completely. It was ice blue, now, and white with clouds. It had happened in an instant, as though all the color and fire had only come from one flame, and then the flame had been put out.

HE HAD TUCKED Cleo's number into his wallet, and at lunchtime on Monday he called her from the lab, but then he hung up when she answered, feeling idiotic. Just before he left for home, he called her again. "Hi," he said. "It's Alexander."

"Why did you hang up before?"

"Before?"

"Twelve-thirty."

He sighed. "I don't really know."

"Well, good for you."

"What?"

"At least you're being honest," she said. "What's on your mind?"

"Not much. I was just wondering if you'd heard something from Alice."

Cleo laughed. She didn't answer him.

"Sorry," Alexander said. "I guess that sounded stupid."

"No, not stupid," Cleo said. "Just incredibly lame."

He laughed.

"Look," Cleo said. "I promise. You will be the first to know."

"Cleo," Alexander said, and realized it was the first time he had called her by her name.

"Yes?"

"How did you know I was scared of the moon?"

"Oh, doll," she said, laughing. "You've got so much to learn."

LINDA LEFT for South Dakota early Tuesday morning.

Alexander felt uncovered, as though a fine light sheet had been lifted away from him in his sleep.

.   .   .

IN THE EVENING, when he came home, he went first to the kitchen and found a note from Linda, pinned with a rabbit magnet to the otherwise sterile refrigerator door. Sighing, Alexander took down the note, reached for a beer, and settled with both on the living room couch.

Dearest Alexander:

I've stocked the refrigerator with food for the week. You've got the number and you know I won't be anywhere else. Don't call later than ten, though. Call.

Please please please take good care of Rogue. Fuss over him the way I do. Talk to him and feed him and tell him I miss him.

As for the plants. The geraniums and marigolds need water three times a week. The rosebush every day. It's new. The impatiens every other day. If you have the time, pluck off the dead leaves. Water at night or in the morning so the water won't boil up. If it rains, you're off the hook.

Hope work went well today. I'm sorry about this last week.

I'll call you when I get in.

Love,
Linda

WILSON PHYSICIST OFFERS NEW "THEORY OF EVERYTHING"

That was the headline. The article made the bottom of the front page of the *New York Times* on Thursday. There was a small photograph of Alexander, which he recognized as his Wilson ID picture. The article explained what string theory was, and told how Alexander's approach took it from ten dimensions to two. It reviewed some of the charges of previous string theory critics, especially those in the Harvard group, who were always saying the theory was too hopelessly esoteric. The article discussed both Einstein and quantum mechanics, and concluded that while no physical proof was possible for Alexander's theory, its beauty and simplicity were bound to make it a theory impossible to ignore. The story gave a brief résumé of Alexander's career and described him as enthusiastic. The words *modest* and *cautious* did not appear, nor did Biner's name. Wilson was only mentioned in the headline and in passing.

Not surprisingly, Alexander heard nothing from Biner all day. He did get a call from the editor at *Nature*, however. The magazine, he said, would be most honored to publish his article.

FOR THE FIRST TIME since the morning in May when he'd known that his theory was going to work, Alexander felt truly excited. He almost wished that Heinz and Talbot were still around. It would have been great, he thought, to go out for a beer with them. He called Heinz at Princeton, but hung up when he got a machine. He called Linda, but she hadn't seen the newspaper yet, and there was something vague and distracted in the tone of her voice. She didn't even say she was proud of him. She asked him about the plants and the cat. She told him how pretty it was out there, and that her parents, who were visiting, too, kept asking about him. "They want to know what you're like," she said.

"Well, tell them to get a *New York Times*."

"No, Alexander. What you're *like*. Not what you *do*."

He sighed.

"I've got to go now," she said.

Alexander called Sam. He let the phone ring twelve times. There was no answer.

He was finally ready to be happy, he thought. So where the hell was everyone?

HE SAT ON the small hill outside the physics building and drank a cup of coffee, despite the early August heat. He was very tired.

He thought about Linda, and he thought about his work. He had not been able to love one, and he had always loved the other. He had not loved Linda because Linda was a goal that he had already reached. He had loved physics more than anything else in his life because it had always seemed to promise something new to want.

Alexander fell asleep in the sun, and when he woke up some hours later, he was in the midst of a downpour. Around him there was the loud hiss of the rain, and laughter and shouts from people who were huddled together, hurrying inside to be warm.

"I'LL BE HONEST with you," Biner said when he finally appeared in Alexander's office late that afternoon. "My first response was outrage. My second response was outrage. Outrage is not a good thing to make me feel."

"You think I wrote that story?" Alexander said. "I had nothing to do with the way that story was written."

"You could at least have mentioned the people who made all this possible. Even actors and actresses do that, you know."

"I talked to that guy for an hour and a half," Alexander said. "He quoted me twice. Anyway, you're the one who called him in the first place."

"All right," Biner snapped. "That's all history now. I don't want to discuss it again."

Alexander sighed. He stared out the window to the path

below. A tour group was approaching. As always, they were
dressed too well, dressed for sterile white laboratories: movie
science. As always, the women lagged behind the men, gingerly
navigating the mud and debris in their ruined high-heeled shoes.
Alexander wondered what they were thinking. Whether the trip
would seem worthwhile to them later. What they would tell
their friends.

Alexander's phone rang, but Biner snatched it up before he
could.

"Mr. Simon is in a meeting at the moment," Biner said
politely. "May I take a message for him?"

Alexander watched, bewildered, as Biner scribbled a number
on a piece of paper and then hung up.

"Who was it?" Alexander asked.

"It was the science editor of *Newsweek*," Biner said.

"And why couldn't I talk to him?"

"Because," Biner said, "we have a strategy to plan."

"A strategy."

"You can't just talk to every damned reporter who calls."

"But that was *Newsweek*," Alexander said.

"Has *Time* called yet? *The Sciences*? Any other papers?"

"No."

"Anyone else?"

"No."

"Good."

"Good? I thought you *wanted* publicity."

"I do," Biner said. "And we're going to get even more on
this than we did on the particle."

"So?" Alexander asked.

"We have to *handle* this," Biner said.

"HE WANTS ME to take three weeks off," Alexander said to
Sam that night over chess.

"Well, what's wrong with that?" Sam asked. "Seems to me you could use the rest."

"He wants me out of the way," Alexander explained. "He's putting a *secretary* in my office to keep track of the phone calls. He doesn't want me to talk to anyone from the press. Not until the lecture."

"What lecture?" Sam said.

"That's the second part of his master plan. He wants me to give a lecture at Wilson. You know. Physicists. Academics. Reporters."

"When?"

"Six weeks or so," Alexander said. "When the article comes out. He'll be the host, and he'll introduce me."

"Well, you have to do that somewhere, right?"

"This way he shares the spotlight."

"This way you get his blessing."

"What makes you think I need his blessing?"

Sam took a sip of his Scotch and shrugged. "Well, don't do it, then, if it bothers you that much."

Alexander moved a pawn and stood up to pace.

"Oh, Ex," Sam said. "You didn't quit, did you?"

Alexander stopped pacing and stared at Sam defiantly.

"Did you?" Sam asked.

"Would it have been so awful if I had?"

Sam shrugged again, studying the chessboard. "I don't know," he finally said.

"I'm going to get lots of offers, you know, Dad. This is a pretty important theory, you know."

"Galileo stood *trial* for what he discovered," Sam said. "People said he was crazy. It didn't matter to him what *Newsweek* thought."

.   .   .

AS A BOY, Alexander had craved his father's respect, somehow confusing respect with love, and thinking that he would need the first in order to get the second.

Then he had been the guilty student surpassing the aging teacher, and he had gone to great condescending lengths to soften that blow for Sam.

It had never occurred to Alexander that he might have gotten it backwards. Maybe, he thought as he walked toward home across the park, it was Sam who had been the real thing all along. Sam had wanted to learn things out of wonder, not fear. Sam had learned about science not to make his mark on the world, but because he loved it when the world contrived to make its mark on him.

ALEXANDER HAD BEEN home for three days. He hadn't shaved, or been outside. He'd written no more than a paragraph of the lecture he was supposed to write. The heat wave had continued, and he sat in the armchair near the air conditioner, watching game shows that he could have won. No one called. Not even Linda. He called no one.

By Monday morning, the heat wave finally seemed to have broken. Alexander woke at eleven and lay on his side, looking out at the roof, amazed both by the hour and by his utter exhaustion. A sharp breeze darted in through the open window, lifting and dropping the half-drawn shades, making the cords that were tied to them dance.

In the bathroom, Alexander turned on the shower and stepped into the bathtub, not stopping to test the temperature.

The water was hot. It was scalding. Pricks of pain washed over him and made it impossible to think. Steam filled the room and fogged the mirror, and when he finally turned off the water and stepped out of the bathtub, there was no one looking back at him.

In the bedroom, shaky from the heat, he felt the need to lie down again. But he pulled on a pair of shorts, went downstairs to make coffee, then climbed back up to the bedroom with a mug in one hand and a notebook in the other.

Outside, on the roof, he read the little he had written and sipped his coffee, trying to concentrate until the words lost their meaning and the coffee's heat was mixed with the sun's. Alexander moved to one of the deck chairs and was shocked by the pallor of his legs. He closed his eyes, raised his chin, and felt the sun on his face. He remembered the tan line on Cleo's left wrist, and he imagined others. Then he imagined Alice lying somewhere in a chaise longue. It felt like a memory, but it wasn't in his usual repertoire.

Alexander opened his eyes and tried to find a pattern in the row of Linda's flowerpots. He'd always been good at sequences. If one, ten, three, nine, five, eight, seven, seven, nine, and six are the first elements in a group, what number continues the sequence? Easy. Five. If small terra-cotta pot, large terra-cotta pot, basket, window box, planter are the first elements in a group . . . No, he thought. There was no pattern, and the petals of Linda's flowers had all curled up in the heat. They were tight bits of shriveled color, like pieces of broken balloons. The parched soil around them looked nearly gray. It hadn't rained since the day that he'd fallen asleep outside the physics building. He had not come up to water once. If he watered now, though, the water would boil. He remembered that he wasn't supposed to let the water boil.

Three hours later, when he woke again, the roof was in shadow. His face was dry and scorched, and the skin was so tight around the corners of his eyes that he knew that he had cried.

The branches of Linda's rosebush stood out, twisted and sinister, and he made the conscious decision to let the flowers die.

. . .

THE MOON WAS so bright that night that it seemed made of metal, perhaps of gold, and it sat against the black night of the city, uncluttered by stars. Sounds came across the street from other apartments—a child's cry, then a woman's, either in passion or pain. There was the whistle of a truck's brakes, and, later, a burst of laughter and a spray of Spanish words.

Alexander lay in bed, watching the moon's subtle progress across the sky. He felt the absence in the bed beside him, but he was glad not to have someone watching him.

He slept when the edge of the moon touched the side of the building across the street.

"You mustn't be scared of the moon," Cleo had said, and she had actually said it quite a long time ago now.

"NOW," Alexander said. "I won't be scared this time."

He didn't try to touch her, though her face was right above his face. Their eyes were matched like four clear points, the corners of a perfect square.

"Touch me," Alexander said.

"Then what will you have dreams about?"

BINER SENT a stack of mail at the end of the week. There were letters from former classmates and former colleagues. There were job offers from three universities. There were notes of congratulations from old professors and the people at the MacArthur Foundation, and a slightly barbed note from Heinz, who wanted to know if his contribution to the theory was ever going to be mentioned. Talbot, of course, had not been in touch. Alexander wondered if Talbot even knew about the article. Sometimes he envied the distance that Talbot put between himself and his life.

Alexander organized the two medicine chests.

He alphabetized the books in the living room.

He cleaned out the files in his computer, but every time he called up the new file named Lecture, he felt overwhelmed and tired.

He was sleeping now for twelve and fourteen hours at a stretch. Sitting in his study, he would listen to the hum of the air conditioner, its rhythm like the presence of another person in the house. Sometimes he found himself studying the lines on his hands.

HE THOUGHT about the famous paradox in mathematics that is known as Zeno's paradox. Zeno lived around Aristotle's time, and like Aristotle, he enjoyed stirring things up.

Zeno said: Imagine a straight line that goes from point *A* to point *B*, and then imagine someone trying to move along this line. In order to get all the way to the end, he first has to pass through a point that's halfway there, right? And to get to the point that's halfway there, he has to pass through the point that's a fourth of the way there. And a sixteenth. A thirty-second. A sixty-fourth. And so on, Zeno argued, right into infinity, since we know that an infinite number of points makes up a straight line. Motion, Zeno concluded, was therefore logically impossible, since anyone trying to get anywhere should be stopped by the infinity that lay between the points.

Moving along a line all his life, Alexander had often thought of Zeno's paradox.

He had finally gotten to *B* now, and all he wanted to do was sleep.

He lay on the bed upstairs, looking for patterns in the dust on the white glass lamp overhead. An hour passed. Alexander went downstairs and reheated the cup of coffee that he hadn't drunk.

"FRIDAY NIGHT," Cleo said when Alexander answered the phone on Wednesday.

"Cleo?" he asked, his voice hoarse.

"You sound awful," she said. "Too much celebrating?"

"Celebrating?" he echoed.

"I do read the newspapers, you know, doll," she said.

"What's Friday night?"

"Your mother."

Alexander started laughing.

"I'm serious," Cleo said.

"Why not? That's *just* what I need."

"You don't sound good," Cleo said.

"I'm fine," he said. "I'm fine."

"Listen, doll, I don't need two flakes on my hands, you know."

"I'll see you Friday night."

"I SEE THAT you're going to travel this year," Cleo said.

It was Friday night, just past eight o'clock, and she was sitting next to Alexander in her now-familiar yoga pose. The cat, Boris, was curled up darkly in her lap, and she stroked him absentmindedly, peering over the coffee table at the prints Alexander had given her weeks before of his hands.

"Right," Alexander said. "And don't tell me. I'm going to meet a tall, dark, handsome stranger."

"Did I say that you had a skeptical nature?"

"Many times."

Their eyes met.

Cleo took his hand in hers and touched the fleshy part of the heel, running a polished fingernail lightly across its net of fine deep lines.

"This means travel," she said. "Look at mine."

Hers was like his, but even more pronounced.

"I've been everywhere, doll," she said, letting his hand drop.

"I hate to travel," Alexander said. "I'm not thrilled to admit it, but I hate to travel."

"I didn't say you were going to be *happy* traveling. I just said you were going to do it."

"My mistake," Alexander said.

Cleo smirked and looked back at his prints.

"You have strong Mounts of Venus and Jupiter," she said. "That suggests exploration of the soul, exploration of reality. I'd say you were spending a lot of time trying to determine what reality is."

Alexander felt a slight flush.

"Now here's the big question," Cleo said. She pushed Boris off her lap and grabbed hold of her ankles. She looked at Alexander expectantly.

"What?"

"What the *hell* are you doing to yourself?"

"Pardon?"

"What are you doing to yourself?" she said. "I mean, look, doll, considering your heart line, which is really pretty spectacular—" Cleo picked up the print of his left hand and pointed to the diagonal line that crossed his palm from the side under the pinky to the place beneath his index finger. The line made a thick ivory channel in the gray ink.

Alexander looked at Cleo, perplexed.

"Look," she said. She put the print back down beside the other one. "Left hand is your potential," she said. "Right hand is what you're doing with it. Now, on your left hand here, this line—you could use this line to draw a straight edge, right?"

Alexander stared again at the ivory-colored line. It was strong and clear and straight.

"*This*," Cleo said, reaching beneath the coffee table into the wicker basket filled with prints, "this is a typical heart line. This is a very nice girl, very warm, very sweet, very typical. But look at yours, doll, look at yours!"

Alexander smiled and felt like squirming.

"Well, this hand," Cleo continued, now picking up the print of his right hand. "Look at this. So what are you doing to yourself?"

The line on the right-hand print was fainter and less straight. It broke in the middle. Alexander thought it must be the paper or the ink. But when he looked down at the actual lines on his hands, the contrast seemed just as great.

"This hand," Cleo said again, taking his right hand in both of hers. "It's like you're being diverted from your true self." She stroked the broken segment of his heart line, stroking it as if the stroke could mend it and set it straight, like a line redrawn in sand, or on a misty window. "You're not using your heart enough," she said. "Magic," she said.

"Maybe you're just not *good* at love," Heinz had said to him one late, lonely night at Wilson.

"You need to get in touch," Cleo was saying. "And the driving force in your life should be some sort of—I don't care what name you put it under—religion, spiritualism, something like that. You need to get in touch with something inside of yourself way down deep."

"I bet you tell that to all the boys," Alexander said nervously.

Cleo smiled. Her eyes showed patience, humor, conviction, and utter superiority. Her eyes looked like small mirrored disks, so bright that he couldn't think what color they were when he tried to remember them later on.

"You're not loving hard enough," Cleo said. "You're letting

your love of ideas get in the way. You're not using that wonderful heart."

HE PUT HIS ARM around Cleo's waist, and, unlike Linda, she
didn't look down. He picked her up and carried her to her
bedroom, and she never once turned her eyes away from his. A
pair of underpants, a slip, and several silk shirts lay in the
rumpled ocean of her sheets. She did not try to push them away.
She let him undress her, and then let him stand back, admiring
her from a distance, not trying to cover her body with embraces.

Alexander's real understanding of sex was based on his knowledge of electrical charges—pluses and minuses, different poles.
The pull was constant. Sex was the only physical thing that he
had ever done well.

In the bedroom, there were mirrors on two facing walls, and
Alexander could see himself above Cleo on the bed, making
love to her a hundred times down the endless silver corridors.

She held his head in her hands and moved beneath him
fiercely. She was perfectly silent, and so was he. Then he listened
to their breathing, and he felt her power. He saw her smile and
then open her mouth and then close her eyes, coming. He
shouted. He didn't mean to.

HER EYES CLOSED, Cleo tossed a theatrical hand across her
forehead.

"Cleo?" Alexander asked.

She opened her eyes and combed her hair with her fingers.
"You're very good in bed," she said.

"Thank you."

"I could tell you were going to be by the bump on the back
of your head."

He rolled onto his side and smoothed the patch of blanket in front of him. He raised his eyebrows at her, smiling.

"The bump on your head," she said again. "Phrenology. Queen Victoria had her children's heads examined by a phrenologist. It's been around since the eighteenth century in Vienna. Every part of the head corresponds to a part of the body."

"Really?" Alexander asked. He reached for her head. "Where are your breasts?" he asked, feeling around.

She moved back slightly. "The back of your head," she continued seriously, "is the center of emotional and physical love. Yours is really very developed."

Now she reached out for him, but didn't move closer. He bent his head toward her hand, like a dog wanting to be petted.

"There," she said, feeling the back of his head. "Clear as day."

He put his own hand on hers, allowing it to guide him, then laced his fingers through hers and wrestled her down into another embrace.

AFTER SHE FELL ASLEEP, he lay beside her, trying not to feel giddy. Science had taught him that little in life could be judged or proven without repetition. Alexander reminded himself of this. He reminded himself of how Blas Cabrera had claimed to have found a magnetic monopole on Valentine's Day, 1982, but how, unable to find a second one, he had never been truly believed.

Without repetition, Alexander thought, nothing he'd done with Cleo should ever have to seem that real.

Alexander fell asleep with his arms around her, and she was the angel again that night in his dream. She hovered above him, as the angel always had, but she was naked and she was laughing.

She had no wings, and yet she seemed to fly around the ceiling anyway. Alexander could actually see her reflected in the mirrors. "Where are your wings?" he asked her.

"My what?" she said, laughing.

"Your wings. You've always had wings."

"I don't need wings," she said.

"Your hair looks different. You used to wear a dress. Why are you naked?"

"Am I naked?" she said.

She darted from one corner of the ceiling to the other. Then she darted back again. She was laughing the whole time.

"Stop moving so fast," Alexander said to her. "I can't keep up."

Then she disappeared. He waited a moment, searching for her.

"Where are you?" Alexander asked.

"I'm right here."

"Where? Where are you? I can't see you," he said.

"Here, cookie. I'm here."

Alexander heard the voice clearly, but no one was there.

"Stop hiding," Alexander said.

"I'm not hiding, cookie. I'm right here. Wake up."

He felt a hand on his shoulder that shook him abruptly out of sleep. When he opened his eyes, he saw a gold locket shining in the dim morning light, and his mother's face above him, peering down.

6

THE TROUBLE

"YOUR AURA IS the most beautiful color when you sleep," Alice said.

She was sitting on the edge of the bed, and she was smiling down at him with a fierce, embracing warmth.

Alexander didn't move. He was waiting to see if he was still dreaming, and trying to think of something to say.

"It's kind of half orange and half pink," Alice went on. "It's changed now. Now it's turned more purple." She raised her hand and gently touched a spot a few inches above Alexander's head. "Yes," she declared. "It's just incredibly purple now." Alice stroked Alexander's cheek. "Oh, cookie," she said softly. "I didn't ever want you to be so angry."

Alexander sat up. "I'm not angry," he said.

Alice laughed, but it was a different laugh than the one he

had always remembered, the one he had always heard when he thought of the night with the ghost by the railroad tracks. This laugh seemed much more kind than cruel. He turned away from her. He wanted to get his bearings. He looked for Cleo, but the bed beside him was empty. He guessed that it was morning, because there was light coming through the drawn blinds, but he couldn't tell if it was early or late.

"Not angry," Alice said, and this time she smoothed the hair away from his forehead. "Then why are you so purple? Cleo!" she called out. Cleo appeared suddenly in the doorway, wearing a long blue satin robe. Alexander felt briefly relieved. "Cleo," Alice said. "Have you ever *seen* anything like the color of my son's aura?"

Cleo looked at them both and grinned. Her eyes met Alexander's, and he looked back, imploring, though he wasn't sure exactly what it was he was asking her for. She seemed to know, though. "Come on, you guys," she said softly. "Alice, why don't you let your son put some clothes on his body and shake the cotton out of his head?"

"Look at how angry he is," Alice said. "Poor darling."

"Let him get dressed, now, Alice," Cleo said.

Alice laughed again as she left the room. "I'll be waiting for you in the living room, cupcake."

Alexander stared at Cleo, who sat down on the bed where Alice had been.

"Well, I told you she promised to come," Cleo said.

"Why didn't you wake me up?"

"She just got here."

"What time is it, anyway?"

"A little after nine."

"She's so different," Alexander said.

"Take a shower," Cleo said. "You smell like sex." She bent over him, and she kissed his neck.

. . .

FIRST THINGS FIRST, he said to himself in the shower. The first thing was Cleo, he said to himself, the perfect island of her body, and the bright silver corridor of her bedroom. And Cleo floating above him. But it had been twenty years since he had seen his mother in any place but his dreams, and Alexander soaped his body furiously, and stepped out of the shower before he had turned off the water, and put on his clothes before his body was really dry, because he was sure now that he had dreamed her again, and that when he emerged from Cleo's bedroom, Alice would be gone.

"COME SAY HELLO to your mother," Cleo said when Alexander, his hair still wet, walked into the living room. Cleo was sitting on the sofa, pouring out tea from a large white teapot.

Alice stood by Cleo's window, twisting the cord of the shade with both hands. The crystal rings she wore on her fingers gleamed in the bright sunlight.

"This must be very difficult for you," Alexander said.

He had chosen the words while he was getting dressed, and he liked the way they sounded.

Alice smiled. "Say that again?" she said to him.

"You heard him," Cleo told Alice. She stood up and brought a cup of tea to Alice. "He said this must be difficult for you. You take sugar?"

"Not for years." Alice took the teacup. "This must be difficult for me?" she repeated, smiling at him.

He nodded, uncomfortable.

"That's terrific, sweetheart," Alice said. "So you like to be in control of things. Or so I gather. You act generous so it'll look like you're above it. I *like* that. I really *like* that. What a great line." She beamed at Cleo. "He's a real survivor, isn't he?"

Cleo shrugged. Alexander was feeling the way he sometimes felt beneath the moon.

He noticed that his mother's face was lined, and that it was more full, and less regal, than he had thought it would be. Her clothes were a surprise to him, too. She was wearing a simple khaki skirt, a black T-shirt, and scuffed black pumps. Her hair fell straight and uncoiffed to her shoulders, an awkward mixture of brown and gray. There was something vaguely unkempt about her, like Linda's school kids at four o'clock when they headed home from school.

She was just a woman, he thought.

He walked across the room and bent down to kiss his mother's cheek. She placed her teacup on the windowsill and put both her arms around him. "My cookie," she said.

Her hair smelled of shampoo, and he remembered that she had shampooed him, though he had never remembered that before. Baby shampoo, he thought. No more tears. His throat felt tight. He could remember his mother kneeling beside him as she bathed him, the bony reach of her long fingers and the sweet smell of the white lather, and the way that she would wrap him up in one of the big bath towels and call him her papoose. "Who's my papoose?" she would ask, tickling him, and he would giggle.

Alexander broke off the embrace. "It's good to meet you. To see you again," he said.

Alice grabbed at the ring-shaped window pull. She lifted it slowly to one eye as if it were a magnifying glass.

THEY SAT ON Cleo's couch, drinking their tea. Alexander knew that he should ask his mother questions before she went away again, but every question he thought of seemed to sound like

an accusation. Why did you leave me? Where did you go? Did
you ever love Daddy? Did you ever love me? Did you find what
you were looking for? What the hell was it, anyway? Was it
really only money? Why was money so damn important? Why
did you keep that creep in your locket? Why did you always
laugh at me? Why did you laugh by the railroad tracks? Why
did you want me to see that ghost? Do you understand what
you did to me? Do you know what you did to my father? Do
you know how long it took me to stop thinking you'd come
back?

Alexander sipped his tea. "How long are you in town for?"
he asked.

"I don't know," Alice said. She shrugged. "I understand
congratulations are in order," she said. "About your theory, I
mean. I read about it in the newspaper, and I was very proud
of you. I know you probably think I don't have a right to
feel proud. But I felt proud anyway. I guess it's a mother's
right."

You have no mother's right, he thought. I didn't have a
mother. "Well," he said, "the *Times* made it sound like everyone
had already accepted it. It still hasn't been published, you know,
and I still have to give the lecture."

"What lecture?" Cleo asked.

Alexander looked at her gratefully. "Well, I've got to present
the paper to a room full of physicists and science writers," he
said. "It's about a month from today. I'm supposed to be writing
it now."

"This minute, you mean?" Alice asked.

"Well," Alexander said. "No. Just generally now."

"Sweetheart," she said. "You're so handsome. No wonder
you've got a thing for him, Cleo. You look just the way I
wanted you to look, cookie. Except who buys your clothes?
Never mind." Alice laughed, shaking her head. "That's just
my old Saks reflex. Some things die particularly hard, you know,

despite everything you do. Anyway, you look just the way I always imagined you'd look. You were so beautiful when you were a baby. I bet you were awkward as hell in your teens, though."

"I was lonely," Alexander said without thinking, and he instantly regretted it.

"Were you?" Alice asked. Abruptly, she stopped smiling, and then everything in her seemed to stop for a moment. She shut her eyes and lifted her chest just slightly. She took several deep, exaggerated breaths.

Alexander looked at Cleo, confused. He was just about to say something when Alice opened her eyes again. Her voice was softer now, and steadier. "I believe that everyone's lonely," she said, "until they learn to be otherwise."

She closed her eyes again, took another deep breath, and when she exhaled she intoned a long guttural note that sounded like AUM. It was very loud and startling, and it almost made Alexander laugh, except that she started to do it again. "AUM," Alice chanted every twenty seconds or so. Alexander looked on, amazed and off balance.

"Doll," Cleo hissed at him. "Doll." She pointed to the kitchen, and they quietly stood up and tiptoed away.

"WHAT WAS THAT?" Alexander asked.

"It's how she meditates."

"In the middle of a conversation?"

"She told me once that a guru had told her to do it whenever she felt she was losing her center."

"Christ," Alexander said. He looked up at the kitchen clock. It was only ten A.M.

Cleo snaked her arms around his waist. "Doll," she said, "I told you she was a flake."

"But you mean she'll just do that in the middle of anything?

Have you ever seen her do it before? I mean with other people? With anyone?"

"You bet."

"Doesn't she care what anyone thinks of her?"

"If she did," Cleo said, "do you think she would have left you in the first place?"

Alexander shook his head. Perhaps, he thought, with a kind of dim fascination, there was actually nothing besides his last name that he had in common with Alice. His last name and a handful of moments. The thought made him strangely exuberant. Like most truly improbable propositions, it was utterly compelling.

Outside the kitchen window, the sky was an extraordinary blue, and when Cleo touched the back of his neck, he turned around and kissed her hard, pinning her against the counter. She kissed back, holding his face in her hands, and her lips tasted of tea and honey.

"I HOPE I DIDN'T embarrass you," Alice said to Alexander when he and Cleo walked back into the living room.

Alexander felt better now, because he'd decided that his mother was crazy, and he figured that he would talk to her as if she were a child. "Of course not. Don't worry," he said to her.

"Well, of course I embarrassed you," she said, and laughed. "But did Cleo explain to you what that sound was all about?"

"The sound?"

"AUM," Alice repeated, but she didn't close her eyes this time.

"She said something about you needing to find your center."

"The sound," Alice said, "is supposed to encompass the whole universe. You'd have to hear the way they do it in Tibet to see what I'm shooting for."

"You've been to Tibet?"

"Plenty."

"That's nice," Alexander said.

"There's a place inside me," Alice said. "You have the same place inside you. When you are there, you know what you are, and what you want, and in fact it's a place where you want very little. It's a place of great joy. It's how you feel alive. Usually you just get glimpses of it in the course of a week or a month. You do something, and it makes you feel particularly proud or happy, but usually you don't know why you're happy, so you don't know how to come back to the place. But if you learn how to say AUM—if you learn how to meditate—then you can find it whenever you need it. It never has to be an accident. That's what I do when I meditate. I look for that place. Of course, sometimes I channel to the astral plane, but that's different. What I'm talking about is really very simple."

Despite himself, Alexander had thought while Alice was talking about how he felt when he was sitting before a page of numbers, looking for a solution. He had thought about how he felt when all the ghosts in an equation were cancelled out. He had thought about how he'd felt while he was working out his theory, and he felt a tug of nostalgia.

"Of course for you," Alice said, "it's probably your work." That was a little startling, and Alexander flinched slightly. "But I've got a secret for you, cupcake," she continued. "It isn't really the work itself that gives you the magic. You only think it is. There's something deeper, beneath the work, and if you meditated, you'd find it."

Now Alice was the one who sounded as if she was talking to a child.

Cleo clapped her hands together. "So," she said, "what do you guys wanna do today?"

. . .

ALEXANDER SAT beside his mother in a taxi heading down-
town. She had told him that there was a place she wanted to
take him to, but she had not said where it was.

"Do you think you can trust me that far?" Alice had asked
him back at Cleo's.

"Trust you?" he'd repeated. "Why not?"

"Because I left you when you were ten years old."

"Eleven," he said.

"Who's counting?"

He had laughed for the first time.

It had been nearly noon when they'd left Cleo's, and it had
felt good to stand outside her building, looking for a taxi and
feeling the breeze from the river. For a moment, he had relaxed.

Cleo had said that she had an armload of clients. She had
said that she would be free by four, and that maybe they could
all have dinner. When Alice went to the bathroom, Cleo had
kissed Alexander good-bye, placing one hand on the back of
his neck and the other between his legs.

"I've got particular plans for you," she'd whispered. "Just
don't let the old bitch get to you."

"Don't call her that," he'd said, and then he had felt confused
and embarrassed.

Now he glanced at Alice out of the corner of one eye. She
was staring out her window as if she'd never seen New York
before. "I really love this city," she said, turning back to him.

Then why did you leave it? he was thinking. He didn't know
what to say.

"I remember that face," Alice told him. "That expression on
your face, I mean. You look just the way you did when you
were seven. You always had so many questions. But there's
never been a brighter, sweeter boy," she said.

Her eyes were fixed on his, unflinching, and he realized that
this was the big difference between then and now. He realized
he'd never really seen his mother's eyes. In all his memories of

her, he was always looking up at her. Hadn't she ever bent down to meet him? Hadn't she ever picked him up? He had only been a little boy, and all he had seen was her locket.

He studied it now, still hanging on its gold chain.

His mother's hand, with its many crystal rings and the liver spots he had just noticed, rose to touch the locket. "There was a man I loved before I met your father," she said.

"What?" he said.

"The locket. You were wondering what's inside it, right?"

"Just remembering it," Alexander said.

Alice smiled at him so sadly that he had to look away. "We've got so little time," she said. "I think you should try to be honest with me."

He looked out the taxi window, wishing he hadn't agreed to come with her. Outside, on Second Avenue, couples were sitting in crowded cafés, leaning across the small tables to talk. He could go back up to Cleo's, he thought, and have a real morning-after. But the taxi was now racing through the empty Saturday streets.

"His name was Mark," Alice was saying, and Alexander knew he was as powerless to stop her as he was to stop the cab. "I was in love with him," she said. "Have you ever been in love?" she asked him.

"No," Alexander said, turning back to face her. He was startled not only to be telling his mother the truth but to realize what he thought the truth was.

"That's too bad," Alice said, "though given the fact that I left when you were so young, it makes a certain amount of sense."

As much as Alexander didn't want to hear about his mother's loves, he wanted much less to talk about his own. "You were telling me about Mark," he said.

"Yes, Mark," Alice said. She closed her eyes. For a moment, Alexander was afraid that she would start her AUMMING again, right there in the taxi, but instead she cleared her throat and turned to face him. "You know, my parents died before you were born," she said. "I don't know if Sam told you much about them, and I'm sure you were too young to remember anything I told you."

With Alexander, Sam had always referred to Alice's parents as Cash and Cary. Alice's mother was Cash because, like Alice, she'd had such dreams of grandeur. Alice's father was Cary because he'd thought that he looked like Cary Grant.

"Daddy never mentioned them," Alexander said. His head was beginning to pound.

"Well, they weren't very intelligent people," Alice said. "At least they weren't very intelligent about how they treated me. I don't really blame them anymore. They were very Old World, you know, first generation here. They were trying to make a living in real estate, but they didn't know the first thing about real estate. They wanted to have a big family, but I was all they could afford."

The taxi lurched, barely missing a huge blue Pontiac that had cut in front of it.

"Fucking idiot!" the cabdriver shouted. "Fucking idiot! Did you see that?" He twisted in his seat to glare at Alexander and Alice. "Fucking asshole!" he shouted at them. His face was flushed and fat and old. He pulled his cab up alongside the Pontiac, which had stopped at a red light. "Hey!" he shouted at the Pontiac's driver. "Heeey!" But the right front window of the cab was shut, and the Pontiac's driver didn't seem to hear. Grunting and panting, the cabbie leaned over in the front seat to roll the window down. By the time he had managed it, the light had turned green, and the Pontiac had pulled away. "Fucking *shvarzes*," he muttered. "Fucking *shvarzes* are taking over the fucking city."

Alexander was looking at the rubber mat on the floor of the cab. If he pressed both his hands against his temples, he thought, maybe the pain in his head would ease up. But he didn't want Alice to see him and to start making a fuss.

"You know," Alice said to the cabdriver, leaning forward, "you obviously have a wonderful sense of right and wrong, and a wonderful amount of energy. If you used that for a good cause, you could be a very happy man."

There was a long, predictable silence. The driver looked at Alice in his rearview mirror. "Lady," he finally said to the mirror, "go piss up a rope."

Alice didn't flinch. She smiled into the mirror, and then sat back in her seat. "I've always wondered," she said to Alexander quietly, "exactly what that expression means. How exactly do you piss up a rope?"

"I don't know," Alexander said quietly.

"Do you think I should ask him?"

"No."

Alice laughed. "Obviously," she said, "you're not crazy about confrontations."

THE CRUCIAL FACT of Alice's childhood, as she described it to Alexander, was the double pressure and double criticism she had had to take from her parents. The double pressure was for Alice to go to college and get married to a nice Jewish boy with a Future. The double criticism was that she would be neither smart nor pretty enough to pull either of these things off.

As the taxi passed Sheridan Square and headed into the heart of Greenwich Village, Alice put her hand on Alexander's left arm. Even that gesture somehow seemed to hurt his head.

"But I did go to college," she said. "I could only go to City, and I had to live at home, but just being with all those people, getting away from my parents . . ." Her voice trailed off. "I wanted to be as different from them as I could possibly be. And then I met Mark. I met him at City. We were in the same art history class together. He was the funniest, wittiest, brightest man I've ever known. Ever. I mean ever. And I've met a lot of people, you know. Oh. We're almost there."

"Where are we going?" Alexander asked.

"You'll see," Alice said. She adjusted one of the rings on her left hand. "I was in love with Mark," she continued, "as I've told you. And he was in love with me, but his goddamn family was a family of goys, and they didn't want their precious one to marry a Jew. I had a nose job. I mean I had an actual nose job. It cost a fortune, but my parents paid for it because I told them I was going to run away from home if they didn't, and so I had a nose job, to look less Jewish, and of course that didn't make any difference to them. His parents told him not to see me anymore, and he didn't."

Alexander remembered suddenly that Alice had bought him crayons once when he was sick—a huge box, with a sharpener in it—and that she had been angry when he had melted six of the crayons down to find out, with his chemistry set, exactly what they were made of.

He remembered that he had gone into the kitchen once, folded a double thickness of cheesecloth into a bag, filled it with flour, and shaken it over a candle flame. A book Sam had bought him had told him that the flour would make sparks. When Alice had walked into the kitchen, she had screamed, and he had dropped the bag of flour and knocked the candlestick over.

"So that's why I keep his picture in my locket," she said now. "And that's why I married your father."

Her last two sentences didn't really seem to follow, but Alexander decided that he would leave it that way. His head hurt so much by now that even the thought of speaking seemed foreign. He wanted to lie down. He wanted to be on Linda's rooftop, sleeping in the sun.

·   ·   ·

ALEXANDER LET Alice pay for the cab, and he got out before she did, sneaking his hands to the sides of his head and pressing hard, the way Linda did when she gave him a head rub. It didn't seem to help. It was already hotter than it had been twenty minutes before outside Cleo's. Alice got out beside him. They were standing on a narrow Greenwich Village street. Tidy brownstones and town houses faced each other on a crooked line. The easy grid of New York City vanished down here, and Alexander had never been able to find his way around.

In the archway of an old firehouse, a man and a woman were kissing, and at their feet a small black dog ran around in circles, tangling its leash between their legs.

"This way," Alice said over Alexander's shoulder, and she crossed the narrow street to an ivy-covered brownstone and walked down four stairs to the sunken entrance. Chimes rang as she opened the door, which was oddly neither locked nor guarded.

The place was cool and dim. Adjusting his eyes after the sunlight on the street, Alexander took a minute to realize that they were standing in a bookstore. He felt profound relief. Books, he thought. Fine, he thought. Let her show me books.

"This is my favorite place in New York City," Alice said almost reverently.

He looked around. He tried to seem both pensive and judicious. "It's wonderful," he said to Alice after what he hoped was an appropriate pause. "I can see why you love it."

"No you can't," she said.

"Oh." Alexander felt stung.

"I mean I haven't shown you yet," she said.

He followed her to the back of the bookstore. The shelves they walked by were labeled not "Fiction" and "Nonfiction" but "Zen," "Tarot," "Crystals," "Alchemy," "Bible," "Koran," "Yoga," "Transcendence." A glass case that they passed held an array of shimmering rocks laid out on velvet, decks of brightly colored tarot cards, and crystal balls of different sizes on neat, black stands.

"I didn't know they *sold* crystal balls," Alexander said with a light laugh.

"Well, what did you think, people make them?"

"I don't know what I thought," Alexander said, and he didn't like the way it sounded.

"VOILÀ!" Alice said.

They had entered a large back room that was draped with rugs and filled with the cloying smell of incense. To Alexander's surprise, it was also filled with people: several dozen stood in three lines that curved out from long tables on three brick walls. The three lines mingled in the center of the room, beneath an incongruous chandelier. These were no Third Avenue movie lines, though the people looked perfectly normal—dressed in Saturday clothes and not particularly young or old. There was something different and startling about them, and Alexander realized that it was simply their quiet, their mellow good cheer. There was a hush, a kind of low hum, in the room that seemed unnatural for so many strangers in one place.

"What are they all doing here?" Alexander whispered to Alice as she steered him toward the center of the room.

"We're all here to get some magic," Alice said.

A beat of pain hit Alexander at the base of his neck. He had to close his eyes. The incense was making him sick to his stomach. "Magic isn't silver, it's gold," he remembered her saying.

Alice was looking closely at his face, but Alexander turned toward the nearest line, which seemed not to be moving at all. He could see a middle-aged man who was grinning as he talked with a short woman behind one of the felt-covered tables. There were a lot of candles lined up on the table. Alexander wondered if the place had a bathroom. He calculated how long it would take him to rush back outside if he started to get sick. He turned to look at the other two tables. No one seemed to be moving there, either.

Alexander remembered sitting on the floor of a bookstore at the age of four or five. He remembered sitting cross-legged beside Alice, who was taking books off the shelves for him, helping him choose what he wanted. "Try this one, cookie," he could hear her saying. She would open a book to a shiny first page and move a finger beneath the large letters as Alexander pressed his face against her shoulder and read the words out loud.

A large black woman was moving through the room now, her arms open toward Alice and her head shaking in happy disbelief.

"I thought it was you," she said to Alice, "but I didn't expect to see you twice in one month."

Alice laughed and embraced the woman. "Julia," she said warmly, then quickly extricated herself. "I want to hear everything," she said, "but first things first. My son has a dreadful headache."

Alexander looked up, stunned. Alice smiled benignly and went on talking to Julia while staring into Alexander's eyes.

"He's really in a lot of pain," Alice continued, "and he hasn't said a word about it, so of course the pressure is just getting worse and worse."

Julia placed a huge, strong hand on the back of Alexander's neck. He started to move away, but he realized that it felt good to have her hand there.

"Julia, you know I never like to push in front of anyone here," Alice said. "But do you think that just this once—"

"Well, of course!" Julia said, and she began to lead Alexander toward one of the long tables, her hand still holding his neck.

She whispered something to one of the women behind the table and scooped up two thick red candles. Then she opened a small door that Alexander hadn't seen before, and she steered him forcefully to a long, low couch.

"Do you think he needs to lie down for this?" Julia asked Alice.

"I don't need to lie down," Alexander said. "Really what I think I need is—"

"Yes," Alice said to Julia. "He needs to lie down."

Firmly, Julia guided him down onto the couch. She sat beside him. His neck was beginning to feel the heat of her hand, and the heat felt surprisingly good, but he wanted to stand up again.

"Really, I'm fine," he said, and was struck immediately by another excruciating beat of pain. At that exact moment, both Alice and Julia laughed.

"How did you know I had a headache?" he asked his mother.

She smiled. "Lie back down," she said. She was standing in the center of a Persian rug, and now she knelt and then sat down, crossing her legs and closing her eyes.

"AUM," she began saying.

Not again, Alexander thought.

Julia's hand had moved to his forehead, and now she was helping him lie down. "How did you get to be such a skeptic?" she asked him softly. "Are you really Alice's son?"

He felt relaxed despite himself, and despite himself, he didn't want the woman to lift her hand away.

"Feels better already, doesn't it?" she asked.

"Yes," he said. "I guess I just needed to get in a quiet place for a minute."

Julia smiled with equal amounts of warmth and condescension, and he wondered if that was how he looked when Linda asked him about his work.

"Don't think about anything but a circle," Julia said.

"A circle?" he said.

"Close your eyes."

"AUM," Alice said in the background.

HE FELT SUDDENLY as if he had been sleeping, and yet he had the sense that no time had passed at all. He sat up quickly, self-consciously, the way he did sometimes with Linda after talking in his sleep.

There was the sweet smell of candles burning, and he saw that they had been placed near the door, on the border of the rug. Julia was gone, and Alice was standing by the one small window, looking out at a brick wall that was covered with ivy and shadows.

"Alice," Alexander said, and realized he'd never said that word to her.

She turned around, and he could see that she was crying, and the sight of her crying struck him as probably the most mysterious thing he'd ever seen.

His headache was gone, and he felt giddy: he knew he was in the presence of a world he didn't understand.

"I didn't think," Alice said softly, "that you could possibly be *this* angry. I knew that you'd be angry, but somehow I didn't think it would be like this."

"What happened when I was asleep?" he asked.

Alice reached into her handbag for a Kleenex and wiped her eyes.

"What happened?" he said again.

"I'll meet you back at Cleo's," Alice said. She bent over with surprising grace and snuffed out the candles with her fingertips. Then she glided quickly past him and out the door.

· · ·

ALEXANDER SAT UP on the low couch and rubbed the back of his neck. He stood and walked to the window where Alice had just been crying, and he tried to judge what time it was by the shadows on the wall. He realized that it could be any time, and the thought was oddly untroubling to him. The shadows before him were as dark and rich as the vines, and it was hard to sort the patterns out and know where each began and each ended, but that didn't bother him either.

The crowd in the main room had thinned markedly, and Julia spotted him immediately when he emerged through the small door. Her smile was enormous, and Alexander found himself moving toward her naturally, and just as naturally letting himself be caught up in her strong, large arms.

"Thank you," Alexander said.

Julia took his right hand in both of hers and looked into his eyes. "I'd like to give you something," she said.

"Oh no. You've already done enough."

"Your mother asked me to," Julia said.

Alexander shrugged and grinned.

Julia led him to one of the felt-covered tables and picked up a huge blue candle, easily twice the size of the red ones that she'd brought into the small room.

"You need to light this tonight in your home," Julia said. "Of course you *won't* light it tonight, and you may never light it, but I'm giving it to you because you should."

"It's very beautiful," Alexander said.

"That's not the point," Julia told him.

Alexander looked down at the candle.

"You've put a kind of a spell on yourself," Julia continued more quietly. "There's a god whose name is Santori, and he's just the guy you need to break it. I know you won't believe all this, but that's one of the reasons you need Santori. For a person with such a large spiritual nature, you've turned yourself into quite some skeptic. There's going to be a time, though, when you will wonder whether you shouldn't try this, so just in case you decide to try it, I'll tell you what to do."

"Santori?" Alexander said.

"Santori."

"What kind of a name for a god is Santori?"

"Try to listen."

"Sorry."

"That's all right," she said. "Santori is someone you need in your life. You need him to break this spell. Santori happens to like chocolate, so it's a good idea to leave a plate of candy for him when you light this."

"Candy?"

"You know—Mars Bars, Snickers, Hershey's Kisses. Something like that. Try not to laugh now. Something sweet and chocolate."

"And the chocolate will be gone when I wake up," Alexander said, "so I'll know that he's been there?"

Julia laughed. "Honey, what do you think this is, Santa Claus? Gods don't eat candy. This one just likes the smell of it."

"Silly of me," Alexander said.

Julia took back the candle and wrapped it in a piece of purple tissue paper. "Go on," she said to him, grinning. "Don't try to understand it now."

AT A CAFÉ on Eighth Avenue, Alexander ordered a tuna salad sandwich and an iced coffee and sat shivering beneath an air conditioning vent. It was nearly four o'clock, and the restaurant was almost empty, but Alexander didn't want to move to another table. He was hoping that the cold air would make him feel less strange. Everything that had happened with both Cleo and his mother had happened either too fast or too slowly.

Alexander thought about Linda, and he felt closer to her than he had felt for months. Our home, he thought. Our bed. Our roof. Our cat. Our life. Since roughly ten o'clock the night before, he had not done one thing that was familiar to him, and he wanted to go straight home, to call Linda and forget about both Alice and Cleo. He thought about his work, and about the speech he was supposed to be writing.

The waitress brought him a cup of coffee. Alexander tried to balance a salt shaker on a crazy angle. When it fell over for the fifth time, he clutched it in his left hand and studied its metal top. In the smallest bit of that metal, he knew, there were more than a billion atoms stacked up like circus acrobats, fixed in known positions. Inside those atoms was the chaos that he'd spent so much of his time trying to fathom. But the world beyond what he held in his hand seemed suddenly even stranger, and he wished, desperately, not to feel that way. He wished he could be back two months before, still struggling to finish his computations. But there was the speech to write, he told himself again. And there was the praise and maybe the fame, and maybe all that would make him feel different after all. He would go to Cleo's, he decided, but only to say he was sorry. He would tell Cleo that sleeping with her had been a mistake, and he would tell Alice that there was no point in trying. He would say good-bye to them both and tell them he had no use for their magic.

AT THE THIRD corner that Alexander reached, he casually dropped the blue candle into a garbage can. Half a block later, he stopped midstride, looking down at the pavement. Of course, he thought, he didn't want to light the candle, but Alice had bought it for him, and she'd probably be furious if he showed up at Cleo's without it.

Alexander glanced in both directions. He saw no one. Quickly he turned and traced his steps back to the garbage can. It was one of the ones that the city had designed to prevent trash fires and scavenging. Made of something that looked like stucco, it had a wide body but a round opening no larger than nine inches in diameter. There was no way of seeing where the candle had landed.

Bracing himself, Alexander slowly put a hand into the hole. He felt only empty space. He moved his hand around: still nothing. He leaned over slightly, reaching farther down. The garbage, he thought, had probably been picked up that morning. His candle was probably sitting at the bottom of an empty barrel.

Alexander removed his hand and tried to look down into the hole. All he saw was darkness.

"Won't help," a voice said from behind him. Startled, Alexander nearly lost his balance.

"Won't help to look in. Won't see nothing. You gotta feel around."

A tall pale man was standing before him, looking down and shifting his weight from one leg to the other. He wore purple jeans and a white T-shirt that was torn at the neck and sleeves. He stank. His face was old, or maybe just seemed to be, and his eyes never stopped moving.

"Got a buck for a cup of coffee?" the man asked. He reached a long arm into the garbage can and, grinning, handed Alexander the candle.

Silently, Alexander reached for his wallet and gave the man a five-dollar bill. He had never done that before, but it seemed right, somehow. The man didn't look surprised at all. He studied the bill intently, as if it were a letter addressed to him, and then he folded it neatly in half and tucked it into his back pocket. "Yes!" the man said, smiling, and quickly walked away.

·   ·   ·

THERE WAS MUSIC coming from inside Cleo's apartment. Alexander stood at the front door, trying to make out voices, but the music was all he could hear. It was something bright and classical, and for the first time since she had left the bookstore, he wondered whether his mother was still upset.

Cleo opened the door for him. She had a dishrag in one hand and the other around Boris, who was slung over her shoulder, and the look on her face was so amused and conspiratorial that he couldn't help smiling back at her.

"I'm going to have to leave," he said after she kissed him.

"Oh I *know*," she said warmly, and he instantly wanted to kiss her again.

In the living room, Alice was sitting on the couch with a small, very tattered book in her hands.

"This book was written by two women," Alice said when Alexander walked in.

"Alice—" Alexander began.

She closed the book and looked up at him. She didn't seem unhappy anymore, but she also didn't seem to be acknowledging him. Alexander wished he didn't care what she was feeling.

"They were both scholars at Oxford at the turn of the century," she went on. "They were academics, and they weren't crazy. I don't suppose you've read this book."

Alexander shook his head. "Listen—" he said.

"It's called *An Adventure*," Alice told him.

Alexander looked at Cleo helplessly, but Cleo was sitting down next to Alice, crossing her legs and grinning.

"These two women who wrote it were old friends," Alice said.

"Wasn't it their first trip to Paris?" Cleo asked.

"I think so. In any case, they didn't know much about it. But they went to Versailles one day in 1901 and had a strange experience that they spent the rest of their lives trying to research and understand.

"They were walking through the grounds, trying to find the Petit Trianon, the little farmhouse where Marie Antoinette had spent a good deal of her leisure time. They got rather lost along the way. Their walk took them half an hour. In that time, they saw eight people. One of them was wearing a heavy cloak, even though it was August. Two of them were dressed in green livery and tricornered hats. Another one seemed to appear from no-where. He wore buckled shoes, acted very agitated, and told the women, in a strange accent, that they should move on. Just before and after he appeared, there was the sound of running footsteps, but each time the women turned around, they saw no one behind them. They saw a strange-looking plow near some deserted farm buildings, and walked past a small kiosk, a wooded area, and a small bridge. They felt what they later described as a profound depression in the place. The grounds where the women were walking were otherwise deserted."

"I can't stay," Alexander said. "I just came to say thank you for showing up finally, and thank you for the candle."

Alice sighed, exasperated. "I would have thought you'd want to know about the ghosts," she said.

"Ghosts?"

"The ghosts."

Unthinkingly, he took several slow steps toward an armchair. "I have to go," he said, sitting down. In his mind, he saw the arc of the lantern swinging in the mist, the light getting closer, and he saw the car door with Sam's foot emerging, and he felt himself running from his mother toward his father's embrace.

"Mind you," Alice said, "all this is true. See, neither of the women spoke about what they'd seen until a week or so after-wards, and then they both admitted to each other that they'd felt a little strange. They decided to write down separate ac-counts of what they'd seen. Those accounts were dated and verified and put in a library. Verified by a lot of very skeptical academics. *Your* kind of people."

Cleo hugged the cat and smiled at Alexander. "This is so great," she said.

"After they exchanged notes," Alice continued, "it turned out that they'd both seen a lot of the same things. But one of them had seen a woman sitting on the terrace of the house, sketching, and the other hadn't. That woman, they found out later, was Marie Antoinette."

Alexander wondered what could have possessed a woman to take an eight-year-old boy to an empty field in the middle of the night and make him think that there was such a thing as ghosts.

"Now here's the weird part," Alice said. "First the women tried to find out if there had been any costume balls then, or historical photographs being taken, and of course there weren't. Then they started doing research—remember, they were scholars—about what they'd seen. Piece by piece, the tableau slowly began to make sense. The costumes turned out to be appropriate for eighteenth-century guards; the plow had been sold in an eighteenth-century auction. The accent of the man would have been Austrian French. And so on. It wasn't until much later, though, that they tried to retrace their actual steps at Versailles. By then it had of course occurred to them that the people were eighteenth-century people, but it hadn't occurred to them yet that the place was an eighteenth-century place. When they went back, the little kiosk was gone; the bridge was gone; the *paths* were gone. Five years after that, they finally got hold of a map of the way Versailles had been in 1789. Sure enough, all those things had existed in the landscape then, and many of them had been destroyed when Marie Antoinette was killed. Her spiritual hold on the place was so strong that everything that had happened around her just kept happening again and again. How about some coffee, Cleo?"

"I don't understand," Alexander said. "That's supposed to prove to me that ghosts exist?"

"Actually, why don't I get the coffee?" Alice said.

"Everything's in the cupboard over the sink," Cleo told her. "Thanks."

"It's nothing," Alice said, and left the room.

Alexander picked up one of Cleo's throw cushions and placed it on his lap. "She's nuts," he said to her.

"Probably."

"All that is supposed to convince me that there's such a thing as ghosts?"

"Don't you believe in ghosts?" Cleo asked brightly.

Alexander looked down at the carpet and shook his head. "Not you, too," he said.

Cleo laughed. "Why not, doll?"

"People die," he said.

"Well, what do *you* think happens to their spirits?"

"Nothing. I don't think anything happens. I think you're born, and I think you die."

"That's not very scientific of you, you know," Cleo said.

Alexander laughed. "Look," he said, "I've really got to go."

"Don't you have some law about conservation of energy?" Cleo asked. "Well, doesn't it make sense that the energy a person has should go somewhere?"

Cleo stood up and walked over to stand in front of Alexander's chair. The metal button on her blue jeans was a few inches from his face, and he wanted her very much.

"Doesn't it make sense to you that if people have said they've seen these things for thousands of years, then some of them might actually have seen them?"

Alexander shrugged.

"Aren't there things in physics that are illogical but true?"

Alexander thought of the way that particles went through the two split screens. He shrugged again. "I think people die," he said.

Alice emerged from the kitchen, carrying coffee cups and

milk. "If he was so sure of that, he never would have become a scientist, you know," she said.

"I know that," Cleo said. "So why is he acting so stupid about it?"

Abruptly, Alice sat on the couch, closed her eyes, and began to chant "AUM."

"Oh, come *on!*" Alexander shouted. "I've had enough! *Enough!*"

The chanting stopped, but Alice's eyes stayed closed. She sat very still, and she was silent for a long time. "I am standing on the astral plane," she finally said in a deep, calm voice.

Alexander wondered whether she had said aster, astro, or astral. In any case, he realized that he didn't know what she'd meant.

"I can see my son and my old friend Cleo, and I can see myself," Alice said.

"That's just amazing," Cleo whispered to Alexander. "Really amazing. Most people can't just pop up there so fast."

"Pop up where?" Alexander asked.

Cleo smiled and went back to sit on the couch.

Alice was silent as well, and Alexander thought about Sam, and he was suddenly eager to tell him about everything that had happened, and to hear Sam laugh, and to play a game of chess with him. Alexander looked carefully at Alice. Her eyes were still shut, and her face looked peaceful and young. He had never guessed that his mother would be this crazy. He felt profoundly empty.

There was a vase on Cleo's coffee table, and in his mind, Alexander began to twist the vase into different shapes, as if it were made of clay. That was the first thing he had learned about the rules of topology, the rules that made it possible to think about strings and the Theory of Everything. The most important thing had been to learn to put away traditional geometry and to think about things that curved and changed. Einstein had made up a space-time that curved, but he'd used a math that was based on straight lines. With topology, things were less rigid than they were in geometry, and outward forms of things were not exactly what they appeared to be. With topology, a vase could be the same as a brick, because by stretching and pulling, you could make one thing from the other. With topology, things were only unequal when you had to put more holes in one to make the other. You couldn't make a pair of scissors from a rubber ball without making two holes. The vase on Cleo's table had no holes—no place you could poke a pencil through—so the vase was the same as a moon, and a moon was the same as a rock, and in that redefinition of spaces and shapes, Alexander's Theory of Everything thrived.

"I see a man," Alice said steadily. "I see a middle-aged man. He's wearing black foul-weather clothes. He's wearing a coat. A policeman's hat. He has a mustache and a tired expression. He's swinging a lantern in his left hand."

Alexander looked at his mother. Her eyes were still closed, her face still calm. "He didn't exist!" Alexander shouted.

Cleo moved quickly across the room and sat on the arm of Alexander's chair. She put a hand on the top of his head and looked at him sympathetically, but he ducked out from under her hand.

"Fine!" he shouted at Alice. "So you remember it, too! Fine! You just made him up to scare me! I was just a little *kid*!"

Alice didn't flinch.

"Don't be scared, doll," Cleo whispered.

"Open your eyes!" Alexander shouted. "I'm not *falling* for this again!" He saw that a moon had come out in the twilit sky, and his thoughts raced with the memory of the gold circling light he had seen in the field so long before. The thought made his heart beat fast. "Open your eyes, goddamm it!" he shouted again.

"And I see an angel beside him," Alice said.

Alexander felt frozen.

"She's wearing a dress," Alice said. "And wings. She's flying around my son's head with wings. And she's very, very beautiful." Suddenly, Alice opened her eyes, and immediately they filled with tears. "I'm so glad you've got an angel," she told him. "I didn't know that you had an angel."

Alexander stood up unsteadily. His mother was crying and smiling at the same time. Cleo was smiling too. "You never told me you had an angel," Cleo said.

Alexander looked down at the carpet, exhausted and terrified. Then Cleo touched his back, and he picked up the vase from the coffee table, threw it against the bookcase, and ran out the front door.

7

THE SEARCH

ALEXANDER HAD NEVER been drunk before. To be drunk had always meant losing control, and that had never seemed logical. In high school, on the few nights when he had found himself with the cool kids, he had drunk Cokes and said they were rum and Cokes, and he'd laughed louder than usual, and slurred his words a bit. In college, he'd stopped pretending.

When he came home from Cleo's, though, Alexander decided that it was time for him to get drunk. He did it very methodically, drinking straight vodka from a small juice glass. After the first glass, he told himself that at least the day behind him would never happen again. After the second glass, he began to laugh. After the third glass, Linda's things were all that he could see: her clothes in the closet, her china on the table, her magnets on the refrigerator, her schoolbooks on the desk. A picture of them from the year before stared out at him from the bookshelf.

He felt less guilty than superstitious, as if by sleeping with Cleo, he had changed the natural order of things. He imagined his life without Linda, and the living room emptied and became a haunted place.

After the fourth glass, Alexander stretched out in the middle of the living room floor and watched in amazement as the ceiling actually spun. He thought about the rotation of the planets, and he recalled that the earth was moving around the sun at about twenty miles a second, and at the same time turning on its axis at about a thousand miles an hour. Maybe when you were drunk, he thought, you were able to sense the motion that you didn't notice the rest of the time. He tried to remember the speed at which the galaxy itself was moving, and then he fell asleep.

IN THE MORNING, he called Linda.

"What's wrong?" she asked him when she heard his voice. "Why are you calling so early?"

He had forgotten about the time difference. His head felt so heavy that he was holding it up with his right fist. "Oh," he said thickly.

"Alexander?" she said. "What's wrong?"

"I don't know," he muttered. He rubbed his forehead, then moved his hand toward the back of his neck, and he wondered how that woman had cured his headache the day before. Julia.

"Is it the lecture?" Linda asked.

"What?"

"The lecture. Are you having lots of trouble writing the lecture?"

"No," Alexander said thickly.

"You mean it's going well."

"No," he said again, stroking the back of his neck, and wanting to be absolved.

"Alexander," Linda said. "What's going on? Is it Sam? Is Sam okay?"

"It's Alice," Alexander said.

"Alice," Linda said. "What happened?"

"She's so crazy. She's my mother, and she's so incredibly crazy."

There was a silence. "You saw her? Are you okay?"

"She took me down to this weird bookstore, and she kept *chanting* every five minutes—"

"A bookstore?" Linda said. "When?"

"Yesterday."

"But you like bookstores."

"This one sold crystal balls."

"Oh," Linda said, and he could hear the smile in her voice.

"It's not funny, Linda," Alexander said.

"Did you—buy one?" she asked, and now she was laughing.

"Linda."

"I'm sorry."

Alexander looked toward the bookshelf, and the photograph of Linda and him he had studied the night before. Then he thought of the pictures in Cleo's bathroom—the picture of Cleo in the evening gown and the picture of her on the mountaintop. Then he thought of how Cleo had looked making love to him in her mirrors, and how she had had her own rhythm, and how good the sex had been.

"What else happened, Alexander?" Linda asked, clearly struggling to sound more serious.

"Did you know," he said, "that I could tell a lot about you by the bumps on your head?"

"What?"

"It's called phrenology," Alexander said.

"Alice told you about that, too?"

"No. Cleo did."

"Cleo. She was there too? Let me guess. She read your palm."

"What's so funny, Linda?"

"I'm sorry, Alexander, it's just you sound like me trying to learn about physics. You know, all this stuff that you don't get, you know?"

He didn't answer her. He had expected her to make him feel either more guilty or less so. He hadn't expected her to make him feel angry.

"Alexander?" she said. "Sweetheart? You're not taking this stuff seriously, are you? You know it's all a bunch of tricks."

He was studying the lines on the palm of his right hand.

"Alexander, I'm sorry," she said. "I miss you, you know."

Maybe if she hadn't left, he thought, he wouldn't have slept with Cleo. Maybe if he hadn't slept with Cleo, none of the rest would have happened. "When are you coming home?" he asked.

"Oh, sweetheart," she said. "Do you miss me too?"

"Yes," he said, missing something.

"Tuesday at the latest."

"Tuesday."

"The day after tomorrow. You know I can't wait to see you, Alexander."

"Let me know when you're coming home," he said.

"I just told you."

She asked about the rosebush. He told her it was fine. She told him that she loved the fact that he'd called her so early. He said good-bye, calling her sweetheart, and hung up before she could say any more.

HE STRETCHED OUT on the couch with the phone on top of his chest. She had heard something frightened in his voice, he knew, and somehow she had extracted from that a hope that he needed her. How blind did love have to be, he wondered, before it was safe to call it something else?

He played with the push buttons on the phone, pretending that they were the key pad on a pocket calculator. He pushed 2, then #, then 2 and then pushed 4. He pushed 4-#-5 and then 20. 42-#-6. He paused. 252. 436-#-754. The numbers danced in his head. He lost them. He closed his eyes. He had always envied the people he knew who could do large calculations in their heads. He had always wondered if that was the kind of talent he needed to have.

HE WOKE UP two hours later, the phone still on his chest. The sky, which he hadn't noticed before, was dark and overcast. He remembered the phone call with Linda and wondered how much of his fear he had let her hear. She didn't have any answers, he thought. He wondered why he had hoped that she would. He fell back to sleep again.

IN THE AFTERNOON, Alexander woke up famished, went into the kitchen, dumped a can of tuna into a large glass bowl, and then remembered that he had no more mayonnaise. In the refrigerator, there were bottles of salad dressing, ketchup, and mustard, some flat tonic water, three shrunken oranges, and one slice of bread that was hard as a cracker.

There was soup in the cupboard, but the two small saucepans were in the sink, unwashed. Alexander poured a can of chicken broth into a large pasta pot and stood, leaning against the counter, waiting for the soup to get hot.

Vaguely, he realized he would have to clean up before Linda came home, and at the same time, he realized that if he didn't clean up, she would.

The soup started to boil. He poured it into a mug and burned his lips when he sipped it. He cursed and put the mug down and went, exhausted, back to the living room couch. Rogue jumped up beside him and stared. Alexander stared back and then he shouted, "What do you want?" and Rogue scampered away.

Back in the kitchen, Alexander remembered that he was out of cat food, too. Rogue was at his feet, tail sweeping the air. Alexander took the bowl of tuna that he'd left on the counter and put it on the floor. Rogue pounced on it, ravenous. Alexander wondered when he'd fed Rogue last, and then he wondered if he was losing his mind. He was trying so hard to hold himself together, but so many things had happened. He wondered if they had changed him already, or if he was still himself. Then he thought about calling Sam. The idea seemed so novel that it almost felt brilliant.

"so," Sam said, smiling, an hour and a half later when he met Alexander at the old front door. "Come on in. You saw her. Tell me. God, you look really awful."

"Got any food?" Alexander asked.

"Sure."

"I could really use some lunch."

"It's five o'clock," Sam said.

"Then dinner."

Sam's kitchen was clean. The refrigerator was filled with fruit and juices, and there was a bowl of leftover pasta. At what point, Alexander wondered, had his father learned to cook? He took the pasta and a fork from the kitchen drawer and began to eat.

"Don't you want to heat that up?" Sam asked.

"No, this is fine."

"Come on, Ex. Take a plate at least. Sit down. It'll taste better."

"This is fine," Alexander said again.

Sam grabbed the bowl away, spooned some pasta onto a plate, took a napkin from the counter, and walked past Alexander into the living room. He stood by the chessboard till Alexander sat in a chair, and then he handed him the plate.

"Tell me everything," Sam said.

"It was weird," Alexander said, and shrugged. He ate for a moment, silent.

"You told me that on the phone. But what happened? You want something to drink with that?"

"No thanks," Alexander said.

Sam watched and waited as Alexander finished the food.

"More?" Sam said.

"Maybe later." Alexander put the plate down on a side table. He looked at the faded blue walls.

"What's wrong with you?" Sam asked.

"Hangover," Alexander said.

Sam laughed. "What'd she do? Did she burn incense? Did she tell you about your aura?"

Alexander reached for the wooden box that held the chess pieces. He slid the top open and closed several times. He wondered why both Linda and Sam thought the whole thing was so funny.

"Ex?" Sam said. "I'm sorry, Ex."

Alexander began to place the chess pieces on the board.

"I'm sorry, Ex," Sam said again. "Was it very rough?"

"Yes."

"I'm sorry."

Alexander began to center the chess pieces inside their squares. "Why did you marry her?" he asked finally.

Sam smiled. "Oh, that," he said. "Well. I was in love."

"And was she—" Alexander began, "was she in love with you too?"

Sam laughed. "Let me guess," he said. "She told you about the goy boyfriend."

Alexander looked up from the chessboard, amazed.

"Oh, you think I don't know about that," Sam said. "Listen. I know. I even knew then."

"Before you married her, you mean?"

"Sure."

"Then why?"

"I told you. I was in love with her. I thought if she married me, she'd fall in love too."

"But—"

"Tell me something," Sam said. "Did she tell you about her necklace?"

"Her necklace."

"That gold necklace. The locket thing. Does she still wear it around her neck?"

Alexander looked at the floor. He felt almost ashamed. "Yes," he said.

"Yeah, I figured. So did she tell you about that, too?"

"Yes."

"There's a picture of him inside it, right?"

"Who?"

"The goy boyfriend. The goyfriend," Sam said, grinning.

"Yes," Alexander said.

"I always thought so," Sam said. "God. Poor Alice."

"Poor *Alice?*"

"Yes, Ex. Think about it."

"How did you know about the necklace?"

"Hey. You live with a woman for thirteen years and she never takes her necklace off, not even in the shower, and you give her other necklaces, and she trades them in for bracelets, you start to figure there's something about that necklace, you know?"

Alexander shook his head.

"Hey, was she wearing a lot of bracelets? She used to make a big deal about wearing all the bracelets. As if that would keep me from noticing her neck."

"Why do you think this is funny?"

Sam stopped smiling. "I didn't think it was funny then. Time passes. That's all. What about the bracelets?"

"I didn't notice," Alexander said. "She was wearing a lot of rings, though. Lots of rings. They sparkled."

"Crystals, probably," Sam said. "Figures."

"Why?"

"There's this whole craze now," Sam said. "Crystals, you know. Health, good luck. Don't you keep up with any of this stuff?"

"She took me to a woman yesterday who cured my headache," Alexander said. "In the evening, she told me all about the dreams I've been having."

"What dreams?" Sam said.

"It doesn't matter what they are. She knew about them, though. Lucky guess, right?"

Sam shrugged. "You never know," he said.

"What do you mean, you never know?"

"More things in heaven and earth, Horatio."

"What?"

"*Hamlet*," Sam said. "Christ, Ex, don't you ever read?"

"Physics," Alexander said.

Sam nodded eagerly. "Right," he said. "The lecture. You can tell me about *that*, at least, can't you?"

"I haven't started it," Alexander said.

Sam put both his hands in the air and shrugged.

"Dad, it *bothered* me that that woman fixed my headache. It *bothered* me that Alice told me all about my dreams."

"I know how it is," Sam said. "Once—this was years ago—she sent me a letter saying, 'Congratulations—you've earned

it,' and that was the week *before* I got my big raise. I know how
it is. Your mother's a little crazy, that's all. I've always told
you that."

"But she was right."

"She can also be right."

Alexander looked down at the chessboard again. "I figured
maybe she overheard me," he said. "About the dream, I mean.
Maybe I was talking in my sleep."

"Your sleep? She was in your apartment?"

Alexander sighed. "She wasn't."

"When did she see you sleep?"

Alexander looked down.

"Christ, Ex, you nailed the palm reader?"

Alexander shrugged, then smirked.

"Where's Linda?" Sam asked.

"South Dakota."

"Marry her," Sam said.

"What?"

"Marry her."

"Dad."

"Have kids."

"*Dad.*"

"I'm telling you, Ex. You want something new to think
about? Marry her. Have kids. You'll have something new to
think about."

WHEN ALEXANDER came home from Sam's that night, he
poured himself a Scotch and slugged it back, and then he
climbed the stairs to the roof. He pushed the door open and
steeled himself and walked out to stand in the clear night air.
The stars danced. They winked. Alexander went over to Linda's
rosebush, touching the soil gently. Dead leaves shook loose like
memories. The branches were dry, reptilian. Buy another rose-

bush, he thought. Then, fuck the rosebush. Screw her. Screw her for laughing.

Screw Sam, too.

Later, in bed, he stared at the private white moon of the round ceiling lamp. He thought about Linda's warmth, and Cleo's heat.

ALEXANDER WOKE the next morning to a blue sky and a faint breeze. He smiled when he realized he hadn't dreamed.

He had met his mother. That was in the past now, and he suddenly understood that if he thought about it that way, he could start to see it as something good. He would shower and shave, he thought, and he would write his lecture and be himself.

An hour later, he was sitting at his desk. The green cursor blinked against the black screen. Clustered on the desk were three cups of half-drunk coffee. The milk in one of them was starting to form mold. Alexander looked back at the screen.

"A Theory of Everything in Two Dimensions," he typed. Then he erased the line, and then the paragraph he had written before. He reached for a copy of his article and started to read it over again. Rogue was at his feet, playing with a dusty sock. Alexander looked up. From where he sat, he could see the bedroom: a pile of dirty shirts on the chair, unmade bed with unchanged sheets, glasses and soda cans on the night table, papers and magazines on the floor. On his desk were stacks of unread mail that Biner kept forwarding from the lab.

He could clean up, he thought, and the idea filled him with sudden joy. First he'd clean up, he thought. Then he'd do work.

Groceries were essential. Alexander started a mental shopping list as he made three trips up and down the stairs, carrying cups and glasses to the kitchen. Really he needed everything. Also there were the shirts to take to the cleaners, and the laundry to do. He would shop and do laundry and cleaning, he thought, and then he would do his work.

On the street, he stood for a moment, undecided. He could get almost everything he needed at the Korean market a block away, but if he went to the grocery store, he'd be able to buy meat. Meat in the freezer, he thought, would be a sign of his stability.

It was a Monday morning, and the grocery store was filled with young mothers. Alexander saw a few old couples doing their shopping together, squinting at lists, but apart from the guys in the checkout line who were packing groceries in bags and boxes, he was the only man under sixty in the place. The mothers wheeled their young children around in shopping carts and called warnings after the older ones as they ran down the crowded aisles. Alexander had never noticed that the carts were made with two holes in back for the children to stick their legs through. He wondered if Alice had ever taken him grocery shopping when he was a child.

A mother in the produce section was letting her son help her pick the ripe fruit. Alexander couldn't remember Alice ever having let him choose anything. He wondered if she had called the apartment while he was over at Sam's. He wondered if she was calling now, and what she had said to Cleo.

He bought juices and fruit and pasta, toilet paper and paper towels, hamburger meat and lamb chops, onions and peppers and fresh tomatoes. He bought ten cans of cat food and a bag of kitty litter. He bought tuna and soup and bread and mayonnaise, and he even remembered to buy celery and carrots for Linda. He didn't think he was really angry at Linda anymore. He was starting to think that to have her back might make everything fall into place again. He told himself that things had been much better before she'd left.

Carrying the bags on the way back, Alexander stopped in front of a small store on Broadway and Sixty-ninth Street. He realized that he must have passed the shop a thousand times doing chores on the weekends—the clean white door and the large picture window, the tarot cards and books laid out like things in a glass box. But he couldn't remember ever having seen the place before. The groceries were getting heavy. He shifted the bags in his hands and walked on.

The phone was ringing when he got back to the apartment, and he answered it unthinkingly.

"Simon?"

"Yes."

"It's Dr. Biner."

Biner, Alexander thought. It seemed very strange to hear his voice. In the nearly three weeks since Alexander had left the lab, Biner had become more a concept than a person. He had become the reason to finish the work, but somehow he'd been disembodied. "How are you?" Alexander asked. His voice sounded giddy, the question somehow inappropriate.

"I'm well," Biner said. "How's it coming?" he asked.

"Oh, fine," Alexander told him.

"What did you think of the *Time* story?" Biner asked.

"The *Time* story? I haven't seen it."

"Haven't seen it!"

"No."

"Did you see *The Sciences?*"

"No."

There was a nervous pause. "When can I read something?" Biner asked.

"As soon as it's done," Alexander said.

"Is it almost done?"

"Yes. It's almost done." Rogue sidled up against his leg, and then scratched viciously at his shin.

"I don't want to push you—" Biner began.

"I'll let you know," Alexander said.

"The lecture is in three weeks."

"I know."

"The eighteenth of September. Monday."

"I know. I'll call you," Alexander said, and hung up. A moment later, he unplugged the phone.

In the kitchen, he opened a fresh can of cat food for Rogue, and he filled the dishwasher with dirty things. The dishwasher was new, and this was the first time that he'd used it, and it took him a while to find the right detergent under the sink. Linda had told him that the dishwasher would change her life. He thought about all the money that they'd spent on the apartment: a good part of both their savings. He told himself not to think of it now.

He cleaned the pots in the sink. He sponged down the counters. He put the food away. He stripped the bed and put all the dirty laundry into a pillowcase. He swept the living room floor, and then he picked up his keys.

"Looking good, huh?" he said to Rogue.

He gathered the shirts in one hand and the laundry in the other and flew down the stairs again.

In the basement, three huge cockroaches skittered across the floor when he turned on the light. Linda hated bugs. He wondered how she forced herself to face this place each week.

He didn't know which dry cleaner she used, so he went to his old one on Broadway. The man at the counter didn't recognize him. The shirts would be ready on Friday, he said.

Out on the street, he was struck again by the sight of so many young mothers. Linda was born to have children, he knew, and the thought made him feel almost angry again. He stopped. There was a small sign at the tarot card place that looked harmless in the sunlight. Five neon letters: TAROT. Alexander told himself the atomic weight and composition of neon. He told himself that if he spent a little time here, then the laundry would be ready for the drier when he was done and he wouldn't have to make an extra trip up and down the stairs. Then he went inside. The room was small but sunny. A white-haired woman with a soft, round face was sitting in an armchair, reading a copy of the *New Republic*. She was wearing a tidy blue suit and navy pumps and stockings. Her hair was permed like a grandmother's, and she looked as if she was waiting at the dentist's.

"Can I help you?" she asked, looking up, smiling warmly.

"No. I—"

"First time?" she said.

"Yes."

"Do you have a question?" the woman asked. Gently she put down her magazine and picked up a pack of large, worn cards.

Alexander stood uncertainly with one hand still on the brass knob behind him. "A question?" he repeated.

"Something you want to know."

He laughed softly. "Everything," he said, and backed out the door.

SITTING AT the computer again, he noticed that the corners of most of the keys were nearly black with grime. He had probably never cleaned them, he thought. He went downstairs to the kitchen and picked up a bottle of cleanser and a roll of paper towels. Upstairs again, he unscrewed the back of the keyboard, took the case apart, and removed each key from its small, tight spring, spraying each one with cleanser and painstakingly wiping it dry. Someone could make a fortune, he thought, by inventing an instrument perfectly shaped for cleaning computer keyboards. Maybe, he thought wryly, that was what he should do when he finished the lecture: start inventing things that actual people could actually use.

The intercom buzzed, but when Alexander pressed the button and asked who was there, he heard only silence. He gathered three quarters for the drier, went down to the basement to transfer the laundry, and then checked the front door. There was a box there with his name on it, and inside was the candle he'd been given by Alice. The note said, "I'm not Alice," and was signed, "Love, Cleo." Upstairs, he plugged the phone in again. An hour later, it rang, but he decided not to answer it. That was the rest of the afternoon: chores for the apartment, and excuses not to write the lecture, and every hour or so the telephone ringing.

AT SEVEN O'CLOCK that evening, Alexander lit the candle and then blew it out, and then lit it again and then blew it out, and then for three solid hours he sat at his computer, writing the lecture and not answering the phone.

AT TEN, Alexander reread what he'd written, which was basically a shorter version of his article with the computations summed up instead of written out. It wasn't exactly thrilling, what he'd done, but he knew it could pass.

He sat at the desk with his head on his arms.

Everything had happened to him that he had ever imagined happening, and he was only thirty-one. Thirty-one had seemed old until now. Now he thought he could see the life that was reeling away in front of him. He would make a big splash with his Theory of Everything, but then he'd become like Biner, yearning for past glory and puffing himself up; he would give lectures, and some young physicists would revere him and others would try to knock him down, and he would have to coddle them. He would marry Linda and have children and not know how to talk to them. He would watch the days replicate themselves, following each other like numbers in sequence.

Alexander felt with complete certainty that he had already had the one great moment of his life. It had been on a subway platform on his way to work three months before, when he'd known what he'd discovered, and when no one else knew about it yet. That had been the moment, and it had come too soon.

At ten-thirty, he called Cleo, feeling that he had always known he would.

THEY SAT cross-legged on the floor of her bedroom. It was just past eleven, and Cleo had filled the room with dozens of burning candles.

"Where'd she go?" Alexander asked.

Cleo shrugged. "I don't know. She's gone, though."

"How did she know?" Alexander asked.

"What?"

"How did she know about my angel?"

"You know, she saw her on the astral plane."

"I don't believe in that stuff."

"Oh, sure you do," Cleo said. She reached for the cat, kissed its neck, and handed it to Alexander, as if they were playing some sort of campfire game, and the one with the cat was the one who had to speak.

Alexander stroked the cat and talked to the wavering flames. "Okay," he said. "I have a memory. It may just be a dream. I don't know. I was eight. It was in North Carolina. I'm telling this wrong."

"Go ahead," Cleo said.

"Once," Alexander said, still not looking at her, "once I saw a ghost. I mean I think I saw a ghost. Thought I did. I was eight. It was a long time ago. I was scared. It's hard to separate what I saw from what I dream I saw."

"What do you dream you saw?"

"A ghost," Alexander said, and laughed, looking up. But Cleo was waiting, watching him, resting her chin on the back of her hand.

"Okay," Alexander said again. "I dream that I saw this man. A guy who was trying to stop a train. He was waving a lantern, and the train ran him over. That was the same guy that Alice was describing last night."

"So it was a violent death," Cleo said.

"Sure. Yeah. I don't know. I was just a kid. Alice took me to see it, of course, and she gave it a really big buildup, and what probably happened is that I just think I saw what I knew she wanted me to see."

"You mean your mind was playing tricks on you."

"Something like that. It was dark. I don't know. There was a lot of mist."

"But what if you really saw it?"

"No. I don't know," Alexander said.

They made love in front of the mirrors again, Cleo bent like a bracket over the side of an armchair. Alexander stood behind her, watching her reflection. Her right hand clutched the arm of the chair as if it were a lifeline. Her forehead was bright with sweat.

"God!" she said when he made her come.

God, he would think later, lying beside her and thinking of Linda and trying to line up objections to Cleo. A hundred magic numbers and Himalayan miracle men, and when all was said and done, this girl cried out for God.

Later still, as Cleo slept, he watched the candles go out, one by one, like people leaving a room.

"THERE *is* an angel," he told Cleo at three in the morning when they woke, inexplicably, at the same moment. "There always has been."

"You see her when you're awake or asleep?" Cleo asked.

"Asleep."

"You dream about her?"

"Yes."

"Since when?"

"My whole life," Alexander said. "At least since I was eight."

"What do you hope for in the dream?"

"I hope," he said, "that she'll touch me."

Cleo smiled and touched his forehead. "What happens then?" she asked.

"Then I know everything."

"Everything?"

"Everything."

"And why is that important?"

Alexander smiled. He thought about the years he had spent working, all the classes he'd sat through in school, all the pages of graph paper that he'd filled with notations, all the politics with people like Biner, and all the trust he'd had that finding the answers would finally transform him. Alexander didn't say anything. He thought that if he spoke he would say something stupid.

"Why hasn't she touched you yet?" Cleo said.

"I guess," he said slowly, "that I haven't deserved the Touch."

"Why not?"

"I don't know."

"Come on, you must."

"I *don't* know," he said. "I mean I thought by now I'd have it. I've written the goddamn Theory of Everything. That's not just some little thing. It's what I always wanted. I thought that it would feel different."

There was a long pause as Cleo looked at him, grinning. "You call it the Touch, huh," she said.

"Yes." He ran a hand through his hair. It was strange, saying out loud what he was really feeling.

"The Touch."

"*Yes*. So?"

"That's a nice name for it," Cleo said.

He shrugged. "That's how I've always thought of it."

"There's another name."

"What do you mean?"

"We'll talk in the morning."

"What do you mean, there's another name?"

"There is," she said.

"Tell me now." He put his arms around her. "Now," he said.

Cleo pressed her hand against the small of his back.

"Tell me," he said again.

She climbed on top of him. She straddled his body, looking down at him intently, her long blond hair like a tent around their faces. There was a lamp on the table beside her bed, and the light appeared behind her head, shining in his eyes every time she rocked forward. He realized his eyes were open. He tried to remember if he closed them with Linda, if he watched her when they made love. He found that he couldn't remember. It was like asking himself whether he dreamed in color.

Cleo was squeezing his body between her knees. Despite himself, Alexander gasped. Cleo grasped for his hands, then stopped and, with one brutal motion, pinned his wrists above his head.

"Oh," Alexander said.

She was grinning, waiting, frozen above him. Her eyes flashed with hunger and power.

"Please," Alexander found himself saying. He pulled, futilely, against her grip.

"Please what?" Cleo whispered cruelly, smiling. Slowly, with terrible gentleness, she started to lift herself away. He raised his hips, straining to stay inside her.

"Please what?" she whispered again.

"You," he said. "Please," he said. "Tell me."

·   ·   ·

IN THE MORNING, she said she would tell him the next day. He knew he was being toyed with, and the thought made him feel better than he'd felt in a long time.

"When can I see you again?" Alexander asked her.

"I don't know," Cleo said, grinning. "When can you?"

"Linda," Alexander said, remembering. "Damn. She's coming home today."

"Hmm," Cleo said.

"Damn."

"Does she know about—what'd you call it last night? The Touch?"

Alexander laughed. "God, no," he said. "She knows I have bad dreams sometimes. That's all." Alexander pulled Cleo close to his body and kissed the back of her neck. "She wouldn't understand the way you do," he said.

"Oh, she wouldn't," Cleo said, drawing back away from him.

"I want to know what you were going to tell me last night," Alexander said.

"Oh, I was never going to tell you last *night*, doll," Cleo said. "You're just not ready yet."

He took three long steps toward her and held her face the same way she'd held his two days before. He kissed her mouth so hard that later he realized he'd bruised his lip.

LINDA CAME HOME at four o'clock, suntanned and apprehensive. She kissed him hello and held him tightly, her face against his chest. Gently, he broke away from her and handed her her mail. She sorted through it, distracted, asking innocuous questions, and when he answered them only in soft, short words, she grew quiet also.

She asked him to carry her suitcases upstairs so she could unpack, and Alexander sat in the bedroom armchair, watching her. When she turned to the windows and looked out at the garden, her eyes narrowed as she focused on one flowerpot and then another. Wordlessly, she walked up the three small steps and shoved open the door to the roof. Braced for her anger, Alexander watched through the window as she stood, taking in the damage that he'd done to her garden. She didn't call for him, though. She didn't say anything. She merely walked to the sooty white chairs and sat, feet up on the table, and stared at the ruined rosebush.

Half an hour later, she carried it indoors and downstairs to the trash, mournful but still silent.

"I DON'T WANT to cook tonight," Linda announced.

"That's fine," Alexander said. "What do you want to do?"

"I don't care."

He called the Chinese takeout place.

His fortune cookie said, "You and your wife will be happy in your life together."

Hers said, "Bottom of well is not as near as moonlight."

"I got the most amazing fortune cookie when I was home," Linda said.

Alexander looked up, grateful, now, that she was talking again.

"I know you won't believe it," she said. "And I meant to save it, but someone threw it away."

"What did it say?" Alexander asked.

"It said, 'He loves you as much as he can, but that is not very much.' "

"I'm sorry, Linda," Alexander said. He didn't want to be with her. He wanted to be with Cleo, and to find out what she knew.

"When are you going to stop this?" she asked. She seemed more sad than angry now.

"I don't know what you mean," he said.

. . .

SHE WATCHED a movie on television, and he read over his lecture, making minute corrections. A sense of pressure was building in him, but it didn't involve the lecture. The lecture, in fact, seemed less daunting to him than it had the week before. What seemed truly daunting was the realization that there was nothing he could do—either with this evening or with the rest of his life—that wouldn't make Linda feel either more happy or more sad. What seemed daunting was that he couldn't get Cleo out of his mind. It was not so much that he was thinking about her directly. It was more the intermittent awareness that *something* was making him feel eager, and then the understanding that that something was the prospect of getting her, and the answers she seemed to have. Cleo had said she knew something important that he didn't know, and the thought that that might be true thrilled him. It made him feel more like himself than being with Linda or even with Sam.

He wondered if what he was feeling for Cleo would simply stop at some point, and if what he had felt for Linda would simply start again.

At eleven-thirty, he took a shower, and Linda went to bed. Fifteen minutes later, the backs of his legs still damp, he walked toward the bedroom and stopped in the doorway. Linda was curled up under the covers, her face nestled against her right arm. Her eyes were shut, her mouth slightly open. Her breaths were long and even.

Alexander hesitated. Linda, he thought. She did this sometimes: lay there as if she was sleeping already, then sprang like a cat when he got into bed. Playing the game by habit, he tiptoed forward, then climbed into bed beside her. He closed his eyes and waited, but Linda didn't move. He tugged on the covers and made the bedsprings squeak. Her breaths continued, steady as a meter. Up on one elbow, he looked at her.

She tilted, just perceptibly, away from him.

"I WANT YOU to hear this," Cleo said on the phone when she called him the next morning. Linda was out on the roof upstairs, trying to salvage her garden. "I found it in a book," Cleo said.

"Is this what you wouldn't tell me yesterday?"

"Hush up and listen."

"Sorry," he said.

" 'Scientific achievement,' " Cleo read, " 'was without value when not accompanied by an ennoblement of the soul. And the mastery was the proof that the Adept was now among the chosen . . .' "

"Yeah," Alexander said slowly. "So?"

"So, you don't get to be a master till you're one of the chosen," Cleo said, "and you don't get to be one of the chosen till you've worked hard enough to deserve it. Sound familiar?"

"I guess," Alexander said. "What are you talking about?"

" 'God has imbued man's soul with a longing for perfection,' " Cleo continued reading. " 'Like nature, man should strive for the divine within him. The best that existed below, the Adept believed, could only be linked to what was lowest above. The most perfect thing on earth was gold; and above, the only body whose rays reached into the heaven of the angels was the sun.' "

"Angels?" Alexander said.

"Angels."

"What are you talking about here?" he asked again.

"Alchemy," Cleo said.

Alexander laughed, but then she said good-bye and hung up, and he wished that he hadn't.

. . .

HE SAT ON the roof with Linda. A faint hot breeze stirred the marigolds and the daisies she had bought that morning, and the empty hanging planters twisted back and forth like shy children.

"Want some iced coffee?" Linda asked him.

He shook his head.

"Iced tea?"

He shook his head again.

"Are we going to talk?"

He said nothing.

She followed his gaze to the water towers that rose in the distance.

"Is it me?" she asked him.

"Why would you think that?"

"Why wouldn't I?"

"It isn't you," he said.

She paused. "I know what we need," she said. "We need some music."

"No we don't."

"Fine."

"It isn't you, Linda," he said.

Two pigeons swooped down and up again, crossing each other like lines on a graph.

Linda settled at Alexander's feet with a large terra-cotta pot and a trowel.

"I think those daisies would look nice in this, don't you?" she asked.

"Sure."

"Well, do you?"

"Yes."

Linda began to dig gently around the roots, painstakingly scraping away each morsel of earth.

"Why don't you just pull it up?" Alexander finally asked.

"You don't just pull something like this up. Root trauma," she said.

"Root trauma," he said, shaking his head. "Maybe that's what I've got."

Linda dug for a few more seconds, then looked up, her eyes catching the light. "What's wrong with you?" she said. "I thought you wanted to find this theory more than anything in the world."

"I did."

"Well, you found it."

"I know."

"So?"

"So. Sometimes I just get scared," he said.

"I know you're scared."

"Okay then."

Alexander lay back in his chair and closed his eyes and tried not to think. His mind kept shifting from Cleo to Linda and back again. A slight change in focus, and the whole world changed. It was like looking at a cube drawn on paper: stare at one set of right angles, and then the front becomes the back; stare at the other set, and then the back becomes the front. Alexander felt a drop of liquid trickle down his face and into his ear. He didn't know if it was a tear or sweat.

"What are you scared of?" Linda asked him.

"I can't talk about it. I don't know," he said.

There was a silence as she reached for a new planter, turned it over, and tapped its base with a trowel. Alexander opened his eyes at the noise. Linda held the plant, with its soil and roots perfectly molded around it, in one hand.

"It's dying," she said, without looking at him.

It took him a moment to realize that she wasn't talking about the plant. He closed his eyes again.

"That's it, Alexander, isn't it? It's dying. You're scared of dying."

He turned his body toward her slightly, rolling onto his side, his face pressed against the hot vinyl slats of the chaise. Try, he thought. Try hard, he thought. "It isn't exactly that," he said.

"Being in pain? Having to—well, having to leave? Knowing someday that you have to leave?"

"No. I don't know," he said.

Linda pulled at a root, examined it briefly, and tossed it away. "I get scared," she said. "But it's not about me. It's about other people dying."

"That's lovely."

"No. It's just as scary. I shouldn't care so much," she said.

"Maybe."

He watched her face darken, even as she tried to smile. A cloud covered the sun. He wondered in which house the sun had been stationed in the easy moment of Linda's birth. He thought about his theory, and the emptiness of arrival. Something would have to change, he knew, but he wished that he could keep her from guessing or acting until he knew what the right change was.

LINDA MADE tuna sandwiches for lunch. She asked him about the lecture, and he told her that it was almost done.

"Do you have to show it to Biner?" she asked.

He told her he did, which was the truth, and that he'd have to spend some time at the lab, which was a lie.

The work, in fact, now seemed to him part of some ancient, distant life, and the steps he needed to go through seemed only the necessary calculations of an equation whose outcome was already known.

"When?" Linda asked him.

"Starting tomorrow night," he said, and couldn't look at her.

After lunch, she worked at the dining room table, making decorations for her classroom, cutting out autumn leaves from heavy construction paper. Several times, she paused to run an errand or to putter in the kitchen. She left Alexander alone. As the late afternoon passed, he realized that he had absolutely no idea what she was feeling. He wondered why she wasn't more angry with him, and if she was. He wondered if she had decided that she was going to wait out the trouble, and why that prospect made him feel as free as it made him feel trapped. It began to dawn on him that he might have to tell her about Cleo at some point—that he might actually have to break up with her. Alexander had never had to break up with anyone before. He had always made them angry, and then they had always left him.

In the darkening apartment, he and Linda worked by separate lamps.

ALEXANDER CALLED Cleo that night when Linda was in the shower. "You know something I need to know," he said.

"Could be."

"You know something about *her*," he said.

"About who?" Cleo said, teasing, laughing.

"About my *angel*," Alexander whispered, perfectly serious.

"Okay, doll, listen to this," Cleo told him. "Wait just a sec, I gotta get the book." There was a clatter as she threw down the phone, and he could imagine her naked, striding across the room to the crooked bookshelf, and grinning the whole time. "You there?" she said when she got back.

"Right here."

"Listen," she said again. He could hear her turning the pages. " 'An angel appeared to him, holding in his hand a large volume bound in copper. He opened it so as to show the title page, saying: *Flamel, take careful note of this book. You will not understand*

any of it at present, nor will many another; but one day you will
discover from it what no one else will be able to do.' "

Alexander was speechless.

"You see," Cleo said slowly, "you're not the only one. You're
not crazy."

"Who were you reading about?"

"An alchemist," she said. "He lived in the fourteenth century.
He had an angel too."

"Oh," Alexander said, deflated. *"Great."*

Cleo laughed. "What?" she said.

"I don't want to sound smug," Alexander told her, "but high
school *chem* students know more about science than, you know,
alchemists do."

"And you know a lot more than that, you mean."

"Well, yeah."

"Why haven't you gotten the Touch then?" Cleo asked
him.

Alexander sighed. He could hear Linda's footsteps as she
moved around the room upstairs, preparing for bed. "I thought
alchemists were just like magicians," he said.

Cleo laughed again. "Who knows?" she said. "Maybe they
are."

"Were."

"Are."

"I thought they just wanted to turn lead into gold."

"Well obviously there's more to it than that," she said.

"This was the big thing that you were going to tell me?
Alchemy?" Alexander asked.

" 'An angel appeared to him,' " Cleo read again, " 'holding
in his hand a large volume bound in copper. . . .' "

"You're serious about this?" Alexander said.

"I'm serious about you," she said.

Alexander sighed. Linda called out to him from the bedroom.

He felt like running. "I think," he whispered to Cleo, "that I need to be with you."

"I'm not going anywhere," she said.

"WHO WERE you talking to?" Linda asked him when he settled into bed beside her.

"Sam," Alexander said.

"How is he?" Linda asked.

"He's fine."

"Do you realize," she said, "that you've never met my parents?"

"Yes."

"They want to meet you, you know," Linda said.

"I want to meet them too," he said. It made no sense, he thought, to tell her anything now. What was he going to say— that there had always been this angel he'd had awkward, hopeful dreams about, and that now he thought he'd met her?

Alexander made love to Linda, thinking of Cleo, and he didn't say a word to her when they were done.

IN HIS DREAM, Cleo floated above him, wearing wings. "You'll have to start learning again," she said.

"I'm ready. I want to start learning again."

There was a bright light around her.

"Is this finally it?" he said.

"Yes."

"Touch me!" he shouted, and woke up knowing that Linda was watching him. He kept his eyes closed and fell back to sleep.

He dreamed about Cleo as the angel again.

He could feel the air above him stir as she flew past his face.

"Magic isn't silver," she said. "It's gold."

. . .

AT SIX O'CLOCK the next afternoon, he told Linda that he had
to go to the lab, and he took a taxi to Cleo's without calling
her first.

She was with a client when he showed up at her door.

"I'll be with you in a minute, doll," she said. She didn't
seem fazed by his sudden presence. She didn't seem thrown by
the look on his face, which he knew must be wild and needy.
"I'm just finishing up with my last pinstriper," she told him.
"It won't take long at all."

Alexander grabbed her by both shoulders and kissed her.

She made him go into her bedroom to wait.

He sat on the edge of Cleo's bed. There was a crystal ball on
the night table that he hadn't noticed three nights before. For
a moment, Alexander wanted to laugh, and to leave, but then
the impulse vanished, and he stared at the round glass globe.
Who was he, he wondered, to decide what was impossible? He
had come up with a theory that said the universe was composed
of tiny vibrating strings, strings that existed in two dimensions,
strings that could never be seen. Who was he, he wondered,
to decide what couldn't be?

He lay on the bed, staring at the lines on the palms of his
hands. When Cleo finally came into the room, his hands grasped
her waist and pulled her down on top of him, and then they
undid the buttons and the zippers on her clothes. He made love
to her recklessly, looking past her to the pentagram that was
hanging on the wall before him. He moved in her with no
pretense of affection; he moved as if he were scrambling away
from a spreading fire.

After he came, she slid out from underneath him and silently left the room. Alexander remained, facedown, hearing
the sound of water running in the kitchen and the gasp of
a truck from the street below. When Cleo came back, she

brought tea and cookies, and the look on her face thrilled
him. She seemed more happy than tender, more wise than
startled. She seemed more full than empty.

Sipping her tea, cross-legged at the foot of the bed, she
listened intently as he told her his dream.

"You said, 'Magic isn't silver, it's gold,' " he told her.

"Oh, I thought this was going to be a sex dream," Cleo said,
and laughed.

"Why did you say it?" Alexander asked, staring at the
pentagram.

Cleo shrugged. "Doll, it was a dream," she said. "I don't
know. I wasn't there. It's probably about the alchemy, you
know. Gold. Silver. Magic."

"Alice said the exact same thing to me."

"When?" Cleo asked.

Alexander looked back at her, then looked down at the bedspread. "When I was eight years old," he said.

Cleo put her cup of tea on the floor beside the bed and crawled
up toward Alexander to kiss the back of his neck.

"I want to know what's going to happen to me," he told
her.

"I know you do," she said.

"I want to know what you've been talking about."

"What, alchemy?" she said. "I thought that made you
laugh."

"Tell me," Alexander said, and then his hands grasped the
headboard of the bed behind him, as if he had said he would
jump somewhere but was still afraid of falling.

APART FROM the few quotes Cleo had read him in the last two
days, all Alexander knew about alchemy was that alchemists
had lived in the Middle Ages and tried to turn base metals into
gold. He knew that some of their experiments had led to early

discoveries in chemistry and physics, but mostly he thought of them as charlatans and con men, white-bearded magician types who preyed on people's greed.

This was not the alchemy that Cleo had in mind.

Alchemy, as Cleo explained it, had more to do with faith than with science, more to do with wisdom than wealth.

Alchemy, as Cleo explained it, was about knowledge, curiosity, a restless passion to learn. Alchemy was about trust that one would find the answers, rage at the prospect that one might not. True, alchemists dreamed of making gold, she told him. But making gold would only be the outward sign of their success. What alchemists really searched for was a substance they called the Philosopher's Stone. Sure, she said, when added to a common metal, it would change it into gold. But when drunk in liquid form as the Elixir of Life, the Philosopher's Stone would give them the answers to all the secrets in the universe. The answers were the real prize.

Alchemists worked for long years in secrecy, she told him. Sometimes they died in poverty. Often they lived alone. They walked along a border, she said, of brilliance and despair. Alchemists believed that the Philosopher's Stone would change them and would change the world. To earn it, they had to be pure of heart. Only those who had worked and waited were granted the true inspiration.

It became midnight.

Alchemy, as Cleo explained it, was exactly like the Touch.

TO HEAR IT ALL was like coming upon some rich, buried past. It was, Alexander imagined, the way that falling in love would be. There was the deep alarm of recognition, and then the mingled emotions of desire, fear, and freedom. Above all, there was the need to know more, the need to stand fixed in a spot forever if it meant he could know more.

. . .

"ALL THE ANSWERS," Alexander said to Cleo.

"Yes."

"All the answers to all the questions in the universe."

"Yes."

"That's just what I've always had dreams about. That's just what my angel keeps saying she has."

He made love to Cleo again, but this time he held her when they were done.

"The Philosopher's Stone. That's the Touch," he said.

"Yes, doll, I know."

"You're making all this up, right?"

"You know better than that," she said.

HE HELPED HER light the candles, and he helped her make the tea. It was late now, he didn't know how late, but he knew that he couldn't call Linda.

"How could this be?" he asked Cleo.

"How could anything be?" she said.

SHE KNEW WHAT he was feeling. She let him have her again. Inside her body, he felt safe. They came at the same moment, and the moment they did, he felt he could make love to her again.

"Did it work?" Alexander asked Cleo.

"What?"

"Did anyone find it?"

"The Stone? Sure."

"Who? When?" he asked her.

"Lots of them. I don't know," she told him. "Aren't you tired?"

"No."

· · ·

"I NEED TO find out more," he told her.

It had started to rain, and the rain was hitting the windows hard. Cleo was under the covers now. Alexander was pacing again. She smiled at him. "There's someone you'll need to meet," she said.

"Who? Tell me."

"Not now."

"Why not?"

"Because it's three o'clock in the morning, and you look a little crazy."

Alexander stopped pacing. He sat on the edge of her bed. He reached out gently to touch her cheek with the back of his hand. "God," he said. "Is it really three o'clock?"

"SO WHAT WOULD I have to do?" he said. He had finally put on his jacket, but he didn't want to leave.

"Go home," she told him. "It's late now."

"Would I have to go to, like, Tibet or something? Would you come with me?"

"He lives in New Jersey," Cleo said.

"Who does?"

"Harold."

"Harold who?"

"Doll, go home," she said.

IT WAS five o'clock in the morning when Alexander woke Cleo's doorman and asked him to unlock the front door. Outside, the rain had stopped, and the air had turned light and clean. Alexander stood on Cleo's corner with his hands in his jacket pockets. Over the East River, the sun was just beginning to rise. He looked out across the blue-brown water, shivering in the open breeze. He felt very cold and very pure. He was seeing the world without the usual cushions of a night's sleep and a day's routine. He turned away from the river and walked west toward the lingering darkness.

THERE WAS a mist in Central Park, and the paths were dark and wet. Vagrants slept on benches and by trees, blankets and bundles around them. There were no voices and few sounds. Alexander walked slowly, savoring the silence and welcoming the sun. He was happy.

It was hard to imagine what form his life was going to take now, but he knew that he would change it. Just staying up all night with Cleo had changed it. He had listened all night to a woman who read palms and believed in magic, a woman who lived by symbols and by candlelight, but he knew and she knew that he had wanted to be there. The hardest part had simply been to ask her what she knew. Now he had asked that question, and her answers had given him other questions, and promise of other answers. He knew that he would follow them. He felt as if he had never known a single thing before.

Part Two

I

THE JOURNEY

IT WAS the middle of December when he finally left New York. Cleo had said that she would drive him to New Jersey herself, and a light snow was falling when she showed up with a borrowed car. She honked the horn on the street below. It was eight o'clock in the morning, and Alexander had been up since six, finishing his packing, feeling sadder than he'd thought he'd feel.

Linda sat on the couch inside a rectangle of sunlight. Her arms and her legs were crossed. "When are you going to come back?" she asked him.

Alexander sighed. "I've told you, sweetheart. I don't know," he said.

She tightened the sash on her terry robe. "You must know," she said. "I mean, you must."

"I don't," Alexander told her.

The car horn honked again, and Alexander put his wallet and his keys into his pocket. Linda stood up quickly and then walked, head down, from the room.

WEEKS BEFORE, he had told her about Cleo, but Linda had not been surprised by that.

"Do you love her?" Linda had asked him flatly.

"I don't think so," he had said.

"Do you love me?" she had asked him.

"I'm not sure about that either."

"What do you love?" she had asked him finally. "Is there anything you love?"

So he had told her about his angel. He had told her about the alchemy.

"What if it's just another theory?" she'd asked. "Another Theory of Everything? What makes you think it'll be any different?"

"Because," he had said, believing it, "this is about the part of me I've always tried to hide."

It had been understood that she would stay in the apartment. So in the intervening weeks, they had gone on living there side by side. It had seemed to Alexander that Linda had withdrawn something new from him each day: sex, grins, dinner, demands, interest in his theory, reports on her classes. Her strength and her growing distance had almost made him want to change his mind. But even in the moments when he'd missed her the most fiercely, he had told himself to go forward. His task would be to learn the things that Harold and Cleo could teach him. His task, he had told Linda, was to find a way to face himself.

"And are you going to call me while you're facing yourself?" she had asked him.

"Linda."

"Are you?"

"I've told you. No," he'd said.

"*Why* aren't you going to call me?"

"Because it'll only make things worse."

Now he looked around the living room. He felt less sure of what he was leaving than of what he was hoping to find. He closed the door behind him, and he walked down the stairs, not counting them.

HAROLD MARKHAM lived in western New Jersey, only an hour and a half from the city. Traffic was backed up for miles over the bridge, though, and Alexander was grateful for the extra time. After all the weeks of planning, and after all the distance from Linda and Sam, and after all the troubles he'd had persuading Harold to take him in, leaving was the only thing that was making leaving seem real.

Cleo drove, singing along with the radio and chain-smoking Salems. The smoke and several strands of her long hair flew out the open window.

"You *are* going to come out and visit, right?" Alexander asked her.

"Doll. Of course I am," she said.

That didn't seem real, either.

"And you don't think I'm crazy, right?" he said.

"Stop pandering," Cleo told him.

Alexander tried to smile. In his mind, he worked an equation, and when he solved it, he thought of a longer one. Naively, he realized now, he had expected to feel elated. He had imagined the car ride as the first part of his freedom. But the things he was leaving were not letting go. The conversations with Sam and Linda flew like ghosts in his mind.

"You're a *scientist* for God's sake!" Sam had shouted when Alexander had told him his plans.

"A scientist? So was Newton!" Alexander had shouted back.

"What has Newton got to do with this?"

"Newton spent three years on his laws and the rest of his life studying pyramids and alchemy."

"Then Newton was an idiot!"

"Roger Bacon was an alchemist. So was Robert Boyle. And Jung."

"Idiots!"

"Look," Alexander had said, "you want to play chess with me or what?"

"No," Sam had said, "I don't want to play chess."

For the last few weeks, Sam had spoken to him as if he was talking to a very sick patient who didn't know what his illness was.

NO ONE BUT Cleo seemed to understand that what he was doing took courage. All his life he had been on one road, and now he was changing everything so that he could start at the beginning of an entirely different road, and all Sam and Linda could do was stand at the end of the first road and say that that was where he belonged.

He had expected hurt and anger from Linda. He had expected more from Sam, though—excitement at the prospect of a new kind of experiment. Sam only looked at him as if he'd suddenly changed into Alice.

Now the landscape was turning white around him, and he tried to ignore his sadness. Cleo was talking merrily about a client who kept making passes at her. Alexander didn't want to listen to her. He wanted to know he had done the right thing. He had felt so certain for weeks now, and he wanted to feel that way again.

. . .

ALEXANDER HAD MET Harold back in September, when Cleo
had finally arranged a first visit.

"*New Jersey,*" Alexander had said to her the first time they'd
driven to Harold's house. "You want me to learn the secrets of
the universe in *New Jersey.*"

"You've got a real streak of snobbism, did anyone tell you
that?"

There had been many surprises that day, most of them in
the need he had felt. But Harold himself had been the main
surprise. Cleo had told Alexander that Harold was over fifty,
but he looked no older than thirty-five, a throwback to the
sixties in old blue jeans and a denim shirt, wire-framed glasses
sliding forward on his sharp, long nose. Harold had shiny black
hair, an angular face, and an unusually tall, thin body. He
walked with a definite bounce in his step. A bright green metal
parakeet was pinned to the brim of his red felt hat.

Their first meeting hadn't gone very well.

"What'd you expect?" Harold had asked him as they stood
in his large, bright kitchen. "White hair? White beard? Long
robes? Mr. Wizard?"

"I don't know what I expected," Alexander had told him,
looking down.

"You don't, huh?"

"I guess not."

Then Harold had looked at him grimly, with exquisite condescension. "So what do you do?" he had asked him.

"Cleo didn't tell you?"

"Sometimes I'll ask things you know I know."

"You like testing people?"

"Sometimes."

"Why?"

"Sometimes I need to."

"Fine."

"I like doing things my way."

"Fine," Alexander had said again, but he had looked over at Cleo. Somehow, he had not expected that he would have to prove himself.

Harold had pushed his glasses up on his nose. "So," he had said. "I assume that you're a twenty-two?"

"Cleo told you that?"

"Well, actually no, I just assumed it. Cleo only sleeps with twenty-twos."

"Harold!" Cleo had shrieked.

Alexander had looked at the ground. Harold had waited a long moment. "This isn't a game, you know," he had said. "And it's not some lab experiment to write notes to. We are talking about a way to understand the entire universe. All its nooks and crannies. All its great, fantastic parts. If I let you stay here, you'll have to want to learn these things more than you've ever wanted anything in your life. If I let you stay, you'll have to want to understand me, too. Sometimes you'll think I'm a sham, but I'm not. Sometimes you'll think I'm cynical, but I can't be, and you can't afford to be, either. There's a truth here. You'd have to be deserving. You'd have to clean yourself up to do this stuff. You'd have to be in a state of grace."

"This is New Jersey."

"Don't be a smart-ass."

They had glared at each other like old enemies.

"Cleo told me you needed some help."

"That all depends," Harold had said.

"Why don't you tell him about your angel, doll?" Cleo had quickly said.

"He has an angel?" Harold had said. "Do you really have an angel, kid?" And then everything had changed, because in a sense Alexander's angel became his résumé with Harold, his ticket of admission. It obviously hadn't impressed Harold that Alexander was a physicist. It obviously hadn't mattered that he had won prizes or that he'd just been published in *Nature* or that he'd been in the *New York Times*. All that had mattered to Harold was that Alexander had dreamed of an angel who would touch him when he deserved to be touched. That was the dream of alchemy, and Harold had recognized it.

"And how long have you been dreaming of her?" Harold had asked with a sudden, quite moving sweetness.

"All my life," Alexander had said. "Well, at least since I was a boy."

"You're very lucky," Harold had said, and then he had looked at Cleo and nodded and grinned, and Alexander had sensed Harold's excitement for the first time.

Harold had turned to face him. "I've been looking for someone to help me for years."

"You'll teach me, then?" Alexander had asked.

"It's too soon to say."

"But the angel—"

"The angel is great," Harold had told him simply. "But there's more to it than that."

"More?" Alexander had asked.

"We'll have to see," Harold had said.

And Alexander had been hooked.

THAT SAME WEEK he'd met Harold, Alexander had given his lecture. Biner had lined up some interviews, several of which Alexander had done. The article had been published the following week. More job offers had come, and then the inevitable backlash. The Harvard group, especially, had weighed in with questions and complaints. Alexander had bought a phone machine and hidden behind it. He had been tempted to stay and defend his work, but the future became more compelling. Biner, of course, had been outraged, threatening Alexander every way he could. But the only leverage Biner had was the office at Wilson, and that had been no real leverage at all. Alexander's horizon had simply shifted, like a slide in a vast projection, and the crucial landmarks of his life no longer had much meaning.

Harold had remained alternately wary and enthusiastic, and Alexander had had to come back to New Jersey twice more before he had talked Harold into letting him stay. By then, of course, he'd completely lost sight of whatever doubts he'd had himself.

CLEO AND HE slipped into the countryside, acres of farmland stretching out before them. The snow had covered everything. Freed of their colors and their detail, the silos and houses in the distance seemed like geometric shapes. They were cylinders, rectangles, boxes, bars. They looked like children's building blocks. Alexander remembered how his schoolmates had stacked those blocks into towers and tunnels, while he had used them to learn about the laws of plane geometry. He had always been different, he thought now, and he was going to be different again. For the first time that morning, he felt the tug of excitement that he'd hoped he would feel.

"We're almost there," Cleo said.

"I know."

He leaned over to her, and kissed her neck.

"You shook it off?" she said.

"What?"

"The funk."

He smiled. "Yes. I shook it off," he said.

When they entered the driveway, the wheels turned up the pebbles that lined the road, spraying flecks of gray against the snow.

The house, which was low and flat, seemed even uglier than it had the first three times. It looked like an airport hangar. The windows seemed filthy. The mailbox was askew. Alexander felt happy at the sight of these imperfections. They made him feel there was something less than holy about Harold.

Cleo parked the car in the driveway. "Ready?" she said.

"I'm ready."

He had brought three suitcases. Cleo carried one of them. He wondered if he had packed enough clothes. He wondered how long he was going to stay, and how he was going to handle the mechanics of his life.

"Come on," Cleo said. "Harold told me last night that we should go around to the back door."

"You talked to him last night?"

"Yes."

"Well, what did he say?"

Cleo smiled. "He said that we should go around to the back door."

"Why didn't he call me?"

"I don't know. He called me."

"Sorry," Alexander said.

"Don't be nervous."

"Sorry."

They walked to the back and knocked and waited. Alexander looked out at the vacant fields. It was colder here in the country, and the air smelled of snow.

"It's going to be great," Cleo said to him, reading his thoughts again. "Didn't I tell you?"

"Yes. You told me." He kissed her again.

"Harold!" she called out. "Come on, Harold! We're freezing our buns off out here!"

They waited for many minutes, breath clouds forming every time they spoke.

Finally Harold appeared at the door. He was still wearing his blue jeans and work shirt and the improbable hat with the parrot pin.

"You made it!" he said. "Come in, come in." He was smiling, and his smile seemed genuine.

He led them into the house, walking through the kitchen, which Alexander had seen before, to the dining room and the living room, which he had not. The house seemed huge, much too huge for two people, let alone for one. There was virtually no furniture in the downstairs rooms, which tumbled after each other like empty railroad cars.

"No doubt," Harold said, "you'll want to see where you'll be staying. I made up the bed this morning. I hope it's okay."

Cleo smiled encouragingly.

"Great," Alexander said. He felt eager but wanted to keep up his guard. There was no way to know how to read Harold's mood.

They took the stairs in single file, Cleo behind Harold, Alexander behind her. The bedroom where he would sleep was at the end of the upstairs hall. Shaped like an L, it had a high four-poster bed, a small wooden dresser, and a large wooden bookshelf. Around the corner, hidden from the entrance, was a long work desk before a small paned window. There was an old red leather desk chair and a tarnished brass lamp. The floors were bare wood, except for a small blue oval throw rug on one side of the bed. The room nearly echoed with Alexander's footsteps, and the walls were white and bare. Instantly, he loved the room's simplicity, its anonymity. He loved its freedom from any past. Not even a mirror hung over the dresser.

There was no mirror in the bathroom either, and that struck Alexander as strange. Hanging over the sink instead was an old black-and-white photograph of Harold. In the photograph, Harold had one hand over his mouth in mock surprise and was gesturing antically with the other to a point outside the frame, just beyond the photographer. There was something in the picture that made Alexander want to turn around to see what was behind him.

"*Why* aren't there any mirrors?" Harold said when Alexander returned. "Because there are other aspects of yourself that are more important to study. Purity is important here. You're trying to make the most perfect metal. You've got to make yourself perfect, too. Ego's out. No mirrors. Of course, shaving will seem a little tricky at first. But you can always grow a beard."

Alexander laughed, but he saw that Harold wasn't kidding. In his mind, he could hear Sam laughing. He could hear Sam saying, "Idiots!" He could hear Sam saying, "Didn't I tell you?" He could hear himself saying, "Yes, Dad, yes."

The power of his father's voice grew stronger inside his mind. But he told himself that he shouldn't be thrown by anything Harold said today. He told himself that all he would learn today was the scope of the experiment—the parameters of the problem. Later, he figured, when he was alone, he could study those parameters and think about the different ways that he could form an approach, or decide if it was better not to take on the problem at all. For now, it was enough that he absorb the information.

"It's a little cold for me to show you the grounds today," Harold was saying. "But there is a greenhouse, where we'll do some work. And there are acres of land that you'll come to know. And then there's the pond, of course." He pointed out the window. In the distance, Alexander could see a small oval pond that sat like a gray disk in the flat white field.

He couldn't help thinking how much Linda would love the place. He could see her rushing out to the pond despite the cold and the snow. But the past, he told himself, was only a prelude now, the means for bringing him to this point. If alchemy was truly the Touch, then all the things he had ever done in the effort to make himself happy were just pages of crossed-out computations, discarded approaches to some difficult equation.

Following Harold and Cleo downstairs, Alexander stopped at the door to the basement, looking at a small iron dragon with a sword in its hand that was fixed to the wall beside it.

"Long-standing tradition," Harold explained. "Supposedly he guards against anyone who would enter with the wrong intention."

Alexander smiled politely and stepped into the room. He thought about his mother, and the crystal rings on her fingers, and the candle she had bought him, and her evident belief that such charms and totems could bring on the needed magic. He was not sorry that she had left again. He was glad neither parent could see him now, being told by a man with a straight face that a silly piece of iron had some power over things.

"So this is where the work gets done," Harold said, and Alexander looked around and finally felt himself relax. He was drawn to the order and the neatness of the place.

Alembics and crucibles and flasks lined one long, low shelf. Another was lined with glass canning jars that were filled with flowers in clear liquid and neatly labeled by date. Shelves above the tables held funnels, stirrers, spoons, brushes, stoppers, and sieves. There was an entire long wall of wooden drawers as well, apparently for ingredients. Antimony was at the upper left corner, and zinc was in the lower right. Alexander stood in the center of the room and took it all in and beamed. "This is amazing," he said hoarsely.

Harold smiled indulgently. "Every afternoon, you'll clean the lab," he said. "You'll wash the beakers and alembics, and you'll put the ingredients away. At night, I'll cook, because I like to cook. At breakfast and lunch, you'll cook, because I do my best work in the morning."

"I don't cook," Alexander said. "I mean, I don't cook very well."

"You'll learn, then," Harold told him.

Alexander nodded.

"By now," Harold said, "you've probably read enough to know that the substance I'm transmuting into gold is referred to as the Prime Matter."

"Yes."

"Well, this is the first rule. You will never touch my Prime Matter unless I specifically tell you you can. To touch someone else's Prime Matter is like trying to raise someone else's child. Do you understand?"

"I understand."

"Someday, if you learn what you're supposed to learn, you'll gather your own Prime Matter. But you'll need my help in finding it, and you won't start looking until I tell you to. Do you understand that, too?"

"Yes."

"Good," Harold said. "Then let's have tea and cookies."

THEY SAT IN the kitchen, a cozy place that was decorated with old blue and white tiles. Harold sang while he made the tea, crooning like Bing Crosby. "Summertiiiime, boobooboo, and the living is eeeeasy . . ."

Alexander laughed.

Harold ate six chocolate chip cookies, grinning like an un-watched child. The sun came in the windows, but the winter light was thin. Alexander's hands felt cold. He tried to warm them on the mug of tea that Harold had placed before him.

"Excited?" Harold asked him.

"Yes."

"Scared?" Harold asked him.

"Terrified."

Cleo touched Harold's shoulder. "You're going to be nice to him, right?" she said.

"Don't you have to get back to the city?"

They talked about one of her clients, someone whom Harold had known in college.

"Where'd you go to school?" Alexander asked him.

"State," he said ambiguously. He went on talking to Cleo, and Alexander clutched his mug and sipped his tea and noticed that the pattern on the curtains over the kitchen sink looked like one of the wave patterns he had studied years ago in his work. He felt worried and ignored now, and jealous of the easy way that Cleo and Harold were speaking. From time to time, Harold looked at him, but Alexander didn't know if Harold was being hostile or being shy.

The words that they were saying began to fade from words into sounds.

ALEXANDER WALKED Cleo to the car that night after dinner. They stood, embracing, under a cloudy, white night sky.

"You'll be fine," she told him.

"I don't think he likes me."

"Of course he does. He let you come, didn't he?"

"I don't want you to go," he said. He held her.

"You're just scared," she said. "You've just got to relax."

He noticed that she was smiling. "What's so funny?" he asked her.

"Nothing."

"Something's making you smile," he said.

"It's just how new you are to all this."

It made him think of Linda, how she had teased him the morning after he'd met Alice, the morning he'd been so hung over.

Alexander wondered why women always seemed to enjoy it so much when he was afraid or confused.

Cleo pulled on her gloves. "I gotta go," she said. "I'm freezing."

"You're coming back out this weekend, though, right?"

"Of course," she said. "I told you." She tugged on his scarf. "You think I'd strand you out here all alone?"

They kissed for quite a long time, standing in the snowfall.

"Don't worry," she whispered when they stopped. He found that he didn't want to let go.

He stood in the snowy driveway, watching as the red lights of her car disappeared.

HE WAS RELIEVED, that night, to dream about his angel. Dreaming of her made him feel more sure. It made him feel less deserted.

"I know that you're not going to touch me now," Alexander said to her.

The angel hovered above him. "How?" she asked him. "How do you know that?"

"I just know," he said. "I'm not ready yet, right? I'm only starting out again."

She banked her wings at a deep angle and flew in perfect circles.

ALEXANDER WOKE in the morning at ten o'clock and panicked. Harold hadn't told him to be up by any particular hour, but Alexander sensed that he had already made his first mistake.

He showered quickly and took out his razor and his shaving cream before he remembered that there was no mirror. The picture of Harold above the sink stared back at him mockingly. He tested the stubble on his face and decided to let it go. He dressed as quickly as he could, and then hurried down the stairs.

.   .   .

HAROLD WAS SITTING at the kitchen table as if he'd known at exactly what moment Alexander would rush into the room.

"Eggs?" Harold said.

"Did I oversleep?"

"Yes," Harold said to him. "Scrambled?"

"Sure. Great. I'm sorry I overslept."

"You won't do it again," Harold said cheerfully. He stood up and smiled and went to the refrigerator. "There's coffee on the counter," he said over his shoulder.

Alexander looked at him nervously.

"Go ahead," Harold said. "There's a mug in the cabinet."

Alexander found the mug in the third cabinet he opened. He was surprised that the others were filled with fancy china and crystal glasses. "You entertain a lot?" he asked lightly.

There was silence, and Alexander almost winced. Cleo could have gotten away with that question, he thought. Nothing was coming naturally. But then Harold turned around and grinned. "No," he said. "Hardly." He beat the eggs in a yellow bowl. "My parents did, though. This was their house. They're both dead now. They died years ago."

"I'm sorry," Alexander said.

"Me too." Harold put a slab of butter into a skillet on the stove. The butter hissed and melted.

"Did they know about the alchemy?"

"Don't call it that."

"What?"

"Don't call it alchemy. It's not done. Just call it the Work."

"The Work."

"And don't call me an alchemist. I'm called an Adept. Accent on the first syllable."

"Am I called an Adept too?"

"Hardly." Harold laughed, but not unkindly. "You're what's

known as a Seeker," he said. "When you figure out what the Prime Matter is, that's when you're called an Adept. Give me a refill, will you?" Harold pointed to his cup.

Alexander stood up and poured the coffee. "So did they know about the Work?" he asked.

"My parents? No," Harold said. "I started after they died."

"How old were you?" Alexander asked.

"About your age," Harold said.

"What had you done before then?"

"Worked for my parents. They were farmers here."

"Really?"

"Really."

Alexander sipped his coffee, momentarily thrilled that Harold had actually answered his questions.

Harold put a plate of eggs before him. "In a way," he said, "the Work is quite a bit like farming. There is planting, sort of, and harvesting, and you need to respect the nature of things."

"The nature of things," Alexander repeated.

"To know what things are. To know what *you* are. I feel a song coming on," Harold said.

Alexander smiled, relieved.

"I meant what I said back when I first met you, though," Harold said. "You do have to be in a state of grace."

Alexander took a bite of his eggs. Harold had mentioned grace before. Alexander had no idea what Harold meant by it. He felt stupid and somehow unprepared. "So what do I do today?" he asked.

Harold stared at him blankly for a moment, then pushed his glasses up on his nose. "Well," he said, "first you get groceries."

"Groceries," Alexander repeated.

"Yes. Groceries. We need to eat. I've left a list and the number. Tell them you're calling for me. They know me. And feel free to add anything you'd like."

"Okay. They deliver?"

"The grocery store, the laundry, and the drugstore all deliver," Harold said. "Going to town wastes time. I get the local paper, too, though to be honest I don't think I've read it all year."

"Fine," Alexander said. "I'll call."

"Don't look so serious. This isn't some sort of cosmic test. This isn't some metaphysical lesson. We just happen to need groceries."

"Okay."

"We'll skip lunch today," Harold said. "From now on, you will wake up at six forty-five every morning. And I mean *every* morning. You may as well get used to it. In the spring, it will be six—that is, if I let you gather the dew."

"What dew?"

"We'll get to that later."

"Sorry."

"I'm not running a boardinghouse. I don't cook breakfast. That's your job now. You've got to earn your keep."

"I'm *sorry*," Alexander said.

Harold glared at him, then seemed to soften. "Look, kid," he said. "It's been years since I've shared this place, you know? We'll just have to work these things out, I guess."

"I'm glad I'm here," Alexander said. "Don't worry. Tell me what I should do today. After I call for the groceries, I mean."

Harold sighed, then put his fork down. "You really want to learn all this stuff?" he said. "You're really not just looking for a little sojourn in the country?"

"Haven't we been all through this?" Alexander said. "Remember about my angel?"

"Okay," Harold said. "Well, where do I start?"

2

THE LESSONS

THE EMERALD TABLET was said to be the oldest existing document about alchemy.

It is true without lie, certain and most veritable, that that which is below is like that which is above and that that which is above is like that which is below, to perpetrate the miracles of one thing.

It had been found on a stone in Egypt, carved in hieroglyphics.

And as all things have been, and come from One by the meditation of One; thus all things have been born from this single thing by adaptation.

In it, the secrets of alchemy were hidden by riddles and metaphors.

The sun is its father, the moon its mother.

It was supposed to have been written by Hermes Trismegistus, the Egyptian god who ruled alchemy and whose name was responsible for the term *hermetically sealed*.

The wind carried it in his belly. The Earth is its nurse. The father of all the perfection of all the world is here.

It was the one text that all alchemists were supposed to begin and end with.

With this knowledge alone you may work miracles.

It went on like that for forty or fifty more lines. Alexander sat at his desk that first long afternoon and learned about the tablet's origin by reading the introduction in the text that Harold had given him. He didn't learn what the tablet meant, though. He wondered what the "it" was that the wind was supposed to carry. He worried that the "One" that all things came from was supposed to be God.

He read the words again and again, and looked out at the snowy fields, and wanted to talk to Cleo, and waited for Harold to call him or for something else to happen.

HE DIDN'T HEAR from Harold until five o'clock. By then, Alexander was exhausted from thinking, and frustrated by the subject. The text was deceptively simple. All he'd figured out was that the tablet was a mystery and that he didn't know enough yet to unravel its clues.

"Kid?" Harold called up to him, and Alexander nearly ran down the stairs.

Harold was eating another cookie. "*This* is my weakness," he said with mock despair. "*This* is my imperfection. Want one?"

"I couldn't deprive you."

"Generous soul."

"Look, I read it," Alexander said. "It's really great. What the hell does it mean?"

Harold eyed him with mock suspicion. "Come with me," he said. "It's lab time now. I'm done, and I want you to clean."

THE SINK IN the basement was filled with glass vials and beakers, and Harold gave Alexander a brush to clean them with, and then showed him where everything went. The lab had a musty odor that Alexander found enticing. He was careful and efficient as he put the things away. He had taken chemistry classes before, and he felt more at home with this sort of work than he had reading the tablet.

He was cleaning off the long metal center table when Harold approached him, carrying a large clay vessel as if it held frankincense or myrrh. Harold placed the vessel on the table and lifted its lid. Inside was a black mossy substance that smelled of rich, fresh earth.

"This is it," Harold said to him. "This is my Prime Matter."

"This is it?"

"This is it."

"This is what I don't touch, right?"

Harold smiled. "That's right."

"I thought the Prime Matter would be a metal," Alexander said. "Tin or lead or something. Isn't that the whole point? To change base metals into gold?"

"The whole point is to make gold," Harold said, "from something that comes from the earth. I use plants."

"Plants?"

"Plants," Harold said. "Sometimes flowers, too. Come on. Finish up here and we'll have an early dinner."

THE GROCERIES CAME at six. Alexander answered the door while Harold was cooking dinner. The icy air surprised him.

"Who are you?" the delivery man asked.

"I'm staying with Harold," Alexander said.

"For how long?"

"For a long time," Alexander said, and shivered.

"SO LOOK, I did read it," Alexander told Harold again when they finally sat down to dinner.

"Good. How many times?"

"I don't know. Probably forty."

"Good. Do you know it?"

"What do you mean?"

"Recite it."

"Recite it?"

"Yes."

"I can't."

Harold frowned. "Learn to," he said, and sipped his water.

"All right. I'll learn to," Alexander said.

"Don't you remember any of it?"

"I remember the part about the moon being its mother and the sun being its father."

"Yes," Harold said warmly. "That's a beautiful line."

"What's the 'it'?" Alexander asked. "Is the 'it' the Prime Matter?"

Harold said nothing.

"What's the 'One'?" Alexander asked. "Am I supposed to believe in God?"

Harold smiled. There was a long silence.

"You're not going to be inscrutable, are you?" Alexander asked him.

Harold laughed. "That depends on you," he said.

IN THE MORNING, Alexander woke at six-thirty, tiptoed downstairs, and took a spoon from the kitchen drawer. Upstairs, he showered and shaved, using the spoon as a mirror and feeling no guilt.

The kitchen was still empty when Alexander returned to it, but he could hear Harold in the basement below. Alexander took four eggs and beat them in the bowl that Harold had used the day before. He put butter in the skillet and called to Harold when the eggs were almost done. He was going to give this his best shot, he thought, and see how far that would take him.

"Good job," Harold said when Alexander served him.

"So what do I do today?" he asked.

"Today," Harold said, "I want you to read the Emerald Tablet."

"I've already read it."

Harold laughed.

"Let me guess," Alexander said. "You want me to read it again."

Harold looked at him. "Listen," he said. "Out of repetition, magic is sometimes forced to rise."

.   .   .

It is true without lie, certain and most veritable, that that which
is below is like that which is above and that that which is above
is like that which is below, to perpetrate the miracles of one thing.

What were the miracles? What was the one thing? Shouldn't
it be the Prime Matter?

He would take this text apart, he told himself: word by word
if necessary. He had done the same for equations that were
fifteen pages long. How could this be more difficult?

It is true without lie, certain and most veritable . . .

What could that first phrase mean, though, other than what it
appeared to mean? It meant that the text that would follow was
true: *really* true. So, swell, Alexander thought. He read on:

. . . that that which is below is like that which is above . . .

It could mean that the heavens were the same as the earth, that
what happened in the sky was like what happened on the
ground. It could be more specific, though: that what happened
at the bottom of some crucible in some experiment would happen at its surface as well. Or it could be more metaphoric: that
what was above was the grace that Harold kept talking about.
Alexander realized that above and below could be in the soul,
the mind, the heart, the lab, the crucible, or the universe.

The more that he thought about it, the more the world
seemed to dissolve into opposites, above and below, high forms
and low forms, perfection and dissipation.

. . . that that which is below is like that which is above.

Well, big deal, Alexander thought. The frustration he felt
was palpable, the anger at Harold for being no help.

He longed for numbers instead of words, a language that he could understand, where symbols had fixed meanings.

HOURS LATER, he put the text aside and tore a page from the notebook that Harold had left for him.

December 16

Dear Dad:

You may have been right. The flake quotient out here approaches infinity. I wish I could tell you what I've been doing, but I don't have the faintest idea.

Alexander stopped writing and read what he had just written and put his head down on his arms. He felt embarrassed and worried. He was not accustomed to failing at new lessons, or with new teachers. He didn't want to go back, but he didn't know if he was going to have the stomach for going forward.

He tore the page from the notebook and began again:

December 16

Dear Dad:

No, I'm not living some weird, phoneless existence here. Harold does have a phone—he's got a dishwasher, too—but I'd feel funny about running up his bill, and frankly I'd rather write to you than call because if you're going to keep telling me I'm an idiot, then I'd rather read it than hear it.

It's very pretty here—very *rural*. I wish I could say that you'd love it here, but I'm not really sure you would. Lots of silence and open spaces.

Harold's a great guy, Dad—not at all what you'd expect. It's been a long time since I've had to depend on anyone else in order to learn something. That's making me feel frustrated, but I don't mind it too much. I keep thinking it's good for me.

Anyway, I'm well, and I hope you'll write back.

Now, set up the chessboard. You play white. I'll assume your usual opening. I play my king's pawn as usual too. Your move, Dad. Write back.

Love,
A.

Alexander sealed the letter and went downstairs to the kitchen. It was still only ten in the morning, and Harold, as usual, was working in the lab. Alexander toyed with the idea of simply walking in on him. Maybe, he thought, that was what Harold wanted: some sign of passionate curiosity on his part. Every teacher he'd ever had had needed to be convinced. "Tell me what the hell it means!" Alexander could shout. Instinct overruled the impulse. He looked for stamps and found them in the kitchen drawer where he'd seen Harold put the bill for the groceries. He took a stamp and placed it on the letter. He put on his coat and went outside. It was warmer than it had been all week, and the snow was finally melting. Down the driveway, Alexander put the letter in the mailbox and raised the small red flag.

In the distance, in every direction, he could not see one thing move.

Alexander thought about watching Cleo's car recede, and he realized with relief that he might see her in a few days. He felt almost desperate to talk with her, or with anyone who knew him.

AT DINNER, Alexander recited the Emerald Tablet to Harold. Harold nodded and asked him to recite it again.

"Can't you tell me what it means?" Alexander asked him.

Harold sipped his wine. "I really don't think I should," he said. "I'm pretty sure it's one of the things you'll have to figure out for yourself."

Alexander nodded. "Could you give me a hint at least?" he asked.

"The hints are all around you," Harold said. "Especially in spring."

"This is winter," Alexander said.

"Not forever."

"Great."

"Ask me other things," Harold said, "things that I can answer."

So Alexander cleared the dishes and poured out the coffee and framed his questions.

He asked Harold what he was living on, how it was that he could afford not to have some kind of job. Harold smiled and explained that the farm had once been four hundred acres, and that whenever he'd needed money, he'd simply sold a small piece of it off.

Alexander asked Harold who'd taken the photograph of him—the one that was hanging over the bathroom sink upstairs.

"Sylvie," Harold said quietly. "Her name was Sylvie. She was my guide to the Prime Matter."

"Your guide?"

"She helped me choose it."

"Do all Adepts have guides?"

"It's common," Harold said. "It's not essential, though."

"Is that what Cleo's supposed to be?"

"What?" Harold said.

"A guide."

"We'll see."

"How will we see?"

"We'll see," Harold said.

"Were you in love with Sylvie?"

"Yes."

"What happened to her?"

"She left," Harold said.

"I can see that. Why did she leave?"

Harold sighed. "Ask me something else," he said.

So Alexander asked him what the Prime Matter really was.

"Kid," Harold said, "that's the ninety-six-billion-dollar question."

"Well, what's it made of?" Alexander asked.

Then Harold told him how different Adepts had always used different methods, but how his method involved working with earth and plants. Technically, his Prime Matter was just soil, he said, just dirt, and anyone with a shovel could go out whenever he wanted to and grab a clump of it. But dawn, Harold pointed out, can look like dusk. Twelve noon and twelve midnight are the same on a clock. The real Prime Matter may have looked like an average lump of earth, but it was made special by the way it was collected, by the position of the planets in the heavens, by the time of day, by the clearness of the weather, and, of course, by the purity and grace of the Adept.

Sylvie had helped Harold find his Prime Matter, he said: she had gone to the fields at midnight, seeing visions of spheres and angels that had told her where the right place was. For nearly twenty years, Harold said, the one lump of earth she'd gathered had been distilled and purified, enriched with dew and ground-up spring plants, left to darken in the sun, heated with special fire. The idea, Harold explained, was to get the Prime Matter to a state called Absolute Black, where all the imperfections were gone and it crumbled like a powder. Then it would be mixed with other things to form what was known as the First Perfection.

"And is there a Second Perfection?" Alexander asked.

"Yes."

"And a third?"

"No, the Second Perfection is it," Harold said. "The Second Perfection is the Philosopher's Stone. With that, you've got the Elixir, and with that you can make the gold."

"And where are you in all this?"

Harold smiled. "I think I'm about a year away from the First Perfection. But it all depends on how good the plants are this spring. The *Farmer's Almanac* says it'll be a good rich year, but they've been wrong before."

Alexander nodded and tried to appear casual. "Twenty years," he said, "and you're not even done with the first part of the thing?"

"Yes," Harold said.

"And I'm supposed to start from the beginning by myself?"

"If you worked on my Prime Matter, the end product would have no real meaning for you."

Alexander thought a moment. "Well, when will I get to find my own Prime Matter?" he asked.

Harold laughed. "What do you think the Prime Matter is?"

"Didn't you just tell me?"

"No."

"But—"

"When you know what the Prime Matter is—what it means—that's when you can find it."

"Why does the whole thing take so long?"

Harold laughed again. "You in some kind of rush?" he asked.

"I just wondered," Alexander said.

"It's simple," Harold told him. "You do the same thing again and again, and eventually something extraordinary happens."

Alexander nodded and sipped his coffee, remembering old chemistry classes, and thinking that he would find shortcuts.

"Out of repetition," Harold said for the second time that day, "magic is sometimes forced to rise."

"Why did you let me come here?"

"Kid," Harold said, and his smile was irresistible. "I think I needed you."

ALL WEEK LONG, Alexander read the Emerald Tablet. Sometimes he plotted methods for making gold by other, quicker means, but other times he was drawn in by the mystique of what he was learning. All week long, Harold worked in his lab alone. But day by day, he placed new books on Alexander's shelf, books with different interpretations of what the Emerald Tablet meant.

The first one Alexander opened had an epigraph that stunned him:

"Angelus Doce Mihi Jus."

Angel, teach me right.

At night, he stayed up late, skimming through the pages of the texts for other signs. It was ridiculous to think that he would spend twenty years doing what could have been done, with an atom smasher, in a single afternoon. But despite that clear conviction, and despite the persistence of Sam's laughter in his mind, the fact was that in three nights of reading, he discovered nearly a dozen Adepts who had written about their angels, and he found sketches and engravings of annunciation scenes in which there were angels blowing their trumpets and whispering their secrets. The coincidences simply seemed too great to be coincidences.

It shocked him that he had spent his whole life reading books and learning theories, but that all along this whole world had existed completely apart from him. It shocked him that he might never have known about it if not for Cleo. And then he thought: No, if not for Alice. Without Alice, he would not be here. He couldn't help wondering where she had gone.

So he tried to keep his impatience at bay, and he looked for pictures of angels, and he thought about his mother, and he wondered if what she had felt when she'd first left was the same sense of nervous awe.

CLEO DIDN'T CALL until Friday morning, and by then his doubt and hope had crossed paths so many times that they had almost seemed to form a new emotion in him. The telephone ringing was an utterly shocking, utterly welcome sound.

She would take the train out the next evening, she said.

It didn't seem plausible to him that he had seen her only a week before. Cleo's voice sounded as strange and somehow magical as his angel's. He felt almost rescued, rewarded for his patience.

"It's okay that she's coming?" he asked Harold when he hung up the phone.

Harold shrugged and smiled, and Alexander decided not to press his luck. He wanted to have sex with Cleo as much as he could recall ever wanting anything. He wanted to feel safe. He wanted to do something physical. For a week, he had been thinking about angels and reading words that were x's and y's in a vast equation he didn't know how to solve. He was aching to do something that wouldn't be open to different interpretations.

ON SATURDAY AT DUSK, he took Harold's old Volvo and drove slowly through the town to the station, feeling as if it were the first time that he'd ever driven a car.

Tacky wreaths and Christmas lights were strung up inside the depot, but the doors were open, and it was cold.

Alexander stood on the platform, his head bowed against the cold wind. It was wonderful to feel the wind and to wait for someone so full of life who was coming there for him.

When Cleo arrived, he nearly ran with her back to the parking lot.

IN THE CAR, he kissed her before she could say anything, pressing her hard against the passenger door. Her gloved fingers made five parallel tracks in the frost of the car's front window.

"So you missed me," she said when she finally caught her breath.

"I missed you," he said, and he kissed her again.

"It's freezing in here," she told him.

Alexander turned on the engine and let it idle. "You have no idea," he said to her.

"What?"

"How strange this week has been."

Cleo laughed. "You're just not used to it yet," she said.

"I have to shave looking into a spoon. I have to cook. I have to read the same thing over and over. I keep finding more angels, but Harold never tells me what anything means."

"It's probably good for you," Cleo said. She lit a Salem and blew out the match. She put a hand on his knee. "Don't worry, doll," she said. "I'm here now."

DINNER WAS LIVELY. Cleo read Harold's palm, and Harold wouldn't stop teasing her. When it came to palm reading, Harold was every bit as skeptical as Sam had been about alchemy. Alexander was amused and delighted to find Harold so discriminating. He realized he'd always assumed that people who bought one kind of occultish science would also buy all the others. He felt the smugness of losing a bias, the thrill of defeating a prejudice.

Cleo held her ground with Harold, flirting and teasing back.

Just as he had the week before, Alexander marveled at the way she seemed to fit in here.

Something was starting to nag at him, though. He was trying to reconcile the jokes and the boisterous laughter with the need for grace and purity that Harold had been describing all week.

He wondered what a guide in alchemy really did, and how he was going to learn whether Cleo was meant to be his guide. Maybe if she was that, he thought, it would make sense for her to be here.

IN BED THAT NIGHT, he had to cover her mouth with his hand to keep her from shouting when she came.

HE WOKE IN the morning to a frigid, bright day. Cleo was standing at the foot of the bed, holding a cup of coffee. For a moment, he thought she was Linda, and he could picture her terry robe, and he could picture the loving, mocking look that had always ended his nightmares. Cleo handed him the coffee, kissed him good morning, and settled in beside him. "Okay, doll," she said. "Tell me everything."

He shook off the thought of Linda and smiled and sipped the coffee, basking in Cleo's protection. "Well," he began, "to start with, do you know that this thing is supposed to take twenty years?"

Cleo laughed. "That's just how long it's taking him."

"Yeah, well, I keep telling myself that. But still—"

"That's not important, doll," Cleo said. "What's next?"

"Well, do you know what the Emerald Tablet is?"

"Sure," she said. "That's the main text, right?"

"Well, I'm not really sure I *get* it."

Cleo smiled. She lit a cigarette and propped up some pillows behind her in bed.

"I don't think you should smoke in here," Alexander said.

"No, it's okay," Cleo said. She blew out the match with a long, confident line of smoke.

"I don't think Harold would like it."

"Don't be so scared of him, doll," Cleo said. "You've got to show him you're not afraid. You've got to show him you know yourself. That's what this stuff is about, you know."

"I know," Alexander said. He envied her joy and her confidence, but he wished that she wasn't smoking.

"Now, what did you do all week?" she asked.

"I read the Emerald Tablet."

"And what didn't you understand?"

"The whole thing."

Cleo laughed, but warmly. "Well, why don't you ask Harold?" she said.

"I did. He wants me to figure it out for myself."

"Let's get some of his other books, then."

"I don't think he'd want us to."

"Let's get them anyway," she said.

"No. Harold—"

Cleo had started laughing again, and this time her laughter seemed less kind.

"What is it?" Alexander said.

"Doll," she said. "He's not the Pope, you know."

THEY SPENT MOST of the day outside. They went for a long walk, and built a snowman, and had a vigorous snowball fight. Her energy astonished him, her missionary zest. Every doubt he expressed, every question, seemed to give her deeper pleasure. She was his savior, and he was her convert, and yet for all her fervor, he knew there was nothing she said that would really help him, nothing that he would be able to work with when she had left again. He would still have to read the texts, he thought. He would still have to solve the riddles, still have to figure out what the Prime Matter was. And when the day was done, he thought, and Cleo had gone back home, then he would still have to dream of an angel who would still refuse to touch him.

It occurred to him for the first time that there was something Cleo wanted from him. He knew that it couldn't just be the sex, and he realized that he didn't think it was love. He didn't know what it was, though, and he wasn't sure that he wanted to.

AT THREE O'CLOCK, they came back to the house, ruddy and cold, large chunks of snow stuck in their hair.

Harold stood at the stove in the kitchen, stirring some soup and singing show tunes. He looked up at their flushed faces and the snow melting off their boots, and Alexander felt silly and self-conscious.

"Have a good time?" Harold asked them. His tone of voice gave nothing away.

"He's such a city boy," Cleo said, laughing. "He's got such lousy aim."

Alexander smiled, embarrassed. "Do I get a lesson today?" he asked Harold.

Harold said, "If you want one, I guess."

"Hey, Harold," Cleo began. "Alexander says there's all this stuff he doesn't understand—"

Alexander shot her a lethal look, and she let her sentence trail off.

"He'll figure it out in time," Harold said, and Alexander felt a first, vital wave of gratitude.

"I DON'T THINK," Alexander said to Cleo after they'd finished their soup and Harold had gone back to the basement, "that what we're doing with each other qualifies as spiritual advancement."

"Our fucking is spiritual," Cleo said, and Alexander found himself looking around to make sure Harold hadn't heard her.

"He's not the Pope, you know," Cleo said.

"You said that already."

"You didn't hear me."

HE WAS ACTUALLY grateful when she left that evening. He stood on the platform and watched her train recede and felt both empty and free.

Just twenty-four hours before, he had wanted her here so intensely that the wanting had filled his whole mind. He suspected that he would want her again, but he needed to be more settled. He needed to know the rules of the game, he thought: to know whether she was some kind of trap, the tangible proof to Harold that he wouldn't be serious enough.

Bursts of laughter and children's cries sprang up all along the railroad tracks. On the platform, wives and children greeted husbands and fathers arriving from the city with last-minute Christmas gifts. Alexander recoiled from the noise and from all the commotion around him. What was it, he wondered, that these people wanted from their lives?

The thought made him feel so empty that he wished he hadn't thought it.

He hurried back to the car.

DRIVING THE ROAD to Harold's house, Alexander passed no other cars. The fields on either side of him were too dark to be visible. The moon was hidden by clouds, and there were no lights along the way.

For a moment, the whole world contracted to the patches of

road moving under his headlights: the straight white lines and the flat black road that didn't change from mile to mile. He panicked. He drove faster. What if he'd come the wrong way? he thought. Or what if the world inside these small lights was not as important as what was outside? He drove even more quickly. His heart raced. He was desperate to feel he was moving, to see something change, to be less afraid. And then in the distance he saw Harold's house, the lights shining brightly, warm and gold.

HAROLD WAS IN the kitchen. He was eating a piece of chocolate cake.

"You caught me," he said, and he held up his fork.

Alexander smiled and took off his coat. He didn't want to show his fear, or his sudden, aching gratitude.

"I gave it up for a whole year, once," Harold said.

"Gave what up?"

"The goodies. The sweets. I wanted to prove to myself that I could. I wanted to make sure that it wasn't a vice that was going to keep me impure."

"You talk a lot about purity," Alexander said.

"I guess."

Alexander filled the kettle with water. His heart was beating more slowly now, but he still didn't feel calm. "What do you mean when you say purity?" he asked. "I really don't think I understand."

Harold sighed. He gathered the last crumbs of cake from his plate. "Well, according to one school of thought," he said, "the real Work has to do with freeing the soul. See, the soul is like a child. It wants to be a grown-up, but it has to learn, eventually, that that doesn't mean just being like its parents. It has to learn that it can be anything, anything at all. In order to do that, it can't be tied down by lots of old rules and expectations. It has to make its own rules. It has to become free. Get it?"

"Yes," Alexander said. "I think so."

"Good."

"Harold, I may be blowing everything here. But I've got to tell you. The prospect of spending twenty years on this—"

"Don't get hung up on the time," Harold said. "If you're meant to do this, then the time will take care of itself. The soul comes first."

"The soul."

"You see, there are actually some very specific disciplines for freeing the soul. Nine of them, actually."

"Nine?"

"Nine."

"Like lessons?" Alexander asked.

"Sort of. More like thought problems. Or, better still, *feeling* problems. It's all about the soul, not the brain."

"Like what?"

"They're hard."

"Like what?"

"Okay," Harold said. "Well, the first one is to contemplate the fourth dimension."

"The fourth dimension?"

"You heard me."

"I know all about the fourth dimension," Alexander said.

"Do you."

"No, I *really* do," Alexander said. "The article I wrote—the research I did—it was all about dimensions. Ten dimensions. Two dimensions. I know all about dimensions. Really."

Harold pushed his chair back and smiled. "Ever been there?" he asked.

"Where?"

"Ever been in the fourth dimension?"

"No. Of course not. What do you mean?"

"Good," Harold said. "Then this should keep you busy."

ALEXANDER KNEW what the problem would be before he even started. The problem was that while he had done his most brilliant work in manipulating dimensions, those dimensions had only been numerical constructs, never physical places. He had made genius equations in ten dimensions that unified the great theories of science, but he was no more capable than Linda would have been of suggesting what those dimensions looked like. They had only been numbers.

Now, trying to imagine the actual world of the fourth dimension, Alexander felt both chastened and unequipped. He took out his notebook and drew a point, a line, a square, and a cube.

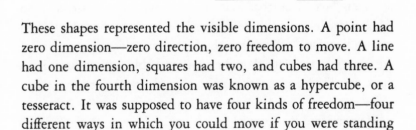

These shapes represented the visible dimensions. A point had zero dimension—zero direction, zero freedom to move. A line had one dimension, squares had two, and cubes had three. A cube in the fourth dimension was known as a hypercube, or a tesseract. It was supposed to have four kinds of freedom—four different ways in which you could move if you were standing around inside it.

In college, Alexander had known lots of budding mathematicians who had spent hours of their free time trying to picture tesseracts. Inevitably, they were the guys who couldn't form a simple sentence if you asked them how they were.

Now Alexander drew the shapes he had seen them draw so often, the shapes he'd sometimes played with in his mind, but had never managed to fix there. The first shape was a cube, drawn as a box inside a box.

The second shape was a tesseract: a cube, by analogy, inside a cube.

It was midnight. It was Christmas Eve. Alexander stared at the shapes he had just drawn in his notebook. The problem was that the cube didn't look a whole lot like a cube. It looked more like a picture frame, flat and two-dimensional. Of course, it was easy enough for Alexander to *imagine* the picture frame as a cube: all he had to do was imagine himself looking into an open box. But that was no help with the tesseract. To Alexander, it looked three-dimensional, just as the cube looked two-dimensional. Whatever the four-dimensional equivalent of an open box was, he thought, you probably had to have it in your mind's eye in order for the second drawing to make any sense at all.

He pondered the lines he had drawn and saw nothing in them that helped him, nothing that called up another world.

In the morning, he thought, he would try again. At least he was working on something that he almost understood.

He went to sleep hoping for dreams.

CHRISTMAS DAY passed without mention. All Alexander did during the week was think about the fourth dimension, and contemplate the tesseract, and strain to imagine its greater depth. On New Year's Eve, Alexander called Sam and was alarmed that there was no answer. Then he remembered that Sam had usually spent that evening with colleagues from school.

Alexander stood in the dark, cold kitchen. He had written to Sam more than two weeks ago, and hadn't heard a word from him yet. Harold had gone to bed early after drinking one glass of champagne. Alexander looked at the silent phone and thought about calling Linda, and then thought about calling Cleo, and then turned and went upstairs to bed. What he needed, he told himself, would not be found on a telephone line.

ON TUESDAY, which was the day after New Year's, Alexander checked the mail and found a note from Sam.

December 28

Dearest Ex:

No time to write. Grading midterms and frazzled. I'm glad you got there in one piece, glad you like Harold. He sounds interesting. Longer letter to follow. Just wanted to say that Linda's been hounded by the people at Wilson, so I gave her your address so she could forward some things to you. Made her swear up and down she wouldn't give them the address. She swore. King's knight to king's bishop three.

Love,
Dad

In the afternoon, a brown UPS truck arrived, and with it, a package from Linda.

Friday, December 29

A:

Here is a bunch of letters sent by Biner. He's been extremely intent about my getting them to you. Sam, after making me promise that I wouldn't catch a train and come out there and picket the lawn, gave me your address. I also promised him I wouldn't sell the address to Biner.

I hope you're well. I'm spending New Year's with my folks. Happy New Year.

Linda

Alexander imagined her composing and recomposing the note, trying to guess what he was feeling, trying to keep her anger back. He told himself not to think about it and opened the package from Biner.

December 18

Dear Mr. Simon:

I am enclosing the mail that has been piling up at the lab. By the time you receive this, I suspect there will be even more.

I gather from your roommate that she is your former roommate, but she assured me that she would find a way to forward these things to you.

As I told you some months ago, I don't know whether you've lost your mind or merely your sense of responsibility. I hope you find one or both soon. I'm not, as you may think, merely concerned about the reputation of this lab. It is still not too late for you to come forward and receive the praise *you* deserve, and sustain your *own* reputation. Please be in touch.

Wishing you the best for the holidays.

Bruce Biner

Alexander knew that if he had been Biner, he would have written the same kind of letter. But somehow all it did was make him want, that much more, to embrace the Work and to dream of the Touch. He took the stack of letters and threw them in the garbage. After a moment, he went back to retrieve the notes from Linda and Sam.

HE WAS GRATEFUL, that afternoon, to see that Harold had left a new book for him. It was called *Transcendental Physics*, and it had been written in 1878 by a scientist named Friedrich Zöllner. It was a book about, among other things, the nature of the fourth dimension, and he was happy to have been given a way to focus on it again.

Alexander knew that scientists had grappled for centuries with the notion of a fourth dimension. What he learned from the book was that in the nineteenth century, the idea had become particularly popular as a way to explain the existence of ghosts. Somehow, after two weeks of finding angels in his reading, Alexander didn't feel all that surprised by the coincidence.

In the book, Zöllner argued not only that spirits clearly existed, but that they did so in the fourth dimension, and that to see a ghost was to have a dimensional door swing open and shut. Zöllner described the experience much the way Alexander's old book, *Flatland*, had described the sight of a sphere passing through flat space. It was just as startling, just as absurd—and just as easy to understand when viewed from the proper perspective.

"Did Cleo tell you that I've got a ghost?" Alexander asked Harold that evening at dinner.

"Gee, I don't think so," Harold said.

"Then why did you give me Zöllner's book?"

"Well, spirits aren't only ghosts, you know. They're also

devils and angels. I was thinking about your angel. I don't know, I thought you'd get a kick out of it."

"A kick," Alexander said.

"Well, sure. But look," Harold said. "This is great. This is great. Do you really have a ghost?"

"Well, sort of. I don't really know."

"Boy," Harold said. "I've never seen a ghost. What the hell does it look like?"

"It was just a light."

"A light?"

"A lantern. Moving in circles. There was this stationmaster in North Carolina. He waved a lantern to stop a train. Supposedly it ran over him."

"What do you see?"

"I told you. A light. I only saw it once."

"When?"

"When I was eight. My mother took me."

"Wow," Harold said.

Alexander laughed.

Harold took off his glasses. "You know, kid," he said, "for someone who doesn't know what end is up yet, you get an awful lot of breaks."

AT BREAKFAST the next morning, Alexander brought Harold his drawing of the tesseract.

"What's that?" Harold said.

"A four-dimensional cube."

Harold shrugged. "Very nice," he said. "And?"

"You've never seen a tesseract?"

"Tesseract," Harold said. "Nice word."

"You've never seen one?"

"No."

"Then how do you know anything about the fourth dimension?"

"Kid," Harold said. "You may be taking this a bit too literally."

"You said to imagine it."

"Wait. I'll be back."

Alexander waited, looking out at the snow-covered driveway and feeling briefly superior.

Harold returned with another old book.

"Listen to this," he said, finding a dog-eared page and reading:

" 'When we look quietly at space, she shows us at once that she has infinite dimensions. And yet, both in magnitudes and dimensions, there is something artificial. . . . We must remember that this apprehension does not lie in the talking about it. It cannot be conveyed in description.' "

"Yeah?" Alexander said slowly.

"The point," Harold said, "is not to think of a four-dimensional body. It's not to think of a body at all. It's not even to *think*. You do this stuff with your heart, not your head. You've got to see yourself floating in space."

"Floating."

"You can do it, kid. I know you can."

"Floating?"

"Want a cookie?"

ALEXANDER BROUGHT the book upstairs. He reread the passage that Harold had quoted, and then he read further on:

That reality where magnitude and dimensions are not, is simple and about us. For passing thus on and on we lose ourselves, but find the clue again in the apprehension of the simplest acts of

human goodness, in the most rudimentary recognition of another
human soul wherein is neither magnitude nor dimension, and yet
all is real.

He wondered if Harold's bringing him here was meant to be
one of those acts of human goodness. He wondered if that was
what grace was. He wondered how he could stop wondering,
and start knowing how to feel.

THE FOURTH WEEK, Harold gave Alexander a seventeenth-
century handbook by a Frenchman named Beguin. It was called
Tyrocinium Chymicum, and it detailed, almost in recipe form,
the ways for making a large collection of old-fashioned medicines. There was oil of wax for burns, oil of cloves for depression,
oil of amber for headache. Tincture of sulphur was said to help
the lungs; tincture of coral cured dysentery.

After a few days of watching Alexander work, Harold left
him alone and spent the afternoons in the greenhouse. Alexander
had the lab to himself, and he learned and practiced the various
methods that Harold had said he would need for the Work.
There was distillation, sublimation, fumigation, calcination,
amalgamation, precipitation—on and on it went. All of these
were methods of what was known as solution, all of them
different ways of breaking different substances down. They were
processes basic to chemistry, but they had first been discovered
by alchemists. Alexander did them in the old-fashioned glass
alembics—three-foot-tall glass vessels—but he heated them over
an electric stove.

"Steady heat," Harold had explained to him when Alexander
asked about it.

"You think Roger Bacon had a self-cleaning oven?"

"You use what you can use," Harold had said.

After the week with the Emerald Tablet, and the two weeks

with the fourth dimension, it was a huge relief to be doing something tangible, something he could do right. At first Alexander had worried that Harold had given up on him spiritually, but Harold had said that precision was also essential in the Work. Practice, Harold said, was important: practice, patience, and repetition.

The lab was dark and dank like any basement, but it was nonetheless filled with wonderful odors: the sweetness of flowers and plants and fresh soil; the sharpness of oils and medicines; the mustiness of powders and stones. Alexander found that he loved the process of learning to recognize these smells, to feel at ease with the work he did.

He was working at tasks that he once would have scorned as too technical, and he felt that if he performed them correctly, he'd have to be rewarded.

He still felt that studying alchemy was the bravest thing he'd ever done, and every time he doubted himself, he told himself to be braver.

Part Three

I

THE WORK

MARCH WAS the month of beginnings, the month of Aries, the ram, the first sign of the zodiac. The earth's cycle began anew in March, as if nothing had ever been born before; as if nothing had died. Aries was a fire sign, and March brought the banked-down warmth from the ground, pushing it up from the roots to the stems, forcing it out in the sap and the buds.

Alexander had never felt close to the earth before. He had loved spring in the city, and the first cool days of autumn, but he had never waited for seasons before; he had never looked forward to them. Now it was the first morning of the first spring he had waited for, and he stood in the driveway with Harold at dawn, looking for the sunrise. A year ago, he thought, he had been sealed away in his office, torturing out his theory in numbers, thoroughly blind to the world he'd kept insisting that they would describe.

Harold and he each held a canvas sack and pair of garden clippers. Harold snapped his open and shut. His eyes were bright with excitement and a look that seemed like tenderness. "Let's go," he whispered softly when the first sunlight appeared.

The hard, dark winter had finally passed, and somewhere along the way, Alexander had ceased to see Harold from Sam's point of view. He had ceased to be bothered by Biner's letters and no longer worried about the time. He'd accepted the fact that he had to stay, and Harold, it seemed, had accepted it too.

This morning, Harold was going to show him how to gather the sap and the new spring shoots. For nearly three months, Alexander had been hoping for this chance, which was his first chance to do something truly useful for the Work. Harold would use the shoots and the sap as nourishment for his Prime Matter.

Their footsteps crunched in the gravel driveway, then rustled the new blades of grass. Harold walked east, toward the widening light. He was eager, and he moved quickly. Half a mile from the house, he stopped in a field where the grass was rich and full, and the wildflowers grew in random clumps. "Follow me," he said quietly, "and do just what I do." He walked toward some yellow flowers and then knelt quickly beside them. He placed a hand on the moist green grass. "Grant us," he said simply, "that we can share in the fiery forces of life that give us this rebirth of springtime."

Alexander looked at the earth and imagined a real fire burning within it. He looked at Harold and felt so beholden that he almost felt blessed. Perhaps it had been luck to have met him, but it felt like grace to have won his trust.

Harold took a deep breath. "Kneel down," he told Alexander.

Alexander knelt beside him.

"Now, the flowers and shoots we want are the green ones," Harold explained, excited. "We want the young plants, the ones filled with sap and dew. You can tell they're filled with sap by how green they are, and how full they look. See, look at these two dandelions—" Harold pointed to two neighboring flowers. "This one is fuller than that one, see?"

"I see," Alexander said.

Deftly, Harold snipped the fuller one at its base and placed it in his canvas bag.

"We're looking for buds," he continued. "They're always good. And shoots that are just coming out of the ground. Weeds or flowers, it doesn't matter, as long as the shoots are new. Look for flowers on trees, too. There are none in this field, but you'll find them in others. White flowers on the dogwoods, and firs—all kinds of evergreens. Broom. You don't want finished flowers, though. You want things that always seem new."

Alexander nodded and scanned the field. The task was so pure and simple that it made him feel giddy and sure.

"Go ahead," Harold told him happily. "Go ahead. Go anywhere you like."

THEY CAME BACK to the house at eight o'clock, their sacks full and their shoes wet. Harold led them down to the lab, where he cleaned off the long center table.

"Carefully," he warned Alexander. "Take them out gently, one by one."

The early sun flooded the room and gleamed off the metal table. Painstakingly, they spread the morning's pickings within its light. Harold hummed. Alexander was dazzled by the sight of the flowers on the table. The pattern they created looked like the fabric of one of Linda's shirts, and he smiled at the thought of what she would say if she saw him with all these flowers.

"Why are you smiling?" Harold asked.

"Because it looks so beautiful," Alexander said, and he wondered if Linda had ever heard him say those words about anything. Beauty had not been a value that he'd ever seen outside the mathematics he'd done.

Harold grinned and elbowed him.

Alexander beamed.

"Now," Harold said. "I don't want to break your heart or anything, but this is a part of life."

"What is?"

"We need to weed out the duds."

"Oh."

Harold reached for a frail daisy and crumpled it in his hand.

"Oh," Alexander said again.

"We just leave the perfect ones, okay?"

Alexander watched Harold for a few moments, then helped him with the weeding. Only half the shoots and buds remained when they were done. It was Alexander, of course, who had collected most of the bad ones, but Harold was sunny and uncritical. "You'll learn," he said simply. "In time, you'll learn."

"What's next?" Alexander asked him.

"Next is we put them in a safe place."

Alexander had often noticed the low shelf in the lab with the jars that were full of flowers.

"It's kind of like pickling," Harold said. "Not that I've got the faintest idea what pickling is actually like."

From the shelf he removed ten of the jars that were filled only with clear liquid.

"Water?" Alexander asked.

"No. Dew. That's gathered under Taurus, you know. The Earth sign. You'll see. That'll be next month."

"Will I get to gather the dew?"

"We'll see."

Together they unscrewed the lids of the jars, and carefully placed the flowers, three or four to a glass, inside them.

"Can I write the labels?" Alexander asked.

"Go ahead," Harold told him. "Knock yourself out."

It was nine o'clock by the time they finished. They placed the jars on the shelf beside the others that Alexander had wondered about so often, and he realized with sincere delight that the world now held one less mystery.

BREAKFAST WAS coffee and crumbcake, and Harold had three slices. Alexander drank his coffee, staring out at the wide, bright morning. He realized that he felt young, and that that was almost a lost sensation. He felt the way he had when he had still believed that Sam knew the answers. He felt the way he had before he had seen the ghost or the angel. "It was great out there," he told Harold.

"I had a feeling you'd like it."

"Will you let me go tomorrow too?"

"Well, it's like this," Harold said. "You can either go every day, or never again. But you've got to choose. You can't just go when you feel like it."

"Repetition?" Alexander asked him.

"Yes."

"Out of repetition, magic is sometimes forced to rise."

"That's right."

"And if I don't go every day," Alexander said, "then I might either miss the magic or not do enough to raise it up."

"Right."

They both smiled a little self-consciously, and Harold looked down at his empty plate.

"Want more?" Alexander asked him.

"No."

There was a silence, and Alexander couldn't decide if Harold was bored or somehow moved.

"Hey," Alexander said to him. "So what's my lesson for the day?"

Harold folded his napkin and looked up again, shaking off whatever his mood had been. "It's a good one," he said.

"Yeah?"

"The best."

"What is it?"

Harold arched one eyebrow dramatically. "The Ouroboros," he said.

"Ouroboros?" Alexander asked.

"*The* Ouroboros."

"Yes?"

"The Ouroboros," Harold said, "is the snake that feeds on its own tail. Its symbolism is crucial. You have pictures of it in your books upstairs. Find out what you think it means."

"That's it? That's the whole lesson?"

"That's what you start with," Harold said.

IN HIS BEDROOM, Alexander stood before the bookshelf, which was filled by now with Harold's texts. Daily or weekly, Harold had snuck up here at odd moments, placing the books on the shelf as Alexander had needed them. It had been one of the few things that Harold had done with complete consistency, and in the more doubtful moments of the last few months, it had seemed to Alexander to be proof that Harold cared.

Accepting Harold's moods had taken a long time for Alexander. All winter long, Harold had been by turns funny and humorless, earnest and condescending. Sometimes he had sung show tunes and he had danced around the lab or the kitchen. Sometimes he had been silent, and there had been no way of coaxing him out of himself.

The strangest things could get through to him. One afternoon, Alexander would simply be cleaning some brushes in the sink, and Harold would look up mistily and say he couldn't remember not having him here, and ask him a personal question with what seemed like real concern. Another afternoon, Alexander would do something truly impressive—make a batch of some complicated compound or cite a very obscure passage—and Harold would not react at all.

Alexander's previous teachers had been more fathomable, more obvious. Diligence and brains had been enough to win them over, no matter how wise or how distant they'd seemed. After three months, Alexander had still not abandoned his hope of converting Harold, but he had come to understand that Harold had reasons for acting the way he did. Harold was going by ancient patterns built up by legends and long-dead men: an Adept with his student was supposed to conform to certain rules. There were some things that Harold could tell him straight out, and other things that would have been wrong to tell. Like the Touch, the Work was secretive, and like the angel, Harold seemed to demand some unnamed combination of virtues. No one Alexander had ever known in the real world had ever promised such knowledge or made him wait so long to get it. No one had ever inspired him so much.

UPSTAIRS, he took down three of the books he had studied already, books that he knew were filled with illustrations and symbols. There was a new book as well, which it took him a moment to notice. It was lying flat on the top shelf, too tall to fit alongside the others. Alexander smiled to himself, remembering the tyranny of his alphabetized bookshelves, and feeling briefly superior to the person he had been. Only three months before, he thought, it truly would have upset him if he'd found a single book too large to be placed in alphabetical order. His old world really had faded, he thought. The letters from Biner were less frequent now, the notes from Linda more businesslike. Sam and he still exchanged letters and chess moves, but they didn't write so often that they'd yet started a second game. Most of their pieces were still standing, uncaptured, on the imaginary board.

Eagerly, Alexander settled at his desk and leafed through the books until he found some engravings of the snake. All of them were roughly the same. They pictured the Ouroboros in the shape of a circle, its tail in its mouth, a crown on its head.

Alexander had seen these engravings before, but he hadn't studied them. He began by reading the different texts, which explained the snake in different ways. One said it symbolized the self-contained nature of alchemy, the fact that it involved work that was meant to be done in solitude. Another text said the Ouroboros had first appeared on the tombs of ancient Egyptians as the guardian of the Underworld. Then there was a Jungian interpretation—for Jung had in fact studied alchemy— that said the Ouroboros symbolized a union of opposites, male and female, into a meaningful flow of life.

Most convincing to Alexander was the last text's interpretation of the snake as the perfect representation of the cycles that never ended: birth from death, death from birth. Life would begin and end again, seasons would come and go. There was one plate of the Ouroboros with a sly, sad look in its eye, and to Alexander it seemed to be the exhausted embodiment of the world's unbreakable chain. Once more, there was repetition.

The thought carried him back to the morning, and the sense of new things rising from the banked-down fires in the ground.

He turned to a fresh page in the spiral notebook that Harold had asked him to keep as a journal. *Solve et coagula*, Harold had written on the cover. That phrase had come up again and again. What it meant was "dissolve and combine," and what that meant to Alexander was that his old ways of thinking and feeling things had to be broken down so new ways could emerge.

It was almost miraculous, he thought sometimes, how change had in fact been possible—how the subtle, fixed patterns of a life could shift, and be lost, and then take a new form. It had been like this in his twenties when, as a student, he'd dreaded the autumns and the prospect of rooming with someone at school, and then how by spring he had dreaded the summers and the prospect of being alone again. It had been like this with Linda, too. Before Alexander had met her, it had been unimaginable to him that he would ever allow someone to alter the rhythm and shape of his days.

Solve et coagula. He had adapted again. In his old life, he had been used to making his own schedule, to enforcing his own silences. He had been used to hiding from Linda, and wrestling with Biner and Heinz and Talbot, and visiting Sam, and not knowing Alice. In his old life, he had been the one whom the others had tried to puzzle out, and had waited for, and had given to. *Solve et coagula.* Now he had the early mornings, the quiet breakfasts, the afternoon lessons. He had learned how to wait for small signs from Harold, and small signs from nature, and important dreams.

In the notebook, Alexander traced a drawing of the Ouroboros, and underneath it he wrote, "Seasons. Spring will always follow winter."

AFTERNOONS had remained his time to work in the lab. After dozens of hours with the *Tyrocinium Chymicium,* he had become all but expert with the methods of making medicines. Harold's laboratory shelves were filled by now with bottles of balsam of sulphur, spirit of nitre, tincture of coral—on and on. Once, when he'd had a headache, Alexander had even trusted himself enough to take some homemade oil of amber. Nothing much had happened to him.

Today, he was planning to make not a medicine but a perfume. Three days before, he had found fresh roses growing in Harold's greenhouse, and he had clipped five or six of them, crushed them in a marble mortar, placed them in a large alembic, and buried them in the cold ground. This afternoon, he went down to the lab and prepared his equipment. Then he went into the backyard and dug up the alembic. As the book had said they would, the roses smelled faintly of acid. Alexander carried them inside, pressed out their liquid, heated what was left, then pressed out more liquid, repeating the process for nearly two hours.

When he was finished, he had a small but potent quantity of rose-scented perfume. Carefully, he poured it into a tiny glass vial. He held it to the light and admired its color and clarity. Cleo would be thrilled, he knew, if he gave her this as a present, and of course he had made it with her in mind. But he hadn't seen her for many weeks now, and he wasn't sure that he wanted to.

HE MISSED Cleo less, and she visited less often. He needed her less, and she was starting to suspect it. She still filled the house with chatter, teasing Harold as Alexander could not. She smoked forbidden cigarettes, leaning halfway out the bedroom window, laughing when he told her she was being impure. She still seemed to revel in the way she had helped to change him, but at times she was strangely irreverent about what he'd become.

In bed at night, she kept trying to find new ways to make him hers.

Taking walks in the morning, she had asked him a few times about becoming his guide, but Alexander was no longer sure that that was what he wanted from her. He wasn't sure she was meant to be so large a part of his future. For Alexander, the future had always been a concept that extended only as far as whatever goal he had, whatever mystery he had to solve. It was really only Harold now who was bound up with that mystery.

Sometime in the middle of February, the angel in his dreams

had stopped looking like Cleo, and Alexander saw that, too, as a sign he could not ignore.

"SO WHAT DID you think of Mr. Snake?" Harold asked Alexander that evening after dinner. Dinner was the one meal Harold still cooked. Harold had remained a much better chef than Alexander, and he seemed to enjoy showing off his skill.

Alexander laughed. "*Mr.* Snake?" he said.

"I love the Ouroboros," Harold said happily.

"I guess he has lots of different meanings."

"No."

"Just one?"

"Just one," Harold said.

There was a long, weighty silence, in which Alexander sighed. He knew he would have to choose one meaning, and he worried that whichever one he chose would be wrong.

"Close that window," Harold said suddenly. "It's *freezing* in here."

Quickly, Alexander rose and walked to the kitchen window. As he fastened the latch, he saw his face reflected in the blackened panes. The windows at night were his only mirror—aside from the spoon he still shaved with—and seeing his face undistorted had become a guilty pleasure. He looked back at Harold quickly, as if recoiling from a former vice.

"Do you ever get cold in the city?" Harold asked. His tone suggested something more profound than conversation.

"Not really," Alexander said carefully. "In the winter, you're only outside long enough to start to get cold, and then the steam heat inside makes you nuts."

"And summer?"

"In summer, that's when you sleep under the blankets, because the air conditioning gets you cold. It's funny, but you stay warm."

"Seasons," Harold said.

"I know."

"Summertime," Harold sang, "and the living is easy."

"I know," Alexander said, settling back into his chair.

"Well, it's a long long time," Harold sang, "from May to December."

"I *know*," Alexander said.

"Seasons," Harold said. "You can't know life if you don't know the seasons."

"That's what I thought the Ouroboros meant. It's just the same thing, again and again. Just like the flowers today. Just like the Work."

"Think of the seasons," Harold said to him.

Alexander thought. He thought of summer and winter and summer again, and he realized that he would still be here the next time there was snow. He thought of being thirty-one, and then turning thirty-two, and he thought how quickly his life was passing and how stunning it was that he'd come to want his life to take place here. He looked up at Harold, distracted.

"Try again," Harold said.

Alexander thought again. This time, he saw tall reeds that were bending toward an ocean in early autumn.

"What are you seeing?" Harold asked him.

"The sea."

"What season?"

"It's fall," Alexander said.

"Are you in the picture?"

"No, I'm not."

Alexander looked up at Harold, brightening. "I'm not in the picture!" he said. "That's good, right?"

Harold smiled and said good night and loped away, humming, down the hall.

.   .   .

ALEXANDER KNEW, of course, that the whole concept of a
seasonal cycle formed the heart of the lessons that he had been
learning; the notion of rejuvenation was something that Harold
had brought up again and again. In the Work, each season was
linked to three of the signs of the zodiac, which were linked
to the elements earth, air, water, and fire, which were linked
to the properties wetness, dryness, cold, and heat. As the seasons
changed, they brought other changes.

Up in his bedroom later that night, Alexander studied the
chart that Harold had drawn for him months before. The chart
had a beautiful balance to it, everything very symmetrical:

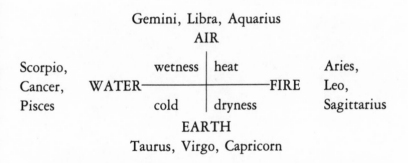

Gemini, Libra, Aquarius
AIR

Scorpio,		wetness	heat		Aries,
Cancer,	WATER			FIRE	Leo,
Pisces		cold	dryness		Sagittarius

EARTH
Taurus, Virgo, Capricorn

Nicholas Flamel, the alchemist Cleo had first told him about,
had written long ago that alchemy should be thought of as
"knowledge of the four elements, and of their seasons and qual-
ities, mutually and reciprocally changed one into the other."
That was the whole point. It was Aristotle who first wrote about
the fifth element, the quintessence, which was the element
containing all the others, the element that made transmutation
possible. Alchemists believed that there could be a rotation of
the elements, that if you could change one element into the
quintessence, then you could change it from the quintessence
into another element.

To Alexander, it seemed exactly like the four forces in physics, and the alchemists' belief in the quintessence was just like the physicists' conviction that there was one universal language, one universal force.

He had not stopped being surprised by such connections, but they had stopped drawing him backward. Now, they drew him on.

2

THE DEW

ALEXANDER HAD GROWN a beard. He had only glimpsed it in darkened windows, at either end of the lengthening days. But he saw it as a kind of badge, the visible proof of his diligence. It had been five weeks since Harold had taken him out and shown him how to gather the shoots and the buds, and every morning since then, Alexander had woken before six, dressed by lamplight, and not bothered to shave.

What he cared about most in the mornings now was reaching the field before the sun did.

This morning, the field seemed to drift with mist. A band of daylight ribboned the horizon, as if a giant dark shade had been partially raised. In country fields, Alexander had learned, it was the sky, not the sun, that seemed to rise.

The early air was damp and unpleasant. Alexander had found

that he didn't much like the cold and chill of dawn. It was hard sometimes, getting up so early each morning, but to think that way meant he might not be deserving.

Harold was always saying these days that he had to be deserving.

"You *do* want your own Prime Matter, don't you?" Harold would ask Alexander.

"Of course."

"And you *do* want to be an Adept," he'd say.

"Of course I do. You know I do."

"Because it would be different if you didn't want to become an Adept," Harold would say. "If you *didn't* want to become an Adept, then that would be *totally* different, because you wouldn't have to fight through quite so many *stages*, you know. But since you *do* want to be an Adept, and since you *do* want to find your own Prime Matter, and since you *do* want to do the Work by yourself—"

"Harold," Alexander would tell him, "you're getting all worked up."

And then Harold would laugh, and Alexander would be left to wonder what he could do that would prove his worth.

He had worked very hard all winter, but since spring had begun, he had doubled his efforts, staying up late to pursue some text that Harold had only mentioned in passing, going back over old lessons he'd learned—the Ouroboros, the fourth dimension, the notes he had written, the lab work he'd done.

Harold acknowledged his efforts but kept repeating his talk of purity, his talk of being deserving; he always implied a greater goodness and a greater depth. At times, Alexander couldn't help but retreat from belief to utter exhaustion, and he didn't always feel sure now that Harold wanted him to succeed.

The sun finally appeared. Alexander looked at the horizon and made himself imagine the morning beginning, hour after hour, beyond the farthest reaches of his sight. Birds pulled worms from the fresh earth and jumped back into the sky.

Alexander took a deep breath and turned, as Harold had taught him to, to face, one by one, the four corners of the world.

In his arms was a folded canvas cloth. At his feet was a large glass vessel.

That which is above, he recited to himself, *is like that which is below. And that which is below is like that which is above . . .*

He took forty steps toward the rising sun, then walked a magic circle on the ground.

With this knowledge alone you may work miracles.

The light was growing brighter, and the sky was clear.

The sun is its father, the moon its mother. The wind carried it in his belly. . . .

Alexander stretched the canvas tight between both hands.

"Taut enough for a painter to paint on," had been Harold's instructions.

Alexander bent slowly over the grass and ran the rigid canvas across the tips of the blades, making sure that the fabric didn't touch the earth itself. Harold said everything vital in the dew would return to the soil if the canvas touched the ground.

Alexander moved the fabric in a half-circle, watching as it grew dark with moisture. When it was heavy enough that his arms could feel it, he wrapped his hands around the cloth and wrung it out into the glass container.

This was the ritual for the dew, which Harold had shown him one week before. For weeks before that, Harold had made it seem as if gathering the dew would be the ultimate spiritual privilege, and Alexander had worked and waited for the chance to learn how it was done. The dew was supposed to be gathered in Taurus, and only on the clearest days, and only with the calmest heart. Harold had made Alexander wait until the last possible moment before he had told him that he could come along. But Harold had never seemed more brusque or more distant than he had that day. In the field, too, he had seemed not only exacting but somehow nervous—critical of the smallest errors, unmoved by Alexander's hope.

"You're going to have to be deserving," Harold had said to him.

"I thought I *was* deserving. I thought that's why you're letting me gather the dew," Alexander had said.

"You have to be able to clear your mind. You have to know how to stop all your thinking. You have to be more deserving if you want to find your own Prime Matter."

"When can I?"

"Not till you know what the Prime Matter is."

It would take nearly two hours before the dew had left the last blade of grass, and during that time Alexander tried to clear his mind of doubts, tried to clear his mind of everything but the words he had learned from the ancient texts, and the need to collect the dew.

He had gone out alone for eight mornings now, straining to find the proper peace. Several times, he had found it, but he had never been able to hold it for long. His thoughts always rushed back, and made him self-conscious, and tied him down. He had learned many things in three months, but he hadn't yet learned how to lose himself.

He bent and straightened and bent again, like a figure on a clock.

Out of repetition, Harold was always saying, magic was sometimes forced to rise.

AT EIGHT O'CLOCK, he returned to the house. He wiped his feet on the scruffy brown doormat and opened the back door quietly. Harold would be in the lab already, not wanting to be disturbed. Just the week before, Harold had told him rather pointedly that "laboratory" was based on the Latin words *labor* and *oratorium*—words that meant "work" and "a place for prayer."

Alexander took the stairs carefully, holding the canvas cloth in front of him so it wouldn't touch the walls or drag along the steps.

The lab smelled of fresh grass and alcohol. Harold was at the stove.

Alexander placed the cloth on the metal table, and he put the heavy glass container on the floor beside it.

"Morning," Harold said to him without looking up.

"Morning," Alexander said.

"Breakfast," Harold said.

"Scrambled eggs?" Alexander asked him wearily.

"Sure. And something sweet. Some pastry. You know. Something good."

Alexander sighed.

"What's the problem?" Harold asked. "Are we out of pastry?"

"No, Harold," Alexander said.

"Good. Then call me when it's done."

BACK UPSTAIRS in the kitchen, Alexander washed his hands, took out a bowl and a frying pan, butter and eggs, and proceeded to make breakfast. Downstairs, Harold would keep working over the other stove, with the more interesting set of ingredients, and Alexander tried to believe that all things would really come in time. He knew that he should still be excited that he'd been permitted to gather the dew. But after all the buildup, he'd found it was really no different from gathering the flowers.

What Alexander wanted, more than anything, was to dig up his own Prime Matter and to start his own version of the Work. He believed that once he was on his own, then everything would become clear to him. The prospect of turning actual soil into actual gold seemed suddenly much easier than the prospect of turning himself into someone who met Harold's standards.

Harold came upstairs whistling and smiled approvingly at the food. He pulled the brim of his felt hat down. "Delicious," he pronounced when he took his first bite.

"Thanks," Alexander said, trying to keep the frustration out of his voice.

"Did you *study* the eggs?" Harold asked him.

"What?"

"Did you study them?"

Alexander laughed. "Oh come on, Harold," he said.

"The eggs," Harold said. "Solution," he said. "Think about it."

Long ago, Alexander had learned from his lab work that what alchemists called "solution" was the process of breaking most substances down into the three basic parts that the Adepts called Mercury, Sulphur, and Salt. Mercury was liquid, Sulphur was vapor, and Salt was the hard substance. The Adepts wrote about Mercury as the Spirit, Sulphur as the Soul, and Salt as the Body.

The lesson about solution had come after the Ouroboros. It was a stale one for Alexander by now, but Harold was trying to distract him with it, like a parent offering an old toy to a bored and restless child.

"Think about it," Harold said again, sipping his coffee happily.

"The white, the yolk, and the shell," Alexander said.

"Yes. Which is which?" Harold asked him.

"The white is the Mercury. The yolk is the Sulphur. The shell is the Salt," Alexander said.

"Yes."

They ate for a while in silence. Breakfast was still the time for lessons.

"I'm tired of lessons," Alexander said, a little surprised that he'd said it.

"That wasn't a lesson," Harold said. "That was extra."

"Couldn't we talk about the Prime Matter?"

"What do you think the Prime Matter is?"

"I think the Prime Matter is what you keep holding over my head."

HE WOKE IN the morning with a sore throat and an aching body. The sky was still dark, and he knew that he had only ten minutes to dress before the sun rose. He knew that he was ill. He thought of Linda, and how she had fussed and cared for him when he was sick, and he thought of how self-conscious it would make him feel to tell Harold that he wasn't well.

He threw back the covers and shivered. He had a fever, and when he stood up, it was as if there was an enormous distance between his head and the floor. He walked slowly toward the bathroom, and the tiles under his feet felt cold, and the room seemed warped somehow in its dimensions. He peed, one hand braced against the nearest wall. His back felt twisted. His eyes felt heavy. He went back to bed and shivered beneath the covers until his mind clouded with thoughts and he fell back into sleep.

"KID," Harold said.

"No."

"Kid."

Harold's face was inches away from him. Alexander started, and tried to sit up.

"Don't," Harold said.

"But—"

"You're ill. You may be very ill."

Harold put his hand on Alexander's forehead. Alexander flinched, embarrassed by Harold's touch.

"Is your throat sore?" Harold asked him. He seemed nervous and eager and awkward, and newly vulnerable.

Alexander shrugged. He felt the same discomfort that he'd always felt with Sam at such times.

"Well, is it?" Harold asked him.

"Yes."

"Does your stomach hurt?"

"No."

"Have you thrown up?"

"No. I'm okay. I just need some sleep."

"You've got a huge fever."

"I'll be all right."

"You need medicine."

"I just need some sleep."

Harold stared at him, silent and tense. He hadn't moved from his spot by the bed.

"Don't worry," Alexander said, but as he drifted back into sleep, he realized that Harold had looked scared.

"HE LOVES YOU," the angel told him in a dream that was almost an hallucination.

"I don't want to be loved. I want to be taught."

"He realizes that he needs you. He's scared," the angel said to him.

"I don't want him to need me," Alexander said.

"You should sleep now."

"I am sleeping."

"You should calm down."

"I am calm."

"Harold isn't calm," she said. "He needs you. He didn't want to."

IT WAS DARK when Alexander woke again, and Harold was sitting in the desk chair. He was looking at his reflection in the darkened windowpanes. His fingertips explored the dark half-circles below his eyes, and he leaned forward intently, seemingly both intrigued and appalled.

"Do you look different?" Alexander asked from the bed.

Harold turned around and quickly moved to Alexander's side. "How are you?" he asked.

"Better."

Harold checked Alexander's forehead again. "You're still burning. God," Harold said.

"Have you changed?" Alexander asked him.

"What?"

"Have you changed? The window. Your reflection."

"You need medicine."

"Have you changed?"

Harold stood up and went back to the desk, where Alexander recognized a small bottle from the lab. "Well, I look older," Harold said. "I'm old."

"You're not old," Alexander said. But Harold did look old, and he also looked very lonely.

"Yes I am. I'm just rocking through my autumn now, and heading into my winter."

Alexander looked away sheepishly.

"Come on," Harold said. "Take your medicine."

"What is it?"

"Oil of amber."

"Swell. Is it my batch or yours?"

"Mine. I made it fresh."

"Good."

"Don't you trust your own?"

"Sure I do."

"Don't be sarcastic. Are you being sincere or not?"

"Harold. Lighten up," Alexander said. "I'm being sincere."

Harold handed him the medicine and a spoon and then watched him after he drank it as if he had just watered a plant and was waiting to see if it would grow.

THE DAWN SEEMED darker than it had four days before. Again, Alexander stood on the crest of the hill, looking down on the field. He had not slept well the night before, though he had no memory of any dreams. He had not dreamed of his angel since the day he'd been so ill, and when time went by without her now, he grew scared that she had gone for good.

He was tired. The thought of bending and straightening for the next hour, dragging the canvas, wringing it out, was thoroughly exhausting. It made his body ache.

He wondered if Cleo would know any more about how he could find the Prime Matter. But thinking of Cleo confused him, and the sun was almost up now, and he knew that he shouldn't be thinking of her.

Alexander turned to face the north.

The people call change death, because the body is dissolved, and life, when it's dissolved, withdraws to the unmanifest. But in this sermon, I say the Cosmos also suffers change—for that a part of it each day is made to be in the unmanifest—yet it is ne'er dissolved.

What it meant was that nothing should ever really die.

Alexander turned to face the east.

Become more lofty than all height and lower than all depth. Collect into thyself all senses of all creatures—of fire and water, dry and moist. Think that thou art at the same time in every place—in earth, in sea, in sky; not yet begotten, in the womb, young, old, and dead.

What it meant was that the world wasn't as finite as it seemed.

Alexander liked the line about being at the same time in every place. It reminded him of quantum mechanics, and the strange way particles had of seeming to be in two places at once.

There were still so many places where things connected, he thought.

He turned toward the south. *Become more lofty than all height and lower than all depth*, he thought again, and then he turned toward the west, and walked in a circle, and stretched the canvas taut in his hands, and bent to collect the dew.

When he was finished, he stood on the hill and looked up at the sky, and he tried to remember if he had ever lost himself in anything. In a way it was like sex, he thought, or at least like the way sex had been at the beginning. The first few times he had made love to a girl, he hadn't been lost in emotion either, or taken somewhere by a fantasy. Most of the time, he had simply been trying to concentrate on doing it right. It had taken a long time before sex had been so natural that it wasn't simply an end in itself. It had taken a long time before sex had become the means to bringing him somewhere else.

Alexander stood very still and waited to feel something vital, and he wondered if all the simple things would always be beyond him.

IN THE AFTERNOON, it rained. Alexander looked out at the pond from his window and was secretly grateful for the change.

The sameness was getting to him. He had had the patience to learn Feynman diagrams, to learn every atomic weight, to compute to the last digit the equations for his strings. But all those had been discrete endeavors whose value he understood.

He thought about what he knew so far.

He knew that there were two separate steps in finding the

Prime Matter. Both were supposed to occur in springtime, both in a state of high inspiration.

The first step was supposed to be taken on a day that the Adept had chosen with the help of his astrological chart and often with the help of a guide. On that night, when the planets were in their proper alignment, the Adept was supposed to find an untouched, fruitful place, a place where things were growing but where no one else had been. Once there, the Adept was supposed to feel that some few square yards of earth were his. He was supposed to be in a state of profound spirituality, often a state that led to brilliant visions and apparitions, a state where angels were said to come. When he found the important place, he was supposed to mark it with a magic circle—walking around it three times.

The second step was to go out on the night of the next full moon and dig up a few pounds of the earth that had been marked.

The second step seemed easier.

None of this information seemed to add up to anything real.

Alexander looked out at the pond, where frogs and muskrats swam back and forth all day, and small white butterflies skimmed the surface. Often in the evenings before dinner, Alexander would sit here, watching the still reflections of the crab apple trees that grew along its banks, trying not to believe that he had been pulled into something ridiculous, trying to will the needs inside him to be as still as the water.

3

THE BEGINNING

A WEEK LATER, Alexander stood in the kitchen with Harold and brandished a plate of Danish over his head. "Tell me when I can find my own Prime Matter, or you will never see this Danish again."

"Tell me what the Prime Matter is," Harold said to him.

Alexander stared at Harold, walked out of the kitchen, and slammed the back door behind him.

For days now, they had been having this nonconversation.

"When can I find my own Prime Matter?"

"Tell me what the Prime Matter is."

Harold said it now as if the answer was perfectly obvious, as if it was Alexander, not he, who had decided to hold something back.

It was not just a riddle when he said it now. It had become a plea.

ALEXANDER LEFT the house and walked down the driveway and out to the flat black road. He walked quickly, furiously, as if he were leaving for good. He was tired of the permanent apology that seemed implicit in everything Harold did: the unspoken *I'm sorry that I can't help you; I'm sorry that you won't help yourself.*

Alexander thought about Sam, and the easy joy with which Sam had always taught him things. Sam's lessons had been gifts, given freely, unambiguously. Sam had never held back anything that Alexander had needed to know.

The spring bulbs had come up along the road—slashes of color, red and pink—and the trees along the pond were showing small green buds. The grass seemed greener, sweeping over the fields, as if the earth moved closer every day to its own perfection.

Alexander stopped walking. He looked back up the road. Harold's house was not visible. He looked ahead, and the view was the same. He was standing in the middle of a country road in springtime, and he felt like a dot on a straight, long line.

He tried to feel something helpful and pure, but all he felt was anger.

AN HOUR LATER, he went back to the house. The breakfast dishes were still on the table. He cleared them and washed them and put them away.

When he finally went down to the basement, he found Harold standing by the stove, stirring a foul-smelling mixture.

"Good. You're here," Harold said softly. "I need two clean alembics."

Alexander nodded and went to the sink and took down a brush. "Just one thing," he said to Harold.

"What?"

"Please don't ask me what the Prime Matter is."

"Fine."

"I mean don't ask me right now."

"Fine. Then don't ask me when you can find it."

There was silence as Harold transferred a mortar of crushed petals into a clean glass vial.

"You want me to learn this stuff or not?" Alexander asked him finally.

"Of course I do," Harold said.

"Do you realize what you're doing to me?"

Harold scraped the remains of the petals from the mortar and looked up at Alexander steadily. "Look, why don't you make some oil of cloves?" he said.

"What for?"

"I just think you should."

"I've made plenty of oil of cloves," Alexander said. "There's a whole bottle on the shelf behind you."

Harold turned to look. Then he turned back. "Suit yourself," he said quietly, and Alexander had to leave the room again.

BY AFTERNOON, he had decided to follow Harold's suggestion. He needed something to help clear his mind, and making oil of cloves was just complex enough to keep him focused.

Alexander began by taking two pounds of Harold's cloves, pounding them into a powder, and mixing them with pure water. Then he added fixed amounts of mace, pepper, coriander, and anise seeds. He placed the mixture in an alembic, and turned the stove to high. The process involved ten or fifteen distillations. Alexander recorded what he had just done in his notebook, and then he sat by the stove to wait.

He found himself thinking of Linda. He wondered if he had made her feel the way that Harold was making him feel now—that there was something that would unlock him, but that he wanted to hide the key from her. He wondered how many times in two years she had started to walk away from him, and what it was about him that had drawn her back each time.

After about an hour, he was startled by the sound of Harold humming on the stairs, but he managed not to look up, even when Harold had come into the room.

Harold was standing behind him now, gazing over his shoulder.

"What is it?" Alexander finally asked.

Harold pulled over another stool and smiled almost politely.

"What?" Alexander asked warily. "Have I done something wrong?"

"Can't I just sit here and talk for a while?" Harold asked.

"I don't know, Harold. You never have."

"Sure I have."

"When?" Alexander asked him.

Harold looked away glumly.

Nervously, Alexander waited. "Sure you can sit here," he said at last.

Harold turned back with the same strange smile. "You know, you do know the answer," he said at last. "You already know what the Prime Matter is."

Alexander looked up slowly, staring back at Harold with all the deliberateness he had learned from him. Alexander gave him hate the way some looks give love or forgiveness.

"What's the matter with you?" Harold asked, as if he truly didn't know.

"Nothing's the matter with me," Alexander said slowly. "What's the matter with you?"

"Nothing's the matter with me."

"Then why don't you fucking tell me what the right answer is?"

"The Great Work can't be taught," Harold said. His voice was almost a whisper. "The Great Work can only be learned." He stood up, turned on the overhead light, then sat back down again. "What are you making here?" he asked.

"Oil of cloves," Alexander said. "Remember? You told me to make some this morning."

"Oh, right. Well, that's good stuff," Harold said. "You should take some yourself. Try it tonight. It might pick up your spirits. It's supposed to dissipate melancholy."

"Sometimes," Alexander said, "I really do think you're crazy."

"I know," Harold said. "But I'm really not."

Alexander stood up to check the alembic. "I'm thinking about leaving, you know," he told Harold.

"I know," Harold said.

"Well?"

"Well, what can I tell you? I don't want you to."

"You can tell me what the Prime Matter is."

"I can't," Harold said. "I want to. But I'd be breaking a pact with every Adept who's ever done the Work. And I'd be using what I know for gain."

"What gain?"

Harold looked away. "The gain of you," he said.

"I thought you wanted to keep me here."

"I do," Harold told him sadly. "That's just the point. Can't you see? It's not that hard to see."

There was so much sorrow in Harold's face that it made Alexander more tired than angry.

"I just hate feeling stupid," he said. "I hate it."

"I know you do," Harold told him. "Be patient. When I was your age, I felt the same way. This is part of the process.

You've got to believe me. And you've got to give yourself over to this. You've got to trust all of its rhythms."

Alexander stared at the stone floor.

"You could definitely use some oil of cloves," Harold said. "Or of course, we could go see a movie tonight."

"A movie," Alexander repeated. "A *movie*? You mean that you'd leave here?"

"That's right. Can't I leave?"

"I don't know, Harold. You never have."

"Sure I have."

Alexander decided that it wouldn't be wise to argue. "What kind of movie, Harold?" he asked softly.

"Who knows? Have you got today's paper?"

"Paper! Harold—"

"I was just wondering," Harold said.

Then he picked Alexander's notebook up and slowly, intently, began to read.

It's just another test, Alexander said to himself. This has got to be some kind of intricate test.

A few moments later, Harold returned the notebook and left the room wordlessly. He never mentioned the movie at dinner and went to his room at the usual time.

Cleaning the kitchen counters, Alexander paused to consider the stack of his unopened mail. There was a letter from Sam that had come that week, and there were three manila envelopes addressed in Linda's neat printing. Alexander had assumed that they were just more things from Biner. Now he sat at the kitchen table and opened the envelopes hopefully. But he'd been right, he saw. Linda had not even written notes.

Alexander heated some coffee for himself and then sat back down to read the most recent of Biner's letters. It was dated in early April, nearly a month before.

Dear Mr. Simon:

By now, I get a perverse satisfaction from sending my letters into this void. It's almost become a compulsion with me to write letters that won't be answered.

Just when we thought the whole thing was finally dying down, along came a fresh wave of publicity. In any case, it suddenly occurred to me that, wherever you are, you might not have seen some of the marvelous press coverage that you—and the lab of course—have recently received.

At this point, I am not going to ask for a reply.

Regards,
Bruce Biner

Biner had enclosed a dizzying stack of Xeroxes from various publications, mostly science journals, but a few national magazines as well. On each, he had circled in red the descriptions of Alexander: "reclusive," "mysterious," "elusive," "enigmatic." It seemed that one of the major critics of his theory, a Stanford physicist named David Merton, had been working on a new approach to string theory himself and had come right out to say that Alexander was a fraud. "The mind can only conclude," Merton was quoted as saying, "that if Mr. Simon had an adequate defense of the inconsistencies in his theory, he would have stepped forward to give it."

Alexander couldn't resist the impulse to scan the journals and learn what the "inconsistencies" were. He read enough to figure out that Merton's problem concerned a truly minor point about topology. Alexander would have been able to clear it up in no time at all. The temptation to do so was killing. Instead, he took a piece of notepaper from the counter and sat down to write:

Tuesday, May 8

Dear Dr. Biner:

I am sorry I haven't written. All I can tell you by way of explanation is that I've become involved in a kind of experiment out here in New Jersey. It is fascinating but not in any way something that the current scientific community would have any patience for. Now that makes it sound somewhat sinister, but though it is somewhat off the beaten track, it isn't sinister. It is simply less about physics than it is about metaphysics.

I think I was as surprised as anyone to find that the hold my theory had on me paled by comparison to this current experiment. I can't pretend I wasn't furious at Merton's pontificating—especially because the point he makes is such a moronic one—but I do need, in an absolute way, to be where I am now, doing what I'm doing.

I told you before I left that I very much regretted whatever difficulty and embarrassment I've caused you and the lab, but ultimately I'm sure that people will understand that what I've done—or not done, from your point of view—is a reflection on myself, and not on you.

Best wishes,
Alexander Simon

Feeling stronger and more self-righteous, Alexander sealed the letter and stamped it, then went back down to the basement and did a load of laundry. While he waited, he reread the most recent pages in his notebook. There had to be a clue to the Prime Matter somewhere, he thought, something that he had missed before. He simply couldn't find it. When the clothes were dry, he folded them, and gathered them in his arms, and then he found himself hugging them to his chest as if they were everything he'd ever lost.

.   .   .

LATER STILL that night, he lay alone in bed and tried to recall what it had been like for him on the brink of finding his Theory of Everything. He remembered the reckless nights of no sleep and no inspiration, just the need to be awake in case an inspiration came.

He went back downstairs. There were shadows on the wall from the moon. He stood alone in the kitchen in his bathrobe and called Cleo. In a strange way, he realized that he thought she was his last chance.

AT EIGHT O'CLOCK the next evening, he drove up to the train depot, half an hour early.

He watched as the eight-fourteen pulled in and the usual wives and children gathered up the men in colors and embraces.

The train was filled with passengers. Alexander could see, inside the bright compartments, other people curled up together, or reading the papers, or staring out. He watched the train pull away and found that he wanted to be on it.

The darkness deepened. There was mist in the air, and he waited. A light flashed down the tracks, and then he was back with his mother and the Railroad Ghost, and he shuddered, remembering everything much more clearly than he had before. He took a few steps back from the tracks, instinctively and fearfully.

There were really only two questions, he thought. The first was: Had there really been a light? The second was: If there had, where had it come from?

He would never know the second answer without knowing the first. And quietly, for the first time, he forced himself to accept the fact that he would never know the first.

A whistle sounded. He saw his mother's necklace as it had

gleamed in the dark above him so infinitely long ago, and he felt something tense inside him that would not give way.

"I WANT TO DO your chart," Cleo said to Alexander.

It was midnight that night, and beyond the window, the moon was a strip in the sky. In two weeks, it would be full again, and full moons were meant to be the time for gathering the Prime Matter.

Cleo was sitting, naked, at the foot of his bed, and she was brushing her hair, which had grown quite long. She used the hairbrush as if it were a paintbrush—as if each stroke were an act of glorious creation.

"My chart?" Alexander said.

"Yes. Your chart," she said.

He had told her about his frustrations with Harold, and as usual she was acting as though she had all the answers he needed.

She brushed her hair forward, covering her face.

"Could you stop that a minute?" Alexander asked.

From behind the veil of her hair, Cleo giggled, then tossed her head back, uncovering her face, and laid the brush on the bed beside her.

He had learned more about alchemy than she had ever known.

"It's no use," Alexander said. "Until I know what the Prime Matter is, it won't matter what a chart would say."

"Bullshit," Cleo said.

"What?"

"Maybe Harold just doesn't want you to do it. Maybe you've just got to do it yourself."

"Don't be ridiculous," Alexander said. "How could I do it myself?"

"I haven't done anyone's chart in years," Cleo said. "Palm reading pays better, you know. Instant gratification. I think people like to walk in and walk out with the answers the same day. They don't like to wait, if the impulse hits them. And, you know, I think they like being able to look at their hands afterwards. It's more tangible somehow than all those planets. But I used to like doing charts. I used to—"

"That's enough," Alexander said.

Cleo froze, then picked up the hairbrush again, then looked at Alexander as if she wasn't quite sure that she liked him. "You need to find out when the planets are right for you to choose the Prime Matter," she said slowly. "Right?"

"I think it's more complicated than that. There's some sort of conjunction of planets or something."

Cleo smiled at him, trying to make him smile. He didn't know what was right. He didn't know if she could help him, or if she was supposed to.

Cleo crawled forward on the bed, stretched out beside him, and grabbed at his shorts. "How about a different kind of conjunction?" she said.

He batted her hand away.

"For the Lord's sake," Cleo said.

They stared at each other angrily.

He jumped off the bed and walked to the bathroom, slamming the door behind him. He tried not to look at the picture of Harold, a picture that had been taken by the right kind of woman on the right kind of day, when the right kind of planets had been whizzing around the sky.

AT THREE O'CLOCK in the morning, Cleo lit a cigarette, and the light of her match went up like a flare.

Alexander lay for a moment, eyes half closed, watching her smoke. The lamp on the bedside table threw a shadow of her two cigarette fingers that looked like rabbit ears. He thought about Linda and the evening he had come home from work and found her in the bathtub with the bunny ears on. For the first time, he admitted to himself that he missed her, deeply, and he reached out to stroke Cleo's hair.

"Leave me alone, doll," she said, but she was smiling.

He pulled her toward him and kissed her. She moved away to put her cigarette out, and then he made love to her, wanting to give her what she wanted, and wanting to get something in return.

THREE HOURS LATER, when they woke again, Cleo persuaded Alexander to let her come and help gather the dew.

"You'll see," she whispered to the small of his neck. "I won't say a word. I'll be so good."

HE LET HER carry the canvas cloth. He carried the glass container. They left the house in silence and walked slowly toward the open field.

The last stars were dimming out of the sky. The birds were calling their morning calls with notes that Alexander knew now by heart. He breathed deeply. Yards from the house, he could still smell the honeysuckle that Harold had planted along the drive. It was the tenth of May, and in the last few days alone, the countryside had changed again.

He and Cleo stopped walking when they reached the crest of the hill.

"It's beautiful," Cleo said.

"I know."

"You do this every morning?"

"Every morning that it's clear."

"It's cold," Cleo said.

"You want my jacket?"

"Yes."

He put the container down, then took off his jacket and gave it to her. He watched as she did the buttons, turned up the collar, and pulled out her long blond hair. He realized that she was still flirting with him. He knew that she was lovely, and he knew that he didn't love her, and he wished, quite sincerely, that he did.

"Look at the horizon," he said quietly. "You see that band of light? Pretty soon, it'll get higher and higher, and there'll be all kinds of colors, and then the blue will turn red, and then the sun will come up."

"I've *seen* sunrises, doll," she said.

A bird screamed from a high tree. Alexander turned toward the sound.

"All right," he said softly. "Let's get to work."

He showed her how to stretch the cloth tight, and how to move it gently over the grass, and then he told her about facing the north, south, east, and west, and he recited the opening lines of the Emerald Tablet to her.

"What does it mean," she said, "The sun is its father, the moon its mother. The wind carried it in his belly. What's *it?*"

"Your guess is as good as mine."

"Okay, doll," she said. "Let's get started."

They worked in silence as the sky grew brighter and the rising sun coaxed out the colors of the day. Alexander was surprised to find that he loved how it felt to have her beside him. He was just about to tell her that when she stopped and touched his arm. She smiled and leaned closer to whisper to him. "You know," she said. "This is really boring."

He heard his old self in her voice, the need for proofs and outcomes, and he took a step away from her.

"It *is*, doll," Cleo said. "Admit it. I know you think it's boring."

"Can't you just concentrate on this?" he asked her.

She shrugged, and went back to the work. He hated in her what he hated in himself—and hated in Alice, too, for that matter—the restless desire for new desires, the total inability to do the things that were simple and to do them again and again.

"Don't you ever just want to *stop* somewhere?" he asked her.

"No," she told him. "Never."

She took a step backward and tripped on the canvas, falling on top of it to the ground.

"Cleo!" Alexander shouted.

"I'm fine," she said, getting to her knees.

"The canvas!" he said. "Christ!"

Cleo rubbed her ankle. "The *canvas?*"

"It's *never* supposed to touch the ground! Not even to *graze* it! I *told* you that!"

Cleo stood up slowly, gathered the canvas, and threw it at Alexander. "What the hell have you turned into?" she said. She strode off across the field, and each step she took seemed deliberately planned to pound the new grass into the earth.

"I KNOW," Alexander said when he finally caught up with her. She was sitting beneath a tree in Harold's backyard. "I'm sorry I yelled at you."

"I'll do the chart," Cleo said.

Alexander settled beside her and gently held her hand. "Thank you," he said. "But I don't want you to."

They were quiet for many moments. Alexander studied the brown dirt marks on the canvas cloth and wondered what Harold would say.

Cleo put her head back against the tree and closed her eyes under the new morning light. "You can be such an idiot sometimes," she said.

.   .   .

HAROLD WASN'T nearly as angry as Alexander had thought he would be. "We'll talk about it later," was all he said when he saw the stained canvas. "Put up a wash. Use some Clorox," he said.

Cleo laughed at him. *"Clorox? Clorox*, Harold? Which of the texts mentions Clorox?"

THEY STOOD TOGETHER at the train station.

"You took it all so seriously," Cleo said to him.

"What did you think I was going to do? What did you want?"

"I wanted some fun."

"You're never going to be happy if you can't ever sit still," he said.

"Don't tell me what I can never be, doll. I don't need sermons from the church of Harold."

"You're jealous," Alexander said. "You're jealous because you think I need him more than I need you."

Impatiently, Cleo looked down the tracks. The train was approaching. She looked back at him.

"You don't understand," he told her. "I'm not sure that Harold can help me either."

"Doll," she said. "I don't think anyone can help you."

Then she stepped onto the train and was gone.

HIS ANGEL FINALLY returned that night. But she didn't come to his room. In the dream, she flew above the city skyline, circling the stars.

"Show me the stars in my chart," he told her.

"That's what you want to know now?" she asked.

"I was born in Gemini," he said. "Which ones make up Gemini?"

"Watch me," the angel said.

She flew higher into the heavens and seemed to pause at a very bright star, and then she flew away from it to another, and then to another, leaving trails of white light between them, sketching a constellation. Dreaming, Alexander told himself to memorize its shape. But then the angel didn't stop. She kept flying around the night sky, going from star to star, from light to light, making the sky one huge shining net that grew brighter and brighter until it was so bright that it engulfed all the stars.

Alexander woke up panicked. He got out of bed and walked to the window and stood for a moment, feeling the thin breeze against his cheeks and his throat. He closed his eyes, trying not to think of his angel or of Cleo, trying to think instead of gold. He thought of his mother's gold necklace, and he thought of the gold light by the railroad tracks, and he thought of Alice, then Cleo, saying, "Magic isn't silver, it's gold."

Dizzily, he opened his eyes and wiped the sweat from his forehead with the heel of his palm. For the first time in his life, he was allowing his chance for succeeding at something to rest with other people, and he wanted to reclaim the conviction that he could help himself. It seemed that Harold didn't want him to remember who he was, what he could do. It suddenly made sense that there were no mirrors in Harold's house. Alexander lunged forward to slam the window shut. Defiantly, he studied his image in the black mirror of the glass.

4

THE THEORY OF
EVERYTHING

AT DAWN, the light pink flowers of the cherry trees matched
the sky. Alexander dragged the canvas cloth over the grass,
trembling from the morning chill, exhausted from the night
before. He recited no passages, faced no poles, and traced no
magic circles. His mind raced instead with his resolutions and
plans and with the giddy freedom of trusting himself for the
first time in many months.

Harold just gave too little, he thought, and Cleo wanted to
give too much. He would seek his own answers, do his own
chart, gather his own Prime Matter, and define it in his own
way. He would find his angel alone, and she would touch him,
and then he would know what to do. She would tell him if he
should stay or should go, and what he should let himself want.

He had always worked best alone, he thought—jotting notes on scraps of paper at odd hours of the day and night, getting lost in the numbers, allowing his mind to become a world from which he could take what he needed and to which he could always retreat.

He had written the Theory of Everything; he could figure out how to pick up some soil.

HE CALLED SAM after breakfast.

"Ex," Sam said.

"Hi."

"Ex."

"Hi, Dad."

It was going to be harder than he'd thought.

"You're calling me," Sam said.

"Sure."

"What's wrong?"

"I missed hearing your voice, Dad."

"I miss you too. Are you all right?"

"I'm fine. Are you?"

"I'm fine."

"What's new?"

"I just wrote you."

"Well, tell me anyway."

"Nothing's new."

Alexander laughed. Sam didn't. "Are you tired of it yet?" he asked.

"Yes."

"You're coming home then," Sam said.

"Maybe."

"When?"

"I don't know. Soon, maybe. I don't know. I need some books."

"Some what?"

"Some books. I need you to get me some books."

There was silence, and Alexander could picture Sam standing in the kitchen at home in a turtleneck shirt and khakis with a look of disgust on his face.

"Dad?" Alexander said softly.

"Linda calls me once a month."

"I know," Alexander said. "You wrote me."

"You haven't talked to her once, have you?"

"No," Alexander said. "She stopped writing."

"What did you expect?"

"I don't know."

"And Cleo? Is that over?"

"Yes."

"*Good.*"

"Dad, you never *knew* her."

"Oh yes I did," Sam told him bitterly.

"Okay, Dad," Alexander said. "Okay."

Sam sighed. "What kind of books?"

ON SATURDAY, Alexander made tincture of sulphur. On Sunday, Harold asked him to gather a half-pound of small white flowers and to crush them in a mortar.

After lunch, Harold asked Alexander to help him wash the kitchen windows, and once, when Harold began to whistle, Alexander was tempted to tell him, point-blank, about the decision he'd made. But then Harold came over and pointed out a spot of dirt that Alexander had missed, and Alexander saw the awkward mixture of hardness and need on Harold's face, and he forced himself to say nothing.

Each morning that week after breakfast, he waited for the mail to come, standing in the kitchen and watching for the truck on the road. He had asked Sam for an ephemeris, which was a book that listed the daily positions of the planets, and he had asked him for anything that would explain how to draw up a chart. He had also asked for a copy of his own birth certificate. Without these things, he could not begin. For the rest of the week, he tried with some success to hide his impatience from Harold.

On Monday, Harold left a small pamphlet in his room. It was divided into seven short sections, one for each of the heavenly bodies that were said to influence the Work. There were Jupiter, Venus, Saturn, Mercury, Mars, and the sun and moon. In each section, there was a list of the herbs that the planets and the sun were supposed to affect. Of course, there wasn't a clue as to what that effect was supposed to be, and Harold had told Alexander only that he should take a long look at the list.

What else is new? Alexander thought: it was just one more little lesson, another hoop that he had to jump through. It was just one more piece of the puzzle whose final image, if it existed at all, was something that Harold refused to show. Alexander flung the pamphlet down on his desk and paced the room. He imagined what it would be like to find his own Prime Matter, to be touched by the angel. He wasn't sure which would come first, but he imagined the joy of telling Harold that he didn't need him anymore. The fantasy gradually calmed him down. He went back to his desk and opened the pamphlet again and looked at the lists. He would need to find some meaning in them in case Harold quizzed him later.

The first section listed the herbs whose growth was influenced by the moon. . . . *The moon is its mother*, he had recited every day, so Alexander looked for the names of herbs that made him think of Alice:

adder's-tongue
cuckooflower
loosestrife

                   mouse-ear
                   stonecrop
                   wallflower

He liked the list. He wrote it into his notebook.

The sun is its father, he thought next, and he looked through the second list. He copied down:

                   angelica
                   lovage
                   sundew

Those names seemed right for Sam, too, as if Sam had known the answers all along.

Alexander didn't know what planet Harold would be. He knew that his own planet was Saturn, though, from all the times in his childhood that Alice had told him that Saturn was in his chart. So he looked under Saturn for himself and wrote down:

                   fluxweed
                   heartsease
                   hemlock
                   melancholy thistle

Alexander considered the simple poetry of the words he had copied. The words were so right and so resonant that they almost drew him back to Harold. Then Alexander made himself look at the words he hadn't copied, the words with no resonance and no magic, and then he tried to decide if he had become the kind of person for whom coincidence had simply become more important than truth.

A LETTER from Biner arrived on Tuesday:

Friday, May 11

Dear Mr. Simon:

Thank you for writing back. I'll confess that your letter, while illuminating in some respects, didn't really give me the kind of answer I had hoped for. I was hoping for something that I could send directly to David Merton. In its absence, I've taken the liberty of circulating a press release that says you will be returning to your post at Wilson at the end of the year, after an extended sabbatical during which time you have been refining your theory.

I realize the odds of this actually happening are slim. But in the first place, this was the best face-saving strategy I could devise. And in the second place, I do continue to hold out some hope. My own belief is that you are by nature too much a scientist to have done the undoable and then to walk away from it. My experience has shown me that theories are a lot like children, and that one can never lose the responsibility for them, even if one chooses to abandon them for a while.

Whenever you do decide to answer your critics and defend your theory, I trust that you will do it under the aegis of this lab. After that, I suppose, we will just have to see.

Regards,
Bruce Biner

Alexander had to smile at what Biner had said about children and theories. He wondered if it was true, and then he thought about how Alice had left him, and about how Harold wanted to take him in, and then he found himself thinking of Linda, and the day she had thrown out the plant he'd let die. He wanted to tell her how sorry he was. He wanted to hear her voice.

THE PACKAGE FROM Sam finally came on Wednesday. Alexander opened it down by the mailbox and read the letter as he walked back to the house.

May 12

Dearest Ex—

The store you sent me to has to be one of the strangest places I've ever seen. I never knew that troubled people could be so hawky and aggressive. Before I managed to get these books for you, I was accosted by half a dozen saleswomen and I was offered candles (did you know that blue is supposedly for success, red is for love, and white is for spirituality?), and crystals, and recipes for love potions and soaps that remove hexes. Hexes! I guess they thought I was an easy mark.

But anyway, here they are, and I hope they're what you wanted because in all honesty, Ex, I can tell you that wild horses couldn't drag me back there. Well, actually they could, because if you really needed something you know I'd never say no.

Write soon and I hope you are well. Queen to Rook 1.

Love,
Dad

P.S. Be careful with the birth certificate. It's the only copy
I've got.

THAT NIGHT, the fireflies by the pond below formed their
own constellations, and Alexander stayed up late, poring over
the astrology books.

Doing a chart, he learned, just involved a lot of mathematical
calculations. The idea was to take the time of birth and find
out where the planets had been in the sky at exactly that moment. To do this, he had to translate the birth time into what
was known as local sidereal time—the time reckoned by the
stars, using Greenwich mean time as a base and taking daylight
savings time into account. The ephemeris would show where
the planets were at noon, local sidereal time, and then all that
was left was calculating the differences between that time and
the birth time for each planet, and then computing what were
called the aspects, the angular relationships of the planets to
each other.

In short, the task would take a long time but for Alexander
would be no more than a finger exercise.

AT BREAKFAST the next morning, Harold grimaced as he
sipped his coffee.

"Something wrong?" Alexander asked.

"It's Cleo, isn't it?" Harold said.

"What's Cleo?"

"The thing that's upsetting you."

"What makes you think that I'm upset?"

"You've been very different since she left."

"*I've* been different?"

"Don't do it."

"Don't do what?"

"Don't love her."

"I *don't* love her," Alexander said, astonished that Harold was trying to pretend that he wasn't the difference himself.

"Love your work, kid," Harold told him, waving a fork. "That's all that really counts. If you learn all this stuff about the Work, if you really study these lessons, then you'll learn about love, too."

Alexander stared at Harold, infuriated by the casual tone, the expansive gesture, the old routine. Rigidly, he stood up to clear the dishes, feeling bitter and speechless. He had ceased to believe that Harold would ever give anything without taking it back.

"Now, sex," Harold was saying, "sex is different. Sex is just fun. But love. Well, that's always going to get in the way of what you're learning. At least when you're starting out—"

Alexander whirled around.

"What?" Harold said. "What's wrong?"

"What the hell do you know about love?"

Harold removed and replaced his glasses, then looked down for a long time. "That's a horrible thing to say," he whispered.

Alexander glared at him. "What happened between you and Sylvie?" he asked.

Harold flinched.

"Where did she go?" Alexander asked. "When did she leave? Why didn't you marry her? Why didn't you ever have children?"

Harold stared back at Alexander. "A horrible thing," he repeated, as if he hadn't heard anything else. He looked, miraculously, close to tears. Alexander was torn between the old anger and a new sympathy. "I'm sorry," he finally said. "I shouldn't have said that, and I shouldn't have asked about Sylvie. Let's forget it. I'm sorry. What's my lesson for the day?"

Harold was silent, acknowledging neither the apology nor the question. Alexander felt a flash of remorse.

Harold pushed his chair back and stood up, crumpling his napkin and letting it fall to the table like a white flag.

"You didn't give me a lesson, Harold."

"Tough shit," Harold said, and walked from the room.

ALEXANDER STACKED the dishes, playing and replaying the conversation in his head. He wanted to go down to the lab, to follow Harold into this new and compelling corner of emotion. He told himself not to go or to care.

Before breakfast, he had hidden the new books under the covers in his bed. Now he went back upstairs, and he retrieved the books resolutely and brought them to his desk. He turned to a fresh page in his notebook and sharpened three new pencils. He felt mean and determined and, having seen Harold's vulnerability, he tried not to feel vulnerable.

He sat at the desk and unfolded the copy of his birth certificate. Sam had sent him a Xerox of an old-fashioned photocopy, with the lines and typed information in white and the background black. To Alexander, there was something truly captivating about this piece of paper. "Full name of child"; "Sex"; "Number of children born of this pregnancy"; "Date of birth"; "Time." The certificate also had spaces for full name of father, and maiden name of mother. Under "Father," it asked for the profession; under "Mother," it asked only for number of children born previously, and number of them still alive.

Alexander read the certificate over and over, as if somehow it could tell him all sorts of things he'd never known. He half expected to find that Alice had had other children, or that Sam had been born in Spain, or that there had been a twin brother. As it was, the stark facts stood on the page as if they were answers to a crossword puzzle that hadn't been completed.

The piece of paper made it seem that he had once been part

of a family. There was something so normal about that, so rich. He thought about what his mother must have been like in those days—how profoundly she must have believed that having a child would make her happy. And then he thought about Harold again, remembering the stark fear that he'd seen the day he'd been sick and he'd understood that Harold had cared. Alexander's anger was gone now, but he still didn't know if it made sense to stay.

He had been born, he saw, at ten forty-eight. Dutifully, he wrote the time down. Then he set to work on the chart, doing the calculations by hand.

HAROLD WAS QUIET and peevish at dinner. Alexander filled in the silences, talking about the list of herbs as if he believed it had meaning. Harold neither challenged nor confirmed what Alexander said.

"It wasn't that big a deal, Harold," Alexander finally told him. "All I asked was what you knew about love."

"I didn't say it was a big deal."

"You're sitting there sulking. You've been sulking all night."

"You hurt my feelings," Harold said, and Alexander wanted to laugh.

"*Your* feelings?" Alexander said. "Do you know how you've made me feel?"

"I suspect," Harold said, "that I've made you feel like a total idiot."

"That's right."

"I'm not *used* to this!" Harold said, and walked out.

Alexander sat alone and in silence. He felt exhausted, and he understood that Harold's life would have four seasons, and no new beginning, and one sure end, and no replica of itself, no seed. Harold could travel only from point *A* to point *B*, and only with profound luck and extreme dedication. Harold's path was an arc, not a circle. It was a broken Ouroboros.

TEN DAYS PASSED. In the mornings, Alexander gathered the dew. In the afternoons, he did the calculations, not trying yet to make sense of them. In the evenings, he ate with Harold and tried not to ask him questions. Harold remained both sad and distant. Alexander struggled to sustain his independence, his belief that Harold's fate and his were meant to be disconnected.

In Alexander's dreams, there was no angel and no promise of an answer.

THE WORK WAS simple and tedious. It was math at its least rewarding, at its oldest and least profound.

Day after day, Alexander sat at his desk, adding and sub-tracting, multiplying and dividing, like a kid in grammar school. His only consolation was a sense of self-conscious pride. He *had* learned to have patience, he thought. Neither Cleo nor Alice would have been able to do anything this dull, and four months ago, he wouldn't have, either. *Out of repetition*, he told himself, *magic is sometimes forced to rise.*

He thought again about Linda, how she had watered the flowers daily, taken the time to trim their leaves back, and he felt surprised by the depth with which he was starting to admire her.

ON THE LAST MONDAY in May, Harold smiled at Alexander after breakfast and asked if he wanted to come to the lab and watch him work.

Alexander tried to feign the proper gratitude. "You mean you'll really let me watch?" he said.

"Sure," Harold told him.

"Why now?"

"Why not?"

"That's great, Harold," Alexander said. "And I promise I won't get in the way."

"Leave the dishes," Harold said. "When opportunity knocks, it's usually wise to leave the dishes."

In the lab, Alexander sat on one of the stools, silently brooding about the fact that his calculations would have to wait.

"You're up to something," Harold said as he poured a jar of dew into the vessel that held his Prime Matter.

"I'd tell you," Alexander said, "but what I'm doing can't be taught. It can only be learned."

"Sarcasm doesn't suit you."

"Neither does failure," Alexander said.

"If all you wanted was to make gold, schmuck, you could have done that in your precious atom smasher."

"It isn't precious anymore."

"You think I'm trying to hurt you, but I'm still trying to help."

Alexander said nothing.

"The thing that breaks my heart," Harold said, "is that you were making a lot of progress. Really. You were learning to feel things instead of think them. Inside you, you have the right answer, you know, but you're just too angry to see it."

"I feel like you just want to keep me guessing," Alexander said.

"Of *course* I want to keep you guessing. How can you learn if you're not going to guess? You have to try," Harold said. "Oh, damn. I've got to stir this thing."

He walked back to the clay vessel, and Alexander tried to

think of his calculations, hoping his thoughts would fill his mind and erase all the words that Harold had said, words that he didn't want to trust anymore but that beckoned like an old embrace.

ALEXANDER FINISHED the chart on the following Friday. It was late morning when he did the last calculations and then sat, with the circle he'd drawn and all the symbols of the zodiac, and he sighed, exhausted by the prospect of trying to figure out what they meant. Part of the point of doing a chart was to learn whether a Seeker was worthy or unworthy of collecting the Prime Matter. All Alexander had to go on were the fortune-cookie paragraphs that were offered by the book.

By evening, he had learned that if Neptune was in the twelfth house, that meant someone with sensitive dreams. If Pluto was in the twelfth house, that meant someone with an interest in psychology or the occult. He had learned that he had an independent nature and a fierce love of wisdom and a hidden attraction to spiritual things and a tendency to dream.

He didn't consider this big news.

Spring was nearly over now. It was the first of June. In less than two weeks, Alexander would turn thirty-two with nothing much to celebrate and no one he really trusted. In less than three weeks, summer would start, and then he would have to wait till the next spring to gather his own Prime Matter.

At one in the morning, he tiptoed downstairs after Harold went to sleep and looked in the *Farmer's Almanac* that was kept on the shelf in the lab. The moon would be full in nine days, he saw. He would choose the spot for his Prime Matter then.

Back upstairs, he closed his notebook and hid the other books under the bed. What would he have done anyway, he wondered, if he had found something in the chart that said he was unworthy?

He would spend the next eight days trying to clear his mind and to cleanse his thoughts.

TWO DAYS LATER, Harold sent Alexander into the fields to gather buttercups. Alexander moved from spot to spot, looking for bits of yellow like a dog chasing a bone. He was at it for several hours, and when he came back, Harold was not in the lab. With a sickening feeling, Alexander climbed the stairs and found Harold, as he'd known he would, standing in his bedroom with his notebook in his hand.

"That's mine," Alexander said. "What gives you the right to read it?"

"You're supposed to be my student," Harold said. "I'm supposed to watch your progress."

"Fine. So help me with the chart."

"What makes you think I can?" Harold said.

"You don't think I'm ready to learn."

"The Great Work can't be taught," Harold said.

"You always say that."

"It's always true."

"I've got Saturn all over my chart. And Saturn's all over the sky now. I don't think it's in the right place."

"Well then, you should wait for it to be farther away."

"That could take months."

Harold sighed.

"Someone must have taught you," Alexander said.

Harold said nothing.

"You just don't want me to start," Alexander said. "You're afraid I'll do it and then I'll leave."

"You really think that?" Harold said ambiguously.

"Why don't you want me to learn what you know?"

"What's the Prime Matter?" Harold said, and Alexander felt the immeasurable relief of having the battle lines drawn again.

. . .

A WEEK LATER, Alexander paced his bedroom and waited for the full moon to rise. The sky was starry and clear, and just after midnight, he peered down the hallway to make sure that Harold had turned out his light. Almost holding his breath, Alexander tiptoed down the stairs to the kitchen. The house was dark and quiet, and he felt both clever and hopeful.

Harold hit the lights in the kitchen the moment that Alexander stepped in.

Alexander gasped.

"Midnight *snack*?" Harold asked demonically.

Alexander was speechless.

"Drink of *water*?" Harold said.

"No."

Harold glared at him menacingly, a troll under a bridge. Beyond him and this room were the open fields, and the promise of answers. "Let me go," Alexander said.

Harold sneered. "Do you know," he said, "do you have any *clue* what is really involved in this process?"

Alexander didn't answer him.

"Listen to me," Harold said. "I waited five *years* to meet Sylvie. Finally I met her. She moved in here. We waited four *months* until the right day for choosing the Prime Matter. Then we chose the right day. It was another six months away. For us it was under Aquarius. That's February."

"I know it's February," Alexander said.

"She had to be on a high spiritual plane," Harold said. He was pacing now. "She had to be in a state of near ecstasy. We meditated. We *fasted*. We took ritual *baths*. Do you understand? When the night finally came, we waited until the precise moment that the sun had set. The sun was supposed to be under our feet, so it would give warmth to the earth. We spent *weeks* purifying the ground in that spot. We traced three magic circles there. She felt the currents. She heard an angel. The angel told her I had to fight with a dragon. This went on for weeks. For *weeks!* It took us two *hours* to take the Prime Matter from the ground. Every *step* was planned." Harold stopped pacing. His eyes were wild.

"So that was how you did it," Alexander said to him quietly. "Maybe you just did it wrong."

"Oh, *Christ!*" Harold shouted, disgusted. "Don't you ever *listen?*"

Alexander was trembling, but he tried to maintain his bravado. "Maybe you just did it wrong," he said again. "It's taken you twenty years."

"I can help you," Harold said.

Alexander walked past Harold and out the back door.

HE RAN DOWN the driveway and kept running until he reached the moonlit fields and he couldn't run anymore. Panting, he turned around to make sure that Harold hadn't followed him. He saw nothing, in any direction, but the long grass and the hollow moonlight. He tried to catch his breath. He looked around him, searching the landscape as if it were hiding his confidence, or his hope. He struggled to drown out what Harold had said with one last wish for magic.

He closed his eyes and waited, certain that he would sense the earth spinning, and sense his place on top of it, and that out of those sensations would come the angel and the answers. Nothing happened. No one appeared. After a while, Alexander opened his eyes again.

Several hundred yards in the distance, the moonlight was shining on a small, low bush, whose leaves seemed to sparkle as a faint breeze blew against them. Alexander realized that he wasn't afraid of the moon anymore.

He wondered if that could be something to go on. He wondered if it could be some kind of sign.

Neither the books nor Harold had said anything about choosing a spot where the moonlight was shining, but Alexander tried one last time to believe that he could make up his own rules and still play at this ancient game.

He kept his eyes focused on the ground next to the bush and walked steadily toward it. Rationally, he knew that he was doing everything wrong, but hadn't Harold told him for months now to follow his instincts instead of his thoughts?

When Alexander reached the spot where the moonlight was shining, a cloud covered the moon. Confused by the darkness, he knelt near the bush and placed his hands on the cool soil beside it. Nothing happened. Nothing changed. He stayed for a long time, hunched in the semidarkness, and then he sat down with his legs crossed and his head held in his hands. He thought about his angel, and he marveled at her power: he marveled at the fact that something he'd dreamed about in childhood could have propelled him to this moment—all on his own in the darkness, needing the moonlight, a scientist waiting for magic.

He realized that he was out in a vacant field past midnight, with the same fear and the same stabbing need that he'd first felt 10,000 midnights before. Then he thought: No, not 10,000. He had been eight years old the night of the ghost. He was nearly thirty-two now. Twenty-four years times 365 days was nearly 9,000.

He had to smile at himself for finding comfort in this computation.

He wondered what other men did when they got what they wanted. He thought of Einstein, who'd done his most important work by thirty, and Newton, who'd done it by twenty-three, and then he thought how ludicrous it was to put himself in that kind of company when he hadn't even stayed in New York to defend the theory he'd written.

He had no idea how much time had passed with him sitting on the ground. The moon had moved across the sky, but it wasn't until the first light appeared that he knew it was already five A.M. He had sat on the cold, damp ground for hours. He watched the round bit of gold in the sky, and felt comforted by it, and almost renewed.

In the new light, Alexander could study the patch of earth that he had been drawn to. It was just a patch of earth, he thought, astonished by the fact that he had hoped until the last possible moment that it was going to be more. He reached down and pulled up a handful of earth. It was just a handful of earth, he thought. The earth was made up of soil, which was made up of minerals, made up of elements, made up of atoms, made up of strings. And then it finally struck him that to change soil into gold, one would have to find a common denominator, the basic stuff of matter—the stuff that had been atoms to the ancient Greeks and had been strings to him. Alexander let a long breath out. In a sense, he had come full circle, but the circle was oddly comforting. Harold knew different names and methods; the goal and the logic remained the same, the need for the world to be hard and sane. Alexander looked at the risen sun. He thought of the coming seasons. Out of repetition, he thought, magic was sometimes forced to rise.

He had come to this place once before, he thought—a year ago, almost exactly now. The calm he felt was staggering.

He threw the handful of earth back to the ground and stood up on stiff legs to face the day. He began to walk through the pale, cold fields. Half a mile or so away, he was strangely unsurprised by the sight of Harold. They stood, staring at each other.

"The Prime Matter," Alexander said. "It's just earth."

Harold sighed and sat down. "Well, *that* I told you on Day One."

"You know what I'm saying," Alexander said.

"Sit down."

Alexander sat. "How did you find me, anyway?" he asked.

"I don't know. I've been looking for hours."

"I don't want to miss my life, Harold," Alexander said.

"I know," Harold said. "I know. You won't. I may not, either."

"The Prime Matter," Alexander said again. "I already found it, didn't I? The Prime Matter is the strings I found. The elemental stuff. The stuff that the world is made of. You've been looking for the same thing I was looking for in New York."

"See, we Adepts," Harold said. "We Adepts can't make gold till we know what the gold is made of."

Alexander sighed, exhausted. "Why couldn't you have just told me?"

"You know why."

"But the Prime Matter is the strings. I've already done it. I've even gone beyond it. You're just starting."

"I've been at this for twenty years."

"I bet you don't want to find it," Alexander said.

"What?"

"God help you if you find it," Alexander said. "You won't know what the hell to do, will you?"

"I don't think I'll be around long enough to find it. I hoped maybe you would. That's all."

"If I did, then I'd miss my life, wouldn't I?"

"Maybe not."

"Didn't you?"

"I don't know yet," Harold said.

"Harold, I can't stay here and be part of your Ouroboros. If I do, then I won't get to make my own."

.   .   .

HE FELL ASLEEP in the late morning and dreamed about his angel. He saw her in the far distance—not in his room, but in a wide, open field.

"Come closer," Alexander called to her.

She flew toward him, making circles in the air, and then he was looking up at her.

"Come down," Alexander told her.

Something she wore seemed to catch the light and gleamed as she hovered above him.

He had thought they were in his midnight field, the field where he'd been the night before, but the light made him think of the Railroad Ghost.

"Where are we now?" he asked her.

"Now we're here," the angel said.

"Are there ghosts?"

"I'm not a ghost."

"Come closer. Please."

The angel smiled and flew down to him. Her wings stirred the air between them.

He saw what it was that was shining.

"That's Mommy's locket," he said, pointing to her neck.

"I know," the angel said.

"Is she dead?"

The angel laughed. "Oh, no, Alexander. Your mother isn't dead."

"Then how did you get her locket?"

The angel smiled. Alexander felt comforted even though she hadn't answered.

"I've missed you," Alexander said. "Why haven't you come to me? I'm still waiting for you to touch me," he said.

"You don't need me," the angel said.

"Of course I need you," Alexander said.

The angel hovered above him. He didn't think he had ever

seen her wings so close up, the gentle layers of small, pale feathers that gleamed in the strange but lovely light. She had never seemed less frightening or more beautiful. She had always been magnificent, but now the sight of her filled him less with awe than with a kind of peace.

He was fighting to make her stay, and yet he felt he knew her so well now that he wouldn't really lose her, even if she really left. "I can imagine you, can't I?" he said in his dream.

"When I'm gone, you mean?" she asked him.

"Yes."

Then she disappeared.

HE WALKED OUTSIDE the house and sat by the pond. The day was brilliant, almost cloudless. Birds seemed to play in the long grass, and a beaver swam in the pond. He watched it move through the still water, only its head visible, and a long wide V trailing out behind it. In the trail that the animal made, and the way it swam without seeming to, Alexander realized he needed to search for no patterns or meanings.

He smelled the lush grass and the noontime heat. It struck him—as a completely unprovable hypothesis—that the world might be extraordinary precisely because of the secrets it hid.

He thought about the fullness of a long life in which things were created, not just understood.

TALL TREES LINED the railroad tracks, but occasionally they would part to reveal other scenes. In the distance were farmhouses and shadowy fields; closer in were trucks and warehouses and other signs of industry. Inside the train, the sunlight flickered against the red vinyl seats.

.   .   .

PENN STATION was hot but not too crowded, and Alexander even felt nostalgia about his former commute. It seemed almost glorious to him that he had ever gone to a place each day that was filled with people.

ALEXANDER STOOD on the roof—Linda's roof, he thought. It was a brilliant day, sunny but dry, and he breathed in the lush smells of the plants and flowers. He hadn't remembered Linda's garden ever being so beautiful. It was crowded with rosebushes, geraniums, marigolds, zinnias—even one sunflower whose head bent heavily against a tall stick. Alexander smiled sadly, thinking of the perfumes and the oils that he could have made for Linda.

An hour passed. He leaned against the railing and stared down at the busy avenue, wanting to belong there, too. In the distance, Alexander could see a band of smoke snaking its way, like Ouroboros, between two buildings.

He stretched out in a chair and closed his eyes against the glare of the sun. He slept without a dream, and when he woke up, Linda was standing above him, gently touching his arm.

ACKNOWLEDGMENTS

A lot of the technical information in this novel derives from
the following books:

Flatland, by Edwin A. Abbott

The Alchemist's Handbook, by Frater Albertus

Gold of a Thousand Mornings, by Armand Barbault

Tyrocinium Chymicum: A Practical Treatise in Alchemy, by Jean
  Beguin

Alchemy, by Titus Burckhardt

The Practical Astrologer, by Nicholas Campion

The Particle Explosion, by Frank Close, Michael Marten, and
  Christine Sutton

Sympathetic Vibrations: Reflections on Physics As a Way of Life,
  by K. C. Cole

*The Second Creation: Makers of the Revolution in Twentieth-
  Century Physics*, by Robert P. Crease and Charles C. Mann

Alchemy, an Introduction to the Symbolism and the Psychology, by
  Marie-Louise von Franz

The Alchemical Tradition in the Late Twentieth Century, edited
  by Richard Grossinger

Alchemy, by Franz Hartmann

Speculations on the Fourth Dimension: Selected Writings, by
  Charles Howard Hinton, edited by Rudy Rucker

Beyond Einstein: The Cosmic Quest for the Theory of the Universe,
  by Dr. Michio Kaku and Jennifer Trainer

Alchemy: The Secret Art, by Stanislas Klossowski de Rola

In Pursuit of Gold, by Lapidus

The Astrology Workbook, by Cordelia Mansall

An Adventure, by C. A. E. Moberly and E. F. Jourdain

Einstein's Dream: The Search for a Unified Theory of the Universe, by Barry Parker

The Morning of the Magicians, by Louis Pauwels and Jacques Bergier, translated from the French by Rollo Myers

Superstrings and the Search for the Theory of Everything, by F. David Peat

The Science of Alchemy: A Treatise on the Science of Soul-Transmutation, by Dr. A. S. Raleigh

The Fourth Dimension: Toward a Geometry of Higher Reality, by Rudy Rucker

Alchemists and Gold, by Jacques Sadoul, translated from the French by Olga Sieveking

Beyond the Quantum, by Michael Talbot

Taking the Quantum Leap: The New Physics for Nonscientists, by Fred Alan Wolf

Transcendental Physics, by J. C. F. Zöllner

The Dancing Wu Li Masters: An Overview of the New Physics, by Gary Zukav

I'd like to thank Gary Taubes and Bruce Schecter for their advice on physics and Cheryl Lee Terry for her advice on palm reading. Any inaccuracies in this book's treatment of these subjects are in no way a reflection of their excellent and generous help.

I'm also grateful to Liz Darhansoff, Victoria Wilson, Betsy Carter, Michael Solomon, Cynthia Stuart, James Sanders, Lee Eisenberg, Roger Rosenblatt, Rebecca Rasmussen, all Grunwalds, and my husband for their criticism and their encouragement.

A NOTE ON THE TYPE

The text of this book was set in a digitized version of a typeface known as Garamond. The design is based on letter forms originally created by Claude Garamond (c. 1480–1561). Garamond was a pupil of Geoffroy Tory and may have patterned his letter forms on Venetian models. To this day, the typeface that bears his name is one of the most attractive used in book composition, and the intervening years have caused it to lose little of its freshness or beauty.

Composed by PennSet, Inc.,
Bloomsburg, Pennsylvania
Printed and bound by Fairfield Graphics,
Fairfield, Pennsylvania
Typography and binding design by
Iris Weinstein